Palgrave Studies in Language, Literature and Style

Series Editors
Rocío Montoro, Department of English and German
Philology, University of Granada, Granada, Spain
Paul Simpson, Department of English, University of
Liverpool, Liverpool, UK

This series offers rigorous and informative treatments of particular writers, genres and literary periods and provides in-depth examination of their key stylistic tropes. Every volume in the series is intended to serve as a key reference point for undergraduate and post-graduate students and as an investigative resource for more experienced researchers. The last twenty years have witnessed a huge transformation in the analytic tools and methods of modern stylistics. By harnessing the talent of a growing body of researchers in the field, this series of books seeks both to capture these developments and transformations and to establish and elaborate new analytic models and paradigms.

Chloe Harrison

The Language of Margaret Atwood

palgrave
macmillan

Chloe Harrison
School of Law and Social Sciences
Aston University
Birmingham, UK

ISSN 2731-8265   ISSN 2731-8273   (electronic)
Palgrave Studies in Language, Literature and Style
ISBN 978-3-031-67639-0   ISBN 978-3-031-67640-6   (eBook)
https://doi.org/10.1007/978-3-031-67640-6

This Palgrave Macmillan imprint is published by the registered company Springer Nature Switzerland AG
The registered company address is: Gewerbestrasse 11, 6330 Cham, Switzerland

If disposing of this product, please recycle the paper.

Writing itself is always bad enough, but writing about writing is surely worse, in the futility department.

Margaret Atwood
On Writers and Writing *(2003, xvi)*

For my fellow detectives and Applied Rhetoricians.

Preface

In September 2015, a friend and I went to a talk given by Margaret Atwood at the Albert Hall conference centre in Nottingham, UK. The talk was part of a tour to promote her then new book, *The Heart Goes Last*. With the preamble of warm-up questions apparently discounted, the first question the interviewer asked was 'What are the perils of a totalitarian state?' We queued up afterwards to say a nervous *hello* and *thank you* and to have our shiny new books signed.

Early the next day, on my way to catch a train home, I saw Margaret Atwood again at the station. She stopped off at the coffee shop in the concourse, where I was sat with a cup of tea and a book, and sat down a few tables away.

Ideally, this opening anecdote would be one in which a meaningful encounter occurred. Perhaps Atwood spotted my dog-eared copy of *The Blind Assassin* on the table and joined me for a cup of tea and a chat. Perhaps I went over to thank her for the talk, and she would have been pleased (and not at all irritated at the interruption of an otherwise quiet morning and momentary respite from a whirlwind book tour) and would ask me to join her for a cup of tea and a chat there.

The reality was nowhere near as exciting. Deciding that, given the hour and the certain unlikelihood of my being able to say something worthy of the interruption, it was more polite to keep a respectful distance and silence.

On the train home, I reflected on the talk from the evening before and the not-encounter at the station. In particular, I thought about the strange kind of communication that takes place between writers and readers. In literary linguistic research, we often talk about the situational context of reading, and the distance in time and space between the moment of writing and the moment of reading. We also discuss the idea that engaging in reading is a deliberate and cooperative interaction in which both writer and reader participate. In reading *The Blind Assassin* in Nottingham in September 2015, while the real-world Margaret Atwood was a few tables away, we were, strangely, both in conversation and not in conversation at the same time.

This book, then, is my verbalised (but quiet, parenthetical) contribution to that conversation that did take place, and continues, all this time later.

Birmingham, UK   Chloe Harrison

Acknowledgements

Like all other plans and projects in recent speculative times, this book was somewhat derailed and ended up taking longer than originally planned. Thank you to the team at Palgrave for their continued patience, assistance and support, and in particular to Cathy Scott and Naveen Dass, and series editors Rocio Montoro and Paul Simpson.

Part of this project has been financially supported by the English, Languages and Applied Linguistics department and the research support funds at Aston University. I am also grateful to have been awarded research leave in 2022, during which time a large proportion of this book was planned and written.

I am lucky to be part of a very supportive stylistics research community. Thank you, in particular, to the Aston Stylistics Research Group, whose members are always supportive and whose enthusiasm and encouragement is unfailing, and unfailingly appreciated.

Thank you to the book group, The ABC Club, for letting me take over your reading choices for a couple of months and for, indirectly, keeping me company while writing this book. It was lots of fun being a fly-on-the-wall to your discussions! Thank you also to Furzeen Ahmed for her careful transcriptions of the book group meetings, which form the basis of the reader analysis in Chapters 4 and 5.

Special thanks to the usual suspects, Marcello Giovanelli, Louise Nuttall, Jess Mason and Helen Ringrow, for being my partners in crime(-solving).

Finally, thank you to my unofficial research assistant, Rob. I am very happy that you are now a Margaret Atwood fan, too.

Permissions

I am grateful to the following for permission to reproduce published extracts which form the basis of the extended analyses in the book.

Dedication

Chapter 2

Chapter 3

Chapter 4

Chapter 5

Chapter 6

Chapter 7

Contents

List of Figures

List of Tables

1

The Language of Margaret Atwood

1.1 Introduction

Throughout a career spanning seven decades, Margaret Atwood has written
well over 50 publications, including collections of poetry and short stories,
prose fiction and series, non-fiction and critical essays, children's fiction, one
graphic novel, one collaborative novel and an unknown contribution to the
Future Library Project (Paterson 2014)—to be released and read in 2114. Her
texts can be regarded as both literary and popular fiction, attracting both critical praise and mass readership alike. Arguably her most popular novel, *The
Handmaid's Tale* (1985) has been adapted and retold across various modes,
including as a film, an opera, a ballet, a graphic novel and, more recently, an
extended TV series. The success of the first series adaptation of *The Handmaid's Tale* meant that the book re-entered bestseller lists in 2017, though
it is argued that this revival in popularity can be traced in part to its reflection of contemporary politics, where it is seen as a symbol of resistance by
many (Valenti 2018). At the same time, the book is (as of Autumn 2024)
included in the UK secondary school English specification[1] as an exemplar
of political and social protest writing. That Atwood's publications continue to
push boundaries and invite such levels of engagement with the contemporary
reading public is a testament to her enduring popularity as an author.

---

[1] *The Handmaid's Tale* is included as a text choice on the English Literature specifications for AQA
B, and the combined English Language and Literature AQA specification.

© The Author(s), under exclusive license to Springer Nature
Switzerland AG 2024
C. Harrison, *The Language of Margaret Atwood*, Palgrave Studies in Language, Literature
and Style, https://doi.org/10.1007/978-3-031-67640-6_1

Unsurprisingly, since her first publications in the 1960s, Atwood has received considerable critical attention. While books have explored her feminist ideologies (Tolan 2007), her use of literary forms such as the *bildungsroman* genre (McWilliams 2009), or specific literary themes within titles (Bouson 2010a, 2010b; Wisker 2002, 2010), the number of extended studies that have explored her use of language—through applied linguistic or applied stylistic perspectives, specifically—is comparatively more limited. Historically, studies that have explored the language of Atwood's writing have taken a philological approach, and in these examples linguistic choice and patterns are treated as a literary theme within her works (e.g., Hutchison 2003), or otherwise framed through a critical or theoretical reading of a text or theme, such as those grounded in psychoanalysis (e.g., Staels 1995a, b). While other more applied linguistic articles or chapters that analyse Atwood's style have touched upon topics such as the language of alienation (Ewell 1981) or the presentation of speech acts (Dodson 1997; Hogsette 1997; Lacombe 1986), these studies often isolate one feature of language, and often in relation to just one text. With reference to key ideas from literary criticism alongside recent literary linguistic forays into Atwood's writing (e.g., Dancygier 2007; Nuttall 2014, 2018; Harrison and Nuttall 2019, 2020), this book explores Atwood's distinctive use of language and style, across a selection of her most recent prose publications, through an extended, reader-centred and cognitive stylistic perspective.

1.2 Cognitive Stylistics

A stylistic approach to language involves the applied and systematic analysis of textual choices and patterns, and the various contexts in which texts are written and received by readers. The emphasis on co-text, context and readers within stylistics means that literary linguistic analysis is both situated and meaningful. In contrast to the mere labelling or counting of instances of linguistic features, the emphasis instead is on *how* these choices both generate and constrain interpretations in reading. While it is not possible to carry out a text analysis that does not start with introspective impressions generated in the mind of the reader-researcher (Stockwell 2021), the exploration of linguistic form and the application of linguistic frameworks developed by stylisticians means that any successful stylistic account will avoid a discussion that is founded on impressionistic, vague or subjective opinions only. Stylisticians have, at their disposal, a range of analytical methods through which to implement a precise, holistic and socially situated analysis of literary reading. These methods are practical tools rather than theoretical positions and enable researchers to generate analyses that are rigorous, transparent and, primarily and most importantly, textually grounded (Carter and Stockwell 2008; Simpson 2014). The prioritisation of practical analysis within stylistics means that it is regarded as a progressive and magpie-like discipline that collects, refines and polishes analytical tools when they become rusty or in need of repair (Carter and Stockwell 2008, 301).

The discipline has undergone a cognitive turn, and cognitive stylistics has emerged as a research strand that references concepts from cognitive linguistics and cognitive psychology for the study of literary texts, adding tools through which to explore processes of the mind. Cognitive stylistics follows the central commitments that underpin cognitive linguistics more generally, such as the 'generalization commitment', which holds that all aspects of language are underpinned by key organisational principles related to the linguistic rank scale. The 'cognitive commitment' is premised on the principle of conceptual embodiment, which argues that all aspects of language are also generated and constrained by our interaction with and experience of the world around as a physical space, through 'species-specific anatomical and neurological structures' (Tyler 2012, 28). These structures create a series of cognitive templates which we draw on in this process of interaction, and these templates derive from our encyclopaedic knowledge and schemas (Schank 1982), the interrelated concepts of domains and frames (Minsky 1975), and of conceptual metaphors (Lakoff and Johnson 1980). In these ways, cognitive stylistics is theoretically and markedly distinct from those theoretical accounts which might inform other linguistic approaches in literary criticism, such as Saussurean linguistics, psychoanalysis or textual deconstruction. As with stylistic study, cognitive stylistics does not present a formalist approach, but instead one which refers to broader facets of the context of literature—such as 'intention, interpretation, social negotiation, history and value' (Harrison and Stockwell 2014, 219)—and which prioritises socio-cognitive concerns. The rigour, systematicity and contextual sensitivity of cognitive stylistics mean that it is first and foremost a 'scientific practice', and one in which the following principles are observed:

1. The analysis is centred on the object of investigation (albeit the literary text or reader response data);
2. The account is supported by appropriate (textual) evidence;
3. Any arguments or assertions made are clear, open and falsifiable;
4. Readings should be replicable and not uniquely idiosyncratic;

5. Applied terms and frameworks have a generally accepted and disciplined currency. (after Harrison and Stockwell 2014, 219).

An overview of the 'applied terms and frameworks' which make up the analytical methods covered in this book is outlined in more detail within each chapter. Given the volume of literary criticism and scholarship that exists on Atwood's writing, it merits emphasising that the discussion in this book does not intend to debate existing literary-critical, theoretical positions on Atwood's work. Instead, such secondary debates will be treated as another type of reader response data and touched upon as a point of departure for discussion of thematic analysis, insofar as it contributes to the stylistic analysis of the language.

1.3   The Language of Writing

Atwood belongs to a long tradition of writers who have critically reflected on the processes of writing and authorship. These reflections have been published throughout her career and appear in both her fiction and non-fiction writings. In the context of her prose fiction, many of these commentaries are centred around what it means to be a successful writer and the social cache and repu-tation that the role carries. *The Blind Assassin* (Atwood 2000; see Chapter 2), for example, comprises three connecting storylines that all reflect on processes of writing and storytelling. The protagonist Iris writes a memoir of her life, in which she describes the bestselling novel written by her sister Laura, and which in turn features an embedded science fiction story. The revelation that Iris, and not her sister Laura, is the author of these stories forms the twist at the end and contributes significantly to the central thematic questions of the perceived authenticity, and the authorship and ownership of stories which underpin the novel. Similarly, the first three interconnected stories in the collection *Stone Mattress* (Atwood 2014a, b) feature Constance, a commercially successful writer of fantasy fiction who worries about appearing 'fatuous' (2014, 33) in interviews, and who seems painfully aware of evalua-tions of snobbery related to genre fiction writing ('There was a small group that confessed to reading The Lord of the Rings, though you had to justify it through an interest in Old Norse', 2014, 25) (Chapter 4). Both *The Blind Assassin* and *Stone Mattress* can be regarded as commentaries on the reception and perception of genre fiction more widely, and both Constance and Iris experience requests from academic researchers and are forced to respond to the 'intrusive critical reader' of their novels (Tolan 2017, 453–454). The experiences of both writing and critiquing genre fiction are presented as ones that can take over someone's identity entirely: *Lady Oracle*, for instance, makes fun of the central character Joan, who writes Gothic romance novels and ultimately becomes a protagonist in her own romanticised story ('I was referred to as a 'key figure' in a mysterious dynamite plot', Atwood 2021, 367).

Another central theme within Atwood's exploration of writing shows a concern with *how* the message of a story is transmitted to audiences, and the spatiotemporal distance that separates narrators and their addressees, or more superordinately, authors and readers. Famously, *The Handmaid's Tale* is a recording of Offred's confession, found in 2195 and some years after the dissolution of Gilead. Critics identify how this novel appraises the processes of storytelling, and the relationship between writing and reading (Bouson 1993; Dvorak 1998). In another account in which the protagonist acknowledges the uncertainty of a future reading audience, *Oryx and Crake* (Atwood 2013) represents the main character Snowman as the potential sole survivor of the human race following the outbreak of a man-made plague. The third-person narration focalises Snowman's voice as his story is told through a series of flashbacks, in which he recounts his former, pre-apocalyptic life as Jimmy. The Snowman/Jimmy divide carries through the story, and at the end of the novel Snowman rereads Jimmy's final missive: 'I don't have much time, but I will try to set down what I believe to be the explanation for the recent ~~extraordinary events~~ catastrophe' (Atwood 2013, 404). The futility of Jimmy's attempt to record the event is derided by Snowman, who acknowledges that '[i]t's the fate of these words to be eaten by beetles' (405). In both *The Handmaid's Tale* and *Oryx and Crake*, the actuality of a reading audience for these impermanent records seems an unsurpassable and unreachable possibility, and in the immediate context, there is no discernible audience other than themselves (Chapters 6 and 7). In other examples of Atwood's writing, this narrative distancing is created through the layering of voices and the mediation between the events that make up the narrative and their reporting by the narrator. The story of the real-world murders in *Alias Grace* (1996), for example, undergoes a process of fabrication and becomes increasingly fictionalised and attenuated in its rendering through its third-, fourth- and fifth-hand reporting (Chapter 3).

Outside of her fictional texts, in *On Writers and Writing* (2015a), Atwood critically reflects on the roles and anxieties that writers will assume and experience across their careers, starting with comments from fellow novelists and writers on what motivates them to write, what it feels like to write, and the associated social expectations. Underpinning this reflection is the metaphor

WRITING IS PERFORMANCE, which is referenced both explicitly and implicitly in the language she uses to describe the activity. Atwood moves from directly commenting on the 'impressive significance' of what is a 'socially acknowledged role', before discussing the public roles of the writer, and the 'costume' they might assume:

> Writing—the setting down of words—is an ordinary enough activity [...] Anyone literate can take an implement in hand and make marks on a flat surface. *Being a writer,* however, seems to be a socially acknowledged role, and one that carries some sort of weight or impressive significance—we hear a capital W on *Writer.* [...] It is not always a particularly blissful or fortunate role to find yourself saddled with, and it comes with a price; though, like many roles, it can lend a certain kind of power to those who assume the costume. (Atwood 2015a, 4)

This description is later refashioned and extended through a more specific MAGICIAN analogy in *Burning Questions* (2022, 38):

> There's knowing what and there's knowing how, and the how comes from years of practice, and failure, and dropping the egg that was supposed to come out of the hat, and crumpling up Chapter One for the twentieth time and throwing it into the wastepaper basket.

Given this foregrounded self-awareness of form across her writing, and the self-reflexivity which underpins her texts, it feels appropriate to start this book on the language of Atwood with a consideration of the language used by the author to describe the writing process. As the quotation in the dedication of this book notes, Atwood might view this enterprise as a futile one, but it is certainly one that has preoccupied her fiction and non-fiction writing over time.

Metaphor analysis is one of the most explored areas at the interface of language and cognition (Gavins 2020, 26) and therefore presents an apt starting point for the cognitive stylistic account that follows in this book. Following the principle of embodiment, in Lakoff and Johnson's (1980) theory of metaphor, the conceptual metaphors we use and encounter in everyday discourse (conversational, non-literary, literary and otherwise) mirror and frame the culturally entrenched ways in which we understand the world. This experience involves conceptualising abstract things or concepts, known as 'target' domains, in reference to more concrete or familiar 'source' domains. The metaphor WRITING IS PERFORMANCE, for example, conceptualises the target domain WRITING in reference to the source domain

PERFORMANCE. The metaphor is created through transferring properties from the source domain to the target domain in a process known as 'mapping'. In this metaphor, mapped properties might include the role of the magician being equated with that of the writer, a wand being compared to a pen, or the stage construed as the writing or the book itself, and so on.

The next three sections outline three important metaphors for writing employed by Atwood, and how these are linguistically and conceptually framed within and across Atwood's critical reflections.[2]

1.3.1 WRITERS ARE CRIMINALS; HANDS ARE (DOUBLE) AGENTS

An associated and recurrent metaphor that appears in *On Writers and Writing* (2015a) is the 'doubleness' that is perceived to be inherently part of writing. Atwood expands on this when she questions:

> What is the relationship between the two entities we lump under the name, that of 'the writer'? The particular writer. By *two*, I mean the person who exists when no writing is going forward—the one who walks the dog, eats bran for regularity, takes the car in to be washed, and so forth—and that other, more shadowy and altogether more equivocal personage who shares the same body, and who, when no one is looking, takes it over and uses it to commit the actual writing. (Atwood 2015a, 30)

The description of the 'two entities' that make up the double roles of 'the writer' and the 'person' here designate two contrasting character profiles. The SPLIT SELF metaphor (Lakoff 1996) occurs where a speaker or writer observes themselves to be divided or duplicated. While Emmott (2002, 156) uses this term to apply to any sense of a different version of the self, Lakoff (1996) uses the term more specifically to designate where selves are attached to intellectual or social roles. In Atwood's commentary, differences between the two writer profiles are modelled in the schematic templates which help elaborate and instantiate these double roles and the social and intellectual functions they fulfil. The 'person' is described in very prosaic terms, and in reference to carrying out daily domestic activities such as walking the dog and eating bran. This role is also described schematically: 'the person' is a definite and yet non-specific noun phrase that does not confer many distinguishing qualities. The person is defined by what they do, and by their existence only in relation to 'that other' through explicit negation ('the person who exists when no writing

---

[2] As with the rest of the book, the examples in this section are selected as representative instances of these metaphors and do not outline an exhaustive list of their representation in Atwood's works.

is going forward'). Since instances of negation foreground the positive counterpart of the denied proposition (Hidalgo-Downing 2000), this works as a
kind of conceptual doubling or comparison which, in this context, emphasises the contrasting and yet inextricable link between the two roles. In other
words, one writer entity cannot be conceptualised without the other.

The contrast between the two writer roles is further carried through grammatically in the comparators in the final half of the sentence. '[T]hat other' is
distinguished through more romanticised descriptions in that they are 'more
shadowy and altogether more equivocal' and exempt from mundane activities. This description, combined with the only activity assigned to 'that other',
marks a genre change which evokes another metaphor. Here, 'the writer'
is attributed criminal or furtive operations; they become the grammatical
subject and agent that controls the shared body and, in fact, more completely
'takes it over'. The final verb phrase ('commit the actual writing') sets up a
domain of CRIME. In other contexts, the verb 'commit' would denote a criminal action,[3] which, used with 'writing' here, maps properties of a covert and
illicit activity.

The conceptualisation of writing as a criminal activity can be observed
thematically across Atwood's oeuvre. In a contemporary example, 'The Dead
Hand Loves You' short story in *Stone Mattress* (Atwood 2014a, b) features
a struggling novelist, Jack, who unwittingly pens a novel that 'started as a
joke' (185) but which becomes an 'International Horror Classic' (187). The
short story describes how, before writing the novel, Jack carelessly signed a
contract with his three housemates which entitled them to share evenly in
the profits from the book. In the focalisation of Jack, the events of the story
are represented as outside of his control: the signing of the contract was an
act of coercion in which '[h]e shouldn't be held responsible' and for which
'[h]e shouldn't be held to terms' (186). Equally, the story he goes on to write
appears as a 'vision', revealed as an animate entity, independent from Jack's
creation: 'Where did it come from, *The Dead Hand Loves You*? Who knows?
Out of desperation. Out from the under the bed. Out of his childhood
nightmares' (200). The horror short story Jack writes features the disembodied hand of a jilted lover who wreaks revenge on his former partner, partly
through writing a letter that imitates her handwriting. A different manifestation of the SPLIT SELF metaphor is therefore presented across both the frame
and the embedded story. In both, Atwood explores the metonymic relationship between the hand as an agent of writing, and the writer herself, and
raises questions of agency and responsibility, questioning who 'is the actual

---

[3] The British National Corpus lists the collocates 'offence', 'crime' and 'crimes' as occurring the third,
fifth and sixth most frequently with instances of the verb 'commit', for example.

perpetrator of the text' (2015a, 38)? Continued ruminations on this relationship mean that hands are considered a leitmotif in Atwood's writing (Staels 2004, 158–159; Murray 2001, 69–70) and indeed, duality, and the division of selves, is also considered a prominent theme and structuring device across her novels (Grace 1980; Vickroy 2015; see also Chapter 3 in this book, which explores the patchwork metaphor in *Alias Grace*, and Chapter 8's examination of June/Offred in *The Handmaid's Tale* TV adaptation).

The short story or prose poem, 'Murder in the Dark' (1994), similarly builds on the WRITING IS A CRIMINAL ACTIVITY metaphor, except here, the crime is conceptualised more specifically, and more ominously, as murder:

> If you like, you can play games with this game. You can say: the murderer is the writer, the detective is the reader, the victim is the book. Or perhaps, the murderer is the writer, the detective is the critic and the victim is the reader. In that case the book would be the total *mise en scène*, including the lamp that was accidentally tipped over and broken. But really it's more than fun just to play the game.
>
> In any case, that's me in the dark. I have designs on you, I'm plotting my sinister crime, my hands are reaching for your neck or perhaps, by mistake, your thigh. You can hear my footsteps approaching, I wear boots and carry a knife, or maybe it's a pearl-handled revolver, in any case I wear boots with very soft soles, you can see the cinematic glow of my cigarette, waxing and waning in the fog of the room, the street, the room, even though I don't smoke. Just remember this, when the scream at last has ended and you've turned on the lights: by the rules of the game, I always lie.
>
> Now: do you believe me? (Atwood 1994, 49–50)

This description starts with a seemingly light and offhand invitation ('If you like, you can play games with this game'), which offers readers different options for interpreting the metaphor. Different parts of the WRITING target domain are spotlighted ('the writer', 'the reader', 'the critic', 'the book') and at the same time, different roles within the CRIMINAL ACTIVITY source domain are analogously specified ('the murderer', 'the detective', 'the victim'). Thus, the description establishes and clarifies several potential mappings within the metaphor. Significantly, though, while the reader's role shifts from 'detective' to 'victim', the writer's role remains fixed. They are the murderer, '[i]n any case', and no matter which way the metaphor is framed. The use of the definite article for the roles and descriptions in this scene ('*the* game', '*the* lamp, '*the* writer', emphasis added) assumes references that are already known and familiar. It appears, therefore, that this game is known to both parties, and that both the narrator and the you-addressee exist within the same shared physical space.

The second paragraph undergoes a stylistic shift to first person, so that the speaking-narrator moves onstage: 'that's me in the dark'. Until this point, the opponent in this game has not been explicitly identified, and with the scene unlit by the 'broken' lamp and the consequent darkness of the space, the specific details of the speaking I-narrator remain ambiguous and open to alternative interpretations: 'I wear boots and carry a knife, *or maybe* it's a pearl-handled revolver' (emphasis added). In addition to the adjustment of props, this conceptual alternativity extends to the parameters of the location of the physical scene (which moves, indiscriminately, between 'the room, the street, the room'), the roles played by the narrator and the addressee, and the negated or ambiguous actions of the narrator ('my hands are reaching for your neck [or] your thigh'—'even though I don't smoke'). The transience and indeterminacies of the facts of the scene are further underscored by the epistemic doubt of speaker ('perhaps', 'maybe'), in the apparent contradiction of facts ('You can hear my foot steps approaching', even though, 'in any case I wear boots with very soft soles'), and in the antithetical, final confession that, 'by the rules of the game, I always lie'.

Despite the uncertainty of the scene, the two roles of the narrator and the addressee are clear. The book's role as conduit is backgrounded in the second paragraph, and the action instead designates how, grammatically, the murderer/writer is an agent who carries out their own physical actions which either supply further Cluedo-esque description as to their appearance ('I wear boots and carry a knife') or else designate actions that impact on the addressee ('I have designs on you'). The reader may be the victim or the detective, and in either case, they are framed as someone who can perceive—they 'can say', 'can hear' and 'can see', and are instructed to 'remember'—but do not have a more physically agentive role. These attributed actions confer the addressee with cognitive or perceptual agency only.

In these two paragraphs from 'Murder in the dark', then, WRITING IS A CRIMINAL ACTIVITY is conflated and blended with a READING IS A GAME metaphor associated with detective fiction. The rules of this game are said to be governed by two central questions: (1) 'Whodunit?' and (2) Who is guilty? (Herman et al. 2005, 103). In this metaphor blend, the identity of the murderer-player is both identified and yet not fully or categorically specified. Because the first-person narrator of 'Murder in the dark' confesses that they are the murderer/writer, then the perceived space between the narrator and the real-world author is reduced (Semino 1995, 145), such that Atwood becomes implicated in the set-up. This is fitting, given the autobiographical frame of the collection (Nischik 2005, 8). At the same time, however, the threatening actions are attributed, grammatically, to the murderer/narrator's hands instead ('my hands are reaching for your neck'). This separation means that 'whodunit' and 'who is guilty' remain distinct, though interrelated, questions (Herman et al. 2005, 103). This discernible authorial presence also invites an extra role for the you-addressee. At the beginning of this story, 'you' might be considered as someone who occupies the same physical space as the narrator. As the authorial and reader's roles are foregrounded, however, the you-address becomes doubly deictic, inviting complicity from both the fictionalised addressee and the real-world reader reading the text. Consequently, then, readers are implicated within, or victims of, these criminal acts.

1.3.2 WRITING IS A JOURNEY

Other metaphors used by Atwood to discuss writing include those that draw on a CONTAINER image schema (Johnson 1987). In cognitive linguistics, an image schema is a schematic representation of activity that derives from our everyday sensory experiences with the world around us (Mandler 2004). The idea that words form containers is part of the conduit metaphor (Lakoff and Johnson 1980; Reddy 1979); a metalinguistic conceptualisation of language as vessels, units or spaces that comprise and can be filled with, and importantly can also transfer, meaning and knowledge. As part of the introductory context for *On Writers and Writing* (2015a). Atwood asks fellow novelists 'what it felt like when they went into a novel' and observes that '[n]one of them wanted to know what I meant by *into*' (Atwood 2015a, xxi). The responses of these other writers featured containers and conduits: a tunnel, a labyrinth, a cave, a lake, a dark room, a deep river, an empty theatre (xxi--xxii).

Aligning with these responses from fellow writers, Atwood's conceptualisations of WRITING IS A CONTAINER change according to different scale of space. At times, the container is very small. Writers might be aware that this space is confined and will be physically constrained or impacted by such close quarters; they may, for example, 'feel struck by the limitations of language' (Atwood 1990). In this framing, language is the limiting container. Language as a container with discrete limits is further elaborated in a more recent essay where Atwood describes writing as a process of visiting the 'word-hoard' (2022, 37–48). She explains how 'hoard' is an Anglo-Saxon word for treasure, and how the phrase can be interpreted as a type of 'well' of inspiration (Atwood 2022, 46). These two conceptualisations represent language as a finite but precious resource for the writer, both limiting and limited in different ways. At other times, writing as a contained space is conceptualised by Atwood on a much larger scale. The examination of science fiction in *In Other Worlds: SF and the Human Imagination* (Atwood 2011), for example, further highlights the metaphorical role of the text itself, and the conceptual sense of place and location that a text designates. As the pun in the title outlines WORDS ARE WORLDS---a mega-metaphor that interrelates with other framings and that also incidentally forms the basis of the cognitive stylistic framework, Text World Theory (Werth 1999) (see Chapter 6).

In Atwood's critical writing memoir, this world is framed specifically as the Underworld, where writing is described as a process of conversing with, and revivifying, voices of the dead. This focus was signposted more explicitly in the original title of the memoir, *Negotiating with the Dead* (2002). She explores the journey made by writers and frames this as a descent that is a compulsive movement, as the repeated deontic 'must' in the following description suggests:

> All writers must go from *now* to *once upon a time*; all must go from here to there; all must descend to where the stories are kept; all must take care not to be captured and held immobile by the past. (Atwood 2015a, 160)

At the other side of the writer-reader exchange, this conceptual movement downwards is mirrored in metaphors for reading. Readers talk about being immersed or pulled into, or volitionally 'diving' into, a story (Nuttall and Harrison 2020). In Atwood's description, though, the downwards movement is framed as one that is finite and bounded in time and space; as a journey with visitor restrictions ('A book is another country. You enter it, but then you must leave; like in the Underworld, you can't live there', 155).

As with the other metaphors for writing mentioned in this chapter, representations of texts-as-worlds can also be found in Atwood's works of fiction. The fantasy world of 'Alphinland', for example, in the recent collection *Stone Mattress*, is navigated by Constance via a gateway screensaver on her computer:

> Over the screensaver gateway is a legend carved in the stone, in pseudo-gothic Pre-Raphaelite lettering:
>
> ALPHINLAND
>
> Constance takes a deep breath. Then she goes through.
> On the other side of the gateway there's no sunny landscape. Instead, there's a narrow road, almost a trail. It winds downhill to a bridge, which is lit – because it's night – by yellowish lights shaped like eggs or water drops. Beyond the bridge is a dark wood.

She'll cross the bridge and move stealthily through the wood, alert for ambushes, and when she comes out the other side she'll be at a crossroads. Then it will be a matter of which of the roads to follow. All of them are in Alphinland, but each leads to a different version of it. Even though she's its creator, its puppet mistress, its determining Fate, Constance never knows exactly where she might end up. (Atwood 2014a, b, 19–20)

For Constance, this is a romanticised and fairy-tale-like place accessible through a portal, much like Alice going through the mirror in *Through the Looking Glass* (Howell 2017, 301). The virtual gateway conferred the physical properties of carved stone, and her retrieval of the story is modelled as a literal journey necessitating physical movement across a threshold: 'she goes through'. Here, the role of traveller is mapped onto Constance's role as a writer. The familiarity of her story is framed as a visible trail, illuminated 'by yellowish lights shaped like eggs or water drops'. Other mappings in the description sketch out the more unfamiliar or hazardous part of this journey that may impede her progress. There are perils in potential 'ambushes' and in the different versions of the land that remain unknown in the absence of a 'sunny landscape'. Constance acknowledges these dangers despite her assumed agency as the orchestrator and 'puppet mistress' (Atwood 2014a, b, 17) of the storyworlds.

This navigation through worlds of fiction represents writing as a journey, more specifically. In cognitive and literary stylistics, READING IS TRANSPORT (sometimes labelled READING IS A JOURNEY) is a metaphor entrenched in readers' conceptualisations of reading fiction (Gerrig 1993; Nuttall and Harrison 2020; Stockwell 2009). Within this metaphor, and like in Constance's trek through Alphinland, readers are mapped as travellers who enter and travel through the fictional world presented by the text. Atwood's conceptualisations of writing as a journey as framed in these examples suggest an additional mapped quality between source and target domains: namely, that writers are fellow travellers. They similarly frame text experiences as processes of visiting and travelling through the world of the text. In Constance's journey described above, this process is one that is established and set out by the text. While she is making the journey, her agency in other ways is questionable in that she is at the mercy of the already established 'roads'. Though this mapping is not one that has been explored in stylistics in the same way as the role of the reader, the pervasiveness of the mapped role of the writer within this conceptual metaphor can be observed in everyday literary discourse such as the word 'plot', both a piece of land and a choice of narrative structure, or in the requirement for writers to 'signpost' writing in order to create greater textual cohesion for readers. In such conceptualisations, writers and readers are fellow travellers, but writers are the ones who chart the course of the journey.

1.3.3 BOOKS ARE CONDUITS

Building on the conceptualisation of writing or texts as creating a location or space, Atwood's fiction explores theoretical questions on the distance between narrators and readers. She reflects on how different types of stories may impact on the perceived proximity of this relationship in time and space, and the different audiences that are addressed within these various genres. She argues that '[f]or the tale-teller, the audience is right there in front of him, but the writer's audience consists of individuals whom he may never see or know' (2015a, 30). In a more recent conversation with fellow author Neil Gaiman, Atwood discusses contemporary changes to reading, writing and publication processes which impact on the perceived distance between writing production and text reception. During their conversation, Atwood and Gaiman talk about the unknown identities of readers, and the distance in space and time between the moment of writing and the moment of reading. Reflecting on current publication processes, she describes how,

> People are learning various other different ways of approaching the whole business of getting from Tin Can A to Tin Can B […] Tin Can A is the writer, Tin Can B is the reader. Everything else in between is string. So, it's the string that's changing. And the fact that the string is changing, is changing the As and Bs to a certain extent, but you're still involved in getting your thing that you have done across time and space to B, The Unknown B. (Atwood 2015b, in conversation with Gaiman)

As the analyses in these sections have observed, the metaphors Atwood draws on to discuss writing clearly position writers in relation to, as opposed to separate from, readers. Each of the metaphors identified here has foregrounded how the sites of textual production and reception might be conceptualised, and the costumes we might need to assume: writers are doubled and duplicitous; they are criminals, murderers and travellers; readers are victims, detectives, competitors, but, at the same time, collaborators and fellow travellers.

This seems a fitting place to begin a book about the language of Atwood's contemporary prose fiction. The chapters in this book focus on the nature of the relationships between Tin Can A (Atwood) and Tin Can B (her contemporary readers). Since stylistics concerns the analysis of linguistic patterns and how these might influence or generate reader interpretation, then, in short, this book is a study of both tin cans, and the string in between.

1.4   The Language of Reading

Stylisticians have always been interested in readers. Alongside the rise of cognitive stylistics in contemporary stylistics scholarship, the turn towards reader response research has similarly burgeoned significantly, with applications drawing on reader data as a means of either supporting the text analysis or as the focus of the analysis itself, with reader discussions spotlighted and the text stimulus a more secondary concern within the research design. This turn towards reader data seems a natural development in the evolution of the discipline, given its fundamental interest in situated and reception-oriented analysis and the offer of 'a reconnection of literary scholarship with natural readers' (Harrison and Stockwell 2014, 219). Stylisticians draw on responses not to argue that readers mentally carry out similar feats of linguistic analysis when they read, but rather as a means of initiating discussion on the way that readers process, model and experience texts via textual or stylistic prompts. In this sense, the use of reader data is an indirect measure of literary experience, and one which forms a valuable springboard for linguistic analysis of those facets of the text that are identified, directly or indirectly, as especially salient in readers' understanding and interpretation of the narrative.

Within stylistics and applied literary studies more broadly, reader response studies can be divided into two approaches: naturalistic and experimental (Swann and Allington 2009). A naturalistic approach collects or generates reader data derived from authentic and naturally occurring reading practices, such that the role of the researcher is backgrounded within the study. Projects that fall into this category include those that explore readers' engagement with literature arising from everyday reading practices, such as discursive discourse generated through participation in book groups (e.g., Long 2003; Peplow 2016; Peplow et al. 2016), or through online book reviews (e.g., Giovanelli 2022a; Nuttall 2018). Unique affordances of naturalistic methods include a consideration of data that are not filtered by a researcher, and which are situated within a collaborative and socially situated experience of reading. Experimental designs, on the other hand, aim to isolate specific parts of the reading experience through controlling the conditions and variables of the reading experience. Experimental protocols have traditionally been the mainstay of cognitive literary studies that are less interested on language and more interested in the psychological processes of reading (Kuiken and Jacobs 2021).

These methods have been taken up in more applied linguistic and stylistic contexts, and methods such as post-reading questionnaires (e.g., Mastropierro and Conklin 2023) and think-aloud protocols (e.g., da Costa Fialho 2007) have been implemented in the generation of text-driven literary linguistic projects. Outside of studies that focus on specific textual stimuli or instances of language, other researchers have employed surveys and questionnaires to elicit reflections on reading habits and practices, for example to explore re-reading habits and preferences (Harrison and Nuttall 2018), or to gather data on practices of reading as altered through wider social circumstances, as in Boucher et al.'s (2020) study on reading habits during the Covid-19 pandemic.

Bell et al. (2021, 9–12) argue that in contemporary scholarship, the choice between the two methodological approaches is dependent on the object of inquiry, with those interested in exploring cognitive phenomena more likely to employ an experimental protocol, and those pursuing a sociocultural analysis more likely to take a naturalistic approach. This divide is less marked in those studies interested in the interrelationship between solitary and social aspects of reading, however, where both cognitive models and situated reading experiences are under scrutiny, and where text choices and patterns in reader responses are both spotlighted. An increasing number of cognitive stylistic projects, for example, draw on naturalistic data where the 'focus is placed on the content of such interpretations, rather than the process of collaborative interpretation itself' (Norledge 2021, 46), or where reader data derived from experimental protocols are used in support of discussions of cognitive phenomena (e.g., Giovanelli 2022b).

1.5   'The Unknown Bs': Reader Response Data

Exploring data derived from naturalistic reader data provides valuable insights into non-academic, everyday experiences and engagement with texts (Swann and Allington 2009) and enables stylisticians to model or contextualise the processes that underpin readers' affective experience of literature (Stockwell 2009, 79). The analyses in this book draw on different types of naturalistic reader responses to Atwood's prose fiction writing, from different groups of readers (including academic, professional and consumers) in support of text analysis. Each chapter will additionally consider reader responses from different sources, as outlined in the summary of the chapters below. The analyses in this book, then, will follow more formal protocols for the study of readers that move the discussion away from an abstracted or implicit notion of an implied or ideal reader and more towards a more 'explicit' study (Whiteley and Canning 2017, 72) of 'ordinary' (Swann and Allington 2009, 247), 'real' (Whiteley 2011) or 'natural' readers (Stockwell 2005). This discussion will therefore depart from the few literary studies of Atwood's reception that have focused on professional or analytical responses.

While acknowledging the popularity of Atwood's writing among the general reading public, existing critical analyses of Atwood's texts have not examined their non-academic audience reception. Indeed, in Nischik's (2017) survey of early reader reviews of *The Blind Assassin* non-critical readers are actively excluded from the dataset. A stylistic approach to Atwood's writing and use of language necessitates a study of readers in different forms, given the discipline's emphasis on how texts produce meaning and generate distinct reading experiences. The discussion in the chapters of this book will outline an account of Atwood's language that is grounded in the experiential processes of reading, and which takes a mixed-methods approach to trace those 'real' reading experiences (Hall 2009) as framed in online and offline reader communication.[4]

1.5.1   Reader Reviews

Chapters 2 and 6 draw on reader data from the online review website, Goodreads, in order to support the text analysis. Launched in 2007, at the time of writing, Goodreads is the largest online community of readers—a website designed to help readers share their thoughts on books they have read and enjoyed. Visitors of the site can browse existing reviews of books more superficially, or else engage more socially by creating an account which enables them to follow friends' virtual bookshelves, to post their own reviews, to respond to others' comments and to participate in various reading challenges. In many ways, this format is a digital echo of an analogue reading book group, and in fact the site is founded on 'a book-club model rather than a journalistic one' (Fay 2012). Such reader review data hold both commercial interest and 'constitute important evidence for how readers read books' (Koolen et al. 2022, 149). Significantly, the rise in popularity of such platforms reflects the changing nature of contemporary reading practices, with the affordances of social media and technology platforms offering readers new opportunities and environments to engage in social reading practices

---

[4] The collection and generation of both the online review and offline book group datasets were approved by Aston University's Business and Social Sciences Research Ethics Committee.

(Allington and Pihlaja 2016; see also Peplow et al. 2016 for a discussion of social and solitary reading).

For the discussion in these two chapters, I collected the top 100 community-rated reviews of *The Blind Assassin* and *Oryx and Crake* as organised by the website's default sorting algorithm. Each dataset was qualitatively coded for themes in NVivo, following the protocol of reader review analysis in contemporary cognitive stylistic practice (e.g., Nuttall 2018; Giovanelli 2022a). While discussions of the ethical implications of the use of online open-access data are ongoing within wider scholarship, the study follows the best practice as outlined at the time of project design and writing. In line with current protocol, the participant contributions have been anonymised and have been assigned an identifier code corresponding with the text choice (e.g., BA1–100 for *The Blind Assassin* reviews; OC1–100 for the *Oryx and Crake* reviews). Where directly quoted, all spelling and punctuation are reproduced as they appear in the original reviews.

1.5.2   The ABC Club

Reading group discourse is 'participant-led, with conversation developing a natural flow in line with habitual discourse practices' (Norledge 2021, 46). Contemporary cognitive stylistic research has drawn on data derived from focus groups that simulate reading group discourse (Lugea 2022; Norledge 2021) or from reading groups already in existence and which are an established community of practice (Long 2003; Peplow et al. 2016). For some researchers, the focus of such analyses is primarily on the language used by the participants, and the text is treated more as a stimulus for discussion (e.g., Nuttall and Harrison 2020). For others, the text is the primary focus, and patterns among reader responses are explored for experiential context or to support the primary textual analysis (e.g., Whiteley 2016). While the emphasis may differ, the interaction between text and readers is always apparent. Researchers in cognitive stylistics acknowledge that reading involves a type of intersubjective communication which takes place, firstly, between a reader and the text as constructed by the author, and secondly between a reader and their fellow discourse participants (Peplow 2016; Peplow et al. 2016; Peplow and Whiteley 2021).

To support the discussion of Chapters 4 and 5 in this book, in spring 2022, I approached an established book group, hereafter referred to as The ABC Club, who agreed to take part in the study. The reading group has been meeting regularly since 2015 and is made up of a group of friends and acquaintances based in the West Midlands, UK. At the time the study took place, six members of the group attended most frequently, with other members joining on a more intermittent basis. The group meets once a month to discuss a book, and they each take turns choosing the text. They read books from different genres and time periods, and their only limiting criterion on text choices, which are suggested and agreed on an annual basis by the group, is the length of the book. Each book must be fewer than 400 pages, and preferably under 350 pages, unless otherwise discussed in advance and agreed by the majority.

Historically, the group would hold their meetings in a local pub. Since the onset of Covid-19 and the first lockdown in the UK in 2020, however, the group switched to meeting online via the video conferencing platform Zoom, and have continued in this format since that time. The discussions typically last 1 hour–1 hour 30 minutes, and take place in the evening, typically starting at 8pm. Since the start of the book group, they had previously read two Atwood novels, *Oryx and Crake*, which was one of the group's earlier text choices, read in March 2016, and *The Testaments* in March 2021.

The group scheduled the two Atwood texts *Hag-Seed* and *Stone Mattress* for the July and August sessions in the summer of 2022. I joined the group for meeting prior to the first Atwood discussion so we were able to meet face to face before the study. At the end of this meeting, I outlined, in broad terms, the contextual information for the research project, and the participants were given the opportunity for questions, before confirming acceptance and consent to take part via an online form. The group were given *gratis* copies of the books which were delivered to the participants in advance of the first meeting. Since the members generally read books in different formats, the participants were offered the choice of audiobook, e-book or physical book for their copies. Four of the participants read the texts as paperbacks and two participants read the texts as audiobooks, in-keeping with their usual preferences. To keep the format as close as possible to the group's typical practice, the participants were not given any specific instructions beyond being asked to read the texts and discuss as they would normally. I also did not prime specific narrative features (cf. Waltonen 2016), in order to capture more naturalised and authentic responses to the texts. To avoid influencing the discussion, I was not present for the two discussions, which were recorded in my absence.

The recorded discussion data were transcribed and coded for patterns, following the same process as for the online reader review data. Following Norledge, emphasis is placed on the content of the interpretations rather than on the sociocultural collaboration of the participants (2021, 46). The participants and discussion have been anonymised when referenced in the analysis. All excerpts from the data are reproduced as they appear in the transcription.

1.6   Structure of the Book

The chapters in this book are organised according to three main topics: *misdirection* (part 1), *ambient storms* (part 2) and *doubling and splitting* (part 3). The theme and focus of each chapter are reader-driven, responding to the recurring points and topics that appear in the reader data and using these as a foundation and context for the text analysis. Each chapter explores Atwood's contemporary prose fiction as a series of exemplars of style choices, though the discussion will, by necessity, refer to other historic and contemporaneous publications written by Atwood. Constraints of time and space, and the scale and volume of Atwood's writing, mean that it is not possible to outline an exhaustive account of her works. For purposes of refining the scope of the book, and to maintain a more homogenous focus for the text analysis, this exploration will exclude Atwood's poetry texts.

The first part of the book explores how stylistic strategies of attentional misdirection are employed in the two earliest Atwood novels that are under consideration in this book. Misdirection is the 'genre-typical set of techniques through which the crime fiction reader is very often deliberately misled away from the precise nature of the circumstances surrounding the crime the fiction features' (Gregoriou 2021, 93). Both *The Blind Assassin* (2001) and *Alias Grace* (1996) are considered variations of the whodunit form, a type of detective or crime fiction driven by a central puzzle. Though Shead (2015) provides a book-length treatment of the theme in Atwood's writing, there is an absence of sustained linguistic or stylistic exploration in this account, as noted by Gregoriou (2015).

Chapter 2 explores the rhetorical strategies and stylistic mechanisms used in *The Blind Assassin* to conceal the central mystery and to maintain its revelation until appropriate moments in the novel. Though written after *Alias Grace* (the focus of Chapter 3), this novel is considered closer to the crime fiction prototype (Ingersoll 2003). *The Blind Assassin* is a complex, layered narrative, which features a story within a story (within a story). Iris's 'retelling of her life is menaced by foreknowledge' (Shead 2015, 21), which invites puzzle solving from the outset. A survey of reader reviews of the novel reveals that the *aesthetic experience of language*, the complex *genre categorisation* of the novel and its *layered structure* are significant parts of the experience of reading the text. Dancygier's (2007) exploration of the novel reveals a number of key mental spaces, what she defines as 'narrative anchors', across the embedded story structures that guide readers to the mystery's solution. The analysis in this chapter extends Dancygier's account by exploring the alternative misdirection strategies within the novel—namely, how crucial pieces of the puzzle are 'buried' (Emmott and Alexander 2014) and hidden from readers' attention—through a series of analyses examining how inferential processing is disrupted, but increasingly clarified, as the story unfolds.

Chapter 3 builds on the concept of misdirection to examine the narrative form and structure of *Alias Grace*. As the oldest novel under consideration in the book, this article draws together themes within the extensive literary criticism on the novel,[5] and particularly the interpretation of the STORY-TELLING IS QUILTING patchwork metaphor that functions structurally and thematically within the novel. Drawing on Cognitive Grammar's construal model (Langacker 2008), and its reconstrual extension outlined by Giovanelli (2022a), the chapter explores narrator retellings: scenes or events that are repeated or reconstrued more than once in the storytelling. Through a series of close analyses, it is argued how this palimpsestic, patchwork quality is not only narratologically, thematically and structurally significant, but also built into the micro-structures of the text itself. This chapter extends contemporary research in stylistics on the nature of narrative retellings and their potential to mystify rather than clarify a story's resolution in cases of uncooperative narration (Harrison 2023). Ultimately, *Alias Grace* 'defeats [the] basic expectation of crime fiction: that the crime will eventually be solved' (Shead 2015, 88).

In the second part of the book, 'Ambient storms', Chapters 4 and 5 explore contextualised reading group responses to two stylistically different Atwood texts: *Stone Mattress* (2014) and *Hag-Seed* (2016). Both texts are examined and situated in reference to discourse from the reading group, The ABC Club, enabling further insights into readers' interpretative activities. Both texts in this section feature stories that are retold. *Hag-Seed* is an adaptation of Shakespeare's *The Tempest*, transposed to a creative-writing programme in a Canadian prison, while *Stone Mattress* is a collection of 'tales about tales' (Atwood 2014a, b, 309), with a self-conscious critical discussion on the nature of storytelling and teller-and-tale relationships across the sequence of stories.

The reading group respond to different facets of the two texts. In the case of *Stone Mattress* (Chapter 4), the focus is on the form of the collection,

---

[5] In the subsequent chapters, literary critics and responses from among literary scholarship will also be referenced in the course of the analysis as a form of expert reader data where pertinent to the topics under discussion.

with The ABC Club readers discussing the structural and thematic connections within and across the short stories. The readers respond, in particular, to the representation of its COLD setting. Chapter 4 extends the application of concepts from Cognitive Grammar (introduced in Chapter 3) to explore the ways *Stone Mattress* networks references to COLD across the collection, and establishes distinctive atmospheric effects in its creation of stylistic ambience. Finally, the analysis considers how representations of perspective and viewpoint subjectify the narration, creating ambient and cohesive effects underpinned by interconnected central themes of ice storms, ageing, and revenge and their metaphorical associations. This chapter additionally contributes to the critical exploration of Atwood's short fiction, which is not as extensively discussed in the critical literature on her writing (Barzilai 2017, 318).

With *Hag-Seed*, on the other hand, the readers spent more time discussing characterisation and reflect on the voice of the unreliable protagonist Felix (Chapter 5). The retelling of this story within a prose context adds another layer to the playwright-readers relationship, which already is pragmatically complex (Feng and Shen 2001, 80). The difference in emphasis across these two reader datasets can be framed in terms of atmosphere and tone, respectively, which cumulatively build ambience in texts (Stockwell 2009). With reference to contemporary research on the stylistics of characterisation, Chapter 5 examines how Felix's distinctive mind style (Fowler 1977) is created in the novel, and how the fantastic and supernatural elements of the original play are instead transposed to his mind style within this retelling.

The third section of the book, Chapters 6 and 7, explores themes of doubling and splitting. Chapter 6 positions *Oryx and Crake* (2003) as a piece of speculative fiction which can be contextualised alongside many of Atwood's prose novels, including *The Handmaid's Tale* (1985), as well as other more recent shorter fictions such as 'Torching the Dusties', the final short story in the *Stone Mattress* (2013) collection, and the story-within-a-story tales of 'Lizard Men' and 'Peach Women' in *The Blind Assassin* (2000). An overview of the codes for a dataset of 100 online reader reviews on the novel reveals a distinctive response of its world-building. Reviewers frequently discuss the world of the text and its development, construction and 'plausibility'. As a speculative text, *Oryx and Crake* invites extended comparison between a reader's real world and the text-world. This chapter explores the various comparisons that readers make at various stages of reading, from the intertexts that form part of a reader's narrative interrelations (Mason 2019) to the building of text-worlds (Werth 1999; Gavins 2007) at key moments in the novel. It is argued that readers' experiences of 'double consciousness'

(Snyder 2011, 470) are invited at all stages and contribute to the lingering what-if questions and felt resonance identified after reading.

With reference to a different type of retelling, Chapter 7 examines the representation of June/Offred's split self in *The Handmaid's Tale* TV series adaptation (MGM and Hulu, 2017). A survey of online newspaper reviews published in response to the first series reveals an audience focus on both thematic and structural choices of the adaptation. Its *political relevance* is discussed, as well as its use of *flashbacks* as a storytelling device and the *division* or *depth* of Offred/June's character. Through linguistic analysis of voiceovers and corresponding cinematic choices, including symmetrical composition and shallow-focus shots, this chapter explores the representation of June/Offred as a divided character, and how the interanimation of style choices foreground key themes of imprisonment, objectification and surveillance.

Chapter 8 contributes a final textual analysis grounded within a different reader response dataset: an introspective account of Atwood's latest (at the time of writing) collection, *Old Babes in the Wood* (2023). This chapter closes with some final reflections on the prioritisation of readers, and future projections of text reception, at the heart of Atwood's contemporary prose fiction writing.

References

Allington, Daniel, and Stephen Pihlaja. 2016. Reading in the age of the internet. *Language and Literature* 25 (3): 201–210.

Atwood, Margaret. 1985. *The handmaid's tale*. Toronto: McClelland and Stewart Ltd.

Atwood, Margaret. 1990. Margaret Atwood: The art of fiction. *The Paris Review* 121 (117).

Atwood, Margaret. 1994. *Murder in the dark*. London: Virago.

Atwood, Margaret. 1996. *Alias Grace*. Toronto: McClelland and Stewart Ltd.

Atwood, Margaret. 2000. *The blind assassin*. Toronto: McClelland and Stewart Ltd.

Atwood, Margaret. 2011. *In other worlds; SF and the human imagination*. London: Virago.

Atwood, Margaret. 2013. *Oryx and Crake*, first edition 2003. London: Virago.

Atwood, Margaret. 2014a. 'Alphinland'. In *Stone mattress: Nine wicked tales*, 1–40. London: Virago.

Atwood, Margaret. 2014b. 'The dead hand loves you'. In *Stone mattress: Nine wicked tales*, 185–232. London: Virago.

Atwood, Margaret. 2015a. *On writers and writing*, first edition 2002. London: Virago.

Atwood, Margaret. 2015b. Neil Gaiman helps Margaret Atwood celebrate her 75th birthday! https://www.youtube.com/watch?v=7Z-DAakpLuM&t=2110s&ab_channel=92ndStreetY. Accessed on 22 April 2022.

Atwood, Margaret. 2021. *Lady oracle*, first edition 1976. London: Virago.

Atwood, Margaret. 2022. *Burning questions: Essays and occasional pieces 2004–2021*. London: Chatto & Windus.

Atwood, Margaret. 2023. *Old babes in the wood*. London: Chatto & Windus.

Barzilai, Shuli. 2017. How far would you go? Trajectories of revenge in Margaret Atwood's short fiction. *Contemporary Women's Writing* 11 (3): 316–335.

Bell, Alice, Sam Browse, Alison Gibbons, and David Peplow, eds. 2021. *Style and reader response: Minds, media, methods*. Amsterdam: John Benjamins.

Boucher, Abigail, Marcello Giovanelli and Chloe Harrison. 2020. How reading habits have changed during the Covid-19 lockdown. *The Conversation*. https://theconversation.com/how-reading-habits-have-changed-during-the-covid-19-lockdown-146894.

Bouson, J. Brooks. 1993. *Brutal choreographies: Oppositional strategies and narrative design in the novels of Margaret Atwood*. Amherst: University of Massachusetts Press.

Bouson, J. Brooks. 2010a. *Margaret Atwood: The robber bride, The blind assassin, Oryx and Crake*. New York: Continuum.

Bouson, J. Brooks. 2010b. *The handmaid's tale, by Margaret Atwood*. New York: Salem Press.

Carter, Ronald and Peter Stockwell. 2008. Stylistics: retrospect and prospect. *The Language and Literature Reader*, 291–301. London: Routledge.

da Costa Fiahlo, Olívia. 2007. Foregrounding and refamiliarization: Understanding readers' responses to literary texts. *Language and Literature* 16 (2): 105–123.

Dancygier, Barbara. 2007. Narrative anchors and the processes of story construction: The case of Margaret Atwood's *The blind assassin'*. *Style* 41 (2): 133–151.

Dodson, Danita J. 1997. 'We lived in the blank white spaces': Rewriting the paradigm of denial in Atwood's *The handmaid's tale*. *Utopian Studies* 8 (2): 66–86.

Dvorak, Marta. 1998. What is real/reel? Margaret Atwood's 'rearrangement of shapes on a flat surface', or narrative as collage. *Études anglaises* 51 (4): 448–460.

Emmott, Catherine. 2002. 'Split-selves' in fiction and in medical 'life-stories': Cognitive linguistic theory and narrative practice. In *Cognitive stylistics: Language and cognition in text analysis*, ed. Elena Semino and Jonathan Culpeper, 153–182. Amsterdam: John Benjamins.

Emmott, Catherine, and Marc Alexander. 2014. Foregrounding, burying and plot construction. In *The Cambridge handbook of stylistics*, ed. Peter Stockwell and Sara Whiteley, 329–344. Cambridge: Cambridge University Press.

Ewell, Barbara. C. 1981. The language of alienation in Margaret Atwood's *Surfacing*. *Centennial Review* 25 (2): 185–202.

Fay, Sarah. 2012. 7 May. Could the internet save book reviews? *The Atlantic*. https://www.theatlantic.com/entertainment/archive/2012/05/could-the-internet-save-book-reviews/256802/. Accessed on 28 April 2018.

Feng, Zongxin, and Dan Shen. 2001. The play off the stage: The writer-reader relationship in drama. *Language and Literature* 10 (1): 79–93.

Fowler, Roger. 1977. *Linguistics and the novel*. London: Methuen.

Gavins, Joanna. 2020. *Poetry in the mind: The cognition of contemporary poetic style*. Edinburgh: Edinburgh University Press.

Gavins, Joanna. 2007. *Text world theory: An introduction*. Edinburgh: Edinburgh University Press.

Giovanelli, Marcello. 2022a. *The language of Siegfried Sassoon*. London: Palgrave.

Giovanelli, Marcello. 2022b. Cognitive grammar and readers' perceived sense of closeness: A study of responses to Mary Borden's 'Belgium.' *Language and Literature* 31 (3): 407–427.

Gerrig, Richard J. 1993. *Experiencing narrative worlds: On the psychological activities of reading*. New Haven: Yale University Press.

Grace, Sherrill. 1980. *Violent duality: A study of Margaret Atwood*. Montreal: Véhicule Press.

Gregoriou, Christiana. 2015. Review of: *Margaret Atwood: Crime fiction writer: The reworking of a popular genre* by Jackie Shead. *Modern Language Review* 110 (1): 230–231.

Gregoriou, Christiana. 2021. Re-writing misdirection: A stylistic approach to crime fiction writing. In *Narrative retellings: Stylistic approaches*, ed. Marina Lambrou, 93–110. London: Bloomsbury.

Hall, Geoff. 2009. Texts, readers—And real readers. *Language and Literature* 18 (3): 331–337.

Harrison, Chloe. 2023. 99 ways to retell a story: Forms and functions of narrator reconstrual. *Style* 57 (2): 163–185.

Harrison, Chloe, and Louise Nuttall. 2018. Re-reading in stylistics. *Language and Literature* 27 (3): 176–195.

Harrison, Chloe, and Louise Nuttall. 2019. Cognitive grammar and reconstrual: Re-experiencing Margaret Atwood's 'The freeze-dried groom.' In *Experiencing fictional worlds*, ed. Benedict Neurohr and Lizzie Stewart-Shaw, 135–154. Amsterdam: Benjamins.

Harrison, Chloe, and Louise Nuttall. 2021. Rereading as retelling: Re-evaluations of perspective in narrative fiction. In *Narrative retellings: Stylistic approaches*, ed. Marina Lambrou, 217–234. London: Bloomsbury.

Harrison, Chloe, and Peter Stockwell. 2014. Cognitive poetics. In *The Bloomsbury companion to cognitive linguistics*, ed. Jeanette Littlemore and John R. Taylor, 218–233. London: Bloomsbury.

Herman, David, Manfred Jahn, and Marie-Laure. Ryan, eds. 2005. *Routledge encyclopaedia of narrative theory*. London: Routledge.

Hidalgo-Downing, Laura. 2000. *Negation, text worlds and discourse: The pragmatics of fiction*. Stamford, CT: Ablex.

Hogsette, David S. 1997. Margaret Atwood's rhetorical epilogue in *The handmaid's tale:* The reader's role in empowering Offred's speech act. *Critique* 38 (4): 262–278.

Howell, Carol Ann. 2017. True trash: genre fiction revisited in Margaret Atwood's *Stone mattress, The heart goes last, and Hag-Seed. Contemporary Women's Writing* 11 (3): 297–315

Hutchison, Laura. 2003. The book reads well: Atwood's *Alias Grace* and the middle voice. *Pacific Coast Philology* 38: 40–59.

Ingersoll, Earl. 2003. Waiting for the end: closure in Margaret Atwood's *The blind assassin. Studies in the Novel* 35 (4): 543–558.

Johnson, Mark. 1987. *The body in the mind: The bodily basis of meaning, imagination, and reason.* Chicago: Chicago University Press.

Kuiken, Donald, and Arthur M. Jacobs, eds. 2021. *Handbook of empirical literary studies.* Berlin: De Gruyter.

Koolen, Marijn, Julia Neugarten, and Peter Boot. 2022. 'This book makes me happy and sad and I love it': A rule-based model for extracting reading impact from English book reviews. *Journal of Computational Literary Studies* 1 (1).

Lacombe, Michele. 1986. The writing on the wall: Amputated speech in Margaret Atwood's *The Handmaid's Tale. Wascana Review* 21 (2): 3–20.

Lakoff, George. 1996. Sorry, I am not myself today: The metaphor system for conceptualizing the self. In *Spaces, worlds, and grammar,* ed. Gilles Fauconnier and Eve Sweetser, 91–123. Chicago: University of Chicago Press.

Lakoff, George, and Mark Johnson. 1980. *Metaphors we live by.* Chicago: University of Chicago Press.

Langacker, Ronald W. 2008. *Cognitive grammar: A basic introduction.* Oxford: Oxford University Press.

Long, Elizabeth. 2003. *Book clubs: Women and the uses of reading in everyday life.* Chicago: University of Chicago Press.

Lugea, Jane. 2022. Dementia mind styles in contemporary narrative fiction. *Language and Literature* 31 (2): 168–195.

Mandler, Jean M. 2004. *The foundations of the mind: Origins of conceptual thought.* Oxford: Oxford University Press.

Mason, Jessica. 2019. *Intertextuality in practice.* Amsterdam: John Benjamins.

Mastropierro, Lorenzo, and Kathy Conklin. 2023. What triggers perceptions of racism in *Heart of darkness*? A reader response analysis. *Language and Literature* 32 (4): 437–457.

McWilliams, Ellen. 2009. *Margaret Atwood and the female Bildungsroman.* London: Routledge.

MGM & Hulu. 2017. *The handmaid's tale* (TV series, series 1). Santa Monica, CA: Hulu.

Minsky, Marvin. 1975. A framework for representing knowledge. In *The psychology of computer vision,* ed. P.H. Winston, 211–277. New York: McGraw Hill.

Murray, Jennifer. 2001. Historical figures and paradoxical patterns: The quilting metaphor in Margaret Atwood's *Alias Grace*. *Studies in Canadian Literature* 26 (1): 65–83.

Nischik, Reingard M. 2005. Murder in the dark: Margaret Atwood's inverse poetics of intertextual minuteness. In *Margaret Atwood's textual assassination*, ed. Sharon R. Wilson, 1–17. Ohio: Ohio State University Press.

Nischik, Reingard M. 2017. Margaret Atwood's reception in Canada and the United States: A comparative analysis of North American reviews of *The blind assassin*. *Contemporary Women's Writing* 11 (3): 354–372.

Norledge, Jessica. 2021. Modelling an unethical mind. In *Style and reader response: Minds, media, methods*, ed. Alice Bell, Sam Browse, Alison Gibbons, and David Peplow, 43–60. Amsterdam: John Benjamins.

Nuttall, Louise. 2014. Constructing a text-world for *The handmaid's tale*. In *Cognitive grammar in literature*, ed. Chloe Harrison, Louise Nuttall, Peter Stockwell, and Wenjuan Yuan, 83–99. Amsterdam: John Benjamins.

Nuttall, Louise. 2018. *Mind style and cognitive grammar: Language and worldview in speculative fiction*. London: Bloomsbury.

Nuttall, Louise, and Chloe Harrison. 2020. Wolfing down the *Twilight* series: Metaphors for reading in online reviews. In *Contemporary media stylistics*, ed. Helen Ringrow and Stephen Pihlaja, 35–59. London: Bloomsbury.

Paterson, Katie. 2014-2114. *The Future Library Project*, public artwork. The Future Library Trust: Oslo, Norway.

Peplow, David. 2016. Transforming readings: reading and interpreting in book groups. In *Scientific approaches to literature in learning environments*, ed. Michael Burke, Olivia Fialho and Sonia Zygnier. Amsterdam: John Benjamins

Peplow, David, Joan Swann, Paola Trimarco, and Sara Whiteley. 2016. *The discourse of reading groups: Integrating cognitive and sociocultural perspectives*. London: Routledge.

Peplow, David, and Sara Whiteley. 2021. Interpretation in interaction: On the dialogic nature of response. In *Style and reader response: Minds, media, methods*, ed. Alice Bell, Sam Browse, Alison Gibbons, and David Peplow, 23–42. Amsterdam: John Benjamins.

Reddy, Michael. 1979. The conduit metaphor: A case of frame conflict in our language about language. In *Metaphor and thought*, ed. Andrew Ortony, 284–297. Cambridge: Cambridge University Press.

Schank, Roger C. 1982. Language and memory. *Cognitive Science* 4 (3): 243–284.

Semino, Elena. 1995. Deixis and the dynamics of poetic voice. In *New essays on deixis: Discourse, narrative, literature*, ed. Keith Green, 145–160. Amsterdam: John Benjamins.

Shead, Jackie. 2015. *Margaret Atwood: Crime fiction writer: The reworking of a popular genre*. London: Routledge.

Simpson, Paul. 2014. *Stylistics: A resource book for students*, 2nd ed. London: Routledge.

Snyder, Katherine V. 2011. 'Time to go': The post-apocalyptic and post-traumatic in Margaret Atwood's *Oryx and Crake. Studies in the Novel* 43 (4): 470–489.

Staels, Hilde. 1995a. Margaret Atwood's *The handmaid's tale*: Resistance through narrating. *English Studies* 76 (5): 455–467.

Staels, Hilde. 1995. *Margaret Atwood's novels: A study of narrative discourse.* Tübingen: Gulde.

Staels, Hilde. 2004. Atwood's specular narrative: *The blind assassin. English Studies: A Journal of English Language and Literature* 85 (2): 147–160.

Stockwell, Peter. 2005. Texture and identification. *European Journal of English Studies* 9 (2): 143–153.

Stockwell, Peter. 2009. *Texture: A cognitive aesthetics of reading.* Edinburgh: Edinburgh University Press.

Stockwell, Peter. 2021. In defence of introspection. In *Style and reader response: Minds, media, methods*, ed. Alice Bell, Sam Browse, Alison Gibbons, and David Peplow, 165–178. Amsterdam: John Benjamins.

Swann, Joan, and Daniel Allington. 2009. Reading groups and the language of literary texts: A case study in social reading. *Language and Literature* 18 (3): 247–264.

Tolan, Fiona. 2007. *Margaret Atwood: Feminism and fiction.* Amsterdam: Rodopi.

Tolan, Fiona. 2017. 'I could say that, too': An interview with Margaret Atwood. *Contemporary Women's Writing* 11 (3): 452–464.

Tyler, Andrea. 2012. *Cognitive linguistics and second language learning: Theoretical basics and experimental evidence.* New York: Routledge.

Valenti, Jessica. 2018. Why *The handmaid's tale* is more relevant one year after the first season. https://www.theguardian.com/commentisfree/2018/apr/25/handmaids-tale-season-2-return-trump-america-2018. Accessed on 12 February 2019.

Vickroy, Laurie. 2015. Re-creating the split self in Margaret Atwood's *The blind assassin* and *Alias Grace*. In *Reading trauma narratives: The contemporary novel and the psychology of oppression*, 33–65. London: University of Virginia Press.

Waltonen, Karma. 2016. 'Atwood's view…is crazy, but very possible': Students reading *Oryx and Crake. Margaret Atwood Studies* 5 (2): 16–35.

Werth, Paul. 1999. *Text worlds: Representing conceptual space in discourse.* Harlow: Longman.

Whiteley, Sara. 2011. Text world theory, real readers and emotional responses to *The remains of the day. Language and Literature* 20 (1): 23–42.

Whiteley, Sara. 2016. Building resonant worlds: Experiencing the text-worlds of *The unconsoled*. In *World building: Discourse in the mind*, ed. Joanna Gavins and Ernestine Lahey, 165–182. London: Bloomsbury Publishing.

Whiteley, Sara, and Patricia Canning. 2017. Reader response research in stylistics. *Language and Literature* 26 (2): 71–87.

Wisker, Gina. 2002. *Margaret Atwood's Alias Grace: A reader's guide.* London: Continuum.

Wisker, Gina. 2010. *Atwood's The handmaid's tale.* London: Continuum.

Part I

Misdirection

2

Burying and Misdirection in *The Blind Assassin*

2.1 Introduction: Structural Complexity and Anchoring in *The Blind Assassin*

The Blind Assassin was first published in 2000, just four years after *Alias Grace* (1996). Both novels are often compared within the critical literature due to their shared narrative features and themes, such as unreliable narrators and an overt preoccupation with storytelling. Significantly, a key part of the comparison and grouping of the two novels concerns the extent to which each text conforms with or challenges the detective genre. As Ingersoll (2003, 543) summarises,

> If *Alias Grace*, the novel just before, may be read as a variety of *anti-detective* novel which draws readers into the expectation that they might discover the extent of Grace's culpability, only to leave them in the end without any confidence that she is clearly guilty or innocent, *The Blind Assassin* is on one level a *"whodunit"* — *with a vengeance* [...] it might be argued that *The Blind Assassin* cues its readers that a major revelation will come as the "climax" of this long narrative by constructing a first-person narrative in which readers are impressed into a race with Iris Chase Griffen to figure out whodunit before she reveals the guilty party. (emphasis added)

In *Alias Grace*, reliability is called into question through Grace's retelling of a significant, criminal event in her past. In contrast, in *The Blind Assassin*, Iris's unreliability as a narrator is marked through the many references to processes of writing, which centre themes of textuality throughout (Staels 2004, 151). Ingersoll's literary exploration of the novel's whodunit structure,

© The Author(s), under exclusive license to Springer Nature
Switzerland AG 2024
C. Harrison, *The Language of Margaret Atwood*, Palgrave Studies in Language, Literature and Style, https://doi.org/10.1007/978-3-031-67640-6_2

and of how Iris withholds and obscures facts and details that relate to the novel's central mystery, creates structural issues of closure within the story-telling, and that these, in turn, mirror the 'very large issue of closure in Iris's emotional life' (2003, 555). Ingersoll considers how the strategic and immediate revelation of the ending invites anticipation from the reader and positions them as detectives from the very beginning of the story (544). *The Blind Assassin*'s whodunit classification is similarly identified in consumer reviews of the novel, which reflect on its structural complexity and invitation to engage in the puzzle or game format, with Iris and Atwood as the reader's potential competitors.

The Blind Assassin is Atwood's longest novel and first to win the Booker Prize. The novel is structurally and stylistically complex, tracking different stories at different diegetic levels. The frame story (hereafter referred to as BA^1) follows 82-year-old Iris Chase as she writes her memoir, recounting her day-to-day interactions with friends and reflecting on her writing progress. Iris's memoir details her younger years and her memories growing up as part of the prosperous Chase family who ran a button factory in Port Ticonderoga. This earlier thread of the story follows Iris's childhood years with her daydreamer sister, Laura, and moves through time to her marriage and adult years. Significantly, Iris describes how she met her love interest, Alex Thomas, at a company picnic, and the story of this introduction is one that is revisited and reframed across the different diegetic levels of the story. As Iris revisits these significant events in her life, such as her marriage to the wealthy and ruthless Richard Griffen, the memoir shifts in time and space, frequently interrupted in its return to her present-day situation. The memoir is further fragmented by the second embedded level of the novel. Iris intersperses her reflections with extracts from the fictional story 'The Blind Assassin' (*BA1*), which describes illicit meetings between two unknown and unnamed lovers and which is understood to be written by Iris's sister, Laura. Finally, within 'The Blind Assassin' is a third story (*BA2*) told by the man to his lover: a pulp, science fiction story about a plot to overthrow a king, which is set on the planet Zycron.

In a cognitive linguistic exploration of the novel's structure, Dancygier (2007) examines narrative prompts, or what she calls 'narrative anchors', which create structure and cohesion across the nested levels of the story. Drawing together ideas from classical narratology and discussions of 'story' versus 'discourse' (Chatman 1980), Dancygier applies mental spaces theory to explore how these points of connection tie together *The Blind Assassin*'s

---

[1] Following Dancygier's (2007) notation system for the three narrative strands.

narrative structure, which she labels as a 'thought-provoking laboratory experiment in narrative spaces construction and blending' (147). She argues that certain expressions signal a mental space and generate reader expectation as to its development at a later stage in the story. Dancygier suggests, for example, that the very opening sentence creates two narrative spaces:

Extract 2.1

Ten days after the war ended, my sister Laura drove her car off a bridge. (Atwood 2000, 1)

Here, the protagonist and narrator, Iris, summarises the details of her sister Laura's death. Dancygier argues that this sentence, as well as the paragraphs that follow within the first chapter, establishes dual *suicide/accident* narrative spaces which are signalled through several language choices. In the sentence above, for example, 'drove' attributes Laura with grammatical agency, which suggests the intentionality of the act. The *suicide* space is evoked later in the inclusion of a witness report that the car was 'turned sharply and deliberately', and by Iris when she observes that Laura 'had her reasons' (1). Following the introduction of the suicide space, when Iris later mentions finding 'the notebooks' after Laura's death which had been left for her to read, readers might assume that they will contain details of her reasons for suicide, but significantly their content is not related by Iris at this stage of the novel. In contrast, Dancygier points out how the adjacent *accident* narrative space is developed in the newspaper clippings, which specifically describe Laura's death as misadventure. She argues that the cross-mapping of spaces invited through the way the characters are referenced within each narrative space—through proper names in *BA*, through pronouns in *BA1* and through more allusive role descriptors only in *BA2*—creates a simple linguistic construction which nevertheless creates coherence across the text as a whole (Dancygier 2007, 145). An exploration of the identity of these characters relates to a KNOWING IS SEEING metaphor at the centre of the text, though the identity of the titular blind assassin is open to interpretation and disputed among critics (2007, 145–146; Bouson 2003; Wilson 2006).

As the analysis in the next section shows, the complexity of the narrative structure of *The Blind Assassin*, and the necessary *puzzle-solving* process it invites, is a prominent theme among the sampled reader reviews. While Dancygier examines the narrative anchors which function as the clues in the mystery and which reveal the identities of the characters, the analysis in this chapter develops these initial observations to explore how the text exhibits stylistic strategies of misdirection and burying. Misdirection is the 'genre-typical set of techniques through which the crime fiction reader is very often deliberately misled away from the precise nature of the circumstances surrounding the crime the fiction features' (Gregoriou 2021, 93). Burying, or backgrounding, on the other hand, is one of the attentional strategies through which writers might mislead audiences (Emmott and Alexander 2014). With reference to key scenes from across the novel, the analysis considers how readers are invited into the DETECTIVE role, and how the second, significant mystery is stylistically concealed in order to maintain the balance between 'the story of the crime' and 'the story of detection' (Todorov 1971)—the latter of which, in this book, takes place at the site of reading. It is revealed that Iris is not, in fact, our helpful fellow detective, but rather an antagonist who actively hides the story's mystery.

2.2   Reading *The Blind Assassin*

Nischik (2017) explores the early reception of *The Blind Assassin*, which she categorises as one of Atwood's 'middle period' novels (356), through a descriptive summary of the themes that appeared in the newspaper and magazine reviews of the novel which were written at the time of the book's publication. The dataset for this study comprises 21 Canadian reviews and 49 reviews from the USA, which are categorised into 'positive', 'negative' or 'in-between' (including 'nonevaluative') reviews (2016, 357). It is found that the Canadian reviews mention the book's commentary on their national history (absent in the American reviews), and that, in contrast, responses to themes of the novel such as gender issues within the American reviews are comparatively more 'perceptive'. Nischik's summary reveals some of the themes among the responses, such as references to 'the infamous so-called Atwood bashing' (358), comments on the physical geography of the story, its gender representation and narrator unreliability. In a summary of academic responses within literary criticism, Staels (2004) found that the early reviews of the novel were similarly contradictory.

Unlike Nischik's study, the analysis of reader reviews in this chapter (and indeed in the rest of this book) will not consider differences in review valence,[2] nor evaluate the quality of a review and whether it is seen as analytical or 'competent' (2017, 367). Instead, the following will explore how the readers frame their reviews of *The Blind Assassin*, and what the

---

[2] For those interested in this data, Goodreads allows reader reviews to be sorted by star rating.

recurring topics within their comments reveal or suggest about the experience of reading this whodunit and its representation of 'the race with Iris Chase Griffen' (Ingersoll 2003, 543). In this chapter, the reader response data comprise 100 reader reviews collected from the open-access website Goodreads, which have been coded for recurring themes.[3] The reviewers have been anonymised and are referred to as BA1–BA100 throughout this chapter. The patterns and key themes in these reviews are used to situate and contextualise the stylistic analysis of the text that follows.

The most prominent coded theme among the reader reviews of the novel was *aesthetic appreciation of language*,[4] with the reviewers commenting on the perceived quality of Atwood's prose.

> (But even though the story was less compelling than others, I found these huge chunks of Atwoodian wisdom between the tangled storylines) (BA35).
>
> Her writing is more delicate and she comes through with a few amazingly written observations about memory and the craft of storytelling itself. (BA38)
>
> I love Margaret Atwood for both her story telling and her writing, and "The Blind Assassin" was no exception. (BA43)

More than commenting on the quality of the writing, however, these readers also contextualise the story in relation to their own reading history of Atwood. There are points of comparison ('less compelling than the others') and, in the cases of BA35, a conceptualisation of Atwood's role as implied author (Booth 1961) and the presence she holds behind that of the story ('I found these huge chunks of Atwoodian wisdom between the tangled story-lines' where 'she comes through' the narrative). Here, the diegetic levels of the narration are separated by the readers, who draw a division between the 'tangled storylines' of the narration and their interpretation of Atwood's authorial presence.

In contrast, others respond more directly to the *voice* and *characterisation of Iris* as the progenitor of the narrative:

> [...] the 50year old [sic] POV narrator was so strong that I can still hear *her voice* weeks after finishing the book. (BA31)
>
> *The voice of Iris*, who narrates much of the story, is so distinct and I loved the language she uses in describing her current life and how she sees the world --

---

[3] See Chapter 1 for a more detailed summary of the reader response methodology in the book.

[4] In an overview of reader reviews of *The Handmaid's Tale*, Nuttall (2018, 68–71) observes the same code among surveyed reader review data and found a distinction between those reviewers attributing style to Atwood and those to Offred, the protagonist.

I especially appreciated how her current views contrast with her lack of insight as a young woman. (BA41)

I did have some trouble, though, with *all the voices of the protagonist*, and with hearing them all as being one and the same person. (BA86)

I totally agree with a friend of mine who observed in her review that the characters are not consistent; of course they aren't, Iris, *the loudest voice* of the novel (for there are many, as we will see), is unable to scrutinize the others, how could she? she's blind – they are for her only Chinese shadows, there, but incomprehensible. (BA90) (emphases added)

For these readers, the mental model of Iris's voice is developed sufficiently that it can be heard 'weeks after finishing the book' (BA31), and indeed all the reviewers listed here comment on Iris's voice as 'strong' (BA31) and 'distinct' (BA41), consistent with rich characterisation. While Iris's voice is seemingly 'loud', some suggest that the plurality of her voices creates inconsistency in the storytelling (BA86, BA90), though others argue that this is part of her development. BA41 observes, for example, how Iris's 'current views contrast with her lack of insight as a young woman'. In these responses, Iris's narratorial presence, and her 'distinct', 'strong' and 'loud' voice, is foregrounded over Atwood's quieter extratextual voice, which is rendered through comparatively 'delicate' writing (BA38) and concealed between the storylines (BA35).

Dancygier (2007) identifies the absence of extended discussion within literary criticism of the significance of the embedded stories to the narrative structure of *The Blind Assassin*, or a sustained consideration of the interaction and interplay between the story levels. The *complexity of structure* of the novel is, however, commented on by nearly half of the reviewers in the dataset. Readers label the embedded levels as 'stories-within-stories' (BA5), and, even more recursively, as 'stories within stories within stories' (BA8). It also gets likened by many to a matryoshka doll narrative (Stein 2005), and to a puzzle (BA2, BA37, BA77, BA91). While not necessarily commenting on the way that the structural choices relate to the novel's themes, many of these reviewers do more indirectly reflect on the impact the structure has on their reading experience. BA39, for example, describes how the opening sections remained 'with me to the final page, which Atwood makes unavoidable by putting the tragedy first - the point of the structure I'm sure'.

Finally, the classification of the novel as a detective text that features a *mystery/twist* is mentioned in over a third of the surveyed reviews. Readers deliberate over the classification of the text, and its mystery component is frequently identified, as highlighted in the reviews below:

Because Atwood only does the slowest of reveals, the reader is forced to pay attention to details as if the book were a *murder mystery* - which in a way is exactly what it is. (BA9)

This novel is a lot of different genres, but most of all I would call it a *mysterious thriller*. The 'thriller' part of it is underrated, but it is there - and Atwood is really good at including scary premonitions in subtle and not so subtle ways. (BA43)

It's a great blend of *mystery*, science fiction and historical fiction that revolves around Laura and Iris Chase. The story told is not always how it seems to be. (BA62)

It's even hard to pin down genre-wise: It's a work of historical fiction, but also a coming-of-age-story, there's a *suspense/mystery* element to the story and then there are chapters of science-fiction. (BA74)

As with many other Atwood texts, the genre is difficult to neatly categorise, and incorporates and blends components of, as the reviewers comment here, science fiction, historical fiction, thriller and *bildungsroman* genres, in addition to the suspense and mystery at the centre of the novel. Even within the detective fiction genre classification, *The Blind Assassin* is said to combine 'spy thriller' and 'murder mystery' subgenres (Shead 2015). Readers additionally describe how the text seems to be masquerading as another type of text. BA62 argues that 'The story told is not always how it seems to be', while BA9 qualifies their 'murder mystery' categorisation, 'which *in a way* is exactly what it is' (emphasis added). The nature of the twist, the revelation that Iris and not Laura is the author of *The Blind Assassin*, and the reasons for Laura's unhappiness, means that an intertextual reference is made by some of the reviewers between *The Blind Assassin* and another contemporary novel. Ian McEwan's *Atonement* features what first appears to be a story told by multiple narrators. At the end of the novel, however, the protagonist Briony is revealed to have written the earlier pages and to be the narrator of the whole story. In this intertext, particular events are disnarrated—revealed to be fabricated by Briony rather than events that authentically happened in the storyworld (Harold 2005 for an extended comparison of these two intertexts). However, BA90 identifies a difference between the two narrators and argues that '[u]nlike Briony of McEwan's Atonement, [Iris] doesn't change the truth to appease reality, she only changes the voice until even she doesn't know whose voice is anymore'. This blurring between representations of Iris and Laura is at the centre of the novel's mystery. At times, readers are not sure whose voice belongs to which character, and indeed they are treated almost interchangeably up until the final revelation.

As part of the discussion of genre categorisation, these reviews addition-ally comment on *the structure of the mystery* and the pacing of the reveal of information. This can be observed in BA43's acknowledgement of the 'scary premonitions' that contribute to the thriller classification, and in BA9's observation that readers do not have much choice in their engagement with this revelation, as they are 'forced to pay attention to details'. Others also comment:

> We gradually learn more about these two girls, their parents, and the men they become involved with. But much of the information is ambiguous, equivocal, obscure – we get clues about something, think ah yes, so that's what's going on, then later well maybe I was wrong, then later yet no, I was right the first time. And new obscurities pop up, casting a veil over things that seemed clear earlier on. (BA18)

> It is all very nicely done, one experiences unease and uncertainty, and says "a-ha" to oneself at the right moments, it has something of the feel of a fin de siecle painting to it, the symbolism at first obscure, then in a heartbeat, heavy handed and obvious. (BA25)

Both reviewers here talk about the obscurity of clues or symbolism, and how the novel establishes the tension between revelation and concealment. They observe that clues are integrated in a measured way, establishing a back-and-forth exchange between the reader and the text until those 'obscure' meanings become 'obvious'. This dynamic is framed by some reviewers as READING IS A GAME, with the resolution of the mystery, the goal or the prize, at the end:

> The entire novel feels like a *treasure hunt* where the truth is the *prize* and, when the reader eventually discovers it themselves, the recoil in horror at how gruesome it is. (BA73)

> I was on page 608 exactly when I realised that everything that I had gathered and concluded about this book was completely wrong. All my conclusions had been based on one assumption and I had merrily skipped through this story thinking with smugness that I knew what the twist was going to be and how it was going to end.
> Well... now I feel like *a reet loser.*
> Because Ms Atwood *won this round.*
> Completely and utterly.
> *Fair and square.*
> In the most remarkable way possible. (BA71)

I particularly appreciated the way that Atwood drew us into the book with the mystery of Laura, and then gradually made us (well, me, at any rate) fonder and fonder of Iris. A beautiful literary *bait and switch*. (BA88) (emphases added)

Within the framing of the novel as a game, many of these reviewers cast Atwood as the other player, acknowledging awareness of the authorial agency in misdirection and attentional manipulation ('Atwood drew us into the book', BA88). The READING IS A GAME metaphor is further framed through a jigsaw puzzle mapping, in which readers fit the pieces together 'until the full picture emerges at the end' (BA37; BA29, BA77). This metaphor is a prevalent one among researchers who discuss crime fiction. Plain (2020), for example, explores the 'clue-puzzle formula' of crime fiction writing, whereas Gregoriou (2022, 408) expands on this metaphor to discuss how certain aspects of the story form different puzzle pieces. A red herring ultimately functions as a spare puzzle piece, while a clue is a piece that reveals the larger picture.

2.3 Burying

In the earliest applications of stylistics, researchers investigated the phenomenon of literary linguistic foregrounding (Mukařovský 1964). Rooted in Gestalt psychology, foregrounding describes how our attention is directed when we consider a stimulus, for example, a picture or painting. Typically, an object or figure will form the focus, or the figure, of the picture, whereas the schematic background of the painting is likely to draw comparatively less attention. Artists will draw attention through painting the figure as larger, brighter, more defined, more detailed, than the background. In texts, foregrounding is achieved through various linguistic means, and particularly through linguistic deviation; that is, any linguistic departure from norms established inside the text or through wider knowledge about texts and genres. Foregrounding impacts on psychological processes of perception and brings about, as Miall and Kuiken (1994) argue, experiences of defamiliarisation, where something everyday is perceived as strange or unfamiliar. Across literary genres, writers can manipulate foregrounded features of language to direct readers' attention in certain ways and to generate specific local effects, such as an increase in aesthetic appreciation of the text (van Peer et al. 2007) or changes in emotional affect (Miall and Kuiken 1994). These effects are brought about through an increase in cognitive demands, where readers attempt to 'refamiliarize' and 'discern, delimit or develop the meanings suggested by the foregrounded passage' (Miall and Kuiken 1994, 394).

Detective fiction is a closed-form and formulaic genre (Todorov 1966) in which these cognitive demands are heightened, and structural conventions and narrative templates are followed to maintain a surprise ending. Doubled storytelling is an inherent part of this form, where the story of the crime and the story of detection both drive the narrative (Todorov 1971). As part of the process of concealing the crime to preserve the story of detection, writers control the release of information and relevant clues through several stylistic strategies. In particular, they are able to deliberately direct and misdirect a reader's attention by foregrounding a detail or world-builder that is 'plot-insignificant' (that is, unimportant to the mystery's solution), and, conversely, by backgrounding details that are in fact 'plot-significant' (Emmott and Alexander 2014, 329; Emmott and Alexander 2010). Sanford and Emmott (2012, 92) label this process of reducing attention as 'burying', where 'an item is placed in the background with the intention that it should not be easily found' (Emmott and Alexander 2014, 331). Though this technique appears in other genres, this is an essential narrative strategy in detective fiction where a text's success is measured by whether information about the twist, the answers to the whodunit mystery, is successfully hidden until the end of the story or an otherwise appropriate moment.

Emmott and Alexander argue that attention may be manipulated through whether an item is given narrative-world salience (for example, if it is cued as important, Mullins and Dixon 2007); its text position, which can encompass choices of '1) whether writers choose to present two connected key pieces of information next to each other in the text, or whether to separate them and therefore disrupt the inferential processing, and 2) presenting a clue immediately after a puzzle has been introduced and when readers are in a 'puzzle-solving mode'; and finally, 3) selective focus, which refers to the depth of processing experienced by readers (Emmott and Alexander 2014, 331). Elaborating on the latter, they argue that '[s]tylistic deviance and standard systemic choices can direct inferencing, but inferencing can also be controlled by the amount and nature of detail given before, during and after crucial points in a text' (331).

The genre blending and structural complexity of *The Blind Assassin* means that, unlike the Agatha Christie examples analysed in Emmott and Alexander's studies, it is not a straightforward detective text, though it does contain two mysteries, as the analysis will explore. In addition to those attentional strategies mentioned above, the clues to these two mysteries are buried through a combination of the following stylistic techniques:

(i) Mention the item as little as possible.

(ii) Use linguistic structures which have been shown empirically to reduce prominence (e.g., embed a mention of the item within a subordinate clause).

(iii) Under-specify the item, describing it in a way that is sufficiently imprecise that it draws little attention to it or detracts from features of the item that are relevant to the plot.

(iv) Place the item next to something that is more prominent, so that focus is on the more prominent item. Hence, when foregrounding is used it may have an automatic effect of downplaying nearby items, like a spotlight that makes items around the light less noticeable.

(v) Make the item apparently unimportant in the narrative world (even though it is actually significant).

(vi) Make it difficult for the reader to make inferences by splitting up information needed to make the inferences.

(vii) Place information in positions where a reader is distracted or not yet interested.

(viii) Stress one specific aspect of the item so that another aspect (which will eventually be important for the solution) becomes less prominent.

(ix) Give the item false significance, so that the real significance is buried.

(x) Get the narrator or characters in the story to say that the item is uninteresting.

(xi) Discredit the characters reporting information, thereby making them appear unreliable and giving less salience to the information they report. (After Emmott and Alexander 2014, 396)

At the same time, details that expose the twist, and clues that hint towards the resolution, cannot be entirely absent from the storyworld. This is because, as Tobin (2018, 16) argues, narratives with a twist or surprise also must have a degree of 'retrospective credibility' to be perceived as successful or satisfactory. Readers need to be able to reflect on the story, or return to or reread parts of the story, to trace the clues. Discussions of *retrospective credibility* appear in the reader dataset where readers comment on this process of looking back through the book, or re-reading it, to clarify or discern the initially hidden clues:

This book has so much scope and so much depth and one that I will need, and immensely enjoy, to read again and again. Mostly so I can see the little

trail of breadcrumbs that Ms Atwood scattered across these pages, little clues that I missed but make perfect sense in hindsight. (BA71)
I intend to re-read it when I have a bit more time on my hands as I think it is one of those books that needs to be read more than once. I expect I may even enjoy the second reading more, as I already know what is going to happen and can appreciate the little clues and significant details much better. (BA77)

The last hundred pages or so are genius. Possibly the best denouement of a novel I've ever read. And because this was a re-read, I knew that already, and spent the whole of the book getting excited for reaching this part. What makes it even better, because I knew the ending, is that I could see the clues coming together, when they completely went over my head first time round. (BA93)

The readers in the examples above discuss the subtle means in which these clues are integrated within the text. Such clues are seen as 'little' (BA71, BA77), and possibly 'missed' (BA71) on a first read. In all three responses, the readers also discuss a sense of heightened attention to textual cues on a re-read which also invites a richer experience and appreciation of its structure, its 'coming together' (BA93) via 'the little trail of breadcrumbs' (BA71) and the way that the 'significant details' (BA77) incrementally reveal the plot.

It is important that meaningful details are framed in a way that obscures connections that are too obvious or that display the twist too early. It is the concealment of these connections and clues that generates a sense of depth for these reviewers, and which build the 'scope' (BA71) and 'denouement' (BA93) of the writing. To manage the revelation of information across the text, Emmott and Alexander (2014, 333) further argue that writers draw on specific rhetorical strategies which are employed at certain stages of the narrative:

1. *At the pre-solution stage*—foreground plot-insignificant items;
2. *At the pre-solution stage*—bury plot-significant items;
3. *At the solution stage*—foreground plot-significant details that were previously buried and make the solution seem credible;
4. *Throughout the text*—manage the reversal in significance.

There are two central mysteries in *The Blind Assassin*: one that is outlined at the beginning, and in fact in the very first sentence, which establishes the mystery of *what Laura really did and why* (Dancygier, 138), and Iris's involvement in it. The second, and related, mystery—*who really wrote BA1*—forms an essential puzzle piece in uncovering the answer to the first. At the *pre-solution stage*, the novel downplays and conceals the existence of this second mystery. Rather than foregrounding plot-insignificant items, though, the story foregrounds and emphasises the first mystery as a distractor, while the existence of the second remains buried. This creates a complex set-up where readers are distracted by the more traditional (not-quite) murder mystery of Laura's death, while the rug-pull surprise relates to the secret, and stylistically buried—but narratively more important—second mystery.

2.4   Pre-solution Stage: Concealing the Second Mystery in *The Blind Assassin*

2.4.1   Authorial Credibility and Curation

The prologue of *BA1* opens with a description of an unknown female character examining a photograph. As the narrator describes, the 'photo is of the two of them together, her and this man, on a picnic' (4). It is later revealed that this picnic is the annual Button Factory picnic, which Iris describes in her memoir. For both Iris and Laura, the picnic is important: it is a high-profile event in the social calendar in that it is the annual company picnic, hosted by the Chase family for the benefit of their factory employees. The picnic is also the site of Laura and Iris's first introduction to Alex Thomas, and therefore establishes the love triangle that persists throughout the rest of the story. The scene of the Button Factory picnic is retold and reconstrued (Chapter 3) within different iterations across the novel:

1. Described as a scene in a photograph by the unnamed female character in the Prologue, 'Perennials for the rock garden' (*BA1*);
2. The original memory of the picnic, recounted by Iris in her memoir (*BA*);
3. Iris's description of the photograph of the picnic, as published in the local newspaper following the event (*BA*);
4. Iris's description of copies of the photograph, edited by her sister Laura (*BA*);
5. Described again by the unnamed female character in the Epilogue, 'The other hand' (*BA1*).

That the scene the photograph depicts is told more than once automatically foregrounds its contents and invites a process of conceptual comparison between the retellings (Toolan 2020; Harrison 2023). Significantly, the description is repeated, or mostly repeated, in the Epilogue, and once readers have knowledge of the twist. On first mention, the photograph is given heightened narrative-world salience. It is identified as having sentimental value for the unnamed character who has kept 'a single photograph of him' in a hidden location, where 'no one else would ever look'. With each reiteration of the depicted scene within the book, this salience increases. In its final position at the end of the novel, at *the solution stage*, it confirms the revelation of the real author of 'The Blind Assassin'. This structural circularity emphasises the thematic equivalence drawn between Laura and Iris. They each represent one bookend, one 'hand', and Laura is described by Iris as her writing 'collaborator' (626).

Firstly, and significantly, the representation of 'The Blind Assassin' as a novel plays with and inverts technique xi, which describes how writers might *Discredit the characters reporting information, thereby making them appear unreliable and giving less salience to the information they report*. Instead, the item—the attribution of the authorship of 'The Blind Assassin' to Laura—is given heightened credibility. This initial description of the photograph in *BA1* appears early in the novel and follows the short chapter, 'The bridge', and an excerpt from *The Toronto Star* that reports on Laura's death. As summarised earlier, 'The bridge' introduces the *What Laura did and why* mystery. In a much less direct way, the description of this photograph introduces the *Who really wrote BA1* mystery:

Extract 2.2

The Blind Assassin. *By Laura Chase.*

Reingold, Jaynes & Moreau, New York, 1947

Prologue: Perennials for the Rock Garden

She has a single photograph of him. She tucked it into a brown envelope on which she'd written *clippings*, and hid the envelope between the pages of *Perennials for the Rock Garden*, where no one else would ever look. [...]

The photo is of the two of them together, her and this man, on a picnic. *Picnic* is written on the back, in pencil – not his name or hers, just *picnic*. She knows the names, she doesn't need to write them down. [...]

The man is wearing a light-coloured hat, angled down on his head and partially shading his face. His face appears more darkly tanned than hers. She's turned half towards him and smiling, in a way she can't remember smiling at anyone since. She seems very young in the picture, too young, though she hadn't considered herself too young at the time. He's smiling too – the whiteness of his teeth shows up like a scratched match flaring – but he's holding up his hand, as if to fend her off in play, or else to protect himself from the camera, from the person who must be there, taking the picture; or else to protect himself from those in the future who might be looking at him, who might be looking in at him through a square, lighted window of glazed paper. As if to protect himself from her. As if to protect her. [...] (Atwood 2000, 4–5)

The introduction, or replication, of paratextual details relating to the title, author and bibliographic information of the embedded book support an impression of its credibility and textual authenticity. In other contexts, '[t]he paratext of novels – such as the front cover and inside title page – usually present clear information about authorship' (Gibbons 2019, 186). The framing information in Extract 2.2 authenticates Laura's identity as author, explicitly specified in the possessive noun phrase and byline, '*By Laura Chase*', and presents this detail as an established fact in the storyworld. In addition to clarifying authorship, Sorlin (2022) argues that paratextual features suggest and signpost authorial presence, as they exist between the text-world of the story and the real world occupied by readers. These features hold a 'transaction function' which 'can be performed with different pragmatic acts – informing, seducing, orientating, allowing to continue reading, but also threatening' (Sorlin 2022, 198; after Genette 1991, 261–262). The co-text and text position of this extract suggests that the paratextual choices both inform and orient readers. Crucially, at this early point, Laura's authorship of 'The Blind Assassin' is integrated as part of the exposition, and framed as a hard fact. Notable, too, is that this extract immediately follows a newspaper excerpt with similarly specific, and spatiotemporally proximal, bibliographic details (Extract 2.3).

Extract 2.3

The Toronto Star, May 26, 1945

QUESTIONS RAISED IN CITY DEATH

SPECIAL TO THE STAR

(Atwood 2000, 3)

Given that the paratextual information of Extract 2.2 is part of the embedded story, *BA1*, questions of the extent of its veracity or authenticity are, much like Iris's photograph, more hidden 'between the pages' of the *BA* frame narrative.

The suggestion that the paratextual and other information may not be fully accurate, however, is indirectly suggested. Though an observant reader may notice that *The Toronto Star* is a reference to a real-world newspaper, the title of the embedded story of Extract 2.2 invites ambiguity. In a study of online reader review data, Bartl and Lahey (2023, 210), summarising Fisher (1984), argue that '[f]irst and most obviously, titles are referential. Like proper nouns, titles have unique reference, providing a label with which we may talk about the works to which they are attached'. This unique referentiality is further complicated in *The Blind Assassin* as the title has a dual reference: *The Blind Assassin* is both the name of the novel more superordinately and, as this prologue confirms, the name of Laura's bestselling novel, the story within the story. Thus, from the beginning, the story plays around with the idea of unique and co-referentiality. Appearing in these early pages of the book, and taken together, these different extracts and story fragments additionally establish Iris's narrating and mediating role. She is presented as the curator of Laura's work and legacy, incorporating these—presumably cherished— 'original' and unmediated extracts and excerpts among her own memoirs which are, seemingly, more subjective and less reliable.

In addition to the paratextual information and the text positioning of Extract 2.2, the presentation of the scene described by the unnamed female character is also noteworthy. Several photographs are described throughout the novel, and the critics discuss the thematic or symbolic role they fulfil. Wilson, for example, refers to these text descriptions as 'verbal photographs' (2003, 274), and while some critics (Bouson 2003) have explored the symbolic suggestions of the colour choices used by Laura to 'tint' these photographs, Wilson goes on to identify different functions that photographs hold in Atwood's texts more generally. On a first reading, Extract 2.1 can be considered 'a neutral recorder of experience' (Wilson 1987, 30–32; Wilson 2003). Much like the reference to the real-world newspaper, the 'neutral recorder' presentation of the scene is a means of conferring credibility, or a more authentic and non-mediated capturing of a particular event in time. Without knowing who is looking at the photograph, or the significance of the photograph, it can be considered as a visually accurate record of an event, which will presumably be elaborated on later. As this photograph, and the scene it describes, becomes repeated across the novel, however, another function comes to the fore. In light of the co-referentiality in this and subsequent description, it becomes a significant scene that alternatively suggest a cause of 'a character's sense of fragmentation' (Wilson 1987, 30–32, 2003). In addition to those listed by Wilson, Dancygier (2007, 141) also attributes a structural function to the photographs in this novel. She argues how, '[i]n reality, photographs, like books, are material anchors for representation spaces', and that '[t]he image in a photograph is like a timeless window to the specific time and space represented, whether identifiable or not' (141). She goes on to say that this 'photograph is in fact the most ambiguous of the anchors in *BA*' (141). Moreover, there are many descriptions of photographs across the novel that each obscure and conceal world-building information, and which also, when explored together, reveal connections and patterns that relate details of character identity. Their role in burying is examined in more detail in 2.5.1.

2.4.2 Distraction and Under-Specification

A second stylistic technique apparent early in the novel 2.2 is the manipulation of text positioning: *(iv) Place the item next to something that is more prominent, so that focus is on the more prominent item.* This can be seen in a very marked way in the stylistic comparison between the very opening page of the novel, 'The bridge' in *BA* (Extract 2.1) and the Prologue of *BA1* (Extract 2.2).

'The bridge' works as a distractor for readers, so that, initially, the photograph and the scene it describes is less sensational and therefore less important. In the sequence of the book, 'The bridge' appears first, which automatically means that it is given greater significance by virtue of its precedence (Rabinowitz 2002). It is also richer in details: it introduces the first mystery specifically and explicitly, and activates readers' puzzle-solving mode from the outset. This is supported in the reader data, where many reviewers acknowledge the impact of the opening passage on their perception of the text. It is described, for example, as especially 'hard-hitting' (BA23), 'remarkable' (BA15) and 'haunting' (BA95) by the readers. A particular moment in time is described ('Ten days after the war ended'), and, in the text that follows Extract 2.1, the characters' names are also revealed: 'Laura' and 'Richard'; and the speaking 'I' narrator is introduced as 'Mrs Griffen'. Clearer ideological information is also attached to these characters 'my sister Laura' confirms their familial relationship, while Iris's marital status is mentioned first. At the same time, Richard's reputation and social standing is established through the reports of other character's reactions: 'His tone was respectful: no doubt he recognised Richard's name'. All these choices help readers begin to build comparatively more rounded profiles for the characters in the *BA* strand.

In contrast, the description of the photograph (Extract 2.2) in the *BA1* story is less attention-grabbing. The details—and particularly the identity of the characters—are under-specified. The publication date of the book is referenced, but the time within the book is not mentioned, though there is an indication that a considerable time has passed since the photograph was taken and the unknown character's examination of it at this moment: 'She seems very young in the picture, too young, though she hadn't considered herself too young at the time'. Unlike 'The bridge', the full names are left offstage as the focalised narrator is referenced through feminine pronouns only, and similarly 'the man' is referenced through masculine pronouns. Because the names of these characters are withheld until much later in the novel, Grishakova (2018, 196) refers to this set-up as a form of 'considerably delayed pronominal reference' which contributes to the polyvocality inherent in the story's narration. This delay of information is even blueprinted at the micro-level of the text. The opening clause in Extract 2.2 works as a cataphoric reference in that 'the two of them together' precedes the, slightly more specific, 'her and this man' in the second clause. The absence of identity of the two characters in the photograph is further attentionally foregrounded in the subordinate clause of the second sentence: 'not his name or hers, just *picnic*', such that the 'picnic' itself becomes the more substantial detail. Significantly, the description of the unknown 'she' here establishes this character as one who will withhold information: 'She knows the names, she doesn't need to write them down'. Of course, as Dancygier points out, knowing the identity of the unnamed female character in this prologue is key to working out the identity of the author of the *BA1*.

Similar distractions, where items or details are positioned next to more prominent ones, or ones that are comparatively more fully specified, appear across the novel. For example, in a later scene, Iris is about to give the presentation of the Laura Chase memorial prize for best short story at the local high school. During a speech about Laura given by a local politician, Iris reflects on the reception of Laura's book when it was released. She comments that '[w]hat people remember isn't the book itself, so much as the furor: ministers in church denounced it as obscene, not only here; the public library was forced to remove it from the shelves, the one bookstore in town refused to stock it. There was word of censoring it' (48). She goes on to say:

Extract 2.4

> But also they wanted to finger the real people in it—apart from Laura, this is: her actuality was taken for granted. They wanted real bodies, to fit onto the bodies conjured up for them by words. They wanted real lust. Above all they wanted to know: *who was the man?* In bed with the young woman, the lovely, dead young woman; in bed with Laura. Some of them thought they knew, of course. There had been gossip. For those who could put two and two together, it all added up. *Acted like she was pure as the driven. Butter wouldn't melt. Just goes to show you can't tell a book by its cover.* (Atwood 2000, 40)

At this point, a different mystery than the one related to the twist is again emphasised by Iris. The question of '*who was the man?*', instead, is the focus of 'the furor'. It is introduced explicitly as the item that carries the most significance—the question that rose '[a]bove all'. It is also grapholog-ically foregrounded through its italicisation, which renders the question as one spoken directly by the 'they' reading audience. The unconfirmed iden-tities of the other 'real people' within the novel, and the reference to those who 'could put two and two together', invite readers to participate in puzzle solving, but attribute narrative salience to the identity of the unknown man, rather than to Laura's role or connection to the book. The mention of Laura's 'actuality' as the author, on the other hand, and that this status is 'taken for granted' by the readers of her books, is a buried hint as to the plot twist. Iris explicitly rules this out as a consideration—'apart from Laura, this is'—and the comment is embedded within a subordinate clause, reducing its atten-tional prominence. This detail is also left unattached from the framing clause 'they wanted', which instead itemises other ambiguous facts sought by the readers. These distractor details acquire heightened importance as themes that impelled a greater reaction among the book's readership. Laura's readers wanted to engage, instead, in discussions of censorship (its 'obscene' content), its associated scandal ('real bodies') and salacious content ('real lust').

At the same time, stylistic choices do not entirely background the 'actuality' of Laura's role. Iris describes how the readers wanted to know the iden-tity of the man '[i]n bed with the young woman, the lovely, dead young woman; in bed with Laura'. Initially, here, 'the young woman' underspec-ifies the identity of the author and instead describes 'her' in broad, general and schematic terms only. As the description progresses, Iris attributes further details which suggest, or presuppose, the sympathetic alignment of the book's readers. The dissonant pairing of 'lovely, dead' creates a derisive or mocking tone, as if Iris mocks the readers' desire to idolise or romanticise Laura. Iris's summary of readers' speculations becomes further evidence her 'mind-modelling' (Stockwell 2009; Chapter 5), that is, imagining and framing the subjective perceptions, of these other voices. In the context of the other strate-gies of misdirection, this creates a deflection from Iris's own and unfiltered assessment of events. Finally, the reported statement, '*Just goes to show you can't tell a book by its cover*', is similarly a cautionary note for the double reading audience: Laura's, and Atwood's. This also, retrospectively, casts doubt over the 'cover' we encountered in the opening pages of the novel.

A clue as to Iris's identity as the author of *BA1* is buried earlier in this same chapter, before Iris's description of readers' questions about the novel 4—and therefore before a puzzle-solving mode has explicitly been invited. She describes how:

Extract 2.5

> [...] I allowed my mind to drift; I knew enough to know that the only thing expected of me was that I not disgrace myself. I could have been back again beside the podium, or at some interminable dinner, sitting next to Richard, keeping my mouth shut. If asked, which was seldom, I used to say that my hobby was gardening. A half-truth at best, though tedious enough to pass muster. (Atwood 2000, 38)

The prologue of *The Blind Assassin* mentions that the treasured photograph is hidden 'between the pages of *Perennials for the Rock Garden*, where no one else would ever look' (4). The world-building significance of 'Perennials for the Rock Garden' is therefore fronted in its mention in the prologue title for *BA1* (Extract 2.2), though this appears some 40 pages earlier than the mention of gardening in this scene in the *BA* narrative. Unlike the title of the story, the book title is a unique reference appearing in both *BA* and *BA1*, though mentioned in the *BA* strand much later. Iris's character profile will be more developed for a re-reader, meaning that Iris's gardening hobby confirms her as someone likely to have a copy of a book of this name. For a first-time reader, however, Iris's memory of discussing her gardening hobby is unlikely to carry the same salience. The mention of this fact is embedded in a flash-back, spatiotemporally displaced in time, and described as unimportant or at least 'tedious enough', perhaps, not to be specially noticed by readers as a salient detail. Iris evaluates the detail as dull and trivial, exhibiting technique (x) *Get the narrator or characters in the story to say that the item is uninteresting*. The connection between the identity of the 'her' character and the hobby of gardening, and more specifically rock gardening, is not clarified until over 200 pages later, where Iris explicitly mentions this particular hobby. She describes how, 'At Winifred's instigation I had taken up gardening: I needed to have a hobby, she said. She'd decided I should start with a rock garden, because even if I killed the plants the rocks would still be there' (296). This delayed but important detail disrupts reader's inferential processing, following burying (vi).

Several techniques of misdirection, then, are working together at the pre-solution stage. Details of other mysteries within the story, such as the circumstances of Laura's death and the identity of 'the young man', are foregrounded and become distractors, while others—such as doubt of Laura's identity or actuality as writer of the book, and conversely Iris's role as author—are buried. These strategies include conferring credibility to Laura's authorship of the novel, pairing more prominent or more interesting topics or scenes along-side less interesting, or less sensational, ones, and under-specifying details so that ambiguity prevails.

2.5   Managing the Reveal: Co-referentiality

The sustained under-specification of identities and details in the *BA1* story means that the novel makes extensive use of co-reference. While this does occur in relation to objects, such as the photograph, pronominal co-reference is more extended with the characters in the novel. Much has been said in the critical literature on the novel about the pairing of Iris and Laura as opposites and yet collaborators, 'an allusion to M. C. Escher's illusionistic lithograph of hands drawing one another into existence' (Grishakova 2018, 197). The unnamed female character, and the feminine pronouns, of *BA1*, creates refer-ential ambiguity and means that Iris's role as author of *BA1* is buried, while the identification of this character as Laura remains the default assumption—though, of course, crucially, the identities can be swapped. Both Dancygier and Grishakova argue that noticing the thematic, and linguistically cued, matches between the *BA* and *BA1* stories, and specifically the recognition of the unnamed 'she' character as Iris rather than Laura, are key to solving the plot. This important mapping, and other potential parallels between the two strands, are buried through the *splitting up of relevant puzzle clues to obstruct inferential processing (vi)*.

2.5.1   Drawing Connections Across Spaces

Another photograph that appears in the *BA* strand describes a young Iris and a baby Laura. Compared to the first description of the picnic photograph in Extract 2.2, this second one is more fully specified, and the identities of the figures, Iris and Laura, are explicitly mentioned. Both photos feature a female character, and both include an additional person who is mostly out of sight, but for their hand. Appearing nearly 100 pages after the presentation of the first photograph in *BA1*, however, the connections between Extract 2.2 and Extract 2.6 are likely to be attentionally less salient:

Extract 2.6

(There I sat on Mother's night table, in a silver frame, in a dark dress with a white lace collar, visible hand clutching the baby's crocheted white blanket in an awkward, ferocious grip, eyes accusing the camera or whoever was wielding it. Laura herself is almost out of sight, in this picture. Nothing can be seen of her but the top of her downy head, and one tiny hand, fingers curled around my thumb. Was I angry because I'd been told to hold the baby, or was I in fact defending it? Shielding it – reluctant to let go?). (Atwood 2000, 85)

Though it appears in the superordinate *BA* narrative, this photograph is attentionally backgrounded at the structural level. Firstly, this occurs through the fact that the event is spatiotemporally displaced from the here and now of Iris's memoir writing, and her position as an older writer in the frame story. The description is further buried through its placement in parentheses. Iris's summary of the photograph is an embedded aside, a fleeting footnote to the main narrative.

Notably, the metaphor describing the subjects' responses to the act of the photograph being taken in both Extract 2.2 and Extract 2.6 echo each other. The photograph is framed as a physical assault in each case. In Extract 2.2, the unnamed man appears to want to 'protect himself from the camera […] or else to protect himself from those in the future who might be looking at him', and similarly, in Extract 2.6, the camera becomes a weapon that is 'wielded' by the photographer, an experience that necessitates the need for the subjects' protection. In both cases, too, the act of protection is presented ambiguously. In Extract 2.6, Iris questions 'was I in fact defending it? Shielding it – reluctant to let go?', and the unknown man's raised arm in Extract 2.2 similarly invites alternate interpretations ('As if to protect himself from her. As if to protect her').

As in Extract 2.2, both Iris and Laura are present in this photograph, though unlike the first, the identities of the two are confirmed. Iris is the natural 'attractor' (Stockwell 2009, 25) in that her physical appearance is described in fuller detail (she appears 'in a dark dress with a white lace collar'), and both her emotional position ('ferocious', 'angry') and her actions ('clutching the baby's crocheted white blanket') are minutely detailed. Most significantly, and in contrast, Laura is mostly out of the frame, as she is in the first photograph. Visual access to her figure is restricted in the partial representation of 'the top of her downy head' and the fingers of 'one tiny hand'. The latter detail mirrors the equivalent representation of Laura in the first photograph, where she, similarly, is just out of sight: 'Over to one side – you wouldn't see it at first – there's a hand, cut by the margin, scissored off at the wrist, resting on the grass as if discarded. Left to its own devices' (8). The tag clause of 'in this picture' in Extract 2.6 is meaningful. It is attentionally backgrounded within a relative clause, but it invites a direct comparison between this one and others. While the 'discarded' hand in Extract 2.2 is unidentified, in 2.6 the owner is acknowledged. The theme of duality that runs throughout the novel is similarly reflected in semantic ambiguity with some of the phrasal choices. In Extract 2.6, 'let go' can be interpreted in a physical sense but also through its metaphorical meaning, in terms of emotional release. This semantic doubling is mirrored in the description of the other hand in the first photograph, following Extract 2.2: 'Left to its own devices' is a comment on dexterity or an act of abandonment.

If readers use these connections to map this photograph onto the first, it can be inferred that, similarly, Iris is the visible person in the photograph, and Laura the one out of sight. In addition to its physical separation within the text from the first description, this inferential processing is complicated again later in the novel, however, in the revelation in *BA* that the photograph has been duplicated so that both Iris and Laura have a copy.

Extract 2.7

> A week after Alex Thomas's departure, Laura came to my room. "I think you should have this," she said. It was a print of the photograph of the three of us, the one Elwood Murray had taken at the picnic. But she'd cut herself out of it – only her hand remained. [...]
>
> I ought to have thrown this mutilated picture away, but I didn't. (Atwood 2000, 220)

Here, and as at other moments in the novel, Alex's full name—'Alex Thomas'—is specified by Iris, but the ambivalence between Laura and Iris's position on either side of him remains. When we consider that Iris earlier raises the question '*Who was the man?*', it can be observed how Alex's identity, and the mystery surrounding it, becomes overreported (Kukkonen 2013, 209; Phelan and Martin 1999) whereas the identity of the 'she' in *BA1* is underreported (Grishakova 2018, 197). This creates complex interplays between revelation and ambiguation which 'encourage the reader to scan and revise available referential frames formed or retrieved in the process of reading – to match them with continuously changing deictic coordinates' (Grishakova 2018, 197). The sustained ambiguity allows the identities of the women within *BA1* and the photographs to be retrofitted by readers at *the reveal* stage.

2.6   The Reveal

The reveal at the end of *The Blind Assassin* can be considered through Emmott and Alexander's third narrative strategy, *At the solution stage: fore-grounding plot-significant details that were previously buried.* There is not space in this chapter to identify and examine all clues in the novel that combine to suggest Iris's identity as author of *BA1*, though other critics have singled out some of these (e.g., Staels' 2004 discussion of Iris's and the unnamed female character's shared knowledge of ancient Greek poetry). The stylistic patterns outlined in the previous analyses combine to maintain *the reversal in significance* across the text and to ensure the clues are present, though not immediately conspicuous. A central part of this process is the disambiguation of earlier references. While critics have commented on the ambiguity of the co-reference between Iris and Laura, the progressive char-acterisation and identification of the addressee of the text, which mirrors the revelation of Iris's authorial role and therefore similarly helps manage this process of gradual reversal, have not been explored.

In the *BA* strand of the novel, Iris ruminates on her readers in her memoir writing. Extracts 2.8–2.10 below show how the addressee is initially unidentified:

Extract 2.8

> For whom am I writing this? For myself? I think not. I have no picture of myself reading it over at a later time, *later time* having become problematical. For some stranger, in the future, after I'm dead? I have no such ambition, or no such hope.
>
> Perhaps I write for no one. Perhaps for the same person children are writing for, when they scrawl their names in the snow.
>
> I'm not as swift as I was. My fingers are stiff and clumsy, the pen wavers and rambles, it takes me a long time to form the words. And yet I persist, hunched over as if sewing by moonlight. (Atwood 2000, 43)

In this early part of the text, Iris is unsure of her audience, as indi-cated through her rhetorical questions, epistemic uncertainty and schematic language ('some stranger'). She proffers some suggestions ('Perhaps I write for no one. Perhaps for the same person children are writing for'), but she appears uncertain and, in some ways, not in control of her story. This is emphasised in her attenuated hold on the writing process: agency is transferred first to her 'fingers', and second to her 'pen', the culprit who 'wavers and rambles'. This lack of clarity and assurance can be attributed to her unreliability as a character-narrator. In these cases where Iris speculates on her readers more explicitly, the novel becomes increasingly metafictional (Ingersoll 2003; Staels 2004; Reed 2009). In Extract 2.8, she further comments on the transience of writing ('names in the snow') as a process that involves fabrication ('sewing by moonlight'), and draws on metaphors that reflexively echo other themes in the text ('I have no picture of myself').

As the novel progresses, however, Iris's audience becomes foregrounded as they become more clearly specified:

Extract 2.9

From here on in, things take a darker turn. But then, you knew they would. You knew it, because you already know what happened to Laura. (Atwood 2000, 417)

Extract 2.10

I must admit it's a surprise to find myself still here, still talking to you. I prefer to think of it as talking, although of course it isn't: I'm saying nothing, you're hearing nothing. The only thing between us is this black line: a thread thrown onto the empty page, into the empty air. (Atwood 2000, 473)

In Extract 2.9, Iris's audience is more precisely characterised as someone who is knowing; as someone who has already second-guessed the solution ('you knew they would') and who are, and have been, complicit with Iris. This exchange becomes more fully detailed in Extract 2.10, where Iris frames her memoir as a spoken conversation between speaker and listener, in which context 'you' is considered a more prototypical choice of pronoun (Fludernik 1993). Even at this late stage of the novel, though, this 'conversation' is presented in ambiguous terms. The syntactic ('isn't') and repeated lexical negation ('nothing', 'empty'), for example, as well as other semantic choices invoking absence ('only', 'air'), suggests Iris's continued reluctance to give complete answers. In the absence of a more fully identified fictionalised addressee, this you-reference can be considered 'apostrophic' (Herman 1994)—a direct address to readers that acknowledges their role in the conversation, or the game.

Finally, the identities of all parties are explicitly revealed, where the author of 'The Blind Assassin' and the intended addressee of the memoir are fully disclosed:

Extract 2.11

> As for the book, Laura didn't write a word of it. But you must have known that for some time. I wrote it myself, during my long evenings alone, when I was waiting for Alex to come back, and then afterwards, once I knew he wouldn't. [...]
> When I began this account of Laura's life – of my own life – I had no idea why I was writing it, or who I expected to read it once I'd done. But it's clear to me now. I was writing it for you, dearest Sabrina, because you're the one – the only one – who needs it now. (512)

Extract 2.11 is the final confirmation that 'Laura didn't write a word' of the story, and that Iris is, in fact, the author Iris's former ambiguity is acknowledged as part of her earlier uncertainty ('I had no idea why I was writing it'), and here, the you-addressee is explicitly revealed as Sabrina. Iris's motive for writing—to expose the truth to her granddaughter—is laid bare in a final act of remediation, where the two missing puzzle pieces, the intended audience and the actual author of the novel, are simultaneously slotted into place.

2.7   'A thread thrown onto the empty page'

The analysis in this chapter has extended the existing narratological research on *The Blind Assassin* and has examined, stylistically, the language choices establishing its whodunit categorisation. This chapter has considered the balance between foregrounding and backgrounding, or anchoring and burying, typical of this genre, and the particular stylistic mechanisms that impact on the revelation of clues. This balance can be observed in the veiled introduction of the central mystery, *who really wrote BA1*, through a conceptual comparison of the representation of photographs across the narrative strands (2.5.1), and in the ambiguation and revelation of references related to scenes, characters (2.4) and the story's addressee (2.6). Rhetorical choices ensure that these clues are distributed and framed in a way that disrupts inferential processing through delaying recognition of the connections between the story strands, while, at the same time, progressively and incrementally collapsing the boundaries between the intercalated narratives. Since burying is an 'inherently deceptive' stylistic phenomenon (Emmott and Alexander

2014, 333), these patterns and structures reveal the duplicitous nature of the potential narrative competitors' Iris and Atwood. Such texts place extra cognitive demands on readers (Emmott 2003, 158–159), but, as the overview of the reader data has explored, these burying techniques form part of the dynamic game of reading this novel and of discovering, or seeing, key details of the whodunit mystery.

References

Atwood, Margaret. 1996. *Alias Grace*. Toronto: McClelland and Stewart Ltd.

Atwood, Margaret. 2000. *The blind assassin*. London: Bloomsbury.

Bartl, Sara, and Ernestine Lahey. 2023. 'As the title implies': How readers talk about titles in Amazon book reviews. *Language and Literature* 32 (2): 209–230.

Booth, Wayne. 1961. *The rhetoric of fiction*. Chicago: University of Chicago Press.

Bouson, J. Brooks. 2003. A commemoration of wounds endured and resented. *Critique* 44 (3): 251–270.

Chatman, Seymour. 1980. *Story and discourse: Narrative structure in fiction and film*. London: Cornell University Press.

Dancygier, Barbara. 2007. Narrative anchors and the processes of story construction: The case of Margaret Atwood's *The blind assassin*. *Style* 41 (2): 133–151.

Emmott, Catherine. 2003. Reading for pleasure: A cognitive poetic analysis of 'twists in the tale' and other plot reversals in narrative texts. In *Cognitive poetics in practice*, ed. Joanna Gavins and Gerard Steen, 145–160. London: Routledge.

Emmott, Catherine and Marc Alexander. 2010. Detective fiction, plot construction, and reader manipulation: Rhetorical control and cognitive misdirection in Agatha Christie's *Sparkling cyanide*. In *Language and style: In honour of Mick Short*, ed. Dan McIntyre and Beatrix Busse, 328–346. Basingstoke: Palgrave.

Emmott, Catherine, and Marc Alexander. 2014. Foregrounding, burying and plot construction. In *The Cambridge handbook of stylistics*, ed. Peter Stockwell and Sara Whiteley, 329–344. Cambridge: Cambridge University Press.

Fisher, John. 1984. Entitling. *Critical inquiry* 11 (2): 286–298.

Fludernik, Monika. 1993. Second-person fiction: Narrative you as addressee and/or protagonist. *AAA: Arbeiten aus Anglistik und Amerikanistik* 18 (2): 217–247.

Genette, Gerard. 1991. Introduction to the paratext, trans. Marie Mackean. *New Literary History* 22 (2): 261–272.

Gibbons, Alison. 2019. Remediation, oral storytelling, and the printed book: the stylistic strategies of Mark Z. Danielewski's *The fifty year sword*. In *The printed book in contemporary American culture: Medium, object, metaphor*, ed. Heike Schaefer and Alexander Starre, 179–202. London: Palgrave.

Goodreads reviews, BA1–BA100. 2022. Reviews: *The Blind Assassin* by Margaret Atwood. https://www.goodreads.com/book/show/78433.The_Blind_Assassin. Accessed on 12 April 2022.

Gregoriou, Christiana. 2021. Re-writing misdirection: A stylistic approach to crime fiction writing. In *Narrative retellings: Stylistic approaches*, ed. Marina Lambrou, 93–110. London: Bloomsbury.

Gregoriou, Christiana. 2022. On the making of Robinson's stylistic 'Fast ones' through the Banks series' early years. *English Studies* 103 (3): 407–427.

Grishakova, Marina. 2018. Multi-teller and multi-voiced stories: The poetics and politics of pronouns. In *Pronouns in Literature*, ed. Alison Gibbons and Andrea Macrae, 193–215. London: Palgrave.

Harrison, Chloe. 2023. 99 ways to retell a story: Forms and functions of narrator reconstrual. *Style*. 57 (2): 163–185.

Harold, James. 2005. Narrative engagement with *Atonement* and *The blind assassin*. *Philosophy and Literature* 29: 130–145.

Herman, David. 1994. Textual you and double deixis in Edna O'Brien's *A pagan place*. *Style* 28 (3): 378–410.

Ingersoll, Earl. 2003. Waiting for the end: Closure in Margaret Atwood's *The blind assassin*. *Studies in the Novel* 35 (4): 543–558.

Kukkonen, Karin. 2013. Flouting figures: Uncooperative narration in the fiction of Eliza Haywood. *Language and Literature* 22 (3): 205–218.

Miall, David, and Don Kuiken. 1994. Foregrounding, defamiliarization, and affect: Response to literary stories. *Poetics* 22: 389–407.

Mukařovský, Jan. 1964. Standard language and poetic language. In *A Prague school reader on esthetics, literary structure, and style*, ed. Paul L. Garvin, 17–30. Washington, DC: Georgetown University Press.

Mullins, Blaine, and Peter Dixon. 2007. Narratorial implicatures: Readers look to the narrator to know what is important. *Poetics* 32: 262–276.

Nischik, Reingard M. 2017. Margaret Atwood's reception in Canada and the United States: A comparative analysis of North American reviews of *The Blind Assassin*. *Contemporary Women's Writing* 11 (3): 354–372.

Nuttall, Louise. 2018. *Mind style and cognitive grammar: Language and worldview in speculative fiction*. London: Bloomsbury.

Phelan, James, and Mary P. Martin. 1999. The lessons of 'Weymouth': Homodiegesis, unreliability, ethics and *The remains of the day*. In *Narratologies: New perspectives on narrative*, ed. David Herman, 88–109. Columbus: Ohio University Press.

Plain, Gill. 2020. Gender and sexuality. In *Routledge companion to crime fiction*, ed. Janice Allan, Jesper Gulddal, Stewart King, and Andrew Pepper, 102–110. London: Routledge.

Rabinowitz, Peter. 2002. Reading beginnings and endings. In *Narrative dynamics: Essays on time, plot, closure and frames*, ed. Brian Richardson, 300–313. Columbus: Ohio State University Press.

Reed, Alison. 2009. Disembodied hands: Structural duplicity in Atwood's *The blind assassin*. *Margaret Atwood Studies* 3 (1): 18–25.

Sanford, Anthony, and Catherine Emmott. 2012. *Mind, brain and narrative*. Cambridge: Cambridge University Press.

Shead, Jackie. 2015. *Margaret Atwood: Crime fiction writer. The reworking of a popular genre*. London: Routledge.

Sorlin, Sandrine. 2022. *The stylistics of 'you': Second-person pronoun and its pragmatic effects*. Cambridge: Cambridge University Press.

Staels, Hilde. 2004. Atwood's specular narrative: *The blind assassin*. *English Studies: A Journal of English Language and Literature* 85 (2): 147–160.

Stein, Karen F. 2005. A left-handed story: *The Blind Assassin*. In *Margaret Atwood's textual assassinations: Recent poetry and fiction*, ed. Sharon R. Wilson, 135–153. Ohio: Ohio State University Press.

Stockwell, Peter. 2009. *Texture: A cognitive aesthetics of reading*. Edinburgh: Edinburgh University Press.

Tobin, Vera. 2018. *Elements of surprise: Our mental limits and the satisfactions of plot*. Harvard: Harvard University Press.

Todorov, Tzvetan. 1966. *The typology of detective fiction*. London: Routledge.

Todorov, Tzvetan. 1971. *The typology of the detective story*, 42–52. The Poetics of Prose. Oxford: Basil Blackwell.

Toolan, Michael. 2020. Narrative retelling in McGahern's 'Swallows': the intensifying power of repetition and return. In *Narrative retellings: stylistic approaches*, ed. Marina Lambrou, 61–76*London: Bloomsbury.*

Van Peer, Willie, Frank J. Hakemulder and Sonia Zyngier. 2007. Lines on feeling: Foregrounding, aesthetics and meaning. *Language and Literature* 16 (2): 197–213.

Wilson, Sharon R. 1987. Camera images in Margaret Atwood's novels. In *Margaret Atwood: Reflection and reality*, ed. Beatrice Mendez-Egle, 29–57. Edinburg, Texas: Pan American University.

Wilson, Sharon R. 2003. Margaret Atwood and popular culture: *The blind assassin* and other novels. *Journal of American and Comparative Cultures* 25 (3–4): 270–275.

Wilson, Sharon R. 2006. Blindness and survival in Margaret Atwood's major novels. In *The Cambridge companion to Margaret Atwood*, ed. Coral Ann Howells, 176–191. Cambridge: Cambridge University Press.

3

Memories and Reconstrual in *Alias Grace*

3.1 Introduction

This chapter explores the earliest Atwood publication under consideration in this book, *Alias Grace* (1996). In a similar way to *The Blind
Assassin* (Chapter 2), *Alias Grace* is a novel that uses strategies of repetition and fragmented storytelling, raising questions about the lines between
fact and fiction, and of the authenticity and reliability of authorship. The
stylistic exploration of Grace Marks' voice outlined examines how Cognitive Grammar's concept of 'reconstrual' (Langacker 2008) can elucidate the
linguistic and conceptual mechanisms that give rise to these central themes,
and which govern reader attention in the revelation and concealment of
significant storyworld details. As a storyteller, Grace repeats and overreports
(Phelan and Martin 1999; Kukkonen 2013, 209) the same events, while
omitting and obscuring the facts of the crime she relates. It is argued that the
reconstrual operations in the descriptions of key scenes, objects and events
form the basis of Grace fragmented, patchworked and, ultimately, uncooperative storytelling style. The stylistic choices of the retold accounts are central
to the novel's categorisation as an 'anti-detective' novel (Ingersoll 2003, 543)
which neither confirms nor denies Grace's culpability.

The chapter opens with an overview of the novel and summarises the
themes that appear in the critical responses to the text. A summary of the
construal model, and how it describes processes of revised storytelling, is
outlined in Sect. 3.4. This framework is applied for the stylistic analysis of
how Grace is first introduced to characters and readers through Dr Jordan's
third-person narration, and secondly of the scene that precedes the 'missing

C. Harrison, *The Language of Margaret Atwood,* Palgrave Studies in Language, Literature
and Style, https://doi.org/10.1007/978-3-031-67640-6_3

memory' (Atwood 2018, 33), which is central to the story and recounted through Grace's first-person narration. The analysis explores how the patch-worked and self-aware storytelling identified within the critical readership is manifested at the micro, linguistic level of the text, and thus creates a stylistic blueprint for the novel that underpins its palimpsestic arrangement.

3.2   Writing and Reading *Alias Grace*

In *Alias Grace*, Atwood re-frames the notorious double murder of Thomas Kinnear and Nancy Montgomery, which took place in Canada in the mid-nineteenth century, as a fictionalised historical account. Alongside other formal choices, such as nested narratives and the inclusion of multiple voices and perspectives, readers are presented with re-examined versions of the same event as outlined by the central character-narrator, Grace Marks. Grace was a servant in the Kinnear household and was charged with being an acces-sory for the double murder and sentenced to life imprisonment. The novel is Atwood's imagined account of Grace's perspective, and the text treads the line between fact and fiction, offering a fictionalised version of Grace's experiences and intertextual references to other second-hand accounts of the case (e.g., Moodie 1854), without deviating too far from the known historical events which make up the main facts of what happened. The story also features Dr Jordan, a medical doctor specialising in psychology, who visits Grace in the penitentiary to help her recover her missing memory of the day of the murder. The novel is classified by some as a murder mystery (Shead 2015), though it departs from the more traditional format of the genre.

In her recent MasterClass on Creative Writing, Atwood (2018) reflects on how she had written the first 100 pages of her first draft of *Alias Grace* before she realised that the mode of person was not right for the book (see also Atwood 2022, 44–45). She had been writing a third-person account of Grace's experiences and had been struggling with the writing, when she realised that the first-person mode would work more effectively. She reflects on how *The Handmaid's Tale*, on the other hand, was written in the first person from the outset, in part because this text belongs more clearly to the genre of 'witness literature', 'in which a first-person narrator tells their story in hope that someone might later find it and learn what happened' (Atwood 2018, 27). In an activity that follows this discussion on the Master-Class course, Atwood asks course participants to compare the following two versions of *Alias Grace*: her original third-person draft manuscript, and the reframed account as narrated through Grace's first-person perspective. In particular, participants are asked to consider the differences between the two versions and reflect on the qualities invited by the first-person form (2018, 27).

Stylistic studies have considered the different affordances offered by these two narrative modes. Third-person narration allows a wider scope of the scene, while also losing the space between the narrator and the character which can be used, for example, to create irony (Simpson 2014, 30). In contrast, first-person narration offers a more limited camera lens in which the reflector mode of the speaker is automatically foregrounded (Morini 2011, 601). The first-person account in the published story enables a closer and less filtered alignment with Grace's point of perception. Her subjectivity is expressed in a more direct and less mediated way, and consequently this closer deictic alignment also removes the possibility for readers to delimit the boundaries of her perception. This choice also positions Grace as an autodiegetic narrator who is automatically duplicated from the outset of the story. In any autodiegetic text, in which the first-person narrator is also a protagonist in the story, dual roles of 'experiencing self' and 'observing self' are established (Cohn 1978; Fludernik 2009). The autodiegesis allows the text to confirm Grace's position as a storyteller (as her observing self) and her position as experiencer (as experiencing self) at alternating points within the storytelling. And, of course, these two perspectives can either align or compete with one another to create consonant or dissonant narration (Cohn 1978; Morini 2011, 600), so that at times readers become more immersed in the story and less aware of Grace's position as storyteller, and at other times this immersion is disrupted through references to the 'constructed' (Michael 2001, 436) nature of her narrative. These tensions enable readers to glimpse the duplicity inherent in Grace's storytelling.

Wisker (2012) summarises the two thematic strands that appear in critical responses to the novel. She notes that the primary topic among the critical responses relates to this perceived sense of duplicity within the storytelling, generating questions of reliability regarding the 'questionable status of all forms of records' (Wisker 2012, 118). In turn, the second thematic strand relates to 'historically contextualising the representation and treatment of women' (2012, 118). Wisker identifies further and related areas of critical interest within these broader themes, including examinations of 'unravelling the truth' (123–124), quilting (124–128) and processes of 'storytelling and murder mystery' creation (129–131). For the purposes of this chapter, this discussion will focus on the first broad category that Wisker identifies: those critical responses that have explored how the novel problematises the representation of fact, as well as those that examine the text's structural and formal choices.[1]

3.2.1 The Patchwork Metaphor and the Nature of Storytelling

Alias Grace is organised into chapters named after quilting patterns, and these labels correspond symbolically with the content and themes of each chapter (Mantel 1996). At the same time, much of the story takes place in the conversations between Grace and Dr Jordan, which occur while Grace is completing needlework, and she often reflects on the various patterns and quilts she encountered at different moments in her life. Many critics of the novel identify the prevalence of this patchwork metaphor, though, as Murray (2001) observes, it holds multiple interpretations and narrative functions.

At the macro-level of the text, the metaphor is seen to signal, more externally, Atwood herself. Grace's role as weaver and storyteller is seen as a metaphorical parallel to Atwood; each is an 'expert quilter' (Mantel 1996), and Grace's character assumes the layered roles of 'writer-novelist-narrator' (O'Neill 2013, 666). This parallel is taken further by Goldblatt (1999), who extends this interanimated metaphor beyond *Alias Grace* to apply to Atwood's writing more generally. In her critical reflections on the processes of writing, this is also a parallel that Atwood acknowledges herself. When describing the resources she might draw on for writing, for example, she describes how 'material, just as in sewing, is anything you use to make the thing you are making' (2022, 42). To return to the analysis of conceptual metaphors (Lakoff and Johnson 1980) outlined in Chapter 1 of this book, this metaphorical parallel can be described in terms of the mapped agentive roles between the domains of STORYTELLING and QUILTING, as summarised in Table 3.1.

Table 3.1 Mappings in STORYTELLING IS QUILTING

Target domain STORYTELLING		Source domain QUILTING
Narrators	←	Quilters
Fragments of story	←	Pieces of fabric
Narrative structures	←	Quilting patterns
Narrating	←	Sewing
Voice/pen	←	Sewing needle
Story	←	Quilt

The mapped properties between the source and target domains within framings of this metaphor underpin the critical discussion of the novel. Within this conceptualisation, Grace is attributed with agency as a storyteller. She is able to both reveal and conceal this agency (Mannon 2014), however, and is considered both a powerful and an empowered storyteller despite her imprisonment in the penitentiary (McWilliams 2009, 94). Given that the fragments relating her story are attributed to different voices, discussion within the critical literature of this structural metaphor extends into debates surrounding reliability, the nature of storytelling and the metafictional status of the novel.

In addition to revealing the symbolic relationship between storyteller and story, many critics have commented on how the patchwork metaphor performs a structural role (e.g., Ingersoll 2001; Tolan 2007; Michael 2001). For instance, Michael (2001, 421) describes the novel's patchwork organisation as a 'spatial construction' (cg. Ingersoll 2001), pieced together in a way that defies more linear storytelling practices. She argues that including and combining fragments of texts from different sources gives each contribution parity in terms of validity and authority. This collection, or curation, is seen to draw equivalence between various modes of narration such as oral storytelling and seemingly more official documents recorded, written and published by authorities (Ingersoll 2001, 425). Consequently, this structure has a dual function in that it 'destabilizes the authority of official documents but also recuperates previously de-authorized texts and discourses' (2001, 426).

More generally, though, the patchwork is regarded as an organisational device that disrupts traditional, incremental forms of storytelling. Murray (2001, 78) indirectly discusses some of the mappings that make up the structural function of the metaphor, including the idea that a story is formed from a unity of disparate fragments, and argues that it is this mapping that leads the novel to be interpreted as an example of 'historiographic metafiction' (Hutcheon 1984). A subset of postmodern writing, historiographic metafiction refers to works which construct and reconstruct history in theoretically self-aware ways, and which tend to investigate the 'relationship between historical fact and the act (and permanence) of writing' (Hutcheon 1984, 233). Murray suggests that, in fact, this patchwork metaphor reflects a genre feature of postmodernity: namely, its '(contradictory) desire for unity and diversity, for freedom and security, for process and closure' (81; Wilson 2003). Other mapped features of the patchwork metaphor inviting this metafictional categorisation includes Grace's overt positioning as storyteller and author, and the lack of narrative closure and resolution in the story (Ingersoll 2001; O'Neill 2013, 655–656). As Ingersoll (2001, 385–386) identifies, within this categorisation, metafictionality does not just mean self-awareness or reflexivity of form, but rather entails a more significant subversion of the way textuality and reality are represented. The absence of narrative resolution transpires in the way that the novel does not paint Grace as wholly innocent or wholly guilty; as in real life, many details of the Kinnear story remain unknown. Grace is presented as an ambiguous character who is at times reliable and at other times unreliable in her account (Vickroy 2015). As expected from Grace's pseudo-authorial role, this unreliability is signposted in a very self-aware way from the very beginning of her story. McWilliams (2009, 103), for example, argues that the opening of the novel echoes *David Copperfield*, similarly highlighting 'the artifice of the story'; 'the fraught relationship between 'real life' and its rendering in narrative'. The question of Grace's unreliability is further evidenced in the central theme of memory in the novel (Wynne-Davies 2010, 60; Mantel 1996; Vickroy 2015).

Its postmodern themes and other style and genre choices mean the novel becomes formally complex and difficult to neatly categorise (O'Neill 2013). *Alias Grace* contains elements of a Bildungsroman story, evokes an intertextual reframing of Tennyson's 'The Lady of Shalott' (McWilliams 2009), and makes references to horror and the Gothic in its depiction of dreams, nightmares and visions (Mantel 1996). Equally, Michael (2001, 424) observes that the emphasis on the trial in Dr Jordan's attempt to uncover the truth of the missing memory resembles the template of a legal narrative as well of detective fiction. At the same time, the novel is labelled as a 'trauma narrative', where the physical activity of quilting is interpreted as a way for Grace to process the traumatic experiences of her past (Vickroy 2015). Drawing similarities between *Alias Grace* and *The Blind Assassin*, Vickroy further observes that the fragmented structure of both novels 'enjoin readers to process and perhaps fill in the gaps in telling' (2015, 35), inviting active participation in narrative comprehension. In the context of *Alias Grace*, these gaps are, in part, created through the 'competing discourses' (2015, 38) of the novel which are manifested in the split selves presented by Grace's character(s).

In summary, the critical reflections on genre classification, structural choices and layered voices within the storytelling are all underpinned by the patchwork metaphor and its constitutive mappings. Grace assumes a number of different roles across the novel, and at the same time, readers are required to enact different roles in their engagement with the story. As noted in Chapter 1 and later developed in Chapter 2 of this book, the detective fiction genre invites readers to participate in solving clues and uncovering facts of the case.

The metafiction elements of the novel, on the other hand, make this a seemingly more marked, direct, and collaborative process between readers and the dual authors, Grace and Atwood. While the patchwork metaphor is particularly salient, therefore, the formal representation of Grace's voice and point of view play a significant role in piecing together the story. The next sections consider the stylistic mechanisms that create this complexity within Grace's storytelling.

3.3 Construal

In Cognitive Grammar, 'construal' (Langacker 1987, 1991, 2008) refers to the way that conceptual content has been organised and represented through linguistic choices and grammatical constructions. Langacker argues that all choices of language production are inherently meaningful, and consequently carry key information about the interpretive impact of the conceptual content. Linguistic producers (writers, speakers) can choose to represent 'the same scene in alternate ways' (Langacker 2008, 43), and readers may also be invited to conceptualise alternate construals based on the linguistic cues they are presented with, and their own encyclopaedic or schematic knowledge. A visual analogy can clarify how construal works, and Langacker uses a stage metaphor to describe the phenomenon (Giovanelli and Harrison 2018). When you visit a theatre, for example, you will see a stage with actors and props. A play director (who analogously takes the role of linguistic producer, in this context) may decide to position the actors or props on stage in particular ways to foreground the salience of certain items, or power relationships, within the play. Your seat in the audience is likely to affect how you interpret what you are watching. If you are seated off to one side, some of those foregrounded choices on stage may not be as salient for you, since you are afforded a different perspective to the stage than if you sat in the centre row.

Langacker describes how this process of conceptual organisation in language and grammar occurs along particular dimensions of construal. Following Giovanelli and Harrison (2018, 34), these can be grouped and summarised as follows:

Specificity	how closely we choose to view a scene or parts of it;
Focusing and prominence	what we choose to look at and pay attention to within the scene;
Perspective	the position from which we view a scene.

While there is not space to give a full overview of the Cognitive Grammar framework here,[2] the next sections will introduce and define those concepts that form the focus of the analysis in this chapter.

3.3.1 Specificity

A scene may be construed with a high level of detail and specificity, or in a vaguer and more schematic way. In language, these different levels of detail can be arranged in taxonomic hierarchies which scale from the highly schematic to the highly specific. Within these hierarchies, each new concept is a further 'elaboration' (Langacker 2008, 17) on the description that precedes it. Shifting levels of specificity in description can be observed, for example, in the following extract:

Extract 3.1

> I'm not looking at the scrapbook now, because they may come at any moment. I sit with my rough hands folded, eyes down, staring at the flowers in the Turkey carpet. Or they are supposed to be flowers. They have petals the shape of diamonds on a playing card; like the cards spread out on the table at Mr Kinnear's, after the gentlemen had been playing the night before. Hard and angular. But red, a deep thick red. Thick strangled tongues. (Atwood 2017, 27)

In Extract 3.1, Grace begins with a more schematic description of 'the flowers', and readers are informed that the abstraction of the pattern invites other associations for Grace. The level of detail offered to readers increases as she embellishes on her description. Further information is provided about where the flowers are located in the prepositional phrase 'in the Turkey carpet', and in the subjective associations Grace attaches to their presence. That they are 'supposed to be flowers' suggests that their form, is unusual, and deviates from Grace's prototype for their usual appearance. Later in the novel, red flowers are often labelled, with greater specificity, as peonies, and these become an extended metaphor across the novel (Gazzaz 2021).

Levels of specificity in literary descriptions have a direct bearing on the reading experience. Vagueness can sometimes disclose a narrator who is unreliable, mentally compromised, or perhaps who wishes to hide something. More schematised descriptions can invite readers to play a more active role in the conceptualisation of the discourse by requiring them to fill in the gaps based on their own schematic knowledge. On the other hand, texts can keep readers at a distance and close off alternative interpretations by more fully specifying descriptions of the conceived scene.

3.3.2   Focusing and Prominence

Another way in which linguistic construals can vary is through 'focusing' (Langacker 2008, 57–65), which describes what we choose to pay attention to within a conceived scene. Lexical choices allow conceptualisers to instantiate 'domains' (Langacker 2008, 44–54), which are knowledge structures enabling access to encyclopaedic knowledge (Chapter 1, Sect. 1.3; Chapter 4). Lexical choices can sometimes instantiate multiple domains, and descriptions in literature can draw on several domains simultaneously. While a FLOWERS domain is initially activated in Extract 3.1, a PLAYING CARDS or associated GAMBLING domain is also introduced in the visual similarity between the forms ('petals in the shape of diamonds'), and in the direct references to 'a playing card' and 'the cards'. Such activation may extend to other language choices such as 'folded' which, on a re-reading, can also evoke a GAMBLING domain. Diamonds in another context, on the other hand, might more prototypically profile domains of MARRIAGE or VALUE for contemporary Western readers (following on from the romantic implications of flowers also mentioned here), before a PLAYING CARDS domain is more peripherally evoked. In the context of this passage, these connections generate darker or more ominous metaphorical meanings.

Focusing and attention can also be directed to refine the 'scope' (Langacker 2008, 62–65) of the conceived scene. Scope is the coverage given by a particular word to its conceptual content. For example, the words 'page' and 'spine' are part of the 'immediate scope' of a 'book', or even a 'library', constituting a 'maximal scope' more broadly (Langacker 2008, 63–65). In fiction, these part-whole relationships can be manipulated to conceal or reveal certain narrative details, in relation to both nouns and verbs. In Extract 3.1, Grace limits her viewing frame to focus on the immediate scope of the Turkey carpet, within the more maximal scope of the room in which she sits. The flowers, in turn, are described maximally, before her viewing frame zooms in on parts of the flower which make up its immediate scope (the 'petals'). In turn, the 'diamonds' are the immediate scope of the more maximal 'playing card', as the viewing frame zooms out again. Through this shifting in focus, it is possible to follow Grace's thought processes closely and track the chains of subjective associations at a micro-level. Again, in the context of this novel, readers might attach narrative or thematic significance to conceptual parallels drawn by Grace.

In verb forms, scope can be further marked in the difference between progressive and non-progressive verb forms. For example, a sentence like 'I sewed a patchwork quilt' is a finite non-progressive form which allows readers to capture the process holistically. In a sentence like this, readers are given access to the action in a maximal viewing frame, where the whole process is described. Comparatively, if the progressive form 'I was sewing a patchwork quilt' were used, then the depicted action becomes more restricted. Readers might assume that the completion of the activity will occur in a future moment to which we do not yet have access, and which might yet be interrupted.

3.3.3   Perspective

Finally, construal can be considered alongside the dimension of 'perspective' (Langacker 2008), which can alter depending on how the conceptualiser is positioned in relation to the conceived situation, and whether they invite or deflect attention. As with the other construal dimensions, perspectival relationships are established through different linguistic mechanisms. Deictic expressions, for example, can encode a vantage point by clearly positioning a conceptualiser in time and space, as well as socially and textually. Grace's first-person vantage point is established in Extract 3.1 through the first-person forms 'I' and 'my', while spatial prepositions such as 'down' indicate where she is physically situated in space. An account where attention is drawn to the conceptualiser places them onstage as the object of attention. Consequently, the conceived scene they are describing recedes into the background and is said to be more subjectively construed (Langacker 2008, 260–264). On the other hand, a conceptualiser can move into the background, and more focus instead can be placed on the conceived scene being described. In these contexts, readers encounter a scene or event which is objectively construed (Langacker 2008, 260–264). Literary texts often move between subjectively and objectively construed accounts, placing greater or lesser emphasis on the perspective of a character to achieve particular effects (see Chapter 4). Extract 3.1 is subjectified through Grace's reference to her first-person perception 'I sit [...] staring', and through her epistemic judgement on what is 'supposed to be' present.

3.3.4 Reconstrual in Fiction

Considered together, construal operations carry meaningful information about the relationship between conceptualiser and scene, and demonstrate how language choices at the micro-level of the text can scale to patterns that similarly operate meaningfully at the discourse level of a text. In his analysis of the writing of Siegfried Sassoon, Giovanelli (2022) identifies how literary revision, the drafting and re-drafting processes undertaken by writers, is a form of 'reconstrual' that can be explored as operating along the linguistic dimensions mentioned above. Giovanelli uses Cognitive Grammar's construal operations to offer an apparatus (Table 3.2) through which to explore linguistic processes of revision and retelling in texts.

Through analysis of different types of rewriting, Giovanelli demonstrates how scenes and events can be re-written to both modulate and empha-sise certain facts, details and identities of the conceptualiser and their relationships with others. He further argues that reconstrual has both a text effect, 'in that it will reshape, at a local level, the text in some way', but that it also has a discourse function: a more 'global phenomenon' in a text which will 'serve some wider and often radical discourse goal in so far as it repack-ages material to profile some previously backgrounded part of the original construal or downplays some aspect or introduces a new perspective into the discourse' (2022, 131).

Readers also play a key role in construing a scene, analogously represented as the audience in the earlier theatre example. It is argued that construal operations form part of the intersubjective relationship between both writers and readers (Harrison 2017; Hart 2011). In a study of reader-centred recon-strual, for example, Harrison and Nuttall (2019, 2021) consider how readers reconstrue Margaret Atwood's (2014) short story 'The Freeze-Dried Groom', which features a narrative twist. In reference to local stylistic choices within

Table 3.2 Reconstrual operations (after Giovanelli 2022, 154)

Construal phenomena	Reconstrual dimensions			
Specificity	*Respecifying* (granular v schematic construals)			
Focus	*Rescoping* (immediate and maximal scope)			
Prominence	*Reprofiling* (onstage attention)	*Refiguring* (figure-ground)	*Realigning* (trajector-landmark)	
Perspective	*Rescanning* (summary vs. sequence scanning)	*Retargeting* (reference points)	*Relocating* (vantage points)	*Reviewing* (subjective and objective construal)

the text, the analysis in the study observes the global effects of reconstrual in this short story: namely, that re-readers become more distanced from the narrating focaliser on a second reading, and that reading this whodunit crime story more than once can create greater ambiguity rather than increased clarity (see Chapter 5). Similar processes or reader reconstrual can be observed in non-literary contexts. Browse (2021), for example, explores how voters are positioned in relation to political speeches, and how reconstrual brings about a process of recentring in a political sense. As Harrison and Nuttall argue, in such experiences of re-reading, the same writer construal is presented, but the reader construal, 'the way individuals respond to these textual cues and draw on their own schematic knowledge in order to conceptualise the fictional world' (Harrison and Nuttall 2019, 14), will alter.

More broadly, and in narratological contexts, reconstrual operations are apparent in examples of narrative retelling (Lambrou 2020). Where a scene is told and retold within the same story, its repetition invites a comparison of the different versions. That it is repeated will automatically increase its narrative salience such that any observable deviations between the two accounts may be interpreted as more significant. Toolan (2020) analysis of the short story 'Swallows' explores narrative retellings of the same scene, as described by different character-narrators. Toolan argues that such intratextual retelling is a type of repetition that has the global function of completing the story or making it satisfactory for readers by offering an alternative form of resolution. In other examples of retelling, of course, the presentation of different details or conflicting accounts holds other discourse functions. Studies of the Rashomon effect, for example, where different and conflicting character accounts of the same event are presented, show how conflicting descriptions, as told by more than one narrator, are seen to play crucial roles in the representation of character unreliability and the obfuscation of plot, placing the reader or viewer in the position of 'negotiator' of the story (Davis and Burnham 2015).

The present analysis of reconstrual in *Alias Grace* departs from the previous studies of both narrative retellings in narratology and accounts of reconstrual in cognitive stylistics, through exploring how scenes and events are retold by the same character-narrator, described by Harrison (2023) as a type of 'narrator reconstrual' (see Chapter 5, Table 5.1). Arguably, these reconstrued scenes work in a similar way to the conflicting descriptions that require an audience to assume the role of 'negotiator' mentioned in the discussion of the Rashomon effect, except in this instance, this negotiation involves a mediation between different enactors of the same character. This reframing is a type of uncooperative narration whereby the character overreports on events but without further clarification of details (Harrison 2023).

The next sections consider how these reconstrual operations take place in *Alias Grace* at key parts of the story: firstly, through Dr Jordan's first and second impressions of Grace (Sect. 3.4), and secondly through Grace's retold accounts of the memory that Dr Jordan is trying to acquire (Sect. 3.5). Following Giovanelli (2023), it is argued that there is a relationship between the local effects brought about by the stylistic choices of reconstrual and the overarching patchwork metaphor at the discourse or thematic level of the novel.

3.4 First and Second Impressions

Only two perspectives are shown in the fictional prose strands of *Alias Grace*: Dr Jordan's and Grace's. This first section of analysis explores Dr Jordan's recollection of his first meeting with Grace, and his construal (Extract 3.2) and reconstrual (Extract 3.3) of her appearance, which occurs both in smaller clausal units and thematically in his wider rumination on her character. As a heterodiegetic reflector, Dr Jordan participates in the events of the main storyworlds of the narrative, and his thoughts are also shown through inner focalisation (cf. O'Neill 2013, 655). Just before this scene, he had been studying an engraved portrait of Grace in a pamphlet reporting the trial. In Extract 3.2, he describes his first encounter with Grace when he arrives at the penitentiary to carry out his initial interview.

Extract 3.2

Preparing himself for his first interview with Grace, Simon had disregarded this portrait entirely. She must be quite different by now, he'd thought; more dishevelled; less self-contained; more like a suppliant; quite possibly insane. He was conducted to her temporary cell by a keeper, who'd locked him in with her, after warning him that she was stronger than she looked and could give a man a devilish bite, and advising him to call for help if she became violent.

As soon as he saw her, he knew that this wouldn't happen. The morning light fell slantingly in through the small window high up on the wall, illuminating the corner where she stood. It was an image almost mediaeval in its plain lines, its angular clarity: a nun in a cloister, a maiden in a towered dungeon, awaiting the next day's burning at the stake, or else the last-minute champion coming to rescue her. The cornered woman; the penitential dress falling straight down, concealing feet that were surely bare; the straw mattress on the floor; the timorous hunch of the shoulders; the arms hugged close to the thin body, the long wisps of auburn hair escaping from what appeared at first glance to be a chaplet of white flowers – and especially the eyes, enormous in the pale face and dilated with fear, or with mute pleading – all was as it should be. He'd seen many hysterics at the Salpêtrière in Paris who'd looked very much like this. (Atwood 2017, 59)

Dr Jordan is regarded as a narrative vehicle for Atwood to bring a different perspective on Grace's character, albeit a perspective that through which she is objectified and which exacerbates gender stereotypes (Vickroy 2015, 37). The context of the scene suggests that his perception is one that should be presented directly and reliably. Visually, the light is 'illuminating' where she is located, and the 'plain lines' confer an 'angular clarity' to the description which prevents ambiguity. Despite his aim to examine Grace from a clinical perspective, however, Dr Jordan's description of Grace suggests a more romanticised perspective. He perceives her as a stereotypical 'hysteric', not unlike those he has encountered previously on his travels. There are some immediate reconstruals of Grace's appearance within the first clauses in which she is described. She is at first, seemingly, 'a nun in a cloister' and then 'a maiden in a towered dungeon'. Listing these descriptions in successive noun phrases, with no verbs and only commas to create an asyndetic list, invites readers to examine each description summatively and via a series of separate viewing frames, emphasising the 'individual salience' of each description (Nuttall 2018, 73). Aligning reader perspective with Dr Jordan here presents cumulative, and at times conflicting, portraits of Grace, as and when they are conceptualised in the narrative.

In both descriptions of Grace's identity ('nun' and 'maiden'), a domain of ABSTINENCE is suggested, though Grace's roles in these initial two scenarios become refigured. She is the figure of attention throughout the scene, but her identity shifts such that prominence is directed differently within her various roles, and that RELIGION becomes superseded by FAIRY TALE. This shift of templates is elaborated with the attribution of a script-reinforcing actions, though it is unclear what role Grace will assume. She is either 'awaiting the next day's burning at the stake, or else the last-minute champion coming to rescue her'. The first option—'the next day's burning at the stake'—brings another shift in domains, indicating a WITCHCRAFT interpretation in Dr Jordan's conceptualisation. The clause that follows, 'or else the last-minute champion coming to rescue her', returns to the medieval timeframe referenced earlier in the scene. In either description, the continuous progressive form of 'awaiting' excludes the resolution from the viewing frame; it is not clear whether the event Grace awaits will or will not happen.

These descriptions are further elaborated with details of CONTAINMENT. In each scenario, the confined space is reprofiled such that the sense of restriction becomes exacerbated ('in a cloister', 'in a dungeon'). This containment schema is enforced in the third sentence which describes her as a 'cornered woman', and evoked later in the contrastive reference to 'escaping'. Grace is construed as confined, but also inactive. There is an absence of verbs in these two initial descriptions which means she is initially cast in a 'zero' clausal role (Langacker 2008, 356); a role that suggests ongoing states of permanence and used for clausal participants that 'merely exist, occupy some location, or exhibit a static property' (Langacker 2008, 356). She remains the object of Dr Jordan's attention and is simply described within her static roles: 'a nun', 'a maiden' and 'a cornered woman'. When Grace is attributed wilful agency through the action of 'awaiting', the semantic profile of this verb continues to foreground her inertia. Even though she is performing this action, both 'the next day's burning' and the visit of 'the last-minute champion' are events or entities that move towards her, rather than the other way round. In other words, she is at the mercy of these external forces. In the context of 'the next day's burning' and the later reconstrual of Grace as a 'cornered woman', this action assumes a menacing rather than a romantic quality. The description generates two potential interpretations: she is literally in the corner of the cell or seemingly 'cornered' by an advancing, unknown enemy.

The rest of Dr Jordan's description in Extract 3.2 elaborates on Grace's physical appearance. In the earlier clauses, the maximal scope of her as a figure is provided in the descriptions of 'a nun', 'a maiden' and 'a cornered woman', though she is described only schematically and indefinitely within these prototypical roles. The fifth sentence, in contrast, starts to further specify some of the physical details through singling out parts of her body (immediate scope) against her appearance as a whole (maximal scope). Each item of clothing or body part is elaborated simply and most frequently through premodification ('penitential dress', 'timorous hunch', 'thin body', 'long wisps', 'auburn hair', 'white flowers', 'pale face'). In these clauses, her body parts are selected for attention ('feet', 'shoulders', 'arms', 'wisps of auburn hair', 'eyes', 'face') and only schematically profiled against the more maximal 'thin body'. Significantly, such foregrounding of body parts in place of more holistic figural descriptions appears in other fictional texts that fall within crime (Kennedy 1982) and romance (Mills 1995) genres, respectively.

Through his physical description of Grace, Dr Jordan demonstrates awareness of the fallibility of his perceptions ('what appeared at first glance'), and of the foregone diagnosis he is imposing on Grace. Assuredly, '[h]e'd seen many hysterics at the Salpêtrière in Paris who'd looked very much like this'. The series of summative images he presents via the asyndetic syntax, and through fronting each clause with specified noun phrases, mean that the stylistic choices in this extract echo those in other pieces of Atwood writing. Nuttall's (2018, 61–86) analysis of *The Handmaid's Tale*, for example, explores the syntactic structure of Offred's description of her room in Gilead, and how the stream of consciousness structure positions readers alongside the world view or mind style of the protagonist. Nuttall outlines how Offred's sustained description of her domestic surroundings, as represented through atemporalised descriptions ('a table, a chair, a lamp'), constructs a series of viewing frames, inviting readers to sequentially process world-builders in the scene but restricting a more holistic understanding or overview of both Offred's situation and the fictional world at the discourse level of the narrative. Because the description in Extract 3.4 is focused on Grace, these style choices create a similar attentional zoom (Tabakowska 1993, 52; Stockwell 2009, 43–44) in the context of this scene, except here, it denies a sense of the depth of Grace's character. Readers experienceDr Jordan's difficulty in drawing together facets of Grace's character, and she prevails as an enigmatic object of scrutiny. Each portrait eschews the overwriting of erroneous information, and this forms part of the tessellated perspective of Grace that remains fractured throughout the narrative.

In contrast, the description that immediately follows (Extract 3.3) shows a more overtly pronounced reconstrual of Dr Jordan's perception of Grace.

Extract 3.3

But then Grace stepped forward, out of the light, and the woman he'd seen the instant before was suddenly no longer there. Instead there was a different woman – straighter, taller, more self-possessed, wearing the conventional dress of the Penitentiary, with a striped blue and white skirt beneath which were two feet, not naked at all but enclosed in ordinary shoes. There was even less escaped hair than he'd thought: most of it was tucked up under a white cap.

Her eyes were unusually large, it was true, but they were far from insane. Instead they were frankly assessing him. It was as if she were contemplating the subject of some unexplained experiment; as if it were he, and not she, who was under scrutiny.

Remembering the scene, Simon winces. I was indulging myself, he thinks. Imagination and fancy. I must stick to observation, I must proceed with caution. A valid experiment must have verifiable results. I must resist melodrama, and an overheated brain. (Atwood 2017, 59–60)

Significantly, it is ironic that moving 'out of the light' invites the mental override of Dr Jordan's perception of Grace's character. In the more holistic reconstrued portrait of Grace' outlined in Extract 3.3, a shift in his perception of her character occurs. This new version of Grace is described by Dr Jordan through an explicit act of comparison with his previous interpretations, and 'the woman he'd seen the instant before' becomes the 'reference point' (Langacker 2008) for this reconstrual. This act of comparison is linguistically signposted in the use of adversative conjunctions such as 'but' and 'Instead', and in the constructions including comparative adjectives ('straighter, taller, more self-possessed') which simultaneously invoke physical features of the figure as construed in Extract 3.2. He also uses explicit syntactic negation, 'no longer there' and 'not naked at all', which emphasises his earlier misconception. In linguistics, negation marks out a mutually exclusive mental space (Langacker 2008, 354), but at the same time 'in order to understand a negated proposition we must be able to conceptualize the positive proposition that is being denied' (Nahajec 2009, 109). The combined structures of comparison and conceptual layering invited through negation means that the iterations of Grace's character remain onstage even while they are categorically altered or denied, contributing to the amorphous, collage-impression of her character.

Overall, Grace and aspects of her appearance become refigured in this reconstrual, and there is a tonal shift from the romantic towards the prosaic. Some of these descriptions undergo a process of respecification in that more precise details of her attire are singled out for attention ('a striped blue and white skirt' of the conventional dress are identified; her feet are 'enclosed in ordinary shoes'), while others are reviewed by Dr Jordan such that his perspective at this point can be considered more objective and comparatively less metaphorical. Consequently, this alters the value judgements attached to particular choices (March 1997, 68–69): her former 'Chaplet of white flowers' becomes reconstrued as, more simply, a 'white cap', for instance. This movement to the prosaic is further seen in the final paragraph in Extract 3.3, where Dr Jordan's present position as a reflector thinking back on the scene, and his initial romanticised assessment of Grace, signals a conceptual difference between his narrating self and his experiencing self. In the present, Dr Jordan narrates how 'Remembering the scene, Simon winces'. While some critics have commented that Dr Jordan's 'use of language in the text is that of a professional', and that 'he attaches linguistic significance to other characters' utterances particularly Grace's, according to the dictates of his medical training' (March 1997, 73), at this point the reconstrual of Grace in Extract 3.3 shows his desire to return to a more purely medical appraisal. He self-consciously reflects on his melodramatic interpretation, and his medical training returns to the fore in his return to science ('[a] valid experiment must have verifiable results'). Notable here, too, is Dr Jordan's hypothetical projection of Grace's thoughts whereby he senses an inversion of the power dynamics between them.

The series of disconnected and alternating descriptions set up though Dr Jordan's introduction to Grace in these two extracts presents a character who is inherently multiplied and fundamentally elusive in details. The constant adjustment of Grace as noted through the analysis of reconstrual operations, and supporting style choices of listing, explicit comparison and the crossovers of semantic domains, creates a palimpsest of character vignettes. Each over-written description remains salient in the 'periphery of consciousness' (Croft and Cruse 2004, 50) to be called up for activation in the text for readers to annex and amend the series of 'contradictory portraits' (Hutchison 2003, 46) of Grace. From this external, first impression of Grace, then, her character is denied depth, clarity and cohesion. At the same time, Dr Jordan's movement from romanticised to more prosaic interpretations of her character forms part of the 'sharper satire' reserved for the doctor (Shead 2015, 91).

3.5   Revisiting the Missing Memory

The scene under consideration in this second section of analysis is a pivotal one in the text; the account that precedes 'the missing memory' (Atwood 2017, 33) that Dr Jordan aims to reveal in his interviews with Grace. This extract forms part of Grace's recollection of the day of the murder, or rather, the recurring dream she is said to have about the day of the murder, which she recounts through interior monologue at the beginning of the story (5–6), and to Dr Jordan later in the novel (312–314). Grace continually revisits the distressing event, thereby also inviting readers to 'emotionally reconstruct the psychological and environmental complexities of, in this case, traumatic experience' (Vickroy 2015, 34). The scene—or, rather, both scenes—describes Grace walking through a grey place with high walls towards Nancy. Both descriptions are disorienting and depict, in detail, flowers that should not be there, and Nancy's appearance as Grace approaches her. An added complexity of this memory is Grace's conflation of details within her retelling. The description blends details of her current position in the penitentiary, the first day she arrived at the Kinnear household and the day of the murder. That Grace continually returns to this event creates heightened salience and partly suggests an awareness of the requirements of 'cooperative' storytelling (Mullins and Dixon 2007); an acknowledgement of the importance and significance of relaying what happened.

The following analysis explores how these representations are construed and reconstrued, and the additional implications this has for representations of time and space, figural prominence and narrator perception. Unlike the reconstrual of Grace in Extracts 3.2 and 3.3, which appear in consecutive paragraphs, the two accounts of this scene appear in pages 5–6 and then much later in the novel between pages 313 and 314 (labelled as Extracts 3.5 and 3.6 in this section). The paragraphs in each of the two scenes have been numbered according to the chronological order in which they appear in the original passages. The reproduction of these extracts in Tables 3.3–3.6 has been paired with the thematic counterpart in the retelling to enable stylistic comparison. The two passages in full and in their original order can be found in the Appendix.

3.5.1 Relocating Grace

The framing co-text of these two extracts, as well as style choices of space, time and setting, provides meaningful information about how the scenes are encountered and subsequently processed by readers. Grace's vantage point— that is, the position in space and time from which she recounts events— changes between the retellings.

Extract 3.5 appears at the very opening of the book. In the first two sentences, Grace describes initially the peonies that are 'growing' and 'testing the air', the buds that are 'swelling and opening', in the present continuous forms, which suggests ongoing and incomplete action experienced by her in the moment, first-hand. Even with the signposted temporal digression where she reminisces about 'that first day', at Mr. Kinnear's, it is not until the end of the passage that it becomes apparent this account is, in fact, a summary that appears later in the novel and not something both experienced and narrated by Grace in the moment. The initial absence of reporting clauses or markers of direct speech means that readers are more likely to attribute this description to Grace's interior thoughts as verbalised through her experiencing self, until this status is revoked by the statement that functions as a reporting clause ('[t]his is what I told Dr Jordan, when we came to that part of the story', 6). Including this final sentence invites readers to reconceptualise the scene as one that was summarised from a spoken account. This final acknowledgement establishes the cataphoric function of the extract within the narrative. Readers do not yet know what 'that part of the story' refers to, and so its reference here, in the opening section, seems ominous. Extract 3.5, therefore, provides a somewhat misleading introduction to Grace's 'confession'.

In contrast, Extract 3.6 occurs much later in the narrative. This retelling is framed through inverted commas which indicate her direct speech to Dr Jordan at this point in the novel, and consequently generates greater immediacy and autonomy to her words. In this description, the distance between Grace's act of experiencing and the act of telling is marked both through the progression of narrative time in the novel and in the shift to past tense. Significant, too, is that the description is explicitly framed as a dream, which impacts on readers' projection into the text (Giovanelli 2013) and their conceptualisation of Grace's (recounted) consciousness. The preceding paragraphs include important co-text for the scene, including details of other dreams Grace experiences. Prior to this account she remembers, for example, how she was afraid to return to sleep, and these 'fears were not in vain, for that is indeed what happened' (313). As in Extract 3.5, the description is also retrospectively reframed by Grace:

Extract 3.4

"You dreamt this before the event?" says Simon. He is writing feverishly.
"Yes Sir", says Grace. "And many times since." [...]
"They said they were not dreams at all, Sir. They said I was awake. But I do not wish to say any more about it." (Atwood 2017, 314)

In this way, her description of the imagined event is reframed as one which is more ontologically real or true.

The framing of each extract, then, generates different reading experiences. The first appears to be an immediate and close telling of a scene as experienced by Grace, though her proximity to the event is revoked at the end. In contrast, the second, retold scene is explicitly introduced as a dream, as a description of events that may or may not have occurred, and then later presented as a more factual account. This relocation and Grace's self-conscious revisions contribute to a feeling of 'epistemic confusion' (Morini 2011, 604) within the narration, such that all possibilities remain fluid and undefined, in terms of time, space and truth status.

3.5.2   Reconstruing Figures and Flowers

A further comparison of the two descriptions reveals several stylistic and thematic similarities, as well as meaningful revisions, at both the local and discourse levels within the text. In terms of local similarities, the peonies are the first 'attractors' (Stockwell 2009, 24) in both renderings. They are described as 'huge', colourful ('dark-red' compared to the 'grey pebbles') and texturally detailed ('shining', 'glossy', 'like satin'). They are also given grammatical agency ('They come/ came up'; 'swelling and opening'; 'they burst') in the first paragraphs. They are also, markedly, out of place: Grace notes that 'peonies don't bloom in April', and that, simply, 'they shouldn't be here'. This incongruity plays a key role in defamiliarising the scene and in signposting Grace's unreliability:

Extract 3.5 in Table 3.3 first outlines the physical position of the peonies more shallowly, where there is one prepositional phrase ('Out of the gravel') to locate them. In contrast, Extract 3.6 contains nested locatives in the first sentence, marked through the two prepositional phrases ('on the ground', 'out of the gravel'), which direct attention more sequentially as that the flowers are incrementally uncovered. Here, a reference point chain (Langacker 2008, 85) is created so that readers' attention is first guided to the 'loose grey pebbles', to the 'gravel', which are both initially more salient, before the peonies are introduced at the end of the second clause. At the same time, a difference can be observed in the representation of the verb processes within the extracts. Extract 3.5 describes an overview of the flowers' growth cycle, with each stage minutely captured through progressive *-ing* forms denoting a more immediate scope of movement (Langacker 2008; Giovanelli 2023), their 'buds testing the air', 'swelling and opening', 'shining', before they 'burst and fall to the ground'. In contrast, Extract 3.6 has fewer verb processes ('They came up [...] and then they opened [...] and then they burst'), which, combined with their finite forms, suggest more maximal, and in this context, comparatively abrupt, actions. Grace seems more interested in isolating the distinct moment in time: namely, the 'one instant before the come part'. The focus similarly shifts in the noun phrases: the parts of the peony are rescoped in Extract 3.6, where the immediate scope of the 'glossy petals' of the peony is described, compared to the maximal description in Extract 3.5 ('red flowers all shining'). Correspondingly, the the domains are reconstrued, redescribing the 'snails' eyes' of the buds as 'unripe apples' in Extract 3.6, evoking more religious connotations. These local style choices combine to alter the focus of attention within these first paragraphs. Grace's reconstrual in the retelling (Extract 3.6) describes more granular details of the physical appearance of the peonies, even while their actions are more summative. This narrowed focus increases their salience and Grace's obsessive re-examination of their significance in the scene and in her memories.

Table 3.3 Peonies as attractors

Extract 3.5 (Atwood 2017, 5)	Extract 3.6 (Atwood 2017, 313)
[1] Out of the gravel there are peonies growing. They come up through the loose grey pebbles, their buds testing the air like snails' eyes, then swelling and opening, huge dark-red flowers all shining and glossy like satin. Then they burst and fall to the ground	[1.2] On the ground there were loose grey pebbles, and out of the gravel there were peonies growing. They came up with just the buds on them, small and hard like unripe apples, and then they opened, and there were huge dark-red flowers with glossy petals, like satin; and then they burst in the wind and fell to the ground
[2] In the one instant before they come apart they are like the peonies in the front garden at Mr. Kinnear's, that first day, only those were white. Nancy was cutting them. She wore a pale dress with pink rosebuds and a triple-flounced skirt, and a straw bonnet that hid her face. She carried a flat basket, to put the flowers in; she bent from the hips like a lady, holding her waist straight. When she heard us and turned to look, she put her hand up to her throat as if startled	[2] "Except for being red, they were like the peonies in the front garden on the first day I came to Mr. Kinnear's, when Nancy was cutting the last of them; and I saw her in the dream, just as she was then, in her pale dress with the pink rosebuds and the triple flounced skirt, and her straw bonnet that hid her face. She was carrying a flat basket, to put the flowers in; and then she turned and put her hand up to her throat as if startled"

The reconstrual of the peonies at the local level contributes to their thematic importance at the discourse level of the text. Structurally, the peonies act as a trigger for Grace's memory of 'Mr. Kinnear's, that first day'. Gazzaz (2021) argues that flowers appear as metaphors in Atwood's writing more generally (for examples, the protagonist is named 'Iris' in *The Blind Assassin*; there are many flowers that appear throughout *The Handmaid's Tale*, and so on), and that the peonies in *Alias Grace* are similarly symbolic. Here, the peonies are said to signify the roles and status of Nancy and Grace, and that they are notably out of place both draws parallels between and suggests the 'displacement and alienation' of the two women (Gazzaz 2021, 11–12). The pairing of Nancy with the peonies is explicitly framed in the second paragraphs in Table 3.4 where she is described as being 'scattered, a drift of red and white cloth petals across the stones'. The description of the 'cloth petals' introduces a further metaphor to the scene, and in fact, there is a chain of related metaphors with shifting domains throughout. WOMEN ARE FLOWERS becomes FLOWERS ARE FABRIC, which in turn relates to the overarching metaphor, STORYTELLING IS QUILTING (Table 3.1). These layered metaphors become interrelated and create spreading activation such that other mappings can be inferred. The interpretation of WOMEN ARE FABRIC PATCHES, for example, is outlined in 'she came apart into patches of colour', but also conceptually aligns with the fragmentary descriptions of the women: they are referred to via constituent body parts ('head', 'eyes', 'hands', 'knuckles', 'toes of shoes', 'throat' and 'waist'), which creates a process of continuous rescoping, and in this context, foregrounds their physical presence.

The metaphorical implications of the peonies then filter into other style choices. The pairs of extracts in Tables 3.3 and 3.4 show how Nancy's actions in relation to the flowers are refigured across the two versions. They are fore-grounded in single clause structures in the first extract (the second sentence of Extract 3.5 in Table 3.3 says simply that 'Nancy was cutting them') and then backgrounded in the retold account of Extract 3.6: 'when Nancy was cutting the last of them' is tagged on the end of the clause. Significantly, though, the realignment from 'cutting them' to cutting '*the last* of them' (emphasis added) gives greater prominence to the final part of the action. It is an action that is nearing completion, which again carries metaphorical value within this context. Within this blended memory, Nancy is 'cutting the last of them' before she is about to be killed.

Table 3.4 Reconstruing figures and flowers

Extract 3.5 (Atwood 2017, 5–6)	Extract 3.6 (Atwood 2017, 313–314)
[4] I watch the peonies out of the corners of my eyes. I know they shouldn't be here: it's April, and peonies don't bloom in April. There are three more now, right in front of me, growing out of the path itself. Furtively I reach out my hand to touch one. It has a dry feel, and I realize it's made of cloth	[3.2] But the peonies were still coming up from the stones; and I knew they shouldn't be there. I reached out my hand to touch one and it had a dry feel, and I knew it was made of cloth
[6] I am almost up to Nancy, to where she's kneeling. But I do not break my step, I do not run I keep on walking two by two; and then Nancy smiles, only the mouth, her eyes are hidden by the blood and the hair, and then she scatters into patches of colour, a drift of red cloth petals across the stones	[4.2] When I was almost up to Nancy, to where she was kneeling, she smiled. Only the mouth, her eyes hidden by the blood and hair, and then she came apart into patches of colour, she scattered, a drift of red and white cloth petals across the stones

3.5.3 Reconstruing Perception and Possibility

As the extracts progress, the reconstrual of the scene becomes more sustained and more noticeable, as the epistemic confusion increases. Grace's positions in time and space becomes blurred and aggregated (Table 3.5). The locations have been respecified across the two versions: in Extract 3.5, Grace describes 'the yard' of the penitentiary as a familiar location, whereas in Extract 3.6, this place becomes defamiliarised. It is introduced indefinitely through expressions that fulfil the role of more salient 'targets' (Langacker 2008). It is referred to, more schematically, as 'a place I had never been before', with 'high walls made of stone', before later becoming the more definite 'the stone yard'. Additional personal significance is added in the introduction of the location in Extract 3.6 when she recounts her past and the reference point 'of the village where' she was born. This defamiliarisation of place blends different vantage points. Grace describes the premonition as she experienced or imagined it in the past, as though the penitentiary courtyard is a place with which she is not yet familiar.

Further and ambiguous revision occurs in the relocation of the retelling, as Grace's vantage point is altered. She initially views the scene as part of a group (Extract 3.5), to instead become a solo conceptualiser (Extract 3.6), Table 3.3. In Extract 3.5, another character is described as belonging to the same vantage point of the speaker: it recounts Nancy's response to 'when she heard *us*' (emphasis added). In contrast, Grace is singled out as the sole conceptualiser in Extract 3.6, as marked through first-person singular pronouns in the clause 'I dreamt I was walking'. This gives Grace greater prominence in

Table 3.5 Reconstruing perception

Extract 3.5 (Atwood 2017, 5)	Extract 3.6 (Atwood 2017, 313)
[3] I tuck my head down while I walk, keeping step with the rest, eyes lowered, silently two by two around the yard, inside the square made by the high stone walls. My hands are clasped in front of me; they're chapped, the knuckles reddened. I can't remember a time when they were not like that. The toes of my shoes go in and out under the hem of my skirt, blue and white, blue and white, crunching on the pathway. These shoes fit me better than any I've ever had before. [...]	[1.1] "In this new dream, I dreamt I was walking in a place I had never been before, with high walls all around made of stone, grey and bleak as the stones of the village where I was born, back across on the other side of the ocean. [...]" [3.1] "Then I was back in the stone yard, walking, with the toes of my shoes going in and out under the hem of my skirt, which was blue and white stripes. I knew I'd never had a skirt like that before, and at the sight of it I felt a great heaviness and desolation"

the second extract, and reviews the scene by heightening the subjectivity of Grace's singular perception. Additional style choices that identify her subjective experience include the higher number of verbs of perception: 'I knew', 'I'd felt', 'I dreamt'. The emphasis on her subjectivity and perception in Extract 3.6 makes the revoking of the dream status at the end of the extract even more pronounced.

Another more obvious change can be observed at the visual level of the text; namely, that the first account is longer and much more embellished than the second (Table 3.6). Extract 3.5 outlines a more detailed account of Grace's 'projected reality' (Langacker 2008) through the hypothetical constructions of what she 'will do'. To save Nancy, she will 'run to help', 'lift her up and wipe away the blood', and 'tear a bandage'. This is followed by a series of clausal constructions in which the attack has been forgotten, and in which the domestic routine will resume: 'Mr Kinnear will come home, and go into the parlour, and have his coffee'. The description undergoes a contrasting shift in tone, from the gory description of Nancy with 'the blood running down into her eyes' at the beginning of the paragraph, to the romanticised and idyllic fireflies, lamplight and music at the end. This imagined scenario is redacted in the reconstrued version (Extract 3.6) which summarises Grace's imagined actions only fleetingly ('I wanted to run and help her'), and via a summative negated form ('but I could not'). Instead of a more sustained description of what she wanted to do, or her possible reactions to Nancy's distress, the scene is reviewed and Grace's more personal evaluations of Nancy and her time at the Kinnears are backgrounded. Instead, Grace returns to and reflects on her physical movement at the time: 'my feet kept walking at a steady pace, as though they were not my own feet at all'. As observed in crime fiction, where grammatical agency is attributed to body parts in order to defer responsibility (e.g., Kennedy 1982), the agency here is assigned to her feet specifically, and is not represented as a purposeful activity. Grace observes the detachment she experiences by describing how 'they were not my own feet at all'. This alienation is a continuation of the description earlier in Extract 3.5, where she describes her clothing and how 'she had never had a skirt like that before', and also echoes her description earlier in Extract 3.6 of her actions occurring outside of her own volition ('The toes of my shoes go in and out under the hem of my skirt').

As before, the combination of these local style choices contributes to key discourse effects in Grace's fragmented narration. Her revisions of the scene highlight different facts of the conceptual distance between her thinking and acting selves, and between her actual and imagined actions, which contribute to the impression of disassociation and the split self divide which is associated

Table 3.6 Reconstruing possibility

Extract 3.5 (Atwood 2017, 6)	Extract 3.6 (Atwood 2017, 313–314)
[6] Then up ahead I see Nancy, on her knees, with her hair fallen over and the blood running down into her eyes. Around her neck is a white cotton kerchief printed with blue flowers, love-in-a-mist, it's mine. She's lifting up her face, she's holding out her hands to me for mercy; in her ears are the little gold earrings I used to envy, but I no longer begrudge them, Nancy can keep them, because this time it will all be different, this time I will run to help, I will lift her up and wipe away the blood with my skirt, I will tear a bandage from my petticoat and none of it will have happened. Mr. Kinnear will come home in the afternoon, he will ride up the driveway and McDermott will take the horse, and Mr. Kinnear will go into the parlour and I will make him some coffee, and Nancy will take it in to him on a tray the way she likes to do, and he will good coffee; and at night the fireflies will come out in the orchard, and there will be music, by lamplight. Jamie Walsh. The boy with the flute	[4.1] "Then up ahead I saw Nancy, on her knees, with her hair fallen over and the blood running down into her eyes. Around her neck was a white cotton kerchief printed with blue flowers, love-in-a-mist, and it was mine. She was holding out her hands to me for mercy; in her ears were the little gold earrings I used to envy. I wanted to run to her and help her, but I could not; and my feet kept walking at the same steady pace, as though they were not my own feet at all"

with traumatic memories (Vickroy 2015). At the same time, the composite quality of the narration, and the suggestion that these revisions are not a clarification but rather a means of further layering ambiguity, suggests that scene reconstrual in this novel buries any definitive answers. As explored in the previous chapter, these stylistic revisions ultimately function to *(xi) Discredit the characters reporting information, thereby making them appear unreliable and giving less salience to the information they report* (Emmott and Alexander 2014, 332).

3.6   'When you are in the middle of a story it isn't a story at all, but only a confusion'

Chapter 2 observed how the repetition and measured exposure of key pieces of information in *The Blind Assassin* helps readers to uncover the resolution of the central mystery and the revelation of Iris's identity as author. In *Alias Grace*, though the repetition and the reconstrual of scenes and events may invite heightened inferential processing, the resolution remains ambiguous while possibilities are not formally closed off, over-written or remediated. This absence of resolution contributes significantly to the novel's 'anti-detective' (Ingersoll 2003, 543) categorisation.

This chapter has examined how stylistic choices of reconstrual can misdirect, and embroider, retold storyworld events and details, and has explored the text effects of these choices at the local level of individual scenes. The divergences between, and the layering of, different accounts—both Dr Jordan's and Grace's, as well as those of other contributing sources in the novel—create salient, meaningful repetition, both signalling and maintaining the reader's role in actively interpreting accounts and in detecting potential discrepancies. As in metafiction more generally, this repetition and reconstrual of events means that, throughout, 'the reader is made hyper-aware of the pragmatics of the text's communicative meaning and of the directed act of interpretation, and in turn is kept overtly conscious of her own constructed reading subjectivity' (Macrae 2019, 8–9). The construction and reconstruction of the story are repeatedly foregrounded, and the palimpsestic, patchwork' quality created through the revision and reframing in these scenes continuously reinstates Grace's role as the creator and curator or the text, and, in metaphorical parallel, maps Atwood's role as the weaver of the story.

Notes

1. As mentioned in Chapter 1, this discussion does not seek to contribute to the already well-established literary critical and theoretical work on the novel. Instead, the discussion will summarise these key arguments to provide context for the novel's reception and how the foregrounded themes and structural elements are perceived within critical readership.
2. For a more detailed summary of Cognitive Grammar and its application for literary linguistic analysis, see Harrison (2017), Nuttall (2018), Giovanelli (2022), and Giovanelli and Harrison (2018).

References

Atwood, Margaret. 2014. The freeze-dried groom. In *Stone mattress: Nine wicked tales*, 135–166. London: Virago.

Atwood, Margaret. 2017. *Alias Grace*, 1st ed.: 1996. London: Bloomsbury.

Atwood, Margaret. 2018. *Margaret Atwood teaches creative writing*. MasterClass online.

Atwood, Margaret. 2022. *Burning questions: Essays and occasional pieces 2004–2021*. London: Chatto & Windus.

Browse, Sam. 2021. 'Hmmm yes, but where's the beef?' Cognitive grammar and the active audience in political discourse. In *New directions in cognitive grammar and style*, ed. Marcello Giovanelli, Chloe Harrison, and Louise Nuttall, 117–134. London: Bloomsbury.

Cohn, Dorrit. 1978. *Transparent minds: Narrative models for presenting consciousness in fiction*. Princeton, NJ: Princeton University Press.

Croft, William, and Alan D. Cruse. 2004. *Cognitive linguistics*. Cambridge: Cambridge University Press.

Davis, Blair, and Jef Burnham. 2015. Screening truths: Rashomon and cinematic negotiation. In *Rashomon effects*, ed. Blair Davis, Robert Anderson, and Jan Walls, 1–19. London: Routledge.

Emmott, Catherine, and Marc Alexander. 2014. Foregrounding, burying, and plot construction. In *The Cambridge handbook of stylistics*, ed. Peter Stockwell and Sara Whiteley, 329–343. Cambridge: Cambridge University Press.

Fludernik, Monika. 2009. *An introduction to narratology*, trans. Patricia Häusler-Greenfield and Monika Fludernik. London: Routledge.

Gazzaz, Rasha. 2021. The effects and functions of setting in Margaret Atwood's *Alias Grace*. *Margaret Atwood Studies* 14: 3–15.

Giovanelli, Marcello. 2013. *Text world theory and Keats' poetry: The cognitive poetics of desire, dreams and nightmares*. London: Bloomsbury.

Giovanelli, Marcello. 2022. *The language of Siegfried Sassoon*. London: Palgrave.

Giovanelli, Marcello. 2023. Cognitive grammar and readers' perceived sense of closeness: A study of responses to Mary Borden's 'Belgium.' *Language and Literature* 31 (3): 407–427.

Giovanelli, Marcello, and Chloe Harrison. 2018. *Cognitive grammar in stylistics: A practical guide*. London: Bloomsbury.

Goldblatt, Patricia F. 1999. Reconstructing Margaret Atwood's protagonists. *World Literature Today* 73 (2): 275–282.

Harrison, Chloe. 2017. *Cognitive grammar in contemporary fiction*. Amsterdam: John Benjamins.

Harrison, Chloe. 2023. 99 ways to retell a story: Forms and functions of narrator reconstrual. *Style* 57 (2): 163–185.

Harrison, Chloe, and Louise Nuttall. 2019. Cognitive grammar and reconstrual: Re-experiencing Margaret Atwood's 'The freeze-dried groom.' In *Experiencing fictional worlds*, ed. Benedict Neurohr and Lizzie Stewart-Shaw, 135–154. Amsterdam: Benjamins.

Harrison, Chloe, and Louise Nuttall. 2021. Rereading as retelling: Re-evaluations of perspective in narrative fiction. In *Narrative retellings: Stylistic approaches*, ed. Marina Lambrou, 217–234. London: Bloomsbury.

Hart, Christopher. 2011. Moving beyond metaphor in the cognitive linguistic approach to CDA: Construal operations in immigration discourse. In *Critical discourse studies in context and cognition*, ed. Chris Hart, 171–192. Amsterdam: John Benjamins.

Hutcheon, Linda. 1984. Canadian historiographic metafiction. *Essays on Canadian Writing* 30: 228–238.

Hutchison, Lorna. 2003. The book reads well: Atwood's *Alias Grace* and the middle voice. *Pacific Coast Philology* 38: 40–59.

Ingersoll, Earl. 2001. Engendering meta-fictions: Textuality and closure in *Alias Grace*. *American Review of Canadian Studies* 31: 385–401.

Ingersoll, Earl. 2003. Waiting for the end: Closure in Margaret Atwood's *The blind assassin*. *Studies in the Novel* 35 (4): 543–558.

Kennedy, Chris. 1982. Systemic grammar and its use in literary analysis. In *Language and literature: An introductory reader in stylistics*, ed. Ron Carter, 82–99. London: G. Allen and Unwin.

Kukkonen, Karin. 2013. Flouting figures: Uncooperative narration in the fiction of Eliza Haywood. *Language and Literature* 22 (3): 205–218.

Lakoff, George, and Mark Johnson. 1980. *Metaphors we live by*. Chicago: University of Chicago Press.

Lambrou, Marina, ed. 2020. *Narrative retellings: Stylistic perspectives*. London: Bloomsbury.

Langacker, Ronald W. 1987. *Foundations of cognitive grammar, volume 1, theoretical prerequisites*. Stanford: Stanford University Press.

Langacker, Ronald W. 1991. *Foundations of cognitive grammar, volume 2, descriptive application*. Stanford: Stanford University Press.

Langacker, Ronald W. 2008. *Cognitive grammar: A basic introduction*. Oxford: Oxford University Press.

Macrae, Andrea. 2019. *Discourse deixis in metafiction: The language of metanarration, metalepsis and disnarration*. London: Routledge.

Mannon, Bethany O. 2014. Fictive memoir and girlhood resistance in Margaret Atwood's *Alias Grace*. *Critique: Studies in Contemporary Fiction* 55 (5): 551–566.

Mantel, Hilary. 1996. Murder and memory. *The New York Review*. https://www.nyb ooks.com/articles/1996/12/19/murder-and-memory/. Accessed 20 April 2022.

March, Christie. 1997. Crimson silks and new potatoes: The heteroglossic power of the object in Atwood's *Alias Grace*. *Studies in Canadian Literature* 22 (2): 66–82.

McWilliams, Ellen. 2009. *Margaret Atwood and the female Bildungsroman*. London: Routledge.

Michael, Magali Cornier. 2001. Rethinking history as a patchwork: The case of Atwood's *Alias Grace*. *Modern Fiction Studies* 47 (2): 421–447.

Mills, Sara. 1995. *Feminist stylistics*. London: Routledge.

Moodie, Susanna. (1854) 1989. *Life in the clearings versus the bush*. Toronto: McClelland and Stewart Ltd.

Morini, Massimiliano. 2011. Point of view in first-person narratives: A deictic analysis of *David Copperfield*. *Style* 45 (4): 598–618.

Mullins, Blaine, and Peter Dixon. 2007. Narratorial implicatures: Readers look to the narrator to know what is important. *Poetics* 32: 262–276.

Murray, Jennifer. 2001. Historical figures and paradoxical patterns: The quilting metaphor in Margaret Atwood's *Alias Grace*. *Studies in Canadian Literature* 26 (1): 65–83.

Nahajec, Lisa. 2009. Negation and the creation of implicit meaning in poetry. *Language and Literature* 18 (2): 109–127.

Nuttall, Louise. 2018. *Mind style and cognitive grammar*. London: Routledge.

O'Neill, John. 2013. Dying in a state of grace: Memory, duality and uncertainty in Margaret Atwood's *Alias Grace*. *Textual Practice* 27 (4): 651–670.

Phelan, James, and M.P. Martin. 1999. The lessons of 'Weymouth': Homodiegesis, unreliability, ethics and *The remains of the day*. In *Narratologies: New perspectives on narrative*, ed. David Herman, 88–109. Columbus: Ohio University Press.

Shead, Jackie. 2015. *Margaret Atwood: Crime fiction writer. The reworking of a popular genre*. London: Routledge.

Simpson, Paul. 2014. *Stylistics: A resource book for students*, 2nd ed. London: Routledge.

Stockwell, Peter. 2009. *Texture: A cognitive aesthetics of reading*. Edinburgh: Edinburgh University Press.

Tabakowska, Elżbieta. 1993. *Cognitive linguistics and the poetics of translation*. Tübingen: Gunter Narr.

Tolan, Fiona. 2007. *Margaret Atwood: Feminism and fiction*. Amsterdam: Rodopi.

Toolan, Michael. 2020. Narrative retelling in McGahern's 'Swallows': The intensifying power of repetition and return. In *Narrative retellings: Stylistic approaches*, ed. Marina Lambrou, 61–76. London: Bloomsbury.

Vickroy, Laurie. 2015. Re-creating the split self in Margaret Atwood's *The blind assassin* and *Alias Grace*. In *Reading trauma narratives: The contemporary novel and the psychology of oppression*, 33–65. London: University of Virginia Press.

Wilson, Sharon R. 2003. Quilting as narrative art: Metafictional construction in *Alias Grace*. In *Margaret Atwood's textual assassinations: Recent poetry and fiction*, ed. Sharon R. Wilson, 121–134. Columbus: Ohio State University Press.

Wisker, Gina. 2012. *Margaret Atwood: An introduction to critical views of her fiction*. London: Palgrave Macmillan.

Wynne-Davies, Marion. 2010. *Margaret Atwood*. Devon: Northcote House Publishers.

Part II

Ambient Storms

4

COLD Revenge in *Stone Mattress*

4.1 Introduction: Macabre Ambience

Atwood's *Stone Mattress* (2014) is a collection of 'nine wicked tales' on the
power of storytelling, and 'several of these tales are tales about tales' (Atwood
2014, 309). As Atwood reflects, the label of 'tales' rather than 'stories' is more
appropriate, as they are 'not from the realm of mundane works and days' but
instead occupy 'the world of the folk tale, the wonder tale, and the long-ago
teller of tales' (2014). Similar to all Atwood texts discussed so far in this book,
the collection can be seen to complicate, layer and interrogate genre templates
(Nischik 2009). Indeed, Howells (2017, 299) argues that '*Stone Mattress* is a
veritable sampler of genre fiction revisited, with one crime story, two vampire
stories, three interconnected fantasy stories, two Gothic horror stories, and
a final dystopia'. Literary criticism on the collection relates to its three main
themes: its *representation of age* (Snaith 2017; Tolan 2017), its *commentary on
genre fiction* (Howells 2017), and, significantly, its preoccupation with *revenge*
(Barzilai 2017; Bruey 2017). Charting the motif of revenge across Atwood's
writing, Barzilai (2017) observes that Atwood's earlier fiction favours retribution plots that focus on women who punish themselves, whereas in her
more contemporary stories, 'by contrast, outer-directed reprisal becomes the
reactive rule' (316). As Barzilai (2017, 317) describes, the theme of *revenge* is
operationalised through Atwood's writing of characters and their motivations.
Consequently, it contributes to readers' perceptions of characters' subjective
position, and to interpretations of narrative voice and tone.

In stylistics research, 'atmosphere' is a specific cognitive phenomenon that 'pertains to the perceived quality of the literary world from a readerly perspective, whereas 'tone' pertains to the quality of the meditating authorial or narratorial voice' (Stockwell 2014, 362). The aggregate effect of these two phenomena is of felt 'ambience', which is the 'cognitive effect of cumulative but diffused associations across discourse' (366). As Stockwell further summarises, 'atmosphere is an effect of objective construal, whereas tone is an effect of subjective construal' (2021, 22).[1] Changes in construal dimensions (Langacker 2008) give rise to ambient effects, where attention is drawn to either the fictional world (atmosphere) or to the voice of the narrator (tone), as outlined in Fig. 4.1.

In a maximally objective text arrangement, attention is directed away from the identity of the viewer and inheres in the object or scene under observation (e.g., *The grey snow cloud*), while, contrastively, in a maximally subjective arrangement, the vantage point of the conceptualiser is foregrounded (e.g., *Brrr, it's bloody freezing!*). Nuttall describes these variations in objective and subjective construal as a type of competitive attentional arrangement which operates like a seesaw: 'as attention to one goes up, the other goes down' (2021, 84).

While tone can be explored through more text-based phenomena such as point of view representation and perspectival arrangements, atmosphere is a more amorphous, psychological phenomenon which invites the application of cognitive poetic models (Stockwell 2014, 362).[2] One way to capture the more nebulous atmospheric effects of a text is to consider how 'dominion

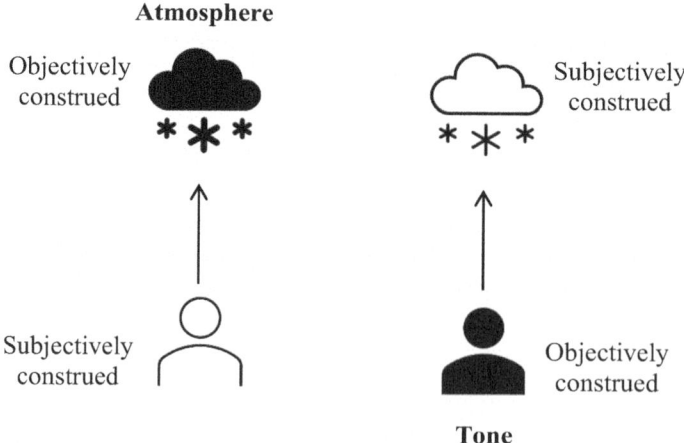

Fig. 4.1 Objective and subjective construal operations in ambience

chaining' works (Stockwell 2009, 2014, 2021). Cognitive Grammar's 'reference point model' (Langacker 2008) describes a process of mental scanning whereby potential meanings are generated and networked through units of language. In this model, a word or phrase functions as a reference point which activates potential meanings and connections with other concepts. These connections create a network of domains which are collectively called the reference point's 'dominion', which build up across a text and accumulate to generate specific atmospheric effects. In Chapter 3, for example, it was observed how Dr Jordan's descriptions of Grace referenced different domains relating to RELIGION, FAIRY TALE and WITCHCRAFT. Part of the challenge in ascertaining details of the story in *Alias Grace*, and in understanding her character, is that many of these associations are contradictory and difficult to reconcile.

In two related studies of first and second reading experiences of one story from *Stone Mattress*, 'The Freeze-Dried Groom', Harrison and Nuttall (2019, 2021) explore how dominion chaining can influence the perceived relationship between tone and atmosphere. Situated fifth in the collection, 'The Freeze-Dried Groom' is a contemporary Gothic tale centred on an unlikeable protagonist, Sam, a con artist who sells fake antique furniture. There is a kind of double narration throughout the story whereby Sam imagines how the police would respond to his own demise, which forms part of the 'mind-game he often plays with himself' (Atwood 2014, 120). He pictures the police interrogating his (soon to be ex-) wife and colleague about his movements that day, and imagines his post-mortem by a 'hot blonde' (Atwood 2014, 139). The story details a day in his life, beginning with his wife Gwyneth breaking up with him at breakfast, and then following him to work where he buys a storage unit with unknown contents. Sam discovers that one of the storage units contains all the items that make up a 'big-ticket wedding' (154), including a cake, some champagne, and, in a dark corner, the eponymous freeze-dried groom. The story ends with Sam in a hotel room with the unnamed 'bride', and finishes with the ominous assurance that 'Nobody knows where he is' (165).

Harrison and Nuttall's (2019) stylistic analysis of 'The Freeze-Dried Groom' argues that, on reading it for the first time, a prominent feature of its fictional world is the references to COLD, which is an observation supported by the book group discussion within the present study (as the next section explores). References to 'the freak cold snap' and 'the polar vortex' (117) in the story's opening paragraph can be linked to the ice storm which traps the main character, Constance, in her home in 'Alphinland' in the first story (Extract 4.1). These references also continue in the stories following

'The Freeze-Dried Groom', most notably in the Arctic setting for the title story 'Stone Mattress' which appears at the end of the collection. Harrison and Nuttall further argue that,

> It is by scanning between such loosely connected reference points across the collection, or drawing connections between specific textual cues – the weather, the women and the murders carried out or imagined – that a sense of the 'dark' world in which these stories take place is progressively enriched. (144)

This progressive enrichment of the chains of associations, brought about through a second reading, is key to the development of the storyworld's ambience. It is suggested that, on a first reading, the title 'The Freeze-dried groom' might trigger more weakly activated domains such as FOOD, STORAGE and DECAY within readers' schematic knowledge, which may then be realised by further references or world-builders within the unfolding story. On a second reading of the text, however, Harrison and Nuttall argue that the readers reconstrue the fictional world such that the intra-textual reference chains become more closely knit, and repeatedly focus specific knowledge of the scene that appears later in the story. An effect of this is the creation of fore-shadowing and a sense of inevitability that did not exist on a first reading. As it transpires, associations of STORAGE and DECAY assume added significance when considered alongside potential connections between the mummified groom and the probable demise of Sam.

The second and follow-on study (Harrison and Nuttall 2021) explores whether these initial intuitions about the experience of reading and re-reading the short story are supported through the responses of real readers. The researchers carried out a re-reading study with a group of undergraduate English students across three UK universities, and captured first and second reading responses through a post-reading questionnaire, designed to gather readers' alignment with, and identification of, the point of view of the story. The results of the study suggested that a first reading of 'The Freeze-Dried Groom' invites greater attention to the tone of the text—and especially necessitates attempts to refamiliarise the voice of the annoying and unlikable protagonist—but that a second reading, and in particular a more attentive second reading,[3] sets up a distancing from the fictional world. As part of this distancing, an additional, and more external, point of view emerged from the story. Notably, the POLICE or INVESTIGATION domain rose in prominence, inviting a recalibration of the ontological status of some of Sam's daydreams of police interrogations and post-mortems. The hypothetical scenarios which form part of his 'mind-games', for example, become a continuation of the story, apparently reframed through a police report ('This is how the day begins'). As part of this second reading experience, the participants identified the point of view as belonging to witness testimonies, interpretations which may have been generated through the preponderance of temporal markers within the story, among other style choices (Harrison and Nuttall 2021).

Building on these initial studies, and in reference to extended naturalistic reader discussion data, this chapter examines how the seesaw balance between atmospheric and tonal effects—and in particular, how the theme of revenge, and its conceptualisation within the collection's COLD setting—is networked in *Stone Mattress*. In addition to analyses of the reference point chains within the stories, the chapter explores the way the text builds metaphorical associations, and other key stylistic features generating heightened tone and emotional immersion. Finally, it is argued that the fictional world of *Stone Mattress* is collectively characterised by its macabre ambience, and the ecological collaborations and connections, distinctive to the short story collection. This chapter additionally contributes to the critical exploration of Atwood's short fiction, which is not as extensively discussed in the literature on her writing (Barzilai 2017, 318).

4.2   Reading *Stone Mattress*

To contextualise the text analysis and to capture the reader-driven experience of the collection's atmospheric and tonal effects, a book group discussion (which took place online in the summer of 2022) of *Stone Mattress* was recorded, transcribed and coded for recurring patterns. The ABC Club are a UK-based reading group comprising around six core members who meet once a month to discuss an agreed upon book. The reading group responses featured in both this chapter and Chapter 5 follow the prototypical pattern observed by Peplow et al. (2016, 21), with members opening their discussion with their personal evaluations of the book. The ABC Club starts every meeting with each member indicating their evaluation to the others by making a thumbs up or thumbs down gesture with both hands, allowing members to indicate mixed feelings with a one-thumb-up and one-thumb-down combination. Everyone indicates their appraisal at the same time so that the group has an overview of the general reception of that month's text. There is also a social chat before moving on to a more detailed and focused discussion of the text. For the purposes of this analysis, the 'off-book' discussion has been discounted from the data in favour of the 'on-book' topics (O'Halloran 2011).[4]

While it can be difficult to neatly isolate topics of discussion in reader discussion data, the group spent most of the *Stone Mattress* meeting exploring—either directly or more indirectly—those thematic elements of the collection that created cohesion as part of a process of 'reticulation' (De Vooght and Nemegeer 2021), an interpretative process guided by repeated linguistic choices suggesting 'that the texts are part of a network, an organization that exceeds them' (Audet 2000, 75–76). In their recent study of how readers analyse and interpret short story collections, De Vooght and Nemegeer (2021) collected readers' free recall of narratives and specific passages to explore this attentional phenomenon, as well as other processes of interpretation, of short stories within a particular collection. They summarise how

> existing reader-oriented approaches to [short story collections] revolve around a number of reading processes, namely, searching and recognising recurring elements throughout the stories (reticulation), which are interpreted (abduction) and synthesised into interpretative hypotheses (totalisation) and confronted with new elements of further stories (verification), potentially modifying the existing hypothesis (modification). (364–365)

The results of their exploratory reader study found that there were 'positive correlations between story appreciation and story recall' (372), but that readers' recollections were also strongly influenced by primacy effect (Perry 1979; Sternberg 1978), the psychological phenomenon that suggests that the first item(s) in a sequence are likely to be remembered better.

The ABC Club readers demonstrate their experiences of the interpretative processes summarised in De Vooght and Nemegeer's study. For the most part, the group discussed processes of reticulation in terms of the atmospheric effects of the short story collection. Unlike the De Vooght and Nemegeer study, however, the group's discussion of more specific passages is not oriented towards the first story, or first stories, only. While the ABC readers did spend time discussing specific extracts from the first three stories (which form one short story cycle in their own right), other passages that received comparable attention spanned the wider collection, with similarly extensive discussion afforded to extracts from the middle story ('The Freeze-Dried Groom'), and stories seven ('The Dead Hand Loves You') and eight ('Stone Mattress'). Rather than necessarily corresponding with the stories they evaluated as their favourite, the readers' more specific recall of key passages related to scenes which invite high emotional involvement (Toolan 2013, 2016), and with more overt tonal qualities, as the analysis in this chapter later explores.

4.3 Atmospheric Conditions: *The ice storm*

An extended part of the book group discussion related to the prevalence of *the ice storm* within the collection, and the way that it builds both cohesion and atmosphere. Narrative world-building is, in part, created through key pieces of textual information which help generate readers' conceptualisation of details within the narrative world. These include textual details that provide information on characters, objects, location and time (Werth 1999). Since atmosphere is inseparable from place or location (Stockwell 2014, 360), the representation of world-building information is instrumental in creating textual ambience.

The readers identified the role of the ice storm as both a feature and object within the fictional world, and as a temporal marker. An illustrative example of this discussion is outlined in the extract in Table 4.1.

In turn 1 (Table 4.1), Olivia demonstrates the desire to spot 'the thing that was connecting them'. She goes on to say that part of reading experience that prevented the cohesive function of the theme was its absence of centrality within all the stories. She notes, for example, how 'The Freeze-Dried Groom' did not fit with the 'ice storm' hypothesis in that the storm was reported as 'happening somewhere else', and demonstrates the progressive realisation of its absence in other stories (turn 3). The other members suggest further evidence that might support the interpretation of the ice storm as a linking event. In turn 4, Angela recalls how the cruise was diverted by some 'ice blocking some of the passages', and the potential cohesive element is reframed, or 'modified' (De Vooght and Nemegeer 2021), more schematically as a 'special weather event' (Olivia, turn 7), and even more generally as 'weather' (Angela, turn 8). This collaborative interpretation leads Olivia to suggest that 'maybe they're all happening at the same time as the ice storm' (turn 9). This discussion indicates the readers' focus on the temporal location as a point of orientation within the short story collection. The presence of this weather event is complicated in their genre categorisation of the stories, however. In turn 10, Stella argues that 'Torching the Dusties' is an outlier within this pattern, as the dystopian element suggests it is separate or othered from the 'reality' of the other storyworlds. As before, however, the group seeks to collaboratively retrofit this thematic connection. Angela speculates that 'maybe there was something on the news' (turn 13) reporting 'the storm or something' (Olivia, turn 12) which prevented Wilma's daughter from visiting (turn 11).

Table 4.1 Thematic connections in *Stone Mattress: The ice storm*

1	Olivia	He didn't know what happened to him like in fact I think like most of them had I guess this is what one of the things that annoyed me a little bit about it is like I really liked the way I kept thinking about spotting the thing that was connecting them all like the whole like *ice storm* is in almost all of them but it's not in all of them so like the Stone Mattress they are more or less on a cruise ship and even in the Freeze-dried Groom Freeze-dried
2	Angela	Freeze-dried Groom
3	Olivia	Freeze-dried Groom like didn't seem at all connected to the other ones but then they kept talking about *this ice storm* that was happening somewhere else and I was like okay I kind of get it you know there's they're not connected but they're sort of happening at the same time and this like relevant cuz it's sort of touching on these things I don't know but then I was like okay I've sussed it and then I was reading the Stone Mattress and I was oh there's *no ice storm* in this one unless I missed it but I don't think there is
4	Angela	No um they do have to take a different route because of something to do with *the ice blocking some of the passages* but yeah it's not an ice storm
5	Olivia	Oh actually you might be because there's that whole thing about why they ended up seeing the like place where she had killed him in the first place
6	Angela	Yeah they shouldn't have
7	Olivia	[inaudible oh you shouldn't be] here because there's some *special weather event* or something that's happening
8	Angela	Yeah so there was *weather*
9	Olivia	So maybe they're all happening at the same time as *the ice storm* but was it in the last one I'm not sure it
10	Stella	The last one was dystopia wasn't it so it couldn't have been happening in *the same storm*
11	Angela	Um I'm trying to think about was there a reason why her daughter didn't come over because they were talking about her daughter wanted to come over
12	Olivia	Oh and you'll never be able to get through *the storm* or something or like I'm fine and don't worry
13	Angela	Yeah there was like I'm fine but I'm wondering whether there was any cuz she listens a lot to the news so maybe there was something on the news but I didn't catch it like

The prominence of *the ice storm* as a key world-builder is established in the first sentences of the first story, 'Alphinland', which opens as follows:

Extract 4.1

> The freezing rain sifts down, handfuls of shining rice thrown by some unseen celebrant. Wherever it hits, it crystallizes into a granulated coating of ice. Under the streetlights it looks so beautiful: like fairy silver, thinks Constance. But then, she would think that; she's far too prone to enchantment. The beauty is an illusion, and also a warning: there's a dark side to beauty, as with poisonous butterflies. She ought to be considering the dangers, the hazards, the grief this ice storm is going to bring to many; is already bringing, according to the television news. (Atwood 2014, 1)

Stylistic analysis of the tonal features of this introduction to the collection allows an exploration of the ways in which the narratorial and character-voices are presented. The evaluation of the first two sentences may be interpreted as belonging to the tone of a third-person omniscient narrator, until Constance's focalisation and reflector position is confirmed in the reporting clause, 'thinks Constance'. Other markers of point of view, including epistemic judgement ('But then, she would think that'), her reflection on her predispositions ('she's far too prone for enchantment') and the deontic modalisation as she notes what 'she ought to be considering', all combine to characterise Constance's voice more closely. From the outset, she is presented as someone who views the world through a romanticised filter—an impression that is supported in the rest of the story, and in the description of her bestselling fantasy series, 'Alphinland' (see also Chapter 1, Sect. 1.3.2)—but also as someone who has an awareness, albeit vague, of the dangers that that this world view might engender, and the subsequent care she must exercise.

Analysis of the atmospheric choices in this opening description is also revealing. Several key reference points that relate to domains of knowledge which include COLD, BEAUTY/ROMANCE, VISIBILITY and, significantly, DANGER, can all be identified in Constance's description of the weather (Table 4.2). Taken together, these domains establish an atmospheric blueprint for the remaining stories, opening dominion spaces to be called up later in the collection. More fleeting targets, which focus parts of domains, also contribute to this network of knowledge. Within the broader BEAUTY/ROMANCE domain, for example, a WEDDING domain is more peripherally evoked in the metaphor of the falling snow as appearing 'like shining rice thrown by some unseen celebrant'. FOOD is also fleetingly referenced through 'rice' and 'granulated coating', and even the verb 'sift' which collocates with

Table 4.2 Intra-textual reference point chains in the opening sentences of 'Alphin-land'

COLD	BEAUTY/ROMANCE	VISIBILITY	DANGER
Freezing rain	Crystallises	Shining	Dark
Ice	Shining rice	Unseen	Unseen
Ice storm	Beautiful	Streetlights	Warning
	Fairy silver	Illusion	Poisonous
	Enchantment	Dark side	Dangers
	Beauty		Hazards
	Butterflies		Grief

icing sugar or flour. As can be seen in Table 4.2, some of these chains become interlinked from the outset where reference points cross domains. 'Dark', for example, semantically denotes an absence of light, with implications for visibility. At the same time, when considered alongside the cluster of other references to 'hazards' and 'grief', its metaphorical associations are more likely to become foregrounded, such that its categorisation within a domain of DANGER is not an unlikely inference. In this way, these associations are initiated and interconnected from the collection's opening sentences.

As Stockwell (2014) demonstrates, associations activated through linguistic expressions or constructions can further be contextualised through, their collocations and extra-textual meanings. Through consideration of the most frequent collocates of a word like *ice*, for example, which appears more than once in Extract 4.1 and is identified by the readers as a particularly salient theme, it is possible to explore some of the wider inferential associations that this description might additionally generate. The BNC lists the top 20 most frequent collocates[5] as in Table 4.3.

Table 4.3 shows how, in wider discourse contexts, *ice* collocates with several different targets belonging to various domains of knowledge, including FOOD (ice cream, ice cubes), SPORT (ice hockey, ice skating, ice rink), distinct periods of TIME (and the geological implications of 'ice age'), and WEATHER or NATURE (snow, water, sheets, sea). In addition, some of these collocates are more widely associated with idiomatic or metaphorical units (e.g., *cold as ice, thin ice, ice breaker*). These targets and their associated meanings may be confirmed or revivified in a text, or, conversely, closed off and decay from readers' working memory. Associations that are not textually realised remain on the 'periphery of consciousness' (Croft and Cruse 2004, 50) to be potentially called up later, however, and it is the lingering or echoic effect of these unrealised associations that create 'textured ambience' (Stockwell 2014, 368).

Table 4.3 Top 20 most frequent collocates of *ice* (BNC)

1	Cream
2	Hockey
3	Age
4	Snow
5	Cold
6	Water
7	Sheets
8	Sea
9	Pack
10	Sheet
11	Rink
12	Skating
13	Thin
14	Cut
15	Break
16	Cubes
17	Creams
18	Cube
19	Ages
20	Dry

To return again to Extract 4.1, it is clear how the associations of *ice* are both cued up in chains within the text (Table 4.2), and simultaneously layered with other extra-textual associations (Table 4.3) generating further nuances and interpretive effects. The readers' discussion of the atmosphere invited by *the ice storm*, and the fact that they opened their conversation by extensively exploring its cohesive function, suggests the salience of this world-builder and the meaningful atmospheric connections it generates.

4.4   Ambient Effects: Physical and Emotional Coldness

The ABC Club readers continue to refer to *the ice storm* as a point of departure for other themes in *Stone Mattress*, as part of their continued processes of reticulation. When discussing the title of the collection, for example, they speculate on other potential title candidates that would accurately capture the text's ambience ('the dark and kind of ominous feel and stuff', Angela, turn 8). A section from this part of the discussion is included in Table 4.4.

The ice storm is considered a world-builder prominent enough to thematically summarise the collection (Olivia, turn 7), while the merits of the other

Table 4.4 Thematic connections in *Stone Mattress*: Title and husbands

1	Jane	What intrigued me was the title story was the same as the second to last
2	Angela	I was just gonna say why did they decide to call it stone mattress and is there something about the title that they like do they think it is the strongest story or like why do people do
3	Olivia	If they think that it's the strongest story don't put it as the penultimate one
4	Angela	No
5	Stella	Yeah but it's just like you know her favourite name or whatever
6	Angela	But then like I don't know I'm trying to look at the names of them I guess any of the others perhaps make it a bit too specific um maybe Alphinland might make it a bit confusing
7	Olivia	Something else that's like they're thematically linked or foregrounds the thematic link that are supposed to be like you know call it the ice storm or something do you know what I mean like
8	Angela	That would work cuz it keeps the dark and kind of ominous feel and stuff that we're going for yeah
9	Stella	The dead husbands
10	Angela	Yeah it could be dead husbands
11	Olivia	Yeah dead husbands in an ice storm and [inaudible] then that's it
12	Jane	Do you know her dead husbands you can go with freeze-dried groom as the title
13	Angela	Yeah

story titles are examined in terms of their referential limitations, either being 'too specific' (Angela, turn 7) or else appropriately schematic ('you can go with freeze-dried groom as the title', Jane, turn 12). The members respond to Olivia's suggestion that 'the ice storm' would work because it accurately captures 'the dark and kind of ominous feel' (Angela, turn 8) of the text, and because it forms a fitting background for the murders and resulting proliferation of 'dead husbands' (turns 9–12). In this sense, the readers seem to suggest that the ambient and symbolic significance of the collection needs to be acknowledged in the title as a label that draws equivalence between the physical setting and the key events within the stories: 'Yeah dead husbands in an ice storm and [inaudible] then that's it' (Olivia, turn 11).

The metaphorical significance of the collection's title is referenced in the collection's penultimate and title story, 'Stone Mattress'. In this scene (Extract 4.2), the main character, Verna, is attending a lecture on stromatolites, a type of Arctic fossil, as part of her cruise holiday. The visiting expert explains the history of the geological formation as part of an upcoming and 'unanticipated stop' to see them:

Extract 4.2

The next day starts with a talk on geology by an energetic young scientist who has been arousing some interest among the passengers, especially the female ones. By great good fortune, he tells them, and because of a change in itinerary owing to ice pack, they'll be making an unanticipated stop, where they'll be able to view a wonder of the geological world, a sight permitted to very few. They'll be privileged to see the world's earliest fossilised stromatolites, clocking in at an astonishing 1.9 billion years old – before fish, before dinosaurs, before mammals – the very first preserved form of life on this planet. What is a stromatolite? He asks rhetorically, his eyes gleaming. The word comes from the Greek *stroma*, a mattress, coupled with the root word for *stone*. Stone mattress: a fossilized cushion, formed by layer upon layer of blue-green algae building up into a mound or dome. It was this very same blue-green algae that created the oxygen they are now breathing. Isn't that astonishing? (Atwood 2014, 216)

Given the connection between this world-building object and the title of both this story and the general collection, this introduction is likely to be attentionally foregrounded. The historical content of his lecture reifies chains of associations that have been introduced elsewhere. It references AGE (noted by the readers in the extract from the discussion in Table 4.5) but also STORAGE and PRESERVATION ('preserved life', 'fossilized') that is similarly discussed in the reader data (e.g., in Jane's observation that 'freeze-dried groom' could work as a title, turn 12, Table 4.4; and in another comment by Olivia that 'there's a lot of dead husbands floating around or so or sitting in storage units'). Additionally, the symbolic meaning of this noun phrase is similarly observed. The speaker's translation of *stroma* as 'mattress' connotes associations of physical sleeping arrangements, which connects to the text's wider theme of sexual desire (Snaith 2017). This interpretation is also modelled later in this story by Verna, who 'gives the word *mattress* the tiniest hint of suggestiveness, and gets an approving twinkle out of Bob the Second' (Atwood 2014, 251). At the same time, the 'stone' undermines associations of comfort that readers might otherwise hold for 'mattress', creating semantic dissonance within this oxymoronic pairing. Finally, that this item is given heightened attention also, and significantly, establishes salience in terms of its function within the plot. As the only crime fiction story in the collection, this description of the fossil, and its utility as a murder weapon, generates wider symbolic meanings. In this way, the act of revenge is equated with humans'

Table 4.5 Thematic connections in *Stone Mattress*: Age, and murder as revenge

1	Olivia	they want to kill everybody
2	Jane	Well that's the [inaudible] plan for one person
3	Angela	Kill all the old people
4	Stella	Just the old people
5	Jane	It's like a group trying to kill all the old people
6	Angela	Well I also wondered isn't it yeah how well say Margaret Atwood she's like in her late eighties now so in two-thousand-and-fifteen when this was was this about two-thousand-and-fifteen or
7	Olivia	Yeah exactly
8	Angela	Yeah she is writing about older people again isn't she mostly and sort of reflecting back and like you said sort of you get to a certain point of life where someone would want to kill don't know what that says about Margaret Atwood about maybe who she would want to kill um but like yeah I guess um it's taking like from the other perspective isn't it like maybe yeah and it didn't get enough time to kind of reflect I suppose the first one has a lot to reflect back on over their lives a bit and how things were um
9	Olivia	Yeah and I like that as well I think like sort of representing for like your older narrators is not a thing you see a huge amount of you know it's done like *Elizabeth Is Missing* and the one that I just recommended uses ideas from *A Hundred Years of Lenni and Margot* it's quite a lot of like character in their very latter years as like the protagonist and not just sort of a thing like I thought that was like I thought that was a theme that linked a lot of them maybe the freeze-dried groom one's and stuff like I liked that that was good

baser natures and necessary biological functions ('It was this very same blue-green algae that created the oxygen they are now breathing'). That these objects are found only in the Arctic circle again is geographically apposite.

4.4.1 COLD Metaphors

This chapter has so far observed that the readers in The ABC Club spend time exploring the role of *the ice storm* as a spatiotemporal world-builder in which many of the events of the stories occur. Given the significance of the storm as a 'special weather event' (Olivia, Table 4.1) and its recurring appearance in *Stone Mattress*, it begins to assume increased metaphorical associations, particularly where it mirrors the emotional or psychological states of the characters and vice versa. In general terms, metaphor is a type of subjectification of discourse, and one which can impact on processes of characterisation (Abbott 2008, 118; Pager-McClymont 2021). A metaphor can colour or filter the perspective of a character or conceptualiser, bringing them to the forefront of attention and, in turn, creating a more subjective construal of the scene they are relating (Fig. 4.1). The networking of metaphors across the *Stone Mattress* collection, therefore, elucidates—in direct and indirect ways—the tone or voice of the conceptualiser or the focalising character.

Considerable research has been carried out on metaphorical representations of the emotions, with anger metaphors one of the most extensively studied (Kövecses 2000, 21). Cognitive linguistic research has shown that ANGER is paired with temperatures and domains of HEAT, such as 'ANGER IS THE HEAT OF A FLUID IN A CONTAINER: She is *boiling with* anger' and 'ANGER IS FIRE: He's doing *a slow burn*. His anger is *smoldering*' (Kövecses 2020). COLD, on the other hand, tends to be associated with 'negative-valenced, low-arousal emotions', more accurately capturing unhappiness and dissatisfaction, as well as passivity and quiet (Barbosa Escobar et al. 2021, 1; Bergman et al. 2014). Unlike the examples of HEAT identified in Kövecses' (2000) research, however, revenge and anger in *Stone Mattress* are conceptualised as a *lack* of heat, as the following analyses will explore. Lakoff and Kövecses (1987; see also Kövecses 2000, 11) describe anger as a 'five stage scenario' comprising a sequence made up of the following events or states: '(1) cause of anger, (2) anger exists, (3) attempt at controlling anger, (4) loss of control over anger, (5) retribution'. Construal of 'retribution' or revenge as COLD profiles the final part of this ANGER scenario, and implies an act that is removed from, or that occurs after, the reactive immediacy of the heat of the moment'. Given the emphasis in *Stone Mattress* on revenge, the retribution end of this cycle is foregrounded and functions as a motivation for the characters in the stories. Retribution as a COLD act is a culturally entrenched construal, observed in idiomatic expressions such as *revenge is a dish best served cold*.[6] In this framing, COLD is associated with psychological distancing, clarity, and an absence of emotion, drawn on in expressions such as *losing your cool*, seeing something clearly in the *cold light of day*, or the *cooling-off period* in legal contexts. Furthermore, these psychological associations of temperature have been shown to filter into people's perceptions of people and emotional assessment in everyday contexts. Williams and Bargh's (2008) study, for example, explored how physical temperatures can impact on how we interpret others in terms of emotional warmth, while the reverse—people's perceptions of a room's temperature being impacted by their feelings of social acceptance—is also an observable interaction (Zhong and Leonardelli 2008).

There are many moments in *Stone Mattress* where the ice storm, or other references to a domain of COLD, and their connections to the emotional states of characters can be seen, as the following analyses of Extracts 4.3–4.8 explore.

Extract 4.3

> "Oh no, not here," she says. "I mean, it's Florida, right? I meant back home." She giggles nervously. *"Ice."*
>
> Gavin, watching the television weather, has noted with interest *the polar vortex* gripping the north, the east, the centre. He's seen the pictures of *the blizzards, the ice storms,* the overturned cars and broken trees. That's where Constance must be right now: in *the eye of the storm.* He imagines her holding out her arms to him, clothed in nothing but *snow,* with an unearthly radiance streaming from around her. (Atwood 2014, 51–52. Emphasis added)

In Extract 4.3 (from 'Revenant'), doctoral student Naveena is researching Constance's writing. She visits Gavin, also a successful writer, in Florida to interview him about his relationship with Constance in his youth. At this moment in the story, Gavin comments on the practicality of Naveena's footwear, which she acknowledges are not suitable for the ice back home in New York. Gavin's focalised narration moves from 'watching the television weather' and its coverage of the physical impact the polar vortex has had on 'the north, the east, the centre', to his daydream about the vortex and Constance's location within it. The tangible chaos wrought by the storm—'the overturned cars and broken trees'—is contrasted with Gavin's mental simulation of Constance. In New York, she is literally positioned in the 'eye of the storm', but, like Constance's view of the ice storm in Extract 4.1, Gavin's picture of her is subjectified. Grammatically, this occurs through his assured epistemic judgement of where she 'must be right now'. In this story, Constance is represented as an object of professional jealousy for Gavin, especially in terms of her comparative and extensive publishing success. His description of her as 'clothed in nothing but snow, with an unearthly radiance streaming from around her' is both romanticised and sexualised, the imagined embrace echoing Constance's erotic dream of Gavin which she recounts in 'Alphinland'. In Extract 4.1, the ice storm can be perceived as an appropriate setting for Constance's grief for her late husband. In 'Revenant', the mirror story to 'Alphinland', Gavin's conceptualisation of Constance as being '*in* the eye of the storm' (emphasis added) evokes the vortex as a kind of container.[7] His description of Constance with 'radiance streaming from her' places her at the heart of the furore, while further enforcing her central role across this trio of stories.

In contrast, Extract 4.4 from 'Stone Mattress' evokes the main character Verna's emotional disposition, rather than her emotional reaction in response to a particular stimulus.

Extract 4.4

> At the outset Verna had not intended to kill anyone. What she had in mind was a vacation, pure and simple. Take a breather, do some inner accounting, shed worn skin. *The Arctic* suits her: there's something inherently calming in the vast *cool sweeps of ice* and rock and sea and sky, undisturbed by cities and highways and trees and other distractions that clutter up the landscape to the south. (Atwood 2014, 201. Emphasis added)

In this story, Verna goes on an Arctic cruise holiday, where she unexpectedly meets her former prom date, Bob, the man who sexually assaulted her in high school. Here, Verna's emotional projection onto her surroundings is more implicit than in Extract 4.3, even while the opening sentence provides an explicit abstract of what is to follow in the crime story: 'At the outset Verna had not intended to kill anyone'. The description of Verna doing some 'inner accounting' evokes a MORALITY IS ACCOUNTING metaphor (Lakoff 2016)[8] that sets the stage for the crimes to follow (Bruey 2017). Verna's focus on her cold physical environment emphasises the neutrality and the absence of emotions it engenders, as a place that is both 'calming' and 'undisturbed'. More direct, too, is the connection in this story between the cold of the geographic location and Verna's act of revenge, more specifically. As Barzilai (2017, 330) observes, it is fitting that the act of retribution takes place here in the Arctic, as an 'icy setting commensurate with the cold-hardened forest floor where the rape occurred'.

The relationship between the physical environment and the characters' emotional position in both Extracts 4.3 and 4.4 can be considered examples of pathetic fallacy, which Pager-McClymont (2022, 435) defines as driven by an EMOTIONS ARE SURROUNDINGS mega-metaphor, and which is textually manifested as a 'projection of emotions onto the surroundings by an animated entity. The emotions and animated entity in question can be featured implicitly or explicitly in the text'. Following the work of Salovey and Mayer (1990, 186), Pager-McClymont defines emotion in this context as a valenced response to an event, which broadly includes 'mood, dispositions, preferences, personality traits, physical feelings, emotional states and effects, lasting any length of time' (435). She goes on to illustrate four observed effects of pathetic fallacy in literary texts, which include the explicit external communication of an implicit emotion, building ambience, characterisation and foreshadowing narrative events (437). Positioned at the beginning of the collection, the metaphorical or symbolic associations of the polar vortex described in Extract 4.1 and Extract 4.3 foreshadow the connections between COLD and the emotions that are to be developed in the remaining stories (Harrison and Nuttall 2019, 2021). As the opening to the penultimate story, on the other hand, the representation of the Arctic as a reflection of Verna's disposition in Extract 4.4 holds a characterisation function. As the story explains, 'The Arctic suits her'. She is in the right place, physically and mentally speaking, to exact her revenge.

Extract 4.5

The next thing is that his car won't start. It's the fault of the *freak cold snap, caused by the polar vortex* – a term that's already spawned a bunch of online jokes by stand-up comics about their wives' vaginas. (Atwood 2014, 117. Emphasis added)

Extract 4.6

Gwyneth isn't snarling or pouting or frowning: *her gaze is glacial*, her voice level. This is a proclamation. (Atwood 2014, 118. Emphasis added)

Pathetic fallacy continues across the collection as the connections between the cold setting and the characters' emotional dispositions intensify. Extract 4.5 is the opening to 'The Freeze-Dried Groom', where the title already cues up associations of COLD, STORAGE and MARRIAGE. The description of the 'freak cold snap' is focalised through the character Sam's point of view, though here the 'polar vortex' is used as a vehicle for his misogynistic perspective. In these opening sentences, he is introduced as the type of character who is likely to acknowledge, and find it humorous, that it is 'a term that's already spawned a bunch of online jokes by stand-up comics about their wives' vaginas', and to direct the 'fault' of the situation to an external cause. This metaphor framing is inverted with the description in Extract 4.6 of his wife, Gwyneth, who is also represented in cold terms. Her announcement of a divorce is described through negated emotional expressions. Notably, 'Gwyneth isn't snarling or pouting or frowning' or otherwise exhibiting an incensed reaction; instead, and more implacably, 'her gaze is glacial, her voice level. This is a proclamation' (136). In this context, the reference to COLD is used as a metaphor for an absence of passion and a lack of affection (Kövecses 1995). As with Extract 4.4, the projection of Sam's emotional disposition on the weather in Extract 4.5, and the projection of the weather onto his description of Gwyneth in Extract 4.6, forms part of his characterisation. In particular, these projections outline his focalised commentary on women, while simultaneously foreshadowing later events. The metaphor assumes more sinister and morbid associations as details of Sam's demise, and the fate he shares with the eponymous 'Freeze-Dried Groom', become apparent.

The COLD domain is referenced differently in Extracts 4.7 and 4.8, where the focus of attention is on the description of the characters rather than on the icy, stormy weather. As with the description of Gwyneth in Extract 4.5, the narration instead draws on the COLD weather to describe the characters, who are more foregrounded within these examples:

Extract 4.7

That's how they go on: like a '30s wisecrackers' movie. The Marxes. Hepburn and Tracy. Nick and Nora Charles, minus the chain-drinking of martinis, which Jorrie and Tin can't handle any more. *They skate over the surfaces, chilled and thin and shiny; they avoid the depths.* It wears Tin out a bit, their doubles act. Possibly Jorrie feels the same, but they both understand that they have to keep up their ends. (Atwood 2014, 78. Emphasis added)

Extract 4.8

"But Noreen. But Jo-Anne. They're still inside. They'll be…" She's clutching – she notices – her own hands. They feel like somebody else's.
   "It was always that way," *he says mournfully. Or is it coldly? She can't tell.* (Atwood 2014, 267. Emphasis added)

Extract 4.7 from 'Dark Lady' describes the relationship between the twins, Tin and Jorrie, and their distinctive means of communication. They have created a shorthand way of speaking that allows them to communicate quick-fire responses to events and situations efficiently. This passage is focalised through Tin's subjective assessment of their conversational strategy, in which, as he observes, they 'skate over the surfaces, chilled and thin and shiny; they avoid the depths'. Tin's assessment of the nature of their conversational exchanges revivifies the link to skating listed in the BNC collocates in Table 4.3. In this framing, the ice foregrounds different mapped properties within the EMOTIONS ARE SURROUNDINGS metaphor, which are listed ('chilled and thin and shiny'). As with the other manifestations of the metaphor, this description suggests that the twins communicate with a lack of emotional warmth. Additionally, it is blended with the orientational metaphor of BAD IS DOWN, evoking a type of emotional shallowness ('they avoid the depths').

Finally, Extract 4.8 from 'Torching the Dusties' contains fewer explicit references to COLD as compared to the penultimate story, 'Stone Mattress' (cf. Extract 4.4). In this part of the final story, the main character Wilma has escaped the violent protest of the care home and is waiting in the grounds with her friend, Tobias. Her description of the tone of his speech ('he says mournfully. Or is it coldly? She can't tell') invites conceptual alternativity, but with two assessments that are disparate. An interpretation of Tobias's speech as 'mournful' suggests an emotional response to the demise of their friends in the care home. An assessment of his words as 'cold', in contrast, suggests a dispassionate and emotionless response to events. Wilma's ambivalent and antagonistic interpretation seems fitting for a final story that considers retribution from a different perspective (see Sect. 4.5.2).

All the examples outlined here draw on the EMOTION IS SURROUND-INGS master emotion metaphor (Pager-McClymont 2022, 436), which more specifically is manifested as EMOTIONS ARE TEMPERATURES, deriving from variations of the base metaphor AFFECTION IS WARMTH (Grady 1997; Lakoff and Johnson 1980)[9] and its reverse counterpart. As explored in the analysis, the examples differ in terms of their 'framing' (Semino et al. 2016), however, and the 'specific entities, roles and relations that are focused in the source domain, or specific scenario' (Nuttall and Harrison 2020, 40). In Extracts 4.3 and 4.4, the physical cold setting is foregrounded, and characters' emotions are construed as a secondary element. In Extracts 4.7 and 4.8, in contrast, this occurs the other way round: the characters are described more directly, and the cold is drawn on in reference to their emotions. The two examples in Extracts 4.5 and 4.6 form a combination of the two, beginning with a focus on the setting before focusing on the characterisation of Gwyneth. In the context of this short story collection, this interaction suggests a conceptual or 'experiential symmetry' (Porat and Shen 2017) between the two domains, with the text fronting either the EMOTION or the TEMPERATURE at alternating points. To return to Fig. 4.1, these different framings are associated with atmospheric and tonal effects, with the foregrounding of atmosphere, in particular, aligning with Pager-McClymont's definition of the phenomenon as a projection of emotions '*onto* the surroundings' (emphasis added); an interaction that physically externalises subjectivity, and further reifies the connection between atmosphere and tone.

4.5   Tone and High Emotional Involvement (HEI) Passages

The overview of the reading group data so far reveals that the group's discussion predominantly focuses on the atmospheric qualities of the fictional worlds of *Stone Mattress*, and particularly the spatiotemporal and symbolic significance of the *ice storm* as a reference point within the stories. This aligns with previous empirical work on reader responses to the collection and particularly with experiences of second reading, or more attentive reading, which found that re-readers attend more closely to its atmospheric connections (Harrison and Nuttall 2019, 2021). The previous section explored how some of these chains of associations rebalance the attention between fictional world and the subjective perspective of the character-narrator so that ambient effects are cumulatively built and networked across the collection. These networks have been shown to establish the theme of revenge, contextualising acts of retribution and demonstrating how characters both project and reflect emotional coldness in meaningful ways. The next and final section of analysis explores the readers' responses to the distinctive and morbid tone of the collection, brought about by an increased subjective construal of story events in key scenes.

Where The ABC Club discuss tonal qualities of *Stone Mattress*, they do so in relation to both Atwood's voice and the voices of particular characters, as can be observed in the extract from the discussion shown in Table 4.5. At this point in the meeting, the readers are discussing the themes of the final dystopian short story, 'Torching the Dusties', which describes a mob of people attacking an old people's home in an act of revenge against their perceived responsibility for global warming. Here, the book group members examine another 'theme that linked a lot of them' (Olivia, turn 9). The readers consider the motivation for the character's actions and the theme of revenge, and specifically murder as an act of revenge. Angela (turns 6–8) comments that this driver is explicitly related to the advanced age of the characters: 'you get to a certain point of life where someone you would want to kill [...] I suppose the first one has a lot to reflect back on over their lives a bit and how things were'. Compared to the other topics discussed by The ABC Club, the extract in Table 4.5 presents a more fleeting reference to the tone of the collection. Specifically, the readers comment on the psychological motivations for the characters' actions, and the point of view through which the narration is filtered, the 'older narrators' (Olivia, turn 9) and the 'other perspective' (Angela, turn 8) they provide. In this part of the discussion, the readers position the older characters as the victims of the acts of revenge (turns 1–5), but also, contrastively, as those who are the instigators of the acts of retribution (turn 8). At the same time, the readers move outside of the text to consider the under-representation of older narrators in contemporary fiction (turn 9), and, finally, the authorial mediation from Atwood herself ('she's like in her late eighties now [...] I don't know what that says about Margaret Atwood maybe who she would want to kill', Angela turns 6–8). In both instances, the attribution of the tone for the collection emphasises the narrator's character profile: someone more advanced in life, who feels reflective and seeks to settle old scores.

As with the discussion of the atmospheric connections, the readers explore the tonal elements that connect the stories and their narration. In addition to the murderous narrators, the readers identify the *hallucinations* of the narrators that unify the opening and closing stories, for example. Jane's comment in Table 4.6 (turn 1) mirrors Le Guin's (2014) view that the opening Alphinland trilogy is, in some ways, 'lightly sketched'. The readers focus on the ending and its ambiguity within the first story. They note how they 'thought that maybe [the main character] died' (Jane, turn 1), but that the differentiation between this interpretation and an alternative resolution ('maybe the releasing of him was when the person he released died', turn 1) is 'hard work' (Olivia, turn 2). Tying together the character profiles and the subjective voices in the collection, the readers draw a connection between the representation of Charles Bonnet syndrome experienced by the character Wilma in the final story, the 'hallucination [of] simple repeated patterns or complex images or people objects or landscapes' (Stella, turn 5), and the extent of Constance's imaginative investment in Alphinland in the first story. Each character, seemingly, 'begins to see things that aren't real' (Stella, turn 3).

4.5.1   High Emotion and Subjective Construal

The tone of each story is heightened at moments of what Toolan (2016) refers to as High Emotional Involvement (HEI). Toolan's (2009) extended narratological exploration considers, through corpus linguistic methods, eight linguistic 'parameters' assisting narrative prospection in contemporary short stories, ranging from sentences that comprise references to the main character as a top keyword, to the presentation of direct speech. In an additional corpus examination of the modern short story form, Toolan (2016) examines how this genre utilises high emotional involvement to immerse readers and to generate specific interpretive effects. He goes on to say (2016, 219) that such HEI passages are stylistically distinctive. This is because,

Table 4.6 Hallucinations

1	Jane	I didn't have a clearer picture of what Alphinland was like and it irritated me because I couldn't quite work out who was who or who these characters were or what was happening in the land like what her books were and at the bit at the end of the first one when she releases somebody I thought she died but then maybe the releasing of him was when the person he released died whose funeral he then you get in the third one
2	Olivia	Yeah I don't know I just feel like we read a lot of books and it shouldn't be such hard work now
3	Stella	I can tell you I just looked up Charles Bonnet syndrome which was what the old lady had in the last one it's a real thing it's the person whose vision has started to deteriorate and begins to see things that aren't real there you go
4	Olivia	That's interesting like
5	Stella	Complex uh two main types of hallucination simple repeated patterns or complex images of people objects or landscapes
6	Olivia	Maybe that's is that supposed to be she's trying to draw a connection like the Constance lady in the first one of like she's sort of it's sounding like she's almost she thought up of Alphinland in her imagination and she like got a bit too much invested in it
7	Angela	Yeah she was very invested

many short stories seem designed to provide, by way of crucial 'consideration' for the reader's performance in investing their mental energies on this complex but soon terminated textualized glimpse-of-a-world, a late-occurring passage where the reader is most intellectually, emotionally, and ethically engaged or taxed. Often the passage functions as a breakthrough, where everything about the characters' situation is seen to be arrestingly more complex, or simpler, or more uplifting, or darker (at any rate, always more thought-provoking) than anything that had emerged in the narrative up to that point – although everything in the narrative up to that point feels all the more clearly a calculated preparation for this moment or arresting insight.

Toolan suggests that these HEI moments are marked by distinctive stylistic choices which tend to include more of the following features (summarised below, after Toolan 2013) when compared against the co-text:

1. Key projecting verbs such as *know, see, feel* and *want*;
2. Negation is widespread;
3. Sentence grammar is comparatively elaborate, complex; or sentences are longer; or use of nominal clauses and clefting is more prominent; mostly, the focalising character will be sentence Subject;

4. Internal sentence rhythms will be more developed and more poetic, with richer tonality or voicing than adjacent text;
5. Much more noticeably than elsewhere in the narration, standard sentence grammar may be departed from;
6. More temporal simultaneity (marked by a *As he did X, he felt y* structures, which typically combine report of a physical or external narrated event with report of a mental or internal event/reaction/insight; hence a double telling); more temporal stating, or multiply-coordinated processes or events;
7. Absolute/ultimate words: e.g., *everlasting, never, rock-bottom,* etc.;
8. Heat, light and dimension words are prominent;
9. A higher density of lexical and structural repetition and para-repetition;
10. Free Indirect Thought.

Building on the exploration of representations of the COLD, the next and final analysis considers the representation of the narrator's voice, and expressions of subjectivity and of emotions, in the closing moments of *Stone Mattress*. As these features are associated with high emotion, they contribute to inciting a more subjective construal of the fictional world, drawing the conceptualiser to the foreground at the pivotal moment of resolution and retribution.

4.5.2 Exacting Revenge

At the end of *Stone Mattress*, 'Torching the Dusties' deviates from the murder-as-revenge template hitherto established. Here, the tables are turned, and the revenge is directed towards, and is not initiated by, the protagonist. The focalised narrator, Wilma, has Charles Bonnet syndrome, a condition affecting her visual processing. In Wilma's case, she sees groups of 'little people' (225) who dance around her, seemingly part of her surrounding physical environment. At the end of the story (Extract 4.9), she and her friend Tobias have fled to the grounds of the care home to escape the protest mob at the front gate.

Extract 4.9

> Now they've gone through the back entrance; they're outside. There are distant voices, there is chanting – it must be coming from the crowd at the front gate. What is it they're saying? *Time to Go. Fast not Slow. Burn Baby Burn. It's Our Turn.* An ominous rhythm.

But it's coming from afar; here at the back of the building it's quiet. The air is fresh, the night is cool. Wilma worries that they'll be seen, mistaken for intruders or for escapees from Advanced Living, though there's no one around. No men with beagles. Tobias uses his flashlight to guide his own steps and by extension hers, switching it on and then off again.

"Are there fireflies?" Wilma whispers. She hopes so, for if not, what are those sparkles of light at the edges of her vision, pulsing like signals? It is some new neural anomaly, her brain short-circuiting like a toaster dropped into a bath?

"Many fireflies," Tobias whispers back. [...]

The flames have taken over now. They're so bright. Even gazing directly, she can see them. Blended with them, flickering and soaring, are the little people, their red garments glowing from within, scarlet, orange, yellow, gold. They're swirling upward, they're so joyful! They meet and embrace, they part; it's an airy dance.

Look. Look! They're singing! (Atwood 2014, 265–268)

Wilma's description contains many of the stylistic features consistent with Toolan's list of HEI features and which subjectify her construal of events. Her anxiety is evidenced in her interpretation of this trip outside as an 'excursion' (264) into the unknown, and referenced through the attributing frame, 'Wilma worries'. The few examples of direct speech relay the exchange between her and Tobias, but otherwise Wilma's account initially focuses on her perception of the physical space and the sounds she hears, while the projecting verbs relate her anxieties. In particular, Wilma 'worries that they'll be seen', and she 'hopes' that her assessments of what is going on is accurate. Outside of the formal verbs of projection, Wilma's subjective and modalised assessment of events is emphasised through other linguistic structures. She describes her and Tobias's physical movement through the gardens of the care home in categorical and deictically proximal terms: 'Now they've gone through the back entrance; they're outside'. Similarly, she relies on her hearing to track the mob, who are grouped as collective 'distant voices' and in the gerund 'chanting'. The source of the sound is construed less categorically, and modalised through her epistemic judgement of the space between them: 'it *must* be coming from the front gate' (emphasis added). Her uncertainty over the 'distant voices' is also apparent in her rhetorical questions ('What is it they're saying?').

The voices of the mob in these final moments remain at a physical distance from Wilma and Tobias's location 'at the back of the building', though the present-tense narration (and temporally proximal 'Now', repeated twice) suggests unfolding or impending threat and danger. While Wilma describes the scene, she also uses syntactic negation to identify absent details. She acknowledges that 'there's no one around. No men with beagles', emphasising her and Tobias's unexpected—and perhaps temporary—solitude. Further negation is attributed to the words she can hear from the mob ('*Fast not Slow*'), while absence is also suggested through lexical choices that lie at one end of an antonymic semantic scale. The building is 'quiet' where they are, denoting an absence of sound that contrasts with the earlier chanting. Equally, the absence of light is used to help guide her progress, while Tobias turns the flashlight 'on and then off again'. Access to Wilma's ongoing assessment of her physical surroundings is further suggested through sentence fragmentation. She uses incomplete or minor clauses (e.g., 'An ominous rhythm'), and clause fragments across sentences that would otherwise be coordinated (e.g., 'But it's coming from afar'), as if she is adding and modiyfng details in the moment. This fragmentation of sentences and shorter clauses in conjunction with longer sentences, and the use of present tense, contributes to the build of suspense or 'narrative *urgency*' at this climatic moment (Simpson 2014).

Finally, and significantly, 'heat, light, and dimension words' are prominent in this closing extract and contribute to its heightened emotional involvement. References to temperature and its emotional valence, as exemplified elsewhere in the collection, are revivified in Wilma's description. As part of her sustained emphasis on perception, she mentions the physical coldness of the evening through repeated copular clauses ('The air is fresh, the night is cool'). In a departure from the previous references to COLD, however, here there is an emphasis on HEAT, instead. The chanting voices of the mob sing '*Burn Baby Burn*', and Wilma's construal draws on the related lexical items 'flashlight', 'fireflies', 'flickering', 'sparkles of light', 'short-circuiting', 'flames', 'bright' and 'glowing', which incite and sustain associations between HEAT and LIGHT. In particular, her description of the mob's activities is rendered through a series of reconstruals (Langacker 2008; see also Chapter 3). She labels the lights, initially, as innocuous 'fireflies'. These lights are later reconstrued and 'retargeted' (Giovanelli 2023) as the more dangerous 'flames'. In these final moments, where the little people are '[b]lended' with the flames, the danger is 'rescoped' (Giovanelli 2023) as harmless and entertaining ('an airy dance'), and as more abstract and visually unformed ('scarlet, orange, yellow, gold'). Wilma's closing directive ('Look. Look! They're singing!') further connects the little people with the chanting protesters at the gates. Her perception ameliorates the murderous acts of revenge taking place around her, and pivots, instead, to her retreat into this fanciful, alternate conceptualisation of the physical environment.

That the collection closes with this subjective construal, and the emphasis on Wilma's illusory interpretation of the otherwise terrifying, 'real' events, fulfils several functions. Firstly, the heightened tone characterises and fore-grounds the voice of the tales' storytellers; the ageing women who are becoming 'increasingly visible' (Tolan 2017, 453) in Atwood's contemporary writing. It also illustrates the connection between Wilma in this final story and Constance from the first story. Both 'become very invested' in the things they imagine, as The ABC Club observe (Table 4.6, turn 7), and this hallucination becomes an enveloping experience for each narrator. At the end of the first story, 'Alphinland', Constance enters the imaginary world she has created, while in 'Torching the Dusties', Wilma is an 'escapee' of the home, and her hallucinations are instead brought into and blended with her conceptualisation of her physical environment. These connections create a type of structural circularity which bookend the collection, replacing a more conclusive resolution associated with longer prose forms (Toolan 2020).

Finally, the foregrounding of HEAT inverts the anger scenario instilled else-where in the stories; a reversal that seems fitting given the directionality of this final act of revenge, which is aimed towards, rather than initiated by, this narrator. In the context of this collection, the title, 'Torching the Dusties', suggests an ANGER IS HEAT framing, and though Barzilai (332) argues the title of the story does not hold metaphorical value, the broader networks within the collection suggest otherwise. The emphasis on a physical fire at the end of *Stone Mattress* counterbalances the environmental *ice storm* identified at the beginning of the collection, offering up a final reification, and denoue-ment, of the TEMPERATURES domain, and the metaphorical associations it precipitates.

4.6   '*Fun* is not knowing how it will end'

This chapter contributes to research on Atwood's comparatively under-examined short story writing (Barzilai 2017), and to the growing scholarship in stylistics on how readers experience and frame responses to short story collections (Harrison and Giovanelli 2022; De Vooght and Nemegeer 2021). In particular, the analysis has explored readers' experiences of the macabre ambience of *Stone Mattress*, and examined how it is stylistically created, and elaborated, across the collection. It was found that the book group discus-sion predominantly focused on the cohesive themes of the short stories, and especially the world-building *ice storm* and the COLD domain it evokes, where readers responded to the chains of associations established within the language of the text and its metaphorical networks. The readers' assessment of tonal qualities similarly sought reticulations across the collection. The second section explored how the storytellers' subjective construal of the fictional world is generated at the end of the stories, where tone is characterised through COLD and HEAT dimension words and through other HEI features. The shifting balance between the emotional state of a character and the physical landscape is instrumental to building the morbid ambience and the 'dark and kind of ominous feel' (Angela, Table 4.4, turn 8) of this short story collection. Significantly, the dialogic relationship between the vengeful characters and the icy setting they inhabit is presented as an innate, and elemental, ecological alliance.

Notes

1. In this shorthand, primacy is given to the fictional world representation (indicated by the snow clouds in Fig. 4.1) as compared to the conceptualiser.

2. Stockwell takes care to separate the concept from the adjacent concept of felt 'resonance', which, instead, 'is what a reader takes away from a striking reading – a definite thread of sensation that persists strongly after the text has been put aside' (2014, 366).

3. To create this extra-attentive re-reading condition, the researchers told one of the groups that the story they were about to re-read had been altered from the original, and to look out for differences in the two versions. The story they were given for the second reading was, in fact, unchanged.

4. I am departing from O'Halloran's (2011) distinction of these labels to widen the classification of 'on-book' discussion to include all literary discussion, even where topics move beyond the actual text to consider, for examples, other texts by the same author, or other texts that the readers identify as being similar to the base text. Topic-shifting in book group discourse is complex, and it can be difficult to differentiate between on-book and off-book discussions in categorical terms (Peplow et al. 2016, 23).

5. The collocations were filtered by ± three tokens.

6. RETRIBUTION as a more specific part of the anger domain is also frequently compared with EATING, as in discussions of revenge being 'satisfying', 'sweet' and generally as a 'dish' that is 'served' or 'eaten'. This blend of COLD and EATING is echoed in *Hag-Seed*, where Felix reflects that 'revenge is a dish best eaten cold, he reminds himself" (Atwood 2016, 151).

7. This container motif appears elsewhere in the collection in both physical and conceptual contexts: Constance locks up Gavin and Marjorie in different places in Alphinland; the wedding of 'The 'Freeze-Dried Froom' is contained within a storage unit, and so on.
8. MORALITY IS ACCOUNTING is also explored in Atwood's (2009) lecture series, *Payback: debt and the shadow side of wealth*.
9. Though COLD in this Western context is associated with unfriendliness and distance, like all conceptual metaphors, this is culturally and geographically varied. Koptjevskaja-Tamm and Nikolaev (2021), for example, observe that, in African languages, COLD has comparatively more positive associations and is drawn on to frame emotional states such as peace, serenity and contentedness.

References

Abbott, Horace Porter. 2008. *The Cambridge introduction to narrative*. Second edition. Cambridge: Cambridge University Press.

Atwood, Margaret. 2009. *Payback: Debt and the shadow side of wealth*. London: Bloomsbury.

Atwood, Margaret. 2014. *Stone mattress: Nine wicked tales*. London: Virago.

Atwood, Margaret. 2016. *Hag-seed*. London: Penguin.

Audet, René. 2000. *Des textes à L'œuvre: la lecture du recueil de nouvelles*. Québec: Nota Bene.

Barbosa Escobar, Francisco, Carlos Velasco, Kosuke Motoki, Derek V. Byrne, and Qian J. Wang. 2021. The temperature of emotions. *PLoS ONE* 16 (6): e0252408.

Barzilai, Shuli. 2017. How far would you go? Trajectories of revenge in Margaret Atwood's short fiction. *Contemporary Women's Writing* 11 (3): 316–335.

Bergman, Penny, Hsin-Ni Ho, Ai Koizumi, Ana Tajadura-Jiménez, and Norimichi Kitagawa. 2014. The pleasant heat? Evidence for thermal-emotional implicit associations occurring with semantic and physical thermal stimulation. *Cognitive Neuroscience* 6 (1): 24–30.

Bruey, Emily. 2017. Pay-up time: (Un)Balanced accounts in Margaret Atwood's *Stone Mattress*. *Margaret Atwood Studies* 11: 17–28.

Croft, William, and Alan Cruse. 2004. *Cognitive linguistics*. Cambridge: Cambridge University Press.

de Vooght, Edward, and Guy Nemegeer. 2021. Reading and analysing short story collections: An empirical study of readers' interpretation process of Benni's *Il bar sotto il mare*. *Language and Literature* 30 (4): 361–380.

Giovanelli, Marcello. 2023. *The language of Siegfried Sassoon*. London: Palgrave.

Grady, Joseph. 1997. Foundations of meaning: Primary metaphors and primary scenes. Ph.D. dissertation, University of California, Berkeley.

Harrison, Chloe, and Marcello Giovanelli. 2022. 'Traits don't change, states of mind do': Tracking Olive in *Olive Kitteridge* by Elizabeth Strout. *English Studies* 103 (3): 428–446.

Harrison, Chloe, and Louise Nuttall. 2019. Cognitive grammar and reconstrual: Re-experiencing Margaret Atwood's 'The freeze-dried groom.' In *Experiencing fictional worlds*, ed. Benedict Neurohr and Lizzie Stewart-Shaw, 135–154. Amsterdam: Benjamins.

Harrison, Chloe, and Louise Nuttall. 2021. Rereading as retelling: Re-evaluations of perspective in narrative fiction. In *Narrative retellings: Stylistic approaches*, ed. Marina Lambrou, 217–234. London: Bloomsbury.

Howells, Coral Ann. 2017. True trash: Genre fiction revisited in Margaret Atwood's *Stone mattress, The heart goes last*, and *Hag-seed. Contemporary Women's Writing* 11 (3): 297–315.

Koptjevskaja-Tamm, Maria, and Dmitry Nikolaev. 2021. Talking about temperature and social thermoregulation in the languages of the world. *Review of Social Psychology* 34 (1): 1–23.

Kövecses, Zoltán. 1995. American friendship and the scope of metaphor. *Cognitive Linguistics* 6–4: 315–346.

Kövecses, Zoltán. 2000. *Metaphor and emotion: Language, culture, and body in human feeling*. Cambridge: Cambridge University Press.

Kövecses, Zoltán. 2020. The concept of anger: Universal or culture specific? *Psychopathology* 33: 159–170.

Lakoff, George. 2016. Language and emotion. *Emotion Review* 8 (3): 269–273.

Lakoff, George, and Mark Johnson. 1980. *Metaphors we live by*. Chicago: University of Chicago Press.

Lakoff, George, and Zoltán Kövecses. 1987. The cognitive model of anger inherent in American English. In *Cultural models in language and thought*, ed. Dorothy Holland and Naomi Quinn, 195–221. New York: Cambridge University Press.

Langacker, Ronald W. 2008. *Cognitive grammar: A basic introduction*. Oxford: Oxford University Press.

Le Guin, Ursula. 2014. Stone Mattress: Nine tales, by Margaret Atwood. *The Financial Times*. http://www.ft.com/cms/s/2/fe6f7aa4-3822-11e4-a687-00144feabdc0.html. Accessed 1 April 2016.

Nischik, Reingard. 2009. *Engendering genre: The works of Margaret Atwood*. Ottawa: University of Ottawa Press.

Nuttall, Louise and Chloe Harrison. 2020. Wolfing down the Twilight series: metaphors for reading in online reviews. In *Contemporary media stylistics*, ed. Helen Ringrow and Stephen Pihlaja, 35–59. London: Bloomsbury.

Nuttall, Louise. 2021. Guilty grammar: See-saw perspective and morality in a poem by E. E. Cummings. In *New directions in cognitive grammar and style*, ed. Marcello Giovanelli, Chloe Harrison, and Louise Nuttall, 75–90. London: Bloomsbury.

O'Halloran, Kieran. 2011. Investigating argumentation in reading groups: Combining manual qualitative coding and corpus analysis tools. *Applied Linguistics* 32 (2): 172–196.

Pager-McClymont, Kimberley. 2021. Introducing Jane: The power of the opening. In *Powerful prose: How textual features impact readers*, ed. R.L. Victoria Pöhls and Mariane Utudji, 111–127. Bielefeld: Transcript.

Pager-McClymont, Kimberley. 2022. Linking emotions to surroundings: A stylistic model of pathetic fallacy. *Language and Literature* 31 (3): 428–454.

Peplow, David, Joan Swann, Paola Trimarco, and Sara Whiteley, eds. 2016. *The discourse of reading groups: Integrating cognitive and sociocultural perspectives*. London: Routledge.

Perry, Menakhem. 1979. Literary dynamics: How the order of a text creates its meaning. *Poetics Today* 1 (1–2): 311–361.

Porat, Roy, and Yeshayahu Shen. 2017. Metaphor: The journey from bidirectionality to unidirectionality. *Poetics Today* 38 (1): 123–140.

Salovey, Peter, and John D. Mayer. 1990. Emotional intelligence. *Imagination, Cognition and Personality* 9 (3): 195–211.

Semino, Elena, Zsófia Demjén, and Jane Demmen. 2016. An integrated approach to metaphor and framing in cognition, discourse and practice, with an application to metaphors for cancer. *Applied Linguistics* 39: 625–645.

Simpson, Paul. 2014. Just what is narrative *urgency*? *Language and Literature* 23 (1): 3–22.

Snaith, Helen. 2017. Dystopia, gerontology and the writing of Margaret Atwood. *Feminist Review: Dystopias and Utopias (Special Issue)* 116: 118–132.

Sternberg, Meir. 1978. *Expositional modes and temporal ordering in fiction*. Baltimore: John Hopkins University Press.

Stockwell, Peter. 2009. *Texture: A cognitive aesthetics of reading*. Edinburgh: Edinburgh University Press.

Stockwell, Peter. 2014. Atmosphere and tone. In *The Cambridge handbook of stylistics*, ed. Peter Stockwell and Sara Whiteley, 360–374. Cambridge: Cambridge University Press.

Stockwell, Peter. 2021. Shelley's dominion: Subliminal and ambient tonal effects across a literary work. In *Cognitive linguistic approaches to text and discourse: From poetics to politics*, ed. Christopher Hart, 20–36. Edinburgh: Edinburgh University Press.

The ABC Club. 2022. Transcribed book group discussion.

Tolan, Fiona. 2017. Aging and subjectivity in Margaret Atwood's fiction. *Contemporary Women's Writing* 11 (3): 336–353.

Toolan, Michael. 2009. *Narrative progression in the short story: A corpus stylistic approach*. Amsterdam: John Benjamins.

Toolan, Michael. 2013. Is style in short fiction different from style in long fiction? *Style in Fiction Today* 4: 95–105.

Toolan, Michael. 2016. *Making sense of narrative text: Situation, repetition, and picturing in the reading of short stories*. New York: Routledge.

Toolan, Michael. 2020. Narrative retelling in McGahern's 'Swallows': the intensifying power of repetition and return. In *Narrative retellings: stylistic approaches*,
ed. Marina Lambrou, 61–76. London: Bloomsbury.

Werth, Paul. 1999. *Text worlds: Representing conceptual space in discourse*. London:
Longman.

Williams, Lawrence E., and John A. Bargh. 2008. Experiencing physical warmth
promotes interpersonal warmth. *Science* 322 (5901): 606–607.

Zhong, Chen-Bo, and Geoffrey J. Leonardelli. 2008. Cold and lonely: Does social
exclusion literally feel cold? *Psychological Science* 19 (9): 831–946.

5

Theatrical Illusion and the Performance of Fictional Minds in *Hag-Seed*

5.1 Introduction: 'The keynotes'

Hag-Seed (Atwood 2016a) is a contemporary retelling of Shakespeare's *The Tempest*. Published in 2016, the book was the fourth to be published in the Random House Hogarth Shakespeare Series, which features other retellings including contemporary versions of *The Winter's Tale* (*The Gap of Time*, Winterson 2015), *The Merchant of Venice* (*Shylock Is My Name*, Jacobson 2016) and *The Taming of the Shrew* (*Vinegar Girl*, Tyler 2016), among others. The story's protagonist, Felix, assumes the role of Duke Prospero, and works as an eccentric Artistic Director at a theatre festival in Makeshiweg, Canada. After being pushed out of his role by a usurping director, Tony (Antonio), Felix vows revenge through the unlikely medium of a theatre production of *The Tempest*. After nine years of 'exile' in which he uses 'the snoop gremlin, Google' (Atwood 2016a, 44) to monitor his adversaries' lives, he takes on the job as a teacher on a Literacy Through Literature programme and rebrands himself as 'Mr Duke'. The story culminates in the Fletcher Correctional Players' performance of *The Tempest*, an adaptation infused with 'dark calamity' (Groskop 2016), whereby the play is performed, twice and simultaneously, in order to trick Tony and exact Felix's long-awaited revenge. *Hag-Seed* thematically aligns with other Atwood narratives in that revenge is a central motif in the story, and it is this theme, as well as the extended wordplay and preoccupation with doubling, which makes the text 'feels so much like something Atwood would have written anyway' (Groskop 2016). As the focalising character, Felix's loose grasp on reality and theatrical world

C. Harrison, *The Language of Margaret Atwood*, Palgrave Studies in Language, Literature and Style, https://doi.org/10.1007/978-3-031-67640-6_5

view forms a key part of the text's critical commentary on 'the relationship between reality and fantasy that theatre provides' (Howells 2017, 309).

This chapter draws on contemporary research in the stylistic representation of fictional minds to consider how Felix's 'mind style' (Fowler 1977), related through his collective characterisation of the prisoners, and via his blurred representation of fantasy, reality and theatrical production, contributes to the exploration and recontextualisation of performance, performativity and illusion at the centre of the original play. Text analysis is contextualised alongside naturalised reader response data in the form of a transcribed discussion from a book group, The ABC Club (2022).[1] The chapter considers how the fantastical and magical elements in *The Tempest* are assigned and confined to Felix's dramaturgical perspective, and the THEATRE frame through which his world view is related.

5.2   Retelling *The Tempest*: Doubled Performance

Narrative retellings assume different stylistic forms. Following Harrison's (2023) taxonomy (Table 5.1), *Hag-Seed* can be classed as a type of rewriting that takes place at the site of text production: an 'inter-writer retelling' (165), which is a story written by one author, as retold by another.

Of course, this is further complicated in that Shakespeare's plays are considered inter-writer retellings of existing stories or myths, sometimes co-authored or produced collaboratively (Sanders 2016, 59–60), though, exceptionally, *The Tempest* is seen as one of Shakespeare's more original play texts (Muñoz-Valdivieso 2017, 113). As part of Atwood's process of adaptation, *Hag-Seed* can be seen to amplify and reappraise themes within the original play. The prison setting, for example, and Felix's role within the

Table 5.1 A taxonomy of narrative retellings (after Harrison 2023, 165)

Text production	Inter-writer	Different writers retelling the same scene, event or story
	Writer	The same writer rewriting the same scene, event or story, e.g., through editing
Text	Inter-narrator	Different narrators recounting the same scene, event or story
	Narrator	The same narrator retelling the same scene, event or story
Text reception	Readers	Shifts in interpretation of the scene, event or story as experienced in re-reading

literacy programme at the Fletcher Correctional Centre, can be interpreted as a reflection on the social issues of the text. In *The Tempest*, Prospero entraps and abuses the island inhabitant, Caliban, while, in *Hag-Seed*, Felix attempts to educate and empower the prisoners on the correctional programme. Additionally, and as the analysis in this chapter will explore, the move from drama to prose allows the development of a narratorial voice and, subsequently, richer development of the characters (see Furlong 2021, 50–56, for a summary of how retellings relate an adaptor's communicative purpose in different ways).

The ABC Club readers briefly discuss the novel as an adaptation, though much like the readers in Bray's (2021) exploration of The Austen Project—commissioned by Harper Collins in 2011, just four years before the Hogarth Shakespeare Series—the ABC readers are not entirely won over by the more explicit intertextual references. They note the incongruity of the synopsis of the play appearing at the end of the text, while Olivia additionally observes the self-reflexivity created by the doubled storytelling:

> I actually don't think that you did need to know *The Tempest* like the way she had written and I felt like there were quite a lot of bits where she was like this is what happens in the plot like in case you didn't know nudge nudge wink wink.

Unlike the retellings within The Austen Project, which came under criticism for too closely resembling the original style of Austen (Bray 2021, 84), however, the transposition of *The Tempest* to a contemporary context in *Hag-Seed* necessitates many key stylistic and narrative changes from the original story. Most markedly, the relocation of the story to a modern prison makes literal one of the central metaphors in the original play: the idea that the island is Prospero's prison, and the place where he has been banished and incarcerated ('Canst thou remember/A time before we came to this cell?', Act I Scene II). The contemporary period in which the action takes place is also foregrounded in *Hag-Seed*, particularly in the central role of 'digital figuration' within the performance of the play (Howells 2017, 310–312). The play is performed at the end by the prisoners, and Felix's contemporary adaptation employs 'one of the oldest theatrical gimmicks in the box' by creating an 'illusion through doubles' (Atwood 2016a, 108). His plan is that '[o]ne version would be the video running onscreen in the rest of the prison', and '[t]he other version would suddenly have real people in it, directed and controlled by himself' (107–108). The prisoners' integration of technical special effects makes this doubled performance possible, while maintaining the boundaries

of realism in the text. In this way, Prospero's magic is replaced with technological sleight of hand. At other moments, the fantastical is rendered through
more everyday, realist descriptions. His magic cloak, for example, 'would be
made of animals – not real animals or even realistic ones, but plush toys that
had been unstuffed and then sewn together' (17).

The heightened self-awareness of the retelling noted by Olivia in the ABC
Club reflections (Table 5.2, turn 2) additionally sets the novel apart from
the original text. While *The Tempest* closes with a wall-breaking Epilogue
where Prospero directly addresses the audience and asks for their pardon in
order that he may be released ('As you from crimes would pardoned be/Let
your indulgence set me free'), this self-reflexivity and meta-commentary on
story construction becomes amplified in the *Hag-Seed* retelling. Firstly, this
is achieved through the play-within-a-play structure. Felix's frame narrative
and story of revenge follows the story of Prospero in *The Tempest*, and he
also delivers a performance of *The Tempest*, which, in turn, is performed
twice. In addition to this nested structure, recursivity is also created through
local choices across the story, such as in the doubled identities of the characters who exist in the frame narrative and also have character counterparts
within the embedded play (Howells 2017, 310–311). Moreover, Mr Duke's
tutor role on the literary programme necessitates many conversations about
the linguistic, thematic and structural choices of the play with his class. For
example, Felix asks the Players to consider its themes and structure through
sharing his 'keynotes' (86) on the original text:

Using the blue marker, he writes:

> IT'S A MUSICAL: Has the most music + songs in Shkspr. Music used for
> what?
> MAGIC: Used for what?
> PRISONS: How many?
> MONSTERS: Who is one?
> REVENGE: Who wants it? Why? (Atwood 2016, 86)

Felix's critical commentary both primes readers to ask these same questions, and establishes the novel's metafictional categorisation. Finally, this
self-reflexive commentary is further reinforced within the structure of the
edition itself. Unlike Winterson's retelling of *The Winter's Tale* in *The Gap
of Time*, which summarises the play at the beginning of the text, for example,
Atwood's '*The Tempest*: The Original' summary appears at the end of *Hag-
Seed*, creating 'her own teasing epilogue in the hall of mirrors that is

Hag-Seed' (Muñoz-Valdivieso 2017, 125). Such choices invite a classification of the text as a critique of *The Tempest*, while also presenting a wider meditation on the process of adaptation itself (Zajac 2020, 339).

At the same time, shared details between *Hag-Seed* and *The Tempest* cue up and overtly mark the intertextual references made within the story to invite a comparison between the two texts in a more straightforward way. Central characters are clearly analogous. Prospero, as Felix, masquerades as 'the Duke' in his new role at the correctional facility in order to hide his identity, and his daughter Miranda also appears throughout the narrative. Other recast characters are labelled through their slightly amended names: Antonio becomes 'Tony', Ferdinand becomes 'Freddie O'Nally', and so on. Key 'world-builders' (Werth 1999) related to time are also transferred to the retelling. In *Hag-Seed*, twelve years have passed since Felix's self-imposed 'exile' (Atwood 2016a, 48), summarised as part of the character's backstory at the start of the narrative. Other 'marked' and 'specific' intertextual references (Mason 2019) are quoted from the original play, and these form part of Felix's discourse presentation (e.g., '"To the elements be free," he says to her', 283), or are otherwise attributed to, and anachronistically adapted within, the speech of other characters (e.g., at the end of the performance, Anne-Marie says, 'The revels now are ended. And that was a fucking good revel!', 275). These references also appear at the structural level of the text, where they are integrated within section headings (e.g., Section one is titled 'Dark backward', quoted from a conversation between Prospero and Miranda in the original play, Act I Scene II). The inter-writer retelling of *The Tempest* that *Hag-Seed* presents, then, both reinstates, and ironically subverts, key structural and stylistic choices of the original narrative.

5.3   Reading Fictional Minds

In drama and dramatic performances, audiences are invited to witness and to overhear conversations between characters in a way that is seemingly unmediated (Short 1989, 149; van Duijn et al. 2015). Stylistic studies have explored how patterns within dramatic conversations can develop the characterisation of the speakers onstage (e.g., Culpeper 2001; Jeffries and McIntyre 2010; Leech 1992; Short 1989). In other cases, characterisation in drama is regarded as deriving from a character's individual actions: as Frye (1957, 171) observes, 'what a character is follows from what he has to do in the play'.

The adaptation from play to prose format enables the focalisation of Felix's voice in a way that would not be possible in a dramatic performance (Howells

2017, 310). In the context of fiction, in contrast to dramatic texts, readers are given additional prompts that go beyond the externalised speech or actions of a character, and are afforded even more direct and telepathic insight into a character's mind through, for example, processes of focalisation and proximal deictic alignment, which can position readers within a character's immanent processes even more closely. Shifting *Hag-Seed* from a play to a prose fiction novel therefore affords a different insight into the characterisation of Prospero. Unlike in a dramatic performance, readers are able to follow his world view more closely, and the inferences they are invited to make about his actions are built on richer textual detail, via more explicit narratorial mediation that is otherwise absent in performance alone.

Regardless of literary genre, research suggests that readers understand and conceptualise fictional characters, and fictional minds, in the same ways that we understand and conceptualise people we encounter in everyday lives (Budelmann and Easterling 2010; Palmer 2004; Zunshine 2006). This conceptualisation is, by necessity, a dynamic and interactive process. We create mental models of people's characters and update these models in response to new or amended information regarding changes in behaviour, disposition, motivations, and so on. These models enable us to second guess what others might do, say, or think, and allow us to speculate on their rationales for particular actions or behaviours. In everyday situations, another person's speech or behaviours are valuable sources of information for building and assembling these character models, which are further developed and elaborated through our own schematic knowledge of the world and understanding of characters, and of how people think and behave. Updating models of characters is therefore a two-stage system, made up of both top-down (i.e., wider knowledge schemas) and bottom-up (i.e., text-driven) processing. This interactive process is therefore both cued up by external cues from the text or from another person, but one that is also dependent on our own interpretation of actions and behaviours (Culpeper 2001; Palmer 2004; Schneider 2001).

Of course, not all characters display minds that are similar to our own, and characterisation can be complicated in those instances where minds we encounter deviate from established or familiar profiles. First coined by Fowler (1977, 103), 'mind style' refers to 'any distinctive linguistic representation of an individual mental self', and explorations of mind styles in literary contexts have increasingly considered those mental selves that present a particularly 'unorthodox conception of the fictional world' (Leech and Short 1981, 188–189). Accounts of character mind styles are, like all stylistic analyses, driven by consistent linguistic patterns and choices distinctive to the text under consideration. In Halliday's (1971) seminal paper, transitivity patterns and syntactic choices are examined as signposts to the Neanderthal world view of Lok in *The Inheritors*. Since this study, stylistic explorations of mind style have branched out to include explorations of pragmatics, schemas and metaphors (as summarised in Semino 2007). In some cases, these unusual perspectives are shown to be manifested through a combination of style choices. For example, Semino's (2014a, 2014b) accounts of *The Curious Incident of the Dog in the Night-Time*[2] consider how pragmatic failure and problems with figurative language processing characterise the neurodivergent perspective of the main character, Christopher. In addition to utilising corpus methods (McIntyre and Archer 2010), mind style studies also increasingly turn to cognitive stylistic frameworks. For example, contemporary projects have demonstrated that changes in construal operations (Langacker 2008) may form part of a highly idiosyncratic world view (Giovanelli 2018; Harrison 2017; Nuttall 2018; Rundquist 2020a, 2020b). By necessity, the study of distinctive mind styles in literary fiction aligns with stylisticians' focus on unusual or challenging texts, containing character perspectives which are perceived as departing from more prototypical or normalised perspectives. As vehicles for perception and relating information about the fictional world, mind styles that are especially distinctive or deviant (Stockwell 2009, 124) can be revealing and stylistically marked in interesting ways.

As the focalising character, Felix displays a view of the world that is markedly idiosyncratic. The characterisation of Felix is central to the experience of *Hag-Seed* and becomes the main topic under consideration in The ABC Club's discussion of the novel. Groskop observes that Felix is presented as both 'utterly idiotic and sometimes despicable', and that the '[t]welve years living in a shack in the wilderness make him more bearable, but only just' (2016). The following sections explore the complex character profile identified by Groskop, and the theatrical mind style which distinguishes his singular voice. This chapter argues that, within this retelling, the fantastical elements of the original play are transposed to Felix's unusual and unreliable account of the world, which is otherwise anchored in a realist, contemporary setting.

5.4   Reading *Hag-Seed*

As in Chapter 4, the reader data for this chapter were generated through a book group discussion. The book group, The ABC Club, were given copies of *Hag-Seed* to read in August 2022. Two members of the group listened to the text via audiobook[3] and the rest via paperback copies. Following the usual protocol of the group, the members met online to discuss the novel, and I was not present during this session. The discussion was recorded, and the transcribed data were coded for recurring themes and topics.

The topics for The ABC Club's discussion included conversations on *the adaptation from the original play*, as well as a briefer consideration of *the prison setting*. The more extensive part of the discussion, which will be drawn on in this chapter, however, explored the *voices and characterisation* of the characters within the text, with discussion of the representation of the prisoners as a collective group (*the prisoners as Chorus*), and of the *characterisation of Felix/Mr Duke/Prospero* collectively constituting the greater parts of the conversation on the book. The emphasis on tone as the distinctive part of the reading experience of *Hag-Seed* departs significantly from the focus of the *Stone Mattress* discussion (see Chapter 4), which comparatively focused on the atmospheric qualities of the fictional worlds of the short stories. This shift within the reader responses to *Hag-Seed* may be traced, in part, to the fact there is 'very little plot' in the original *Tempest* (Muñoz-Valdivieso 2017, 110), which contrastively brings characterisation into greater focus.

5.4.1   Characterisation of *Felix/Mr Duke/Prospero*

Mind-modelling captures the dynamic process by which readers keep track of characters 'across embedded worlds', and, as Stockwell (2022, 135) argues, sometimes this process extends beyond the text to include the imagined authorial mind.

> The feeling of literary reading is largely a consequence of mind-modelling, and where authorial, narratorial, poetic persona and character minds are spread across embedded worlds, a reader's experience of immersion and emergence, engagement and disengagement, empathy and cold rationality are also matters that can be explored by considering how these minds are modelled.

Significant, too, is that characterisation processes can be complicated by readers' evaluations and judgements of the character and their actions. Immersion, engagement and empathy are all markers of a successful proximal, emotional alignment between a reader and a character, whereas emergence, disengagement and cold rationality may be the result of greater emotional distancing in those cases where characters are deemed unlikable, or morally or ethically dubious in some way (Nuttall 2018).

The ABC Club spend a large part of their meeting on *Hag-Seed* 'mind-modelling' Felix and his role within the narrative. As Groskop (2016) observes, Felix's characterisation is not unproblematic, and much like the dislike of Prospero's character among the prisoners in *Hag-Seed*,[4] The ABC Club readers are not predisposed to like him: 'I didn't feel like the character development of the main dude Felix was like that interesting or relatable' (Nancy, Table 5.2, turn 1). Research has shown that sharing a character's point of view during reading can impact on readers' interpretations of that character's actions or disposition (van Peer and Pander Maat 2001), though unlikeable or ethically dubious points of view can problematise these feelings (Harrison and Nuttall 2021; Nuttall 2018). Nancy qualifies some of the ethical considerations that made up her negative assessment of Felix, taking issue with being encouraged to feel 'benevolently superior to [the prisoners] the whole way through', and in the social or class cache attached to 'understanding Shakespeare' (Table 5.2, turn 1). As Olivia also comments, the emphasis on Felix's perspective is perhaps the reason why the prisoners were not characterised as fully; it is 'because he's not really interested in them' (Table 5.2, turn 2).

The readers further explore the distorted version of the story that is presented by Felix and how it complicates the ontological status of the events throughout the story. In the extract from the discussion in Table 5.3,

Table 5.2 Mind-modelling Felix

1	Nancy	Well the whole way through we were just set up to kind of take like even though we well I didn't particularly I don't know I didn't feel like the character development of the main dude Felix was like that interesting or like relatable but we saw everything from his point of view so all the prisoners it was just like we were supposed to feel sort of like benevolently superior to them the whole way through and then like pat them on the back for doing well and understanding Shakespeare [...]
2	Olivia	I agree with that like I felt cuz I kept thinking it was gonna go down this sort of and I feel this is sort of what I maybe have missed and maybe if I'd have read *Tempest* and understood it all and done it recently I felt there was a vibe that the whole book was sort of kind of a meta-adaptation of like the plot or there was some sort of commentary on it and I thought like there was sort of lot of stuff foregrounded about you know Prospero being really unreliable and like you can't really trust him and stuff and I was like oh maybe it's gonna be like Felix is telling you a story but he is like an unreliable narrator when actually cuz like cuz exactly what you said like Nancy the prisoners felt like really underdeveloped and like I was like maybe because he's not really interested in them [...]

the readers question the extent to which Felix's narration, and in particular the story's resolution, is an erroneous account, or a 'misreporting' (Phelan 2007), of events. The perceived open-endedness of the story's resolution is suggested in Olivia's proposal for an alternative ending ('that is what I choose to believe', turn 2), and in Angela's question that this alternative ending is not precluded, 'So this is the message to Margaret then is like was it really all in his head' (turn 3). This speculation is marked in the focus on Felix's thoughts throughout this section of the group discussion ('made up in his head'; 'all in his head'; 'went a bit mad', 'pretend daughter', 'imagined himself a job', 'imaginary play', Table 5.3). Notable, too, is that The ABC Club's discussion of alternative resolutions or endings mirrors the assignment task Felix sets his class at the end of the novel, where he asks the prisoners to extend the narrative and the storylines of the characters beyond the end of the play.

These impressions of Felix's character are driven by specific textual cues. Stockwell (2020, 179) identifies five stylistic patterns which readers respond to as part of the process of mind-modelling, which include the physical description of a character, their speech presentation and the representation of thought, as well as external reactions of other characters, and any deictic markers or choices of social register that suggest 'all the divergences of characters' viewpoints from your own. The introduction to Felix establishes these

Table 5.3 '[W]as it really all in his head': The ending of *Hag-Seed*

1	Jane	Do you know when that guy got released early from parole and he was gonna go with him on the cruise I was like that doesn't like surely you're under probation or parole or have restrictions and you're not allowed to go up on a boat and have a jolly
2	Olivia	Which is why if it had been a whole thing that Felix had made up in his head that would have like all been fine and maybe it was and that is what I choose to believe that like
3	Angela	So this is the message to Margaret then is like was it really all in his head
4	Olivia	Yeah
5	Angela	But yeah
6	Olivia	And that none of it ever happened but he liked sat and went a bit mad and with his pretend daughter and imagined himself a job and went on to perform his imaginary play so that he could leave his little shack thing and then he went off and went on a cruise on his own that's what I like to believe had happened just like a superior ending

patterns, and introduces his unusual world view, from the beginning of the story, as Extracts 5.1–5.4 (Atwood 2016a) demonstrate:

Extract 5.1

Felix brushes his teeth. Then he brushes his other teeth, the false ones, and slides them into his mouth. Despite the layer of pink adhesive he's applied, they don't fit very well; perhaps his mouth is shrinking. He smiles: the illusion of a smile. Pretense, fakery, but who's to know? (9)

Extract 5.2

"Mi-my-mo-moo," he tells the toothpaste-speckled mirror over the kitchen sink. He lowers his eyebrows, juts out his chin. Then he grins: the grin of a cornered chimpanzee, part anger, part threat, part dejection. (10)

Extract 5.3

That devious twisted bastard, Tony, is Felix's own fault. Or mostly his own fault. Over the past twelve years, he's often blamed himself. [...] Worse: he'd trusted the evil-hearted, social-clambering, Machiavellian foot-licker. He'd fallen for the act: *Let me do this chore for you, delegate that, send me instead.* What a fool he'd been.

His only excuse was that he'd been distracted by grief at that time. He'd recently lost his only child, and in such a terrible way. If only he had, if only he hadn't, if only he'd been aware...

No, too painful still. Don't think about it, he tells himself while doing up the buttons of his shirt. Hold it far back. Pretend it was only a movie. (11)

Extract 5.4

"Unfortunately," said Tony now. There was a pause. He had an odd expression on his face. It was a downturned mouth with a smile underneath. Felix felt his neck hairs prickling. "Unfortunately," said Tony at last in his suavest voice, "the Board has voted to terminate your contract. As Artistic Director." (19)

Firstly, Felix's social roles are clearly established. Readers are informed that he is a father (Extract 5.3), and that his previous employment was as Artistic

Director (Extract 5.4). He also reveals, indirectly, details of his social background. He is educated and erudite, even when it comes to his insults, e.g., Tony is described as a 'Machiavellian foot-licker' (Extract 5.3). Felix's physical appearance is also schematically outlined. The opening sentence describes an everyday and familiar domestic activity: 'He brushes his teeth'. The second sentence, in contrast, immediately defamiliarises and duplicates this activity: 'Then he brushes his other teeth, the false ones'. That he is wearing false teeth that perhaps do not fit his 'shrinking' mouth suggests his more advanced age, but also creates a sense of duplicity. He is physically doubled, and these 'false ones' are part of the 'fakery' of his physical appearance. His physical description is further defamiliarised in Extract 5.2, where he describes his 'grin of a cornered chimpanzee'. Here, his mouth and smile are focused in the description, mirroring the introduction of Tony (Extract 5.4) which appears in the chapter that follows. Additionally, the chimpanzee metaphor moves Felix towards a more primal, animalistic representation. The addition of 'cornered' carries associations both of being sized up for a physical fight but also of being imprisoned.

The exposition of Felix's life and background at this point in the novel means that the examples of direct speech are more limited. Felix talks to his reflection in the mirror as he carries out his vocal training exercises, 'Mi-my-mo-moo' (Extract 5.2), which contributes to the initial perception of his character as one who is doubled in some way. Where he does speak in these early descriptions, he is talking only to himself, and the speech here is purely for the purposes of 'warming up' rather than as a meaningul inter-action with another person. Another form of direct speech appears later in Extract 5.3, where Felix summarises the sycophantic responses he had given to Tony's demands: '*Let me do this chore for you, delegate that, send me instead*'. These summaries of speech are layered with the tone of his present self, who evidently feels frustration for '[w]hat a fool he'd been' in the past'. This frustration is evidenced through the schematic summaries of the demands as 'this chore' and 'that'. The details of the commands are seemingly secondary to the fact that he had 'fallen for the act' and done Tony's bidding in the first place.

Of course, even more revealing in these opening descriptions of his character is the representation of Felix's thoughts. The third-person narration allows readers 'telepathic ability' (Stockwell 2020, 179) and focalises Felix's point of view. Readers are positioned proximally close to his physical and emotional perspective. Where Felix recounts the painful memories of his departure from the Makeshiweg Festival, for example, he narrates the memory as an event that is occurring 'now' (Extract 5.4). Extract 5.1, is the opening to the novel, and the external description of his physical appearance switches to foreground his immanent thought swiftly. This is marked through his epistemic judgements ('perhaps his mouth is shrinking') and rhetorical questions framed through instances of free indirect thought ('who's to know?'). The close emotional alignment continues in Felix's dysphemistic and evaluative description of 'That devious twisted bastard, Tony' (Extract 5.3), and in his qualification of the extent of his responsibility in events: 'Or mostly his own fault'. This contrasts in tone with his emotive backstory ('He'd recently lost his only child, and in such a terrible way') (Muñoz-Valdivieso 2017, 119) and is sustained in his rumination on what-if scenarios, whose repetition and fragmentation suggest their prominence in his thoughts and the associated guilt he continues to experience ('If only he had, if only he hadn't, if only he'd been aware...'). The reactions of other characters are limited in these earlier extracts, though the focus on 'That devious twisted bastard, Tony' and Felix's presentation of Tony's direct speech—with the repetition of 'Unfortunately', spoken in his 'suavest' voice (Extract 5.4)—confirms his position as Felix's adversary, and relates their mutual evaluation of each other.

Significantly, the emphasis on performance threads through all these extracts, illustrating Felix's idiosyncratic mind style and the theatrical lens through which he views the world. His lexical choices suggest duplicity and artifice ('false', 'Pretense, fakery', 'illusion', 'devious twisted', 'pretend'), while other descriptions foreground the THEATRE frame filtering his perspective, and through which he tries to create some emotional distance. Tony had presented an 'act' that Felix had 'fallen for', and while revisiting these 'painful' memories he instructs himself to 'Pretend it was only a movie' (Extract 5.3). Finally, Felix's 'illusion of a smile' (Extract 5.1) is echoed later in his description of Tony's 'odd expression'; 'a downturned mouth with a smile underneath' (Extract 5.4). Within the wider context of performance, the doubled smiles evoke the tragedy/comedy, Thalia/Melpomene theatre masks for these two characters, who are, in Felix's view, mirrored antagonists. As the tragic figure, Felix inserts his teeth to create the 'illusion of a smile', while Tony assumes 'a downturned mouth with a smile underneath'. The opening section of *Hag-Seed*, then, sets the scene for these characters. Felix's backstory is swiftly established, his vocal warmups completed; the two antagonists have assumed their masks and are ready to take the stage.

5.4.2 'Prospero's Goblins': *The Prisoners as Chorus*

Critics observe the comparative 'flat' characterisation of the prisoners in *Hag-Seed* (Charlebois 2023). The ABC Club similarly explores the characterisation of the prisoners and their 'lack of character development' (Angela, turn 6) in relation to Felix. In the extract from the book group discussion in Table 5.4, the readers consider the prison location of the narrative. Unlike the cohesive setting of the *ice storm* identified by the readers with *Stone Mattress* (Chapter 4), here they argue that the institutional setting of *Hag-Seed* could be treated interchangeably with others[5] ('it could have been in a children's home and troubled children it could have been in a hospital or anywhere' Lis, turn 5). This observation aligns with the critical view that the novel's prison setting is 'more of a central conceit than a vehicle for social commentary' (Charlebois 2023, 112). Instead, the readers suggest that the location is secondary to the motivation of Felix's character, in that 'the whole point of the book is this man and the revenge he was taking on these people it wasn't even about the prisoners' (Lis, turn 5). At this point, Lis references top-down categorisation of Felix in the form of 'personal categorisation', the grouping of characters by their idiosyncratic habits, preferences, and goals (Culpeper 2001, 75). She notes that one of Felix's key, defining traits, which drives the narrative, is his goal of revenge. The recognition of Felix's principal aim, and what this suggests about the characterisation of 'this man', aligns with Schneider's observation that, while empirical research on processes of characterisation favours short texts comprising more 'eventful situations' for characters to react to, 'readers of novels focus their attention *predominantly* on psychological traits, emotions and aims of characters that are more abstract and less dependent on the immediate circumstantial conditions of individual situations' (2001, 610). Felix's obsession with revenge categorises him as a moral agent (Gray et al. 2007); someone who is focused on planning, scheming and plotting a detailed plan for vengeance.

Angela's reflection on a lack of felt character resonance in the extract from the discussion in Table 5.4 ('I don't think any of the characters actually they hadn't stayed with me', turn 6) suggests a comparative, more simplistic characterisation of the prisoners. As part of this process of disengagement from the characters, the readers examine how the doubling of names problematises the charting of the 'character constellations' (Smeets 2021) within the story ('it was like what was I gonna call him now', Angela, turn 6).[6] The consideration of the prisoners' characterisation continues in the extract in Table 5.5, where the readers reflect on another Atwood retelling, *The Penelopiad* (2005), a rewrite of *The Odyssey* from Penelope's perspective. Nancy observes the

Table 5.4 Character development in *Hag-Seed*

1	Jane	Yeah it didn't feel like it had to be set in a prison they could have been a group or community [act] or something I mean yeah
2	Lis	The other prisoners seem to be incredibly behind it right even from the start there wasn't much push back or much you know it was all oh this is lovely and it may have played out like that but then in real-life settings but then I don't suppose that was the whole point of the book was it the whole point of the book is this man and the revenge he was taking on these people it wasn't even about the prisoners like you said it could have been in any setting it could have been in a children's home and troubled children it could have been in a hospital or anywhere
3	Angela	I know I think it's really good what you said about the current lack of character development in terms of it you only really get was it Filo I don't know the main person [it gets it yeah]
4	Lis	I don't know too
5	Jane	[Filo gets that] Even Filo has multiple names
6	Angela	I know it was like what am I gonna call him now um but like yeah you get him but not really anyone else I I had I read this like ages ago and I couldn't remember it and I didn't know why and then when I got started I was still slightly struggling to remember it and I actually think it was the character bit what you were saying I don't think any of the characters actually they hadn't stayed with me whereas like yeah I think you are right there

connection between the level of reader investment and the lack of return on character development (turn 5), and draws a parallel between the Chorus of the Twelve Hanged Maids in *The Penelopiad* and the prisoners' voices within *Hag-Seed*. She understands them as a homogeneous group without 'distinct personalities' (turn 7), and argues that, as a group, the prisoners collectively 'serve a function' which might be to 'move the plot along' (turn 7). The readers' reactions to the prisoners similarly acknowledge their lack of authenticity, assessing them as a group who do not behave as they would expect in 'more real-life settings' (Lis, turn 2).

In *Hag-Seed*, the first introduction to the prisoners is, as with the narration throughout the novel, focalised through Felix's perspective. Felix's profiling of their characters has the double effect of building his characterisation further and forms a key part of his mind style representation. Consequently, their representation reveals more about his world view than it does about their individual characters. As Olivia observes, Felix's shallower characterisation of the prisoners may be 'because he's not really interested in them' (Table 5.2,

Table 5.5 The prisoners as Chorus

1	Nancy	It felt a little bit like *Persephone* [sic] by her
2	Angela	Oh yeah
3	Nancy	Kind of
4	Olivia	Oh I haven't read that one
5	Nancy	That's a telling of it's a short it's like a novella but telling the story of Odysseus' wife like from her point of view essentially but again I was a bit like I don't really like you don't get very much character development you're not very invested it's quite short
6	Angela	Is that the there's quite a lot of chorus line in that as well
7	Nancy	Lots of chorus line yeah but in that way it's kind of like that's a more extreme example but like if you compare it to this the prisoners were kind of the chorus right they don't have a distinct personalities they are there to kind of move the plot along or to serve a function I don't know

turn 2). Extract 5.5 describes the first class of the new semester, where Felix meets his cast of *The Tempest*:

Extract 5.5

> He scans the room. Familiar faces, veterans of his previous plays: these nod at him, offer half-smiles. New faces, blank or apprehensive: they don't know what to expect. Lost boys all of them, though they are not boys: their ages range from nineteen to forty-five. There are many hues, from white to black through yellow, red and brown; they are many ethnicities. The crimes for which they've been convicted are assorted. The one thing they share, apart from their imprisoned state, is a desire to be in Felix's acting troupe. Their motives, he expects, are varied. (Atwood 2016a, 83)

In Felix's description of his troupe, the prisoners are grouped as a collective who are depersonalised from their individual identities and characteristics. Felix scans 'the room' as a whole, and the noun phrases he draws on initially assemble the prisoners through pluralised count nouns. They are, conversely, 'veterans' and 'boys', and also detached and bodiless 'faces' within the room. The group is separated between the 'familiar faces' of the veterans, who are described in more deictically proximal terms ('these nod at him'), and the 'blank' faces of the new joiners, who are more distant ('they don't know what to expect'). Even where more specific details of age are conferred, these are presented as a 'range' and with no direct assignation of ages. Repeated syntactic constructions, comprising a list of varied physical features ('There are many hues, from white to black through yellow, red and brown'), paired with a summative categorisation ('they are many ethnicities'), further suggest Felix's cataloguing of their details as part of a more general directory. Their distinguishing features are summarised ('their ages range from nineteen to forty-five', 'they are many ethnicities', and their crimes 'are assorted'), and they are given one common desire: 'to be in Felix's acting troupe'. In this way, Felix confers a generic goal on the class as a single, shared motivation and an intermental objective (Nuttall 2015; Palmer 2004).

As the story progresses, the prisoners are individually named and singled out through their physical and social descriptions. Felix encourages them all to have a 'stage name' (85–86), which forms part of the doubling and double-casting. When Felix deliberates over the assignation of roles within the play, he summarises his cast as a 'tentative list' (85), complete with notes on their convictions, to be shared with his colleague Anne-Marie, who is drafted in to play Miranda:

Extract 5.6

ARIEL: 8Handz. Slight build. East Indian family background. About twenty-three. Very bright. Agile with a keyboard. Highly knowledgeable in tech matters. *Conviction*: Hacker, identity theft, impersonation. Forgery. Feels justified in his activities, as he believes he was playing a benevolent Robin Hood versus the evil King John capitalists of this world. Betrayed by an older colleague when he wouldn't hack refugee charities. Played Rivers in *Richard III*.

CALIBAN: Leggs. About thirty. Mixed background, Irish and black. Red hair, freckles, heavy build, works out a lot. A vet, was in Afghanistan. Veterans Affairs failed to pay for PTSD treatment. *Conviction*: Break-and-enter, assault. Drugs- and booze-related. Was in addiction treatment but the program's been cancelled. Played Brutus, Second Witch, Clarence. Excellent actor but touchy. (Atwood 2016a, 133–134)

As in Extract 5.6, these seemingly more individual profiles become generic in their formulaic constructions and in the type of attributed details listed. Felix's descriptions in his list again rely on schematic categorisation processes. Proper names and nicknames in stories serve a referential function to help readers track characters through time, but they can also provide rich background knowledge for characters (Dancygier 2011). The aliases the prisoners have selected double up as aptronyms relaying details of their crimes. '8Handz' seems appropriate as an alias, for example, given that hacking and forgery form part of his convictions (see Chapter 1 for further discussion of hands, agency and authorship in Atwood's writing). Their 'group member-ship categories' (Culpeper 2001) are identified by Felix first in these profiles: their physical appearance ('slight build', 'Red hair, freckles, heavy build'), their approximate ages, and their nationality and race ('East Indian', 'Mixed background, Irish and black'). Details that suggest their dispositions are also documented as part of the 'personal categories' (Culpeper 2001) to which they belong ('Very bright', 'Excellent actor but touchy'). Where the char-acters are rounded with additional details that might partly mitigate their convictions or actions, this empathetic alignment is based on brief and unde-veloped backstories. 8Handz was 'Betrayed by an older colleague when he wouldn't hack refugee charities', while Leggs 'Was in addiction treatment but the program's been cancelled'. Though it is argued that '[a]s soon as the involved minds are 'labeled', attributes can accumulate' (van Duijn et al. 2015, 154–155), Felix's assessment of the prisoners continues to note their singular qualities in ways that homogenises them, solidifying their depiction as secondary, 'background' characters (Harvey 1965).[7]

The prisoners are described only in relation to Felix and what they contribute to his performance. They are, functionally, his 'agents of retribu-tion' (Muñoz-Valdivieso 2017, 112). As the rehearsals for the play continue, the totalising experience of the performance inflects Felix's description of the prisoners further, as can be observed in his concern about the cast's lack of cooperation later in the story (Extract 5.7):

Extract 5.7

> Gremlins conspire against him. There have been two defections among the minor Goblins, though he talked one of them back. Another Goblin's in the infirmary with an unspecified injury: some sort of payback involving a nail file, Leggs told him, "nothing to do with any of us". (Atwood 2016a, 152)

Felix's labelling of the prisoners as 'Gremlins' and 'minor Goblins' here suggests that his experience of the magical world of the play is beginning to seep into his impressions of reality. Compared to the more specific marked reference to Peter Pan's 'lost boys' of Extract 5.5, these noun phrases evoke a more generic FAIRY TALE template that sustains his fantastical perspective. Earlier, he mentions that 'everyone in our play will have two roles: their own role and one of Prospero's goblins'; and that these will be 'played by whoever wasn't already onstage in that scene' (131). The labelling of the misbehaving prisoners here as 'minor Goblins' more fully designates their 'offstage' roles.

Finally, to close the course, Felix asks the actors to deliver a 'last assignment' (243); 'presentations on the post-play lives' (246) of the characters, delivered by each of the character 'teams':

Extract 5.8

"This is the report of Team Ariel," he says, "which is me, WonderBoy, Shiv, PPod, and Hotwire. We did it together. We all put in some ideas. You guys rock," he says to his teammates.

"We were supposed to figure out what happens to your team's main guy after the end of the play. So, our team's guy is Ariel. I know we all said at the beginning he's an alien from outer space, but we changed our minds. Like Mr. Duke said, this play is about changing your mind, from revenge to forgiveness, because despite the crap they did, he feels sorry for the bad guys and what they've been put through, once they've suffered enough, so we take it that's okay – to change our minds." (Atwood 2016a, 247)

8Handz's report in Extract 5.8 summarises the views of 'Team Ariel'. Felix's assignation of the prisoners as character teams creates additional polyvocality and contributes to the Chorus-like classification identified by Nancy in Table 5.5. In classical theatre, the Chorus has multiple functions which include setting the mood including adding 'dynamic energy' to the narrative, in some cases 'giving advice to characters', and setting up an 'ethical [...] framework' for the story (Brockett and Hildy 2008, 19–20). They can also contribute summarising, lyrical interludes (Jung 2014); and indeed, the *Hag-Seed* prisoners frequently contribute rap numbers to the performance. While in a broader sense the prison, and the prisoners by extension, are regarded as the social context for the text (Jayendran 2020), here they also provide a moral reflection on the story. Significantly, in the closing discussions of the play (Extract 4.8), they model Prospero's mind on behalf of the (reading) audience; emphasising how, despite appearances, ultimately it is likely that 'he feels sorry for the bad guys' (Budelmann and Easterling 2010, 297). In this way, the assignment, and Team Ariel's contribution towards it, underscores its ethical position ('this play is about changing your mind, from revenge to forgiveness') in a reflective, and partly wall-breaking, manner. It collectively summarises the group's shared, intermental review ('We did it together'), while critically and metatextually reflecting on the themes of the intertext.

5.5 'Artistic immersion'

The final marker of Felix's mind style considered in this chapter is how the THEATRE frame is manifested in his apparent misreporting of events and situations, and particularly in his interactions with and conceptualisation of the ghost of his late daughter, Miranda. In the extract from the group discussion in Table 5.6, The ABC Club readers consider *Felix's unreliability* in further detail and discuss to what extent it is signposted in other characters' responses. In particular, they reflect on the early episode where Tony terminates Felix's contract as Artistic Director of the Makeshiweg Festival (Extract 5.4) and orders security to wait outside:

The readers question whether the choice to have security can be interpreted as a 'comment on the character' (Angela, turn 1), suggesting that there is a general expectation that Felix 'was gonna go mental' (Olivia, turn 9). The choice to appoint security suggests an event in the backstory or a character trait that Felix does not provide within the text. Angela speculates, for example, on whether his boss has 'gently been trying to break this to him for quite a while' (turn 1). Here, Felix's version of events is categorised as a potential 'underreporting' (Phelan 2007) of the full context of what happened. In this exchange, the readers move beyond the perspective of Felix, and the explanation of the events that he has offered, to mind-model the choices of the other characters. This mind-modelling is apparent in Olivia's comment in turn 7, where she says 'actually they were just like if he goes ahead with this production it's gonna ruin us'. The framing of this comment demonstrates a 'psychological projection' (Lahey 2003, 2005) into the text. The change in pronoun (it's gonna like ruin *us*', emphasis added) performs Olivia's reaction from the same shared position as Felix's adversaries.

The accumulation of situations of this nature within *Hag-Seed* has led the readers to summarise that, ultimately, 'there were a lot of concrete things that you can point to in the text where [Atwood] is sort of saying like don't make maybe this guy's account is like super accurate or reliable' (Olivia, Table 5.7, turn 7). Other evidence is drawn on to support this interpretation. They query the extent to which his response to being fired is disproportional ('is it like go and sit for a shack for nine years shit', turn 1), the apparent and unquestioned ease with which he was recognised and given a job nine years later (Table 5.7, turn 5), and Tony's decision to hide the 'odd complaint' from him (Table 5.7, turn 9), against their own standards of appropriate behaviour. Finally, they also acknowledge those moments where Felix professes his own unreliability. Olivia comments, for example, that 'there were a few bits where it's like a little bit late on and he's just like oh you know now I look back on it

Table 5.6 Felix's unreliability

1	Angela	And yeah like as well they do get rid of him in like they don't get rid of him in like a measured way they had the security outside the door which is like does that comment on the character that he is that they need that or that or is it just like that they are orchestrating a bit like you know you're like yeah how bad has it been or for how long or what has he been up to or like have they gently been trying to break this to him for quite a while
2	Stella	Yeah but it was a bit shit like writing the sort not in the middle of the production but he wasn't really
3	Angela	Yeah
4	Stella	The production was under way wasn't it that seems that also seems a bit unrealistic really 'cause then you got a
5	Olivia	Well does it though unless it was about the production and he'd been trying to tell him not to do stuff and actually they were just like if he goes ahead with this production it's gonna like ruin us
6	Stella	Fair enough
7	Olivia	So you so actually like that is sort of it just I do think there were a lot like of concrete things that you can point to in the text where she is sort of saying like don't make maybe this guy's account is like super accurate or reliable
8	Jane	Could you um
9	Olivia	Why would you have the security outside the door if you didn't know he was gonna go mental which he promptly did
10	Jane	I didn't know why at the end when he'd got his revenge why they agreed to it cuz if he released that video footage that's evidence that he'd drugged them all and like surely then he'd be in trouble and not the politicians
11	Angela	Oh I think he found this complete thing like doesn't work
12	Nancy	Why didn't they jump out of the window[8]
13	Stella	Yeah
14	Olivia	Why didn't they jump out of the window
15	Stella	I don't know I feel like yeah saying you're gonna murder people is probably
16	Nancy	Yeah I agree I don't think there's much
17	Stella	Worse than giving someone some grapes

I did go a bit over the top sometimes well not actually sometimes like maybe a lot' (turn 9). All these examples are ones that researchers note as playing a role in characterisation and in building unreliability. The reactions of other characters can impact on conceptualisations of character (Stockwell 2020, 179), while self-referential comments and explicit discussions of a narrator's own believability are listed by researchers as a significant textual cue of unreliability (Nünning 1997; Olsen 2003, 98).

As narratological research has identified, 'the general effect of what is called unreliable narration consists of redirecting the reader's attention from the level of the story to the speaker and of foregrounding peculiarities of the narrator's psychology' (Nünning 1997, 88). This is particularly apparent in Felix's description and hallucination of his late daughter, Miranda, which is mentioned in The ABC Club conversation (Table 5.7, turn 7) and returned to elsewhere in the book group's reflections.

Table 5.7 Character reactions to Felix

1	Olivia	They all knew they all were like the gobliny things like the book I think it is really interesting and maybe this is some sort of like clever comment when she was like actually he wasn't a great guy because like they thought it was to do with continuing the programme right not his weird like vengeance on them which like I also felt like right they were a bit shit to him like pushing him out of his job but is it like go and sit in a shack for nine years shit like I get why his [inaudible wife has recently died]
2	Stella	No absolutely no
3	Olivia	But it was just like that's shit not nine years in a shack shit
4	Stella	It's not like he was you know the [inaudible lighting] director or something or everyone ganged up against him and sacked him or bad-mouthed or anything he was like the artistic director of the entire festival surely he was employable somewhere else quite easily
5	Olivia	Like after nine years he went and spoke to one woman and she recognised him who she was and gave him a job
6	Stella	Yeah yeah
7	Lis	[Inaudible and this goes with] your theory Olivia about his mental breakdown that you know he could have gone off and live you know a normal life but because he had mental issues after that dismissal then it leads him to kind of hallucinating in a shack about his daughter
8	Stella	We've all been there
9	Olivia	And maybe they weren't actually and like yeah I told you this was maybe they actually weren't out to get him at all yeah and there were a few bits where it's a little bit a later on and he's just like oh you know now I look back on it I did go a bit over the top sometimes well not actually sometimes like maybe a lot like I thought that his account of like how well his plays were being received and felt quite unreliable and was like oh yeah there is the odd complaint about you know and Tony deals with when someone gets splattered with blood in the audience or something so maybe it was actually [inaudible]

Extract 5.9 is an illustrative example of an episode in which Felix's interacts with the ghost of his late daughter. The scene describes how he returns home after work to find the house empty, and his search for Miranda.

Extract 5.9

Better to abdicate. Give up his plans for retribution, for restoration. Kiss his former self goodbye. Go quietly into the dark. What has ever accomplished in his life, anyway, beyond a few gaudy hours, a few short-lived triumphs of no importance in the world where most people live? Why did he feel entitled to special consideration from the universe at large?

Miranda doesn't like it when he's depressed. It makes her anxious. Maybe that's why she's rendered herself invisible, though she's usually invisible anyway. Is that her, in the other room? Does he hear a humming? Or is it only the bar fridge?

The bedroom has a medicinal smell, as if someone's been ill in it. An invalid, for a long time. No, she's not in here. Only the photo in its silver frame: the small girl on the swing, frozen in Time's jelly. Visible but not alive.

He switches on the bedside lamp, opens the door of the large armoire. There's his wizard's garment; it's been waiting for him now for a dozen years. Must it go to waste, after all? Its many eyes glint, alive, aware.

"Not yet," he tells his magic animals. "Not quite yet. It is not the hour".

Their hour will be his hour. His vengeful hour. There must be a way he can make it work. Surely he still has a few tricks left.

He moves back into the front room. "Dear one," he says out loud; and there she is, over in the corner. Luckily she's wearing white: she glimmers. What is this fretful energy he's feeling? She's picked up on his worries, and now she's worrying herself.

"There's no harm done," he says. "And there won't be, I promise. I will do nothing but in care of thee."

But what has his care amounted to? He's protected her, true, but hasn't he overdone it? There are so many things he should be able to offer her. She should have what other girls her age take for granted, not that he knows what those things are. Clothes, certainly. Pretty clothes, more clothes than she has at her disposal now. She seems to go around in makeshifts, fabricated out of cheesecloth and old bed sheets. She ought to have silks and velvets, or miniskirts and those tall boots girls these days seem so fond of. She ought to have an iPhone, in a pastel shade. She ought to be painting her nails blue or silver or green, chattering with her friends, listening to music through her pink ear buds. Going to parties.

He's been such a failure as a parent. How can he make it up to her? It's a wonder she isn't sulkier, cooped up here with nobody but her shabby old father; but then, she doesn't know what she's missing. Still, he's been able to teach her a lot of things that most girls her age would never have a chance of learning.

"What have you been up to all day?" he says to her. "Would you like a game of chess?"

Reluctantly – is that reluctance? – she moves to the chess board, set up as usual on the red Formica table.

Black or white? she asks him. (Atwood 2016a, 108–110)

As identified in the analysis in Sect. 5.4.1, a sense of anticipation for the forthcoming performance is similarly established in this extract, such that the shack becomes a stand-in for Felix's green room. He advises his 'magic animals' that the performance is 'Not quite yet. It is not the hour'. As in the rest of the story, Felix's focalised description juxtaposes archaic, theatrical language with more contemporary and prosaic choices. The passage begins with his reflection on whether he should 'abdicate' and '[g]ive up his plans for retribution, for restoration', a process which is interrupted by the presence of more tangible, domestic objects and concerns. He hears a 'humming', for example, that may well be attributed to the 'bar fridge' rather than to anything more spectral. His commentary moves between acknowledging Miranda's continued presence as shadowy and indeterminate, her solidity filtered through uncertain epistemic judgements ('*Maybe* that's why she's rendered herself invisible, though she's *usually* invisible anyway', emphasis added), and presenting her in more concrete, unmodalised terms. The move between the theatrical and the domestic, and linguistic degrees of certainty and uncertainty, suggests the seeping of his delusions into his perception of reality.

Miranda's character and her physical presence is reified through various linguistic means. Felix describes her in immediate, present-tense terms suggesting ongoing, fact-permanence. He states how 'Miranda doesn't like it when he's depressed', and summarises their established habits and the ongoing status quo of their domestic routine (she is '*usually* invisible'; and the chess board is 'set up as *usual* on the formica table', emphasis added). In this description, he mind-models her emotional reaction to his, as he notes that his low mood 'makes her anxious'. The attribution of an emotional response suggests his active and ongoing engagement with her psychological traits. When she does appear, her physical presence is construed categorically ('There she is, over in the corner'). Felix also later confirms that his mind-modelling of her emotional state is accurate. He reflects how 'She's picked up on his worries, now she's worrying herself'; this psychological attribution mirroring his own feelings in this moment.

In Felix's reflections on their family life, he frames his previous care and protection of her as fact, and as something that has taken place over a period of time. Similarly, his thoughts are projected towards the future care of his daughter and through self-recriminations on his role as a father. His commentary on duties are shaded with deontic modality and through expressions relating what he should be doing ('There are so many things he *should* be able to offer her', emphasis added), and what she should be doing or what she ought to be given ('She *ought* to have silks and velvets', 'She *ought* to have an iPhone', 'She *ought* to be painting her nails', emphasis added). In these descriptions Felix schematically builds a rounded profile for Miranda based on his perception of what a prototypical teenager has and does ('chattering with her friends, listening to music through her pink ear buds. Going to parties'). This profile anachronistically clashes with his more archaic conceptualisation of her, however. His direct speech verbally addresses her in Shakespearean language ('I will do nothing but in care of thee'), and he imagines her as 'wearing makeshifts, fabricated out of cheesecloth and old bed sheets'. Though he acknowledges that she 'ought to have an iPhone', he asks her if she would like a game of chess. Notable, too, are the colours that he references in the list of hypothetical scenarios. In her more immediate but ghostly form he perceives Miranda as wearing 'white', but as part of the idealised, real-world scenario he sketches out, she would be rendered in richer and more varied colours, in 'a pastel shade', in 'blue or silver or green' and 'pink'.

While these choices characterise Miranda and confirm her continued presence in Felix's thoughts, her impermanence is also and simultaneously suggested, primarily through the epistemic modality expressing Felix's uncertainty. His assessment is subjectified through *verba sentiendi* that mark the potential fallibility of his perceptions. He questions his 'feeling', though frames some of his reflections with high certitude ('Certainly'), and generally acknowledge being at the mercy of external forces of fortune bestowed by 'the universe at large' ('Luckily'). These judgements are additionally rendered through language of estrangement which distance him from the judgements he raises. For example, he reflects on how she '*seems* to go around in makeshifts', and also assesses that the 'bedroom has a medicinal smell, *as if* someone's been ill in it' (emphases added). He further acknowledges his own lack of knowledge about 'girls her age', as he admits 'not that he knows what those things are'. The high number of rhetorical questions additionally contribute to the impression of his lack of conviction. At the same time, he also partly answers the questions he raises: 'What is this fretful energy he's feeling? She's picked up on his worries, and now she's worrying herself'. In this way, his inner monologue becomes framed as a back-and-forth conversational exchange with himself, a habit established from the very beginning of the story (see Extract 5.1). With the absence of an explicit addressee, he models both parts of the conversational exchange, echoing the hypothetical conversation he has with Miranda. Finally, though Miranda is attributed with free direct speech at the end of the extract, unlike Felix's speech, her words are not enclosed in inverted commas and appear instead in their freest form ('Black or white? She asks him'). The idiomatic suggestion of Miranda's question, 'Black or white', is also suggestive within this context. As The ABC Club readers commented, it is clear that Felix does not see the world in black and white terms.

Other thematic and metaphorical suggestions contribute to the blurring between Felix's perceptions of fact and fiction. The theme of dark and light, and the metaphorical associations this contrast holds, is apparent throughout Extract 5.9. In reference to giving up on his plans for retribution at the beginning of the passage, for example, Felix reflects on how he might 'Go quietly into the dark'. In this conceptualisation, the darkness represents an enveloping CONTAINER which is othered from 'the world where most people live' and which, in contrast, comprises brightness: 'a few gaudy hours'. Associations of visibility are also referenced in this scene. Though normally 'invisible', Miranda's appearance in the room is visibly noticeable, 'wearing white: she glimmers'. This visual description mirrors Felix's earlier observation of his 'wizard's garment', which is made of plush animal toys, and whose 'many eyes glint, alive, aware'. Finally, and significantly, Felix also differentiates between and doubles versions of both himself and Miranda. When he opens the bedroom door, for instance, he observes how it 'has a medicinal smell, as if someone's been ill in it. An invalid, for a long time'. The vague perception of 'someone' who is an 'invalid' disassociates the room from his possession, as if it belongs to someone else. This is an interpretation supported in the SPLIT SELF metaphor (Lakoff 1993, 1996) he draws on earlier in Extract 5.9 to describe how he might 'Kiss his former self goodbye'. This disassociation of self can also be seen in his conceptualisation of Miranda. When he enters the bedroom, he confirms that 'she's not in here', but references the presence of 'the photo in its silver frame: the small girl on the swing, frozen in Time's jelly. Visible but not alive'. Here Felix construes 'the small girl' as a separate being; a mirrored version of the ghost daughter with whom he interacts, who is alive but invisible.

In summary, the combined metaphors and the shifting style choices of modality, perception and speech presentation both reify and abstract Felix's conceptualisation of Miranda. These stylistic choices combine to establish the theatrical delusion which dominates his perspective and which, in turn, invites reader assessment of the extent of his unreliability, further enacting the 'artistic immersion' (233) and duplicity inherent in his mind style.

5.6 'A con man playing an actor. A double unreality'

This chapter has explored the stylistic representation of Felix's mind style in *Hag-Seed*. The recentring of the text on his voice and perspective places him as driver of the narrative, and a prominent part of readers' experiences of the story. His mind style is manifested in the blurring of illusion and reality he displays, for example, in the potential misreporting of events and in his interactions with his late daughter, Miranda. Further, his homogeneous characterisation of the prisoners confirms his perception of their secondary, functional roles as 'Prospero's goblins' within his acting troupe. Stylistic choices of characterisation within the text establish mind-modelling processes as a significant part of the experience of reading the novel. Collectively, these style choices establish a THEATRE frame through which Felix's perspective is filtered, foregrounding both the original dramatic mode of the text and sustaining the play's thematic focus on illusions (Atwood 2016b) within this prose recasting.

Notes

1. Chapter 1 provides a more detailed overview of the reader data used in this book.
2. *The Curious Incident of the Dog in the Night-Time* (Haddon 2003) is a text which has, incidentally, undergone the reverse adaptation to *Hag-Seed*, first published as a prose novel and then adapted to a stage play.
3. Given the musicality of *Hag-Seed* and the high number of rap songs it features, reading this novel via audiobook likely engendered a different engagement with the story. Unfortunately, exploration of the musicality of the text is beyond the scope of this chapter, though discussions of the rap choices are discussed elsewhere in the literary criticism (see, e.g., Howells 2017).

4. "Okay, you don't like Prospero," says Felix. "And there are some reasons why you wouldn't. We'll talk about that later" (Atwood 2016a, 121).
5. This contrasts with the argument put forward by critic Jayendran (2020), who argues that the prison space contextualises the text's exploration of creativity and agency.
6. It is notable, too, that Angela and Jane both conflate the names 'Felix' and 'Prospero' in the amalgam 'Filo' (turns 6 and 8, Table 5.4).
7. The backgrounding of the prisoners as secondary characters within the retelling is another duplicitous choice. Despite his reference in the title of this retelling, Caliban, 'Leggs', is not the main character or the focus of the adaptation (Charlebois 2023, 112).
8. This phrase recurs in The ABC Club reading group discourse and is used as shorthand by the readers to reference overlooked plot holes in stories. It relates to an event in a previously read book where it was unclear why a group of characters did not, in fact, just 'jump out of the window' to escape their untimely demise.

References

Atwood, Margaret. 2005. *The Penelopiad*. London: Canongate Books.
Atwood, Margaret. 2016a. *Hag-Seed*. London: Penguin.
Atwood, Margaret. 2016b. A perfect storm: Margaret Atwood on rewriting Shakespeare's *The tempest*. https://www.theguardian.com/books/2016/sep/24/margaret-atwood-rewriting-shakespeare-tempest-hagseed. Accessed 19 April 2023.
Bray, Joe. 2021. Modern retellings of Jane Austen. In *Narrative retellings: Stylistic approaches*, ed. Marina Lambrou, 77–92. London: Bloomsbury.
Brockett, Oscar G., and Franklin J. Hildy. 2008. *History of the theatre*, 10th ed. Boston: Pearson.
Budelmann, Felix, and Pat Easterling. 2010. Reading minds in Greek tragedy. *Greece and Rome* 57 (2): 289–303.
Charlebois, Elizabeth H. 2023. Prospero in prison: Adaptation and appropriation in Margaret Atwood's *Hag-Seed*. In *Shakespeare and cultural appropriation*, ed. Vanessa I. Corredera, L. Monique Pittman, and Geoffrey Way, 112–129. London: Routledge.
Culpeper, Jonathan. 2001. *Language and characterisation: People in plays and other texts*. London: Routledge.
Dancygier, Barbara. 2011. Modification and constructional blends in the use of proper names. *Constructions and Frames* 3 (2): 208–235.
Fowler, Roger. 1977. *Linguistics and the novel*. London: Methuen.

Furlong, Anne. 2021. Adapting *Pride and prejudice*: Stylistic choices as communicative acts. In *Narrative retellings: Stylistic perspectives*, ed. Marina Lambrou, 45–60. London: Bloomsbury.

Frye, Northrop. 1957. *Anatomy of criticism: Four essays*. Princeton, NJ: Princeton University Press.

Giovanelli, Marcello. 2018. 'Something happened, something bad': Blackouts, uncertainties and event construal in *The girl on the train. Language and Literature* 27 (1): 38–51.

Gray, Heather, Kurt Gray, and Daniel M. Wegner. 2007. Dimensions of mind perception. *Science* 315: 619.

Groskop, Viv. 2016. *Hag-Seed* review: Margaret Atwood turns *The Tempest* into a perfect storm. https://www.theguardian.com/books/2016/oct/16/hag-seed-rev iew-margaret-atwood-tempest-hogarth-shakespeare. Accessed 19 April 2023.

Halliday, Michael A.K.. 1971. Linguistic function and literary style: An inquiry into the language of William Golding's *The inheritors*. In *Literary style: A symposium*, ed. Seymour Chatman, 330–368. Oxford: Oxford University Press.

Harrison, Chloe. 2017. Finding Elizabeth: Construing memory in *Elizabeth is missing* by Emma Healey. *Journal of Literary Semantics* 46 (2): 131–151.

Harrison, Chloe. 2023. 99 ways to retell a story: Forms and functions of narrator reconstrual. *Style* 57 (2): 163–185.

Harrison, Chloe, and Louise Nuttall. 2021. Rereading as retelling: Re-evaluations of perspective in narrative fiction'. In *Narrative retellings: Stylistic approaches*, ed. Marina Lambrou, 217–234. London: Bloomsbury.

Harvey, William J. 1965. *Character and the novel*. London: Chatto and Windus.

Howells, Coral. 2017. True trash: Genre fiction revisited in Margaret Atwood's *Stone Mattress, The heart goes last* and *Hag-Seed. Contemporary Women's Writing* 11 (3): 297–315.

Jacobson, Howard. 2016. *Shylock is my name: The merchant of Venice retold*. London: Hogarth.

Jayendran, Nishebvita. 2020. 'Set me free': Spaces and the politics of creativity in Margaret Atwood's *Hag-Seed. Journal of Language, Literature, and Culture* 67 (1): 15–27.

Jeffries, Lesley, and Daniel McIntyre. 2010. *Stylistics*. Cambridge: Cambridge University Press.

Jung, Susanne. 2014. 'A chorus line': Margaret Atwood's *Penelopiad* at the crossroads of narrative, poetic and dramatic genres. *Connotations* 24 (1): 41–62.

Lahey, Ernestine. 2003. Seeing the forest for the trees in Al Purdy's 'trees at the arctic circle'. *BELL: Belgian Journal of Language and Literatures* 1: 73–83.

Lahey, Ernestine. 2005. Text-world landscapes and English Canadian national identity in the poetry of Al Purdy, Milton Acorn and Alden Nowlan. Unpublished PhD thesis, University of Nottingham, UK.

Lakoff, George. 1993. The contemporary theory of metaphor. In *Metaphor and thought*, 2nd ed., ed. Andrew Ortony, 202–251. Cambridge: Cambridge University Press.

Lakoff, George. 1996. Sorry, I'm not myself today: The metaphor system for conceptualizing the self. In *Spaces, worlds and grammars*, ed. Gilles Fauconnier and Eve Sweetser, 91–123. Chicago: University of Chicago Press.

Langacker, Ronald W. 2008. *Cognitive grammar: A basic introduction*. Oxford: Oxford University Press.

Leech, Geoffrey. 1992. Pragmatic principles in Shaw's *You never can tell*. In *Language, text and context: Essays in stylistics*, ed. Michael Toolan, 259–278. London: Routledge.

Leech, Geoffrey, and Michael H. Short. 1981. *Style in fiction*. London: Longman.

Mason, Jessica. 2019. *Intertextuality in practice*. Amsterdam: John Benjamins.

McIntyre, Dan, and Dawn E. Archer. 2010. A corpus-based approach to mind style. *Journal of Literary Semantics* 39 (2): 167–182.

Muñoz-Valdivieso, Sofia. 2017. Shakespeare our contemporary in 2016: Margaret Atwood's rewriting of *The tempest* in *Hag-Seed*. *Sederi* 27: 105–129.

Nünning, Ansgar. 1997. 'But why will you say that I am mad?' On the theory, history, and signals of unreliable narration in British Fiction. *AAA: Arbeiten aus Anglistik und Amerikanistik* 22 (1): 83–105.

Nuttall, Louise. 2015. Attributing minds to vampires in Richard Matheson's *I am legend*. *Language and Literature* 24 (1): 23–39.

Nuttall, Louise. 2018. *Mind style and cognitive grammar: Language and worldview in speculative fiction*. London: Bloomsbury.

Olsen, Greta. 2003. Reconsidering unreliability: Fallible and untrustworthy narrators. *Narrative* 11 (1): 93–109.

Palmer, Alan. 2004. *Fictional minds*. Nebraska: University of Nebraska Press.

Phelan, James. 2007. Estranging unreliability, bonding unreliability, and the ethics of *Lolita*. *Narrative* 15 (2): 222–238.

Rundquist, Eric. 2020a. The cognitive grammar of drunkenness: Consciousness representation in *Under the Volcano*. *Language and Literature* 29 (1): 39–56.

Rundquist, Eric. 2020b. Literary meaning as character conceptualization: Reorienting the cognitive stylistic analysis of character discourse and free indirect thought. *Journal of Literary Semantics* 49 (2): 143–165.

Sanders, Julie. 2016. *Adaptation and appropriation*. London: Routledge.

Schneider, Ralf. 2001. Toward a cognitive theory of literary character: The dynamics of mental model construction. *Style* 35 (4): 607–639.

Semino, Elena. 2007. Mind style 25 years on. *Style* 41 (2): 153–173.

Semino, Elena. 2014a. Pragmatic failure, mind style and characterisation in fiction about autism. *Language and Literature* 23 (2): 141–158.

Semino, Elena. 2014b. Language, mind and autism in Mark Haddon's *The curious incident of the dog in the night-time*. In *Linguistics and literary studies*, 279–303. Berlin: De Gruyter.

Short, Mick. 1989. Discourse analysis and the analysis of drama. In *Language, discourse and literature*, ed. Ron Carter and Paul Simpson, 139–168. London: Unwin Hyman.

Smeets, Roel. 2021. *Character constellations: Representations of social groups in present day Dutch literary fiction*. Leuven University Press.

Stockwell, Peter. 2009. *Texture: A cognitive aesthetics of reading*. Edinburgh: Edinburgh University Press.

Stockwell, Peter. 2020. *Cognitive poetics: An introduction*, 2nd ed. London: Routledge.

Stockwell, Peter. 2022. Mind-modelling literary personas. *Journal of Literary Semantics* 51 (2): 131–146.

Stockwell, Peter, and Michaela Mahlberg. 2015. Mind-modelling with corpus stylistics in *David Copperfield*. *Language and Literature* 24 (2): 129–147.

The ABC Club. 2022. Transcribed book group discussion.

Tyler, Anne. 2016. *Vinegar girl: The taming of the shrew Retold*. London: Hogarth.

Van Duijn, Max J., Ineke Sluiter, and Arie Verhagen. 2015. When narrative takes over: The representation of embedded mindstates in Shakespeare's *Othello*. *Language and Literature* 24 (2): 148–166.

Van Peer, Willie, and Henk Pander Maat. 2001. Narrative perspective and the interpretation of characters' motives. *Language and Literature* 10 (3): 229–241.

Werth, Paul. 1999. *Text-worlds: Representing conceptual space in discourse*. Harlow: Longman.

Winterson, Jeanette. 2015. *The gap of time: The winter's tale retold*. London: Hogarth.

Zajac, Paul J. 2020. Prisoners of Shakespeare: Trauma and adaptation in Atwood's *Hag-Seed*. *Studies in the Novel* 52 (3): 324–343.

Zunshine, Lisa. 2006. *Why we read fiction: Theory of mind and the novel*. Columbus: The Ohio State University Press.

Part III

Doubling and Splitting

6

Double Consciousness and Speculative Worlds in *Oryx and Crake*

6.1 Introduction: 'Not real can tell us about real'

As a genre, speculative fiction can be differentiated from science fiction in its concern with human rather than technological problems, and in its exclusive focus on possible futures (Gadpaille 2018), on the psychological effects of these forecast physical and cultural environments (Nuttall 2018, 9) and, significantly, in its eschewal of Martians (Atwood 2011a, 6). *Oryx and Crake* (Atwood 2003) presents a possible future where a lone survivor, Snowman, watches over the new species of humans and animals that have survived, and reflects on the physical, cultural, and technological events that led to the demise of the world. Like other speculative texts, and science fiction more generally, *Oryx and Crake* is built on a complex process of conceptual comparison. The layering and blending of world representations is regarded as characteristic of the genre, which is acknowledged by Atwood (2011b) in her own critical reflections on speculative fiction as a type of 'ustopia'. Blending utopia and dystopia, the term captures 'the imagined perfect society and its opposite—because in [her] view, each contains a latent version of the other' (Atwood 2011b).

This chapter explores the interaction between the latent worlds that make up *Oryx and Crake* (Atwood 2003). Set in a post-apocalyptic near-future, this latency is cued up in the novel's creation of text-worlds and the continued and layered processes of conceptual comparison it engenders. Through stylistic analysis of reader reviews and of key extracts from the opening and the

© The Author(s), under exclusive license to Springer Nature
Switzerland AG 2024
C. Harrison, *The Language of Margaret Atwood*, Palgrave Studies in Language, Literature
and Style, https://doi.org/10.1007/978-3-031-67640-6_6

close of the novel, this chapter argues that the readerly experience of plausibility and the resonant effects of reading, as suggested through lingering *what if* questions noted by the reviewers, is invited by the 'double consciousness' (Snyder 2011, 470) inherent in speculative text-world creation. As in Chapter 2 of this book, the text analysis of the beginning and end of the novel is contextualised alongside naturalistic reader data comprising 100 reviews collected from the open-access reader review website, Goodreads. This reader dataset was coded for recurring topics and themes. All reviewers are anonymised and referred to as OC1–OC100 within this chapter.[1]

6.2   *Oryx and Crake* as Speculative Fiction

Oryx and Crake presents a speculative future in which a man-made plague has nearly wiped out humankind. This novel is the first of the *Maddaddam* trilogy, which follows the lives of different characters in this post-apocalyptic world. The third-person narration features Snowman, who is initially introduced as the sole survivor of the pandemic. He is living alongside a group called 'the Crakers', who are the 'floor models' (135) of bio-engineered humans. Through a series of flashbacks, Snowman recounts his former life (as 'Jimmy') and the events that led up to apocalypse. It is revealed that Jimmy was friends with Crake, who synthesised a deadly viral pathogen and distributed it among the population via BlyssPluss pills, advertised as something that increased libido and prolonged life, and yet also sterilised the user. As part of his Paradice project, Crake designed the Crakers and brought in Jimmy to help run the advertising campaign. Both Crake and Jimmy have a relationship with the elusive Oryx, who helps teach the Crakers about the world around them. In the present day, Snowman is forced to return to Paradice, the dome where the Crakers were first created, due to running low on supplies. This proves to be a difficult journey, as Snowman is forced to navigate the perils and dangers of this new world, including pursuit by killer animal splices such as woolvogs and the concerningly intelligent pigoons, and the threat that an infected cut might pose on his chances of survival. The two parallel timelines progressively converge: as Snowman reaches the Paradice complex in the present, he recalls the day that Crake unleashed the virus. Snowman returns to the Crakers at the shore and sees a small group of other human survivors. At the end of this first novel, his fate remains uncertain.

The storytelling is driven by 'unfinished business' (Atwood 2011, 94), raising questions relating to consumerism, environmentalism, and the impact of developing technologies on our everyday lives. Atwood's on-record labelling of the series as 'speculative' has invited debates within the literary criticism about its classification and associated labels of dystopia, utopia, science fiction and the Anthropocene (e.g., Thomas 2013; Glover 2009; Winstead 2017). In an article pairing and comparing *Oryx and Crake* with *The Handmaid's Tale*, Atwood (2004, 513; see also Laflen 2009) describes a heated exchange on a recent radio show where she renounced her position as a science fiction writer, and caused upset within the community for winning the *Arthur C. Clarke Award for Science Fiction.* She goes on to describe her response:

> I said I liked to make a distinction between science fiction proper – for me, this label denotes books with things in them we can't do yet or begin to do, talking beings we can never meet, and places we can't go – and speculative fiction, which employs the means already more or less to hand, and takes place on Planet Earth.

In Atwood's view, speculative fiction ruminates on 'the consequences of new and proposed technologies in graphic ways by showing them as fully operational' (2011a, 62). Through an exploration of the key themes and questions related to the impact of new technologies, social organisation and issues of humanity within science fiction more widely, and speculative fiction more specifically, she argues that this genre is closer to romance rather than it is to social realism (Atwood 2004, 515–516). The social commentary that makes up the 'half prediction, half satire' (Le Guin 2009) blend of these stories occludes more prototypical interpretations of the 'romance' genre, however. As one Goodreads reviewer notes, quoting from the blurb:

> **Oryx and Crake is at once an unforgettable love story and a compelling vision of the future.**
> Even the book description is complete satire. If you read the book expecting this, you will read a very grim story. (O41; original emphasis)

6.2.1 Speculative Fiction in Stylistics: Alternativity and Comparison

While all literary texts are said to generate defamiliarisation through a process of 'making strange' familiar subjects (Shklovsky 1965), the psychological experience and effects of defamiliarisation are particularly heightened and powerful in reading speculative fiction (Nuttall 2018). Speculative fiction invites readers to conceptualise worlds which are recognisable, and yet simultaneously defamiliarised and estranged from their own reality (Suvin 1979). This magnified sense of defamiliarisation can be traced, in part, to the continuous conceptual comparison invited by the genre. As Snyder (2011, 470) observes,

> In order to grasp the caution offered by the tale, we must see the imagined future actual present and also recognize the difference between now and the future-as-imagined. Thus, the reader of such fiction must sustain a kind of *double consciousness* with respect both to the fictionality of the world portrayed to its potential as our own world's future. (emphasis added)

Stockwell's (2000) research on the *Poetics of Science Fiction* similarly describes this double consciousness as a process of comparison, arguing that '[s]ince every science fictional text (by definition) has an element of alternativity about it which differentiates it from our reality, any reading of a science fiction narrative involves an act of generic isomorphism between the real world and the text world' (185). It could be argued that this act of comparison is further layered in the context of post-apocalyptic narratives, a category into which *Oryx and Crake* also falls. When reading post-apocalyptic texts, Caracciolo (2018, 226) describes a type of 'double vision' and mental juxtaposition in that readers will automatically be primed to consider the *pre*-apocalyptic state of the fictional world (which, depending on the text under consideration, may also be 'othered' from the reader's current reality). In short, and as Norledge (2021, 43) argues, '[d]ystopian worlds are therefore purposefully refracted, depicting events and places that are necessarily recognisable yet fundamentally different to our own in one or more meaningful ways'.

Contemporary stylistic analyses of speculative and dystopian fiction have explored how processes of defamiliarisation and conceptual alternativity are generated through responses to character world view, impacting, for example, how readers mind-model a character's ethical choices (Norledge 2021, 2022), or how they may experience a character's mind style (Nuttall 2018). When readers experience defamiliarisation in a text, it is suggested that this also invites a process of refamiliarisation: 'an intra and/or extra textual revision or re-evaluation in order to discern, delimit or develop the novel meanings suggested by the foregrounded passages' (Miall and Kuiken 1994, 394). It invites an interactive process of 'feedback oscillation' (Suvin 1979), whereby the reader draws on their experience and understanding of their real-world situation in order to interact with the dystopian fictional world presented within the text. In stylistics research, this processes of refamiliarisation and comparison can be best explored through an application of Text World Theory.

6.3   Text World Theory

Text World Theory is a cognitive stylistic framework premised on the container metaphor, the TEXT IS A WORLD. While Atwood has conceptualised writing in cartographic terms (Chapter 1, Sect. 1.3.2), readers also frequently draw on this metaphor to frame reading experiences. A search through the reader datasets which form the basis of the analyses across this book, for example, reveals that this metaphor frames readers' metaphorical movement into and through a text:

> I remember stopping a little after reading this first sentence and preparing myself for the immensely melancholic world that this book was going to immerse me into. (BA95)

> We begin in a post-apocalyptic world, barren and seemingly unpopulated except for sheet-clad protagonist Snowman and a group of naked, multi-hued green-eyed beings called the Children of Crake. (OC22)

First devised by Paul Werth in 1999 and later expanded by Joanna Gavins in 2007, Text World Theory is one of the most widely applied cognitive stylistic frameworks. While other cognitive stylistic models offer adjacent apparatus for discourse-level analyses (e.g., possible worlds theory [Ryan 1991]; contextual frame theory [Emmott 1997]), Text World Theory aligns with the principles of cognitive linguistics to prioritise reader experience as an interactive, negotiated and embodied process (Gavins and Lahey 2016). Following these principles, Text World Theory outlines reading as an embodied experience that is attenuated from real-world interactions, with readers conceptualising and responding to world-building details—characters, objects and settings—using the same cognitive processes as in real-world life (see Chapter 5, Sect. 5.3).

Text World Theory divides the discourse architecture of reading into three superordinate levels. The first world encountered by readers is called the discourse-world. This world comprises all facets of the context of the communicative exchange between authors and readers. Any discourse event comprises at least two co-participants: a speaker or writer, and a hearer or listener. In spoken discourse, it is likely that the discourse-world context will be shared between speaker and listener. When I bought an ice tea at a café earlier this afternoon, for example, I shared the same discourse-world context as the barista. My request for a drink was spoken and heard instantaneously, and details of the setting were also shared, both in terms of time (lunch time on a sunny day in July 2022, during a heat wave), and physical location (a busy café in South London). Within the context of reading, the act of communication is spatiotemporally divided in that the act of writing takes place at an earlier stage in time than the act of reading. It is also likely that the physical context in which a reader engages with the text will be very different from the setting in which the text was written. In some cases, this division or 'split' (Gavins 2007, 26) in time and space can be more distal than proximal. The discourse-world of any reading event is individual and dynamic, changing and evolving according to each reader's experiential baggage, set of knowledge schemata and contextual situation of reading.

When readers begin reading, the text-world describes reader's mental and dynamic conceptualisation of the content of the narrative. All text and linguistic choices encode information about the way the text-world will be built up and developed. This information can be grouped according to 'world-builders', which describe the entities—the objects, the characters—that populate the world, and key facts regarding the time and location of the narrative event. 'Function-advancers' are verb phrases describing the action within the world, and which therefore serve to advance and progress the plot in some way. World-building and function-advancing information combine to flesh out the text-world and cue up key inferential processing in readers' minds. Importantly, this information is 'text-driven': readers' background knowledge and schemata are activated when cued through specific choices of language. This principle of text-drivenness 'provides a manageable route into the systematic examination of context by acting as a control valve on the massive sum of personal knowledge which each participant carries with them to the discourse-world' (Gavins 2007, 29); a way of constraining and directing reader interpretation such that only those relevant and meaningful schemas are activated. As Gavins and Lahey (2016, 1) summarise, '[l]anguage thus provides a blueprint for the imagination, a set of textual prompts that allows human beings to build rich conceptual models of their own reality and alternative realities'.

To see how these concepts work in text analysis, consider this six-word story:

Longed for him. Got him. Shit. (Atwood 2006)

Though minimal, this text comprises details that enable readers to conceptualise a rich text-world. Like in all reading events, the discourse-world context is split in that there is a distance in time and space between Atwood writing this story and me reading it in 2022. Readers can identify the speaker, a first-person enactor, who is discussing another character we know to be male ('him'). According to each reader's own prototypes for romantic relationships, the speaking persona may be female or male. Temporal information is also sketched out: both 'longed for' and 'got' are presented in their past participle forms, suggesting that both events have already occurred outside of the current timeframe. Finally, the expletive 'Shit' reveals the character's negative evaluation of events, confirming that this union is not turning out as expected or hoped.

Different facets of discourse-world knowledge will be cued up by readers to develop interpretations of the story and to fill out and complete the absent or implied parts of the text. For me, this short story reads as a parody of the romance genre, in which typically much of the story is concerned with the key narrative action of a protagonist 'longing' for a particular partner. The 'Shit' spotlights a part of the story that is traditionally not previewed within the romance genre, however: the protagonist's evaluation and what happens after the couple has united. Readers will draw on their own knowledge of relationships and romance schemas to fill out potential reasons for the negative reaction, and to characterise, more richly, the speaker and their situation.

The complexity of more extended literary narratives tends to mean that texts create worlds that shift away from the central text-world encountered, known as the 'matrix' text-world (Gavins 2007, 108). Changes in the parameters of a scene, brought about through linguistic markers denoting a shift in time or space, for example, will generate a 'world-switch' (Gavins 2007, 48) to a text-world populated by new world-building details. To continue the travel metaphor, these worlds are more conceptually remote, inviting readers to travel further into the text re-orientation. Texts may also outline hypothetical or possible scenarios, termed 'modal-worlds' (Gavins 2007).

In reading *Oryx and Crake*, readers enter a split discourse-world which is anchored in the moment of reading, and, at the production end of the tin-can string, Atwood's moment of writing (Chapter 1, Sect. 1.3.3). Notably, many of the reviewers in the data acknowledge this split context of the book, and comment that, despite the time that has elapsed since the text's production, the world it describes feels worryingly familiar and proximal. Within the reader reviews, this resonance forms part of an explicit comparison between the world as represented in the novel and the readers' own. This impression can be observed in the use of first-person plural possessive, 'our', highlighted in the following responses:

Our post-apocalyptic fate will surely be a wonder to behold. (OC10)

Her characters are relatable, their struggles are *our* own, and the outcomes of their decisions have the unintended consequences that *our* own do […] I want to see and feel what that world is there through the filters of this book that presages all of these things about our species that have the potential of going really, horribly wrong. (OC25)

And she does this by showing the horrors that could easily become *our* reality. (OC28)

The story is also about the online world we have created for ourselves. (OC34)

And as far as I can tell, it takes place around the year 2070. That's within *our* lifetimes and that's one of the things that makes it disturbing. (OC42)

The world is well detailed and described, and very much like *our* own. (OC51)

Because the scary thing is…we're already on *our* way to the world Atwood describes in this book. (OC54)

The world feels like *our* own with a few children running on a white beach […] It opens with Snowman, who lives in a world we could easily recognise as being related to *ours*. (OC57)

Interesting perspective on how genetic engineering can destroy *our* reality and turn the world upside down. (OC58)

But there is plenty in it to inspire us to change *our* ways. (OC63)

In these examples, 'our' assumes several referents. Firstly, readers describe the *process of comparison* between the world of the text and their own world, described as 'our reality' (OC28, OC58), 'our own' (OC25, OC51) and being 'related to ours' (OC57). In other examples, they situate themselves collectively alongside the characters within the novel, and in some cases, the reviewers confer collective agency or causation within this shared location. The events presented in the book occur because of 'our ways' (OC63), brought about by the collective situation 'we have created for ourselves' (OC34), suggesting a shared culpability in the generation of our collective 'post-apocalyptic fate' (OC10). These references further suggest that readers are aware of this act of comparison, and actively incrementing it as part of their discourse-world knowledge. This is further indicated by the reviewers' discussion of *plausibility*, which similarly predominates the reviews and which is often paired with readers' 'evaluative feelings' (Miall and Kuiken 2001) of the novel. In their evaluations, reviewers describe the text as being 'scary' (mentioned by 4 reviewers), 'terrifying' (12 reviewers), 'disturbing' (5 reviewers) and 'strange' (9 reviewers). In context, these readers suggest that the worlds are scary and terrifying *because of* the plausibility, and directly mention this connection: 'the story felt scarily plausible' or 'Terrifyingly plausible'. It is this continued intercalation between the text-world and the readers' own world that justifies Atwood's reputation for prophetic storytelling (Mead 2017); her spooky prescience (Allardice 2018).

In a review of literary criticism on speculative fiction, and drawing on the work of particular literary scholars (Delany 2009; Hills 2013; Moylan 2000; Spencer 1983), Nuttall (2018, 9) argues that processes of world-building are given greater attention in speculative fiction, with readers having to carefully attend to the world-builders that make up the background of the text in order to conceptualise and reify the 'other' world presented in the text. Such experiences of world-building and refamiliarisation are governed by particular rules: readers will follow the principle of minimal departure (Lewis 1983; Ryan 1980), for instance, which describes how they will default to their own everyday knowledge of the world in the interpretation of new and unfamiliar worlds. This forms part of the processes of conceptual comparison described in Sect. 6.2.1; '[w]henever we interpret a message concerning an alternate world, we reconstrue this world as being the closest possible to the reality we know' (Ryan 1980, 403). Sometimes this closest reality is that established within another text, as the analysis in the next two sections explores.

6.3.1 Intertextuality and World-Building

Within literary scholarship, intertextuality is a nebulous and much debated phenomenon, with many critical theorists divided as to its exact provenance and definition (Allen 2000). Generally, though, and across disciplines, 'researchers agree that intertextuality concerns links and connections between texts' (Mason 2019, 2). In cognitive stylistic research, the exploration of intertextuality has much to offer a situated and contextualised account of reading experience, not least because it is such a pervasive phenomenon in contemporary and postmodern literature (Allen 2000; Jameson 1991), and intrinsically subjective and idiosyncratic.

Drawing together different strands of contemporary research in cognitive linguistics supported by extensive empirical evidence, Mason (2019) presents a framework for the linguistic and stylistic analysis of intertextuality in both fiction and within reading discourse, or 'booktalk' (2019, 11; Erikkson 2002). As a starting point for exploring intertextuality from a stylistic perspective, Mason (2019, 21) differentiates between 'intertextuality' and 'narrative interrelations', arguing that the former is the 'examinable product of narrative interrelation' which exists in texts, and that the latter is 'the cognitive act of making a link between a narrative and at least one other'. The narrative interrelation framework draws on schema theory (Bartlett 1932) to explain how readers build up a 'mental archive' (Mason 2019, 72) of narratives they have encountered in their reading history and wider engagement with stories, and how they respond to textual cues in creating and delineating the connections between the text under consideration and those stored in the mind. As with other cognitive stylistic models, this framework departs from the privileging of authorial intention or 'expert readers' who will be able to identify all the intertextual references, and instead allows an examination of reading which is more situated and contextualised (Mason 2019, 2–3). Mason's framework offers a model for researchers to linguistically analyse intertextuality in literature in a text-driven, reader-centred and systematic way.

For the purposes of the analysis of *Oryx and Crake* presented in this chapter, my application of the narrative interrelation framework will maintain a reader-centred account of narrative interrelation (Gavins 2020), focusing on the intertextual references made by readers within the review data (Sect. 6.4), and those cued and triggered by text choices (Sect. 6.5). This involves the exploration of references in terms of degree of 'markedness' (i.e., whether the connection is identified in clear terms, such as through reference to a title of the book), or 'specificity' (i.e., whether a reference refers to one particular text or a more general group or genre).[1] As Mason (2019) explores, intertextuality in reading discourse and fiction has particular functions, including the framing and creation of simile, metaphor and synecdoche, disanalogy, and finally, and most importantly for the analysis in this chapter, in the generation of world-building information; helping readers reify characters and conceptualise rich, vivid text-worlds.

Before the story of *Oryx and Crake* formally starts and the matrix text-world is first encountered, paratextual information activates pertinent

---

[1] A comprehensive overview of the narrative interrelation framework can be found in Mason (2017; Gavins 2020).

knowledge schemas which readers may or may not, depending on their individual mental archive, increment in the world-building process. Epigraphs contribute to the store of paratextual world-building information in that they both form part of the text and establish key discourse-world knowledge that precipitates the matrix text-world introduced, traditionally, on the first page of the novel.

> I could perhaps like others have astonished you with strange improbable tales; but I rather chose to relate plain matter of fact in the simplest manner and style; because my principal design was to inform you, and not to amuse you.
> Jonathan Swift, *Gulliver's Travels*

> Was there no safety? No learning by heart of the ways of the world? No guide, no shelter, but all was miracle and leaping from the pinnacle of a tower into the air?
> Virginia Woolf, *To the Lighthouse*

Applying Mason's (2019) meta-language, both epigraph quotations in *Oryx and Crake* form intertextual references that are both 'specific' and 'marked'. This means that readers encountering this novel are invited to negotiate the relevance of these quotations for the purposes of the reading experience, creating associations that will either attentionally decay or else become revivified while reading via the realisation of a 'point of narrative contact' (Mason 2019, 100–102). Readers familiar with *Gulliver's Travels*, for example, might acknowledge the satire that underpins this intertext, and which is signposted explicitly in this first epigraph quotation. The designation of co-participant roles, the you-address in the quotation, is significant: the narrator reflects on the 'principal design' of *Gulliver's Travels* 'to inform you, and not to amuse you'. You-address in fiction can designate several addressee roles (see Herman 1994 for an overview), implicating multiple potential referents. Reproduced as an epigraph quotation here, this conflates the discourse-world set-up of *Gulliver's Travels* with that established in the discourse-world of *Oryx and Crake*, such that this also addresses the specific 'you' reading *Oryx and Crake*. This address is further reinforced in the rhetorical questions that make up the second epigraph quotation, referencing *To the Lighthouse*, and in turn activating associations of philosophical introspection for those familiar with the Woolf novel. In this way, knowledge that the original text is satirical foregrounds readers' role as the addressee of the text. This becomes incremented in the discourse-world structure, as '[s]atirical texts are understood as utterances which are inextricably bound up with context of situation, with participants in discourse and frameworks of knowledge' (Simpson 2003, 1). The salient 'context of situation' in satire means that the writer retains heightened prominence as co-participant. At the same time, the layered 'you' overtly introduces the co-participant, collaborative role of the novel's readers. In constructing the communicative event, then, readers of *Oryx and Crake* are primed for conceptual comparison from the very beginning of the story.

6.4   Building the Castaway Narrative

This next section of analysis explores the opening to the novel, and how the speculative world of *Oryx and Crake*, and the CASTAWAY or 'Robinsonade' narrative schema on which it draws, is first introduced to readers. Section 6.4.1 considers the reader responses that have noted the intertextual connections in the narrative, and Sect. 6.5 explores how these interrelations are invited and cued by world-building details within the text.

6.4.1   Reader Interrelations

The review data for *Oryx and Crake* clearly show readers engaging in processes of narrative interrelation, drawing on narrative schemas within their mental archives to conceptualise the speculative world established and developed. Readers comment on the relationship between this novel and others written by Atwood, and specifically the speculative text, *The Handmaid's Tale*; and other dystopian, science fiction or post-apocalyptic texts more generally. These observations are often connected with other codes of the data related to *(dis)engagement with characters*, and the novel's *speculative world creation*.

A specific marked intertextual reference articulated by many of the reviewers is the genre connection between *Oryx and Crake* and Atwood's first speculative novel, *The Handmaid's Tale*. The dataset shows that the reviewers draw points of narrative contact between these two novels based on different facets of the world-building experience distinctive to the speculative genre:

> For me, this was even more powerful than The Handmaid's Tale because of how effectively Atwood incorporates the global nature of what is happening. (OC80)

> Oryx and Crake, in the same vein as The Handmaid's Tale, is a novel that speculates about the near future of humanity. [...] As in The Handmaid's Tale, the narrative takes a biblical turn: Atwood provides a parody of the fall of

man, cast out from the Garden of Eden (see the Book of Genesis), with Crake standing for Yahweh and the post-human Crackers playing a comical version of Adam and Eve. (OC15)

I was reminded of the scrabble game in The Handmaid's Tale, Atwood I feel has a fondness for word games. (OC45)

The themes within speculative fiction, the language of the storytelling and the religious motifs in the text are particularly salient for these reviewers. The connections between these narrative schemas are made apparent through each reviewer's scope refinement. For OC15, for example, this intertextuality is apparent in the substitution and interchange of character roles or archetypes ('Crake standing for Yahweh and the post-human Crackers [sic] playing a comical version of Adam and Eve', OC15). For others, the potential points of connection and common ground between the two narratives create a space for readers to explore those divergent parts of the fictional world creation:

If we think of The Handmaid's Tale as a religious dystopia, then this book is a scientific dystopia. (OC48)

The Handmaid's Tale was an excellent dystopian novel with compelling, if heavy-handed and not entirely plausible politics; Oryx and Crake, which takes aim at corporate states, consumer capitalism, and genetic engineering, is an eco-apocalypse in which mad scientists wipe out humanity and replace it with. something else. (OC84)

This is Atwood's second successful work of speculative fiction. But where The Handmaid's Tale focused on gender and reproduction in a totalitarian regime, Oryx And Crake examines genetic splicing and disease. (OC22)

These readers acknowledge the themes of the referenced text ('scientific dystopia', 'genetic engineering', 'gender and reproduction') but also refine the scope of their interrelation to consider the thematic points of departure. In the context of these latter three excerpts, these include those scientific world-building details which set the novel up as an 'eco-apocalypse' narrative and which comprise a comparatively 'scientific' examination of 'genetic splicing and disease'. More broadly, such points of connection are generated by extratextual systems of categorisation of which readers might be aware: its prototypical genre features (as a speculative or dystopian text, as identified specifically by OC15, OC22, OC48 and OC84), and its placement within the Atwood oeuvre.

Marked references among the reviews similarly observe connections with other speculative or dystopian novels outside of Atwood's work, which include *Brave New World, 1984, Lord of the Flies, The Windup Girl, The Road, Never Let Me Go* and *I am Legend*. As in the previous comparisons with *The Handmaid's Tale*, these range from the more general and genre-level points of contact, where such texts are considered as prototypical artefacts of the genre (e.g., 'It belongs on everyone's bookshelves right alongside Anthem, Brave New World, 1984', OC79), to the identification of more specific world-builders and events within *Oryx and Crake* and a given intertext (e.g., 'Reminiscent in some ways to Orwell's 1984, this is a world of check-points and 24-hour guards and disappearances and interrogations that masquerade as investigations', OC79). On a yet more granular level, many of the reviews refine the scope of their interrelation through focusing on the role of the protagonist Snowman, and the relationship he bears to his intertextual counterparts. He is described variously as, for example:

'A middling Mad Max named Snowman'. (OC18)

'Castaway'. (OC49, OC24)

'Poor imitation of Robinson Crusoe'. (OC45)

The specific marked intertextual reference to *Robinson Crusoe* is considered by other reviewers who identify the 'Robinsonade' template (OC24; Phillips 1996), which, at its centre, comprises a lone character isolated from civilisation. This template is indirectly referenced in reviewers' identification of Snowman's role as a 'lone survivor' (OC28), his being 'alone' (OC32, OC66) and the 'loneliness' of this position (OC6, OC47, OC56). Such equivalence further reinforces the text-driven nature of the more generic intertextual references to *Lord of the Flies, The Road* and *I Am Legend*, for example, which similarly feature isolated character(s) forced to survive in a hostile location. The analysis in Sect. 6.5 of this chapter considers how these readerly intertextual connections are generated by several marked and unmarked textual prompts.

6.5 'Nobody nowhere'

In stylistics and narratology, the opening to a text is seen as particularly fore-grounded (Rabinowitz 2002). Attentionally, the scene in the opening extract is the first that readers are likely to encounter, which means that it becomes an attractor in its newness (Stockwell 2009). It is also cognitively the first shift into the text-world, as readers align their perspective with a speaking narrator. In the context of dystopian fiction, Norledge (2022, 67) argues that opening sentences relate key pieces of world-building information, which may include details of a threatening situation, the representation of a character who is afraid, description of a bleak environment, and linguistic choices heightening estrangement. Consequently, it can be seen as a particularly immersive part of the reading experience for some readers, a metaphor fittingly acknowledged by one reviewer who describes how 'Atwood drops us in a lagoon' (OC18) in the first chapter.

Extract 6.1

Mango

Snowman wakes before dawn. He lies unmoving, listening to the tide coming in, wave after wave sloshing over the various barricades, wish-wash, wish-wash, the rhythm of heartbeat. He would so like to believe he is still asleep.

On the eastern horizon there's a greyish haze, lit now with a rosy, deadly glow. Strange how that colour still seems tender. The offshore towers stand out in dark silhouette against it, rising improbably out of the pink and pale blue of the lagoon. The shrieks of the birds that nest out there and the distant ocean grinding against the ersatz reefs of rusted car parts and jumbled bricks and assorted rubble sound almost like holiday traffic.

Out of habit he looks at his watch—stainless-steel case, burnished aluminum band, still shiny although it no longer works. He wears it now as his only talisman. A blank face is what it shows him: zero hour. It causes a jolt of terror to run through him, this absence of official time. Nobody nowhere knows what time it is. (Atwood 2003, 3)

The CASTAWAY or desert island narrative is established in the opening chapter title, 'Mango', which instantly references knowledge schemas relating to FOOD, and FRUIT more specifically. For some Western readers, this also introduces a TROPICAL schema; this is not a fruit naturally indigenous to my location in the United Kingdom, for example, and is more typically associated with sunnier climes. The introduction of 'Snowman', therefore, creates conceptual dissonance and estranges this focalising character. Readers are more likely to imagine a snowman as being situated in a cold and icy location. Introducing the protagonist with the name 'Snowman' also suggests that this enactor of the main character lacks human qualities. A snowman as an inanimate entity, something that resembles a caricature of a person, but also ultimately is a transient object. The style choices of these first two words, and the departure from established knowledge schemas that they evoke, create a linguistic blueprint for the world-building in the rest of the novel, and specifically one that is founded on defamiliarisation and conceptual dissonance. In other words, it is clear from the very beginning of *Oryx and Crake* that the worlds outlined in the text will depart from or juxtapose domains from within readers' encyclopaedic, real-world knowledge.

This opening description additionally establishes the temporal parameters of the world, and, like other dystopian texts, it is anchored in a future point in time, after the catastrophe has already taken place (Norledge 2022, 71) (see Sect. 6.5.1). The focus on the nature—or the defamiliarised nature— in Snowman's surroundings is similarly observable in this scene. Readers are informed that 'Snowman wakes before dawn' and so the time of day is specified, albeit a time inferred by his assessment of the haze of the colour on the horizon, and not specified more exactly on a wristwatch. The present-tense narration ('wakes', 'lies') invites readers to align with Snowman's focalised perspective and his unfolding experience of events more closely. Present tense in third-person narration additionally closes the distance between the narrated and the narrating time (Shigematsu 2022), so while a third-person narrator tells the story, this narrator is similarly proximal to Snowman, recounting events as and when they occur.

The text-world location at first supports the interpretation of a desert island setting, and the TROPICAL schema signalled by the world-building title 'mango' is re-activated in additional descriptions of the objects that populate the world: 'the tide', the audible 'wish-wash' of the waves, 'the lagoon', the 'shrieks of the birds', 'the distant ocean' and the 'reefs' (see Fig. 6.1). The spatial deixis positions Snowman in clearer terms within this coastal location. The movement verb phrase 'coming in' depicts the waves as moving towards his fixed perspective where he 'lies unmoving', suggesting he is positioned near or on the shore. Prepositional phrases similarly provide information about how the features of this scene are positioned around Snowman. The 'lagoon', the 'offshore towers' which 'stand out in dark silhouette' against the horizon and the birds 'out there' are further away from his deictic centre, as are the 'distant ocean' and the reefs. These descriptions also increase in scale and scope in the second paragraph to display a more sweeping panorama. The perspective moves from Snowman to the wider of the 'eastern horizon' and the large-scale objects (the towers, the reefs and the ocean) that fall in between. The scope narrows abruptly in the third paragraph, however, returning to Snowman and the physical action of checking his watch, where the absence of time is rendered significant, and 'zero hour' feels more immediate and more ominous. This literal 'zeroing in' from the expanse of the world is contrasted with the smaller and contrastively insignificant space Snowman inhabits within it.

To return to the narrative interrelations made by readers, it is clear how the world-builders of this opening scene evoke other dystopian texts identified in the reviews. These points of narrative contact can be traced to the intertexts through shared world-builders that designate details of location, objects and time, as the following examples demonstrate:

> The boy with fair hair lowered himself down the last few feet of rock and began to pick his way toward *the lagoon.*
> *Lord of the Flies* (Golding 2005 [1954]. Emphasis added)

> 'No! I don't want the *mangosteen.*' Anderson Lake leans forward, pointing.
> *The Windup Girl* (Bacigalupi 2009. Emphasis added)

> It was a bright cold day in April, and *the clocks were striking thirteen.*
> *1984* (Orwell 2000 [1984]. Emphasis added)

> On those cloudy days, *Robert Neville was never sure when sunset came,* and sometimes they were in the streets before he could get back.

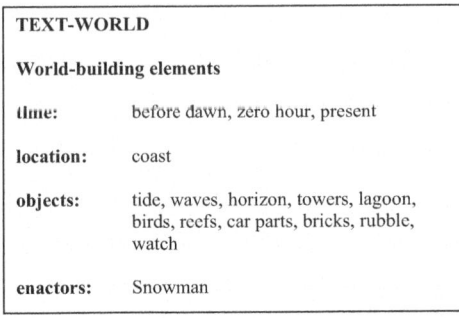

TEXT-WORLD	
World-building elements	
time:	before dawn, zero hour, present
location:	coast
objects:	tide, waves, horizon, towers, lagoon, birds, reefs, car parts, bricks, rubble, watch
enactors:	Snowman

Fig. 6.1 Building the castaway narrative in *Oryx and Crake*

I am Legend (Matheson 2001 [1954]. Emphasis added)

The intertextual traces activated in the first part of the novel are cued in an explicit way (for example, where Snowman acknowledges that he 'too is a castaway of sorts' (45), which is a generic marked reference to his Robinsonade role), and in the world-building information included in this introduction which, conversely, is specific and unmarked: no titles are mentioned, but there are shared world-builders which can be seen in a brief survey of the first sentences and paragraphs within the intertexts. For example, *Lord of the Flies* similarly mentions 'the lagoon', and *The Windup Girl* also describes 'mangosteen' fruit. More thematically, both *1984* and *I Am Legend* foreground temporal references: Winston marks the specific and unfamiliar time ('the clocks were striking thirteen', Orwell 2000); Neville observes that he has to mark time by the sun, and that his understanding of the time is important ('sometimes they were in the streets before he could get back', Matheson 2001). While the reviewers' discussion of the intertextual connections responds more holistically to the genre of the text and more general points of narrative contact, these connections and potential schema activations can be traced within the world-building level of the text at these more local, textual levels.

6.5.1   Snowman/no man

Outlined in Sect. 6.3, the principle of minimal departure dictates that readers will assume all new worlds are like their own unless otherwise stated. The introduction to *Oryx and Crake* reinforces familiarity with readers' own worlds through Snowman's actions, which align with those that might appear as part of a Western domestic and everyday routine: that is, waking up (but wanting to go back to sleep), listening to the sounds outside the window, checking the time. Other meteorological (e.g., the sun rising in the same place) and biological (e.g., His heart is beating steadily) facts schematically reinforce the familiarity of this new world. At the same time, other lexical choices create alterity. The 'distant ocean' contains 'reefs', but these are 'ersatz', and substituted by man-made substances such as 'rusted car parts and jumbled bricks and assorted rubble' bearing little resemblance to the natural flora they replace. Established in this description is a semantic clash between domains of the natural and the urban, echoed in the unlikely position of the 'offshore towers' within the lagoon. The cinematic and vivid world-building details that saturate this introduction are related through the semantic choices describing visual imagery (e.g., the various associated colour descriptions, such as 'greyish', 'rose', 'glow', 'dark silhouette', 'pink', 'pale blue', 'aluminum'), positioned alongside other descriptors that suggest decay ('rusted', 'rubble', 'burnished', 'blank'), and those that create a sense of foreboding ('deadly', 'tender', 'shriek', 'grinding', 'terror'). The juxtaposition of commonplace routines and objects alongside anomalous descriptions are instrumental in the defamiliarisation of this first chapter.

Significantly, the figural absence in Extract 6.1 creates a strong sense of isolation that marks and establishes Snowman's 'lone survivor' (OC28) status. This is built up stylistically in several ways. While Snowman is dehumanised by his name, his surroundings are comparatively animated. The waves move to the sound of the 'rhythm of heartbeat', and, though other people are notable in their absence, they are figuratively suggested in the comparison of the sound of the reefs as 'holiday traffic'. Equally, the inanimate objects and buildings are attributed grammatical agency: 'the tide coming in', 'wave after wave sloshing', the 'offshore towers stand out'. The absence of other figures is further emphasised in the negation in the final paragraph. The final sentence, 'Nobody nowhere knows what time it is' (Atwood 2019, 3) is stylistically striking. First, in the double affixal negation of 'nobody nowhere', which creates two distinct counterparts: somebody somewhere. This conceptual layering is further reinforced through the phonetic iconicity within the line; 'knows' sounds like 'no', and is similarly phonetically echoed in the name 'Snowman' (OC45).

There are also suggestions in the description that the current state of affairs has not always been as represented here. There is a comparison of a time before, where the colour of the sky was similarly 'tender', but where perhaps the original location of the looming offshore towers was not 'improbable', and when Snowman's watch *was* working. This comparison is reinforced through the creation of negated text-worlds. The narration describes how his watch 'no longer works', which, in text-world terms, invites readers to conceptualise an alternate reality where his watch does work. In cognitive linguistics, negation foregrounds the positive counterpart of the absent description. Here, then, the 'blank' watch and the 'absence of official time' are more likely to be foregrounded in readers' conceptualisation. The clustering of cognitive processing surrounding this final sentence foregrounds the figural absence within the scene; his isolation, and temporal dislocation, is brought to the fore.

Caracciolo et al.'s corpus analysis of patterns of metaphor in Anthropocene fiction (2019) finds that the predominant type of metaphor in *Oryx and Crake* features the human as a target, and an inanimate object as the source (and specifically as FOOD, in many cases). The researchers argue that this holds a specific function, which is to 'demote' the human characters 'by comparing them to things and objects that rank lower on the animacy scale' (Caracciolo et al. 2019, 229). In those cases where an inanimate object forms the target of the metaphor, however, it can be observed that the opposite is also true. In the final paragraph in Extract 6.1, for example, Snowman's watch 'shows him' a 'blank face', and is animated through the agency conferred in the act of showing and also in the reference to 'face'. The absence suggested through the semantic 'blank' is echoed in the subsequent 'nobody nowhere', and the figural quality of the watch face is further evoked in the description of it as a 'talisman'. In this way, while Snowman's animacy is demoted, other world-building objects are promoted to a more human-like status, such that the entities that populate this strange world are attributed with more equal status. Such a convergence between human and non-human entities homogenises the sentient status, and perceived agency, of the story's world-builders, additionally interanimating their respective object/ enactor classifications.

The argument of human demotion put forward by Caracciolo et al. (2019) is further referenced in the reviewer data. Another theme among the reader responses was the reference to *(dis)engagement with characters*, particularly in relation to the protagonist, Snowman/Jimmy. He and other characters in the novel are perceived by many as schematic types that hold purely functional roles in the text. He is described as a 'De facto priest' (OC31), existing purely to lead the Crakers, but even more predominantly as an 'Everyman character' (OC14, OC32, OC41, OC43, OC91), who 'represents all the dirtiness of the human collective' (OC28). The identification of the character 'type' of Snowman/Jimmy is similarly identified in the critical literature. Le Guin (2009) argues that *Oryx and Crake* is more satirical than its sequel, *Year of the Flood*, and that the characters are consequently more flat and less developed; 'these were figures in the service of a morality play'. This 'deprioritisation' of characterisation is another genre feature of dystopian and speculative texts (Nuttall 2018, 10; Stockwell 2000).

The analysis has observed how the opening to *Oryx and Crake* is built on multiple and layered processes of comparison. Intertextual traces to other stories, and in particular to the Robinsonade template, establish Snowman as a lone survivor and castaway. Equally, his descriptions of his environment are founded on comparisons with his experiences in a pre-apocalyptic world, and the rendering of familiar objects and places as strange and defamiliarised within this new reality. Finally, Snowman's reduction to a more schematic character type opens up processes of 'feedback oscillation' (Suvin 1979) for readers to construe Snowman as a more generic representation of 'the human collective' (OC28).

6.6   Possible Endings

Like introductions to stories, endings are seen as perceptually salient, inviting an interpretive convention which requires readers to seek out a conclusion, even in those cases where a satisfactory resolution has not been offered (Richardson et al. 2002, 304). While all stories have some kind of formal ending, stories are said to offer narrative closure in those cases where the narrative has a clear outcome (Chandler and Munday 2011, 89), or where a resolution to a complicating action has been outlined (Habermas and Berger 2011, 208; Klauk et al. 2016). *Oryx and Crake*'s categorisation as a 'what if narrative' (Howells 2017, 298) is confirmed in the closing moments of the story.

This final section of analysis considers the closing of *Oryx and Crake*, in which an injured Snowman/Jimmy finally encounters a group of other people at night by a fireside, and considers how to determine whether they are friend or foe. The two strands of the story prior to this point follow Snowman's existence in the present post-apocalyptic world where he watches over the Crakers, and also outline flashbacks to his pre-apocalyptic life as Jimmy. In the present, Snowman travels back to the Paradice project to search for supplies. As he nears the centre of the facility in the RejoovenEsense Compound, he reveals more information about the run-up to the apocalypse, and what actually happened to his friends Oryx and Crake.

Extract 6.2

What next? Advance with a strip of bedsheet tied to a stick, waving a white flag? *I come in peace.* But he doesn't have his bedsheet with him.

Or *I can show you much treasure.* But no, he has nothing to trade with them, nor they with him. Nothing except themselves. They could listen to him, they could hear his tale, he could hear theirs. They at least understand something of what he'd been through.

Or, *Get the hell off my turf before I blow you off,* as in some old-style Western film. *Hands up. Back away. Leave that spraygun.* That wouldn't be the end of it though. There are three of them and only one of him. They'd do what he'd do in their place; they'd go away, but they'd lurk, they'd spy. They'd sneak up on him in the dark, conk him on the head with a rock. He'd never know when they might come.

He could finish it now, before they see him, while he still has the strength. While he can still stand up. His foot is like a shoeful of liquid fire. But they hadn't done something bad, not to him. Should he kill them in cold blood? Is he able to? And if he starts killing them and then stops, one of them will kill him first. Naturally.

> "What do you want me to do?" he whispers to the empty air.
> It's hard to know.
> *Oh Jimmy, you were so funny.*
> *Don't let me down.*
> From habit he lifts his watch; it shows him its blank face.
> Zero hour, Snowman thinks. Time to go. (Atwood 2003, 373–374)

Discussion of *the ending* of the novel was a prominent theme among the reader review data (explicitly mentioned in one in five of the surveyed reader responses). In particular, the reviews comment on the absence of a resolution or satisfactory ending within the novel. Readers describe it as feeling 'anti-climactic' (OC22, OC93), as 'open' (OC36) and 'unresolved' (OC77), and a 'cliffhanger' (OC84) that feels 'abrupt' (OC52) and 'unsatisfying' (OC92). The ambivalence and ambiguity of the ending is reinforced through the hypothetical and modalised scenarios imagined by Snowman in the text. These alternative scenarios are framed in possible terms, indicated through rhetorical questions ('What next?', 'Should he kill them in cold blood?'). As before, Snowman's solitary status is confirmed in the self-reflexivity of his monologue. Much like in Felix's discourse in *Hag-Seed* (Chapter 5, Sect. 5.5), the rhetorical questions enact Snowman's role as both addresser and addressee, and the only direct speech that he does vocalise has an absent recipient ('"What do you want me to do?" he whispers to the empty air'), evoking the figural absence established in the opening passage (Sect. 6.5). Similarly, the other examples of direct speech ('*Oh Jimmy, you were so funny*' and '*Don't let me down*') appear in their free direct forms, meaning that they are not explicitly attached to a speaker and instead form part of Snowman's imma-nent monologue. The representation of speech revivifies the voices of Oryx and Crake, with '*Don't let me down*' echoing Crake's final directive to Jimmy.

In text-world terms, the introduction of possibility generates a modal-world which shifts attention away from the matrix text-world. In this extract, modalised language invites readers to conceptualise alternative and equally possible options for the continuation of the story. The first two scenarios are originally introduced as conceptual alternatives, signposted through the conjunction 'or'. Snowman's deliberations cue several generic marked references. Each possible scenario is introduced through headers evoking schema-activating world-building details or function-advancing actions, only to be ruled out or determined an impossibility. A generic PEACE schema is first initiated by the world-building description of objects ('a strip of bedsheet tied to a stick'), and by the function-advancing act of 'waving a white flag', for example, which is then ruled out because 'he doesn't have his bedsheet with him'. The second alternative scenario in turn signposts a generic marked reference to a superordinate ADVENTURE script, with the function-advancing act of displaying '*much treasure*' indicating a potential material trade. As before, though, this is revoked in Snowman's conclusion that, in fact, he has 'nothing to trade'. The final alternative intertextually references a WESTERN FILM script, reinforced through lines from the anticipated dialogue ('*Get the hell of my turf before I blow you off*') and specifically acknowledged by Snowman as a familiar script ('as in some old-style Western film'). Each intertextual scenario becomes increasingly more violent as Snowman considers the potential physical options available to him; he could wave a peace flag or talk to the strangers, or he could threaten them with physical assault. The devolution into violence underscores Jimmy's Hobbesian reflections on human nature: 'And if he starts killing them and then stops, one of them will kill him first. Naturally'.

Finally, the last lines intratextually repeat the 'zero hour' call to action referenced at the beginning of the novel (Extract 6.1). This cyclical structure is echoed structurally in the sequel, which also ends at the point of this scene, but is narrated from the perspective of the figures by the fireside. This circularity and lack of linear resolution arguably contributes to the sense of non-closure identified by the reviewers, while retaining the possibilities for the continuation of the story in the next novels: 'There are so many themes she can address and so many interesting places she can take this' (OC6).

6.7 'Time to go'

The analysis in this chapter has demonstrated how *Oryx and Crake* builds text-worlds from familiar narrative schemas and templates, comprising latent versions of other stories that are cued up through textual prompts and intertextual traces. It has examined how experiences of conceptual comparison persist across different facets of world-building, which constitute the processes of 'double consciousness' (Snyder 2011, 470) essential to the genre. These intertextual traces both 're-voice' the words and worlds of other writers

(Gavins 2020, 74), and also perform the narrative alternativity central to Snowman's discourse. It has been observed how readers attempt to refamiliarise and reify the novel through these intertextual connections, and in particular, by comparing the world-building details against both their current real-world position and against their mental archive of story schemas.

Analysis of the *Oryx and Crake* reader review data suggests that such processes of conceptual comparison, and the the felt resonance of the story, linger after the book has finished. Several of the reader reviews in the surveyed dataset were published since the start of the COVID-19 pandemic in 2020, for example, and make explicit reference to the relevance of the novel to, and its reflections on, this global event:

> "Oryx and Crake" is one of Margaret Atwood's novels from 2003, and yet it sets an eerie and all too-realistic tone on 2020 [...] I think had I read this book at any other time, it would not have resonated as it did. Atwood, like Stephen King, seems to have some pretty crazy premonitions (or a time machine). The believability of this novel is, sadly, a lot higher now than it would've been when it was released. (OC60)

> Having been living through the Covid-19 pandemic, her description of the spread of virus through this fictional world seemed spot on. The attempts to quarantine people, the hysteria, and the desire to flee the sites of contagion have all been evident over the last couple of years. (OC62)

> there was just something that didn't capture me like the handmaids tale did all those years ago. Perhaps it is because I am so much older now...Or perhaps it is because the talk of the pandemic and devastation is hitting a little too close to home right now... (OC75)

> This is a strange, yet delightful novel, only made all the more frightening by the current state of the world [...] Her clear criticism of the direction of society, and her almost prophetic writings (hello, pandemic) truly terrify me, and I can only conclude she is some form of harbinger (OC91)

Given the shared subject-matter of the novel—a deadly, worldwide pandemic—it is clear how the text-worlds of *Oryx and Crake* sustain and extend readers' experiences and conceptualisations of world comparison, confirming both the portentous, echoic quality of speculative fiction more widely and, by extension, Atwood's prophetic, 'harbinger' (OC91) reputation.

Note

1. Chapter 1provides a more detailed overview of the reader data used in this book.

References

Allardice, Lisa. 2018. Margaret Atwood: I am not a prophet. Science fiction is really about now. https://www.theguardian.com/books/2018/jan/20/margaret-atwood-i-am-not-a-prophet-science-fiction-is-about-now. Accessed 2 February 2023.

Allen, Graham. 2000. *Intertextuality*. London: Routledge.

Atwood, Margaret. 2004. *The handmaid's tale* and *Oryx and Crake* 'in context.' *Modern Language Association* 119 (3): 513–517.

Atwood, Margaret. 2006. Very Short Stories. *Wired Magazine*.

Atwood, Margaret. 2011a. *In other worlds: SF and the human imagination*. London: Virago.

Atwood, Margaret. 2011b. Margaret Atwood: the road to ustopia. https://www.theguardian.com/books/2011/oct/14/margaret-atwood-road-to-ustopia. Accessed 2 February 2023.

Atwood, Margaret. 2013. *Oryx and Crake*, 1st ed. 2003. London: Virago.

Bacigalupi, Paolo. 2009. *The windup girl*. London: Little, Brown.

Bartlett, Frederic. C. 1932. *Remembering: A study in experimental and social psychology*. Cambridge: Cambridge University Press.

Caracciolo, Marco. 2018. Negative strategies and world disruption in postapocalyptic fiction. *Style* 52 (3): 221–241.

Caracciolo, Marco, Andrei Ionescu, and Ruben Fransoo. 2019. Metaphorical patterns in anthropocene fiction. *Language and Literature* 28 (3): 221–240.

Chandler, Daniel, and Rod Munday. 2011. *A dictionary of media and communication*. Oxford: Oxford University Press.

Delany, Samuel. R. 2009. *The jewel-hinged jaw*, Middletown: Wesleyan University Press.

Emmott, Catherine. 1997. *Narrative comprehension: A discourse perspective*. Oxford: Oxford University Press.

Erikkson, Katarina. 2002. Booktalk dilemmas: Teachers organisation of pupils' reading. *Scandinavian Journal of Educational Research* 46 (4): 391–408.

Gadpaille, Michelle. 2018. Sci-fi, cli-fi or speculative fiction: Genre and discourse in Margaret Atwood's 'Three novels I won't write soon.' *English Language Overseas Perspectives and Enquiries* 15 (1): 17–28.

Gavins, Joanna. 2007. *Text world theory: An introduction*. Edinburgh: Edinburgh University Press.

Gavins, Joanna. 2020. *Poetry in the mind: The cognition of contemporary poetic style.* Edinburgh: Edinburgh University Press.

Gavins, Joanna, and Ernestine Lahey. 2016. *World-building: Discourse in the mind.* London: Bloomsbury Academic.

Glover, Jayne. 2009. Human/nature: Ecological philosophy in Margaret Atwood's *Oryx and Crake. English Studies in Africa* 52 (2): 50–62.

Golding, William. 2005. *Lord of the flies* (originally published 1954). London: Faber & Faber.

Goodreads reviews, OC1–OC100. 2022. 'Oryx and Crake by Margaret Atwood'. https://www.goodreads.com/book/show/46756.Oryx_and_Crake. Accessed 12 April 2022.

Habermas, Tilmann, and Nadine Berger. 2011. Retelling everyday emotional events: Condensation, distancing and closure. *Cognition and Emotion* 25 (2): 206–219.

Herman, David. 1994. Textual 'you' and double deixis in Edna O'Brien's 'A Pagan Place.' *Style* 28 (3): 378–410.

Hills, Matt. 2013. The 'world sharing' pleasures of SF: from expansive universes to miniscule details', Deletion, episode 1. https://www.deletionscifi.org/episodes/episode-1/the-world-sharing-pleasures-of-sf-from-expansive-universes-to-minisc ule-details/. Accessed 13 June 2023.

Howells, Coral Ann. 2017. True trash: Genre fiction revisited in Margaret Atwood's *Stone mattress, The heart goes last,* and *Hag-seed. Contemporary Women's Writing* 11 (3): 297–315.

Jameson, Frederic. 1991. *Postmodernism, or the cultural logic of late Capitalism.* Durham, NC: Duke University Press.

Klauk, Tobias, Tilmann Köppe, and Thomas Weskott. 2016. Empirical correlates of narrative closure. *Diegesis* 5 (1): 26–42.

Laflen, Angela. 2009. There's a shock in this seeing': The problem of image in *The Handmaid's Tale* and *Oryx and Crake. American Studies* 54 (1): 99–120.

Le Guin, Ursula. 2009. *The Year of the Flood* by Margaret Atwood. https://www.theguardian.com/books/2009/aug/29/margaret-atwood-year-of-flood. Accessed March 24, 2023.

Lewis, David. 1983. Truth in fiction. In *Philosophical Papers*, Vol. 1, 261 –280. New York: Oxford University Press.

Mason, Jessica. 2019. *Intertextuality in practice.* Amsterdam: John Benjamins.

Matheson, Richard. 2001. *I am legend*, [1954]. London: Orion.

Mead, Rebecca. 2017. Margaret Atwood, the prophet of dystopia. *The New Yorker.* www.newyorker.com/magazine/2017/04/17/margaret-atwood-the-prophet-of-dystopia. Accessed 13 June 2023.

Miall, David and Don Kuiken. 1994. Foregrounding, defamiliarization, and affect: response to literary stories. *Poetics* 22: 389–407.

Miall, David, and Don Kuiken. 2001. A feeling for fiction: Becoming what we behold. *Poetics* 30 (4): 221–241.

Moylan, Tom. 2000. *Scraps of the untainted sky: Science fiction, utopia, dystopia.* Oxford: Westview Press.

Norledge, Jessica. 2021. Modelling an unethical mind. In *Style and reader response: Minds, media, methods*, ed. Alice Bell, Sam Browse, Alison Gibbons, and Dave Peplow, 43–60. Amsterdam: John Benjamins.

Norledge, Jessica. 2022. *The language of dystopia*. London: Palgrave.

Nuttall, Louise. 2018. *Mind style and cognitive grammar: Language and worldview in speculative fiction*. London: Bloomsbury.

Orwell, George. (1949) 2000. *1984*. London: Penguin Books Ltd.

Phillips, Richard. 1996. *Mapping men and empire: Geographies of adventure*. London: Routledge.

Richardson, Brian, James Phelan, and Peter Rabinowitz, eds. 2002. *Narrative dynamics: Essays on time, plot, closure, and frame*. Ohio: Ohio State University Press.

Ryan, Marie-Laure. 1980. Fiction, non-factuals, and the principle of minimal departure. *Poetics* 9: 403–422.

Ryan, Marie-Laure. 1991. *Possible worlds, artificial intelligence, and narrative theory*. Bloomington: Indiana University Press.

Shigematsu, Eri. 2022. Is it narration or experience? The narrative effects of present-tense narration Ali Smith's *How to be both*. *Language and Literature* 31 (2): 227–442.

Shklovsky, Viktor. 1965. Art as technique. In *Russian formalist criticism: Four essays*, ed. Lee T. Lemon and Marion J. Reiss, 3–24. Lincoln: University of Nebraska Press.

Simpson, Paul. 2003. *On the discourse of satire: Towards a stylistic model of satirical humour*. Amsterdam: John Benjamins.

Spencer, K.I. 1983. 'The red sun is high, the blue low': Towards a stylistic description of science fiction. *Science Fiction Studies* 10 (1): 35–49.

Snyder, Katherine V. 2011. 'Time to go': The post-apocalyptic and post-traumatic in Margaret Atwood's *Oryx and Crake*. *Studies in the Novel* 43 (4): 470–489.

Suvin, Darko. 1979. *Metamorphoses of science fiction: On the poetics and history of a literary genre*. New Haven: Yale University Press.

Stockwell, Peter. 2000. *The poetics of science fiction*. Harlow: Pearson Education.

Stockwell, Peter. 2009. *Texture: a cognitive aesthetics of reading*. Edinburgh: Edinburgh University Press.

Thomas, Paul L. 2013. *Science and speculative fiction: Challenging genres*. Leiden, NA: Brill Academic Publishers.

Werth, Paul. 1999. *Text worlds: Representing conceptual space in discourse*. Harlow: Longman.

Winstead, Ashley. 2017. Beyond persuasion: Margaret Atwood's speculative politics. *Studies in the Novel* 49 (2): 228–249.

7

Voiceover Narration and the Split Self in *The Handmaid's Tale* TV Series

7.1 Introduction

The analysis of *Alias Grace* in Chapter 3 explored how, in Atwood's 'autobiographical "I"' narratives, the narrating subject 'speaks with increasing confidence and authority' while at the same time recognising 'its own multiplicity' and 'its indissoluable connections with others' (Grace 1994, 202). As Chapter 3 further examined, the narration in such 'I' narratives sets up a speaking narrator who is automatically multiplied: the narrating self can be separated from the experiencing self at different parts of the narrative, and this separation can be traced through an account of style choices such as reconstrual operations. *The Handmaid's Tale* and *Alias Grace* are often paired together in critical readings due to several shared features, including their first-person narration which marks them out as resembling witness testimonials (Atwood 2018), albeit ones in which the validity of the testimony, and the reliability of the witness, are called into question.

While cognitive stylistic tools have been applied in the investigation of literary texts, their application to TV, film and screen has been more limited. This chapter examines the cognitive stylistic features of the voiceover narration in the first television series adaptation of *The Handmaid's Tale* (2017) to explore the representation of June/Offred's enactors and how these are mediated through a prominent filmic composition device. Through analysis of voiceovers and corresponding production choices in the adaptation of the series, this chapter explores, first, how the different modes of communication—both choices of visual production (such as shallow-focus shots) and linguistic features (such as you-address and container metaphors)—combine

© The Author(s), under exclusive license to Springer Nature Switzerland AG 2024
C. Harrison, *The Language of Margaret Atwood*, Palgrave Studies in Language, Literature and Style, https://doi.org/10.1007/978-3-031-67640-6_7

to show Offred's split perspective; and second, how these stylistic elements work to foreground the series' key themes of imprisonment, objectification and surveillance.

7.2   Viewing *The Handmaid's Tale*

The first series adaptation of *The Handmaid's Tale* (MGM & Hulu 2017) is set in a dystopian future America and follows June, also known as Offred, and her life as a Handmaid—a woman who is forced to bear children for wealthy families—under the theocratic totalitarian regime of Gilead. June/Offred has been placed in the household of one of the leaders of this regime, Commander Fred Waterford, and his wife Serena, and the first series follows June/Offred as she adjusts to her new life. Since its release the series has received great critical acclaim, winning eight Emmy Awards from thirteen nominations as well as two Golden Globe awards for Best Television Series and Best Actress for Elizabeth Moss (who plays June/Offred).

The novel on which the series is based features June/Offred as the first-person narrator who recounts her experiences in short sections that detail her present day and her previous life, as well as some of the events leading up to the inception of Gilead. In contrast to the sustained first-person narrative in the text, the TV series adaptation focalises the narrative through multiple characters—such as her friends, Ofglen and Moira; her husband, Luke; and the Commander's Wife, Serena. June/Offred's story remains prominent, however, and she is the only character given a voice through interior monologue. The focus on June/Offred in the series serves to personalise her voice and story, but 'because of the torturous training she's subjected to under Aunt Lydia (Ann Dowd), she conveys her deepest and most personal thoughts via voiceover only' (Fienberg 2017). As the analysis later in this chapter will explore, the voiceovers are often accompanied by 'lingering close ups' which create a strong sense of 'claustrophobia' for viewers (Hinds 2017).

A survey of ten online UK newspaper reviews of the first TV series reveals several recurrent patterns among the critical responses. Unsurprisingly, given its speculative label, the reviewers comment on the *political relevance* of the series. Critics describe it as particularly timely and prescient, representing themes and social issues which on occasion move a bit 'too close' to those in the current political climate (Fienberg 2017), with reviewers framing these connections as not just resonating with our own (Debnath 2017) but being completely aligned with contemporary reality. Chandler (2017) observes, for example, how 'the horrors of the *The Handmaid's Tale* are happening right here, right now', while Rees (2017) similarly notes that 'this riveting adaptation has mapped itself onto the contemporary news cycle'. Indeed, when talking with *The Guardian* (2017) in an interview about her inspiration for the content of the book, Atwood acknowledges that '[w]hen it first came out it was viewed as being far-fetched'. She went on to add, 'when I wrote it I was making sure I wasn't putting anything into it that humans had not already done somewhere at some time'. For this reason, Atwood refers to *The Handmaid's Tale* narrative as speculative fiction rather than science fiction, and labels it, more specifically, as an Orwell-inspired 'classic dystopia' (Atwood 2004, 516). Such connections have led the reviewers to acknowledge the cautionary tone of the story. Some view it as a 'warning' (Rowney 2017); 'a potent reminder of what we have to lose' (Ross 2017). As with the responses to with *Oryx and Crake* (see Chapter 6), the reviewers also respond to the frightening nature of the narrative, though with *The Handmaid's Tale* this is taken further, with critics discussing its *horror* elements. The content is described as 'horrifying' (Chan and Tingle 2017; Billen 2017) and 'terrifying' (Chandler 2017), creating a 'chilling' (Ross 2017) story that presents a 'nightmarish vision' of the world (Stacey 2017). This horror categorisation is evoked in the political and social resonance of the series, which presents 'frightening possibility, and [...] a terrifying reality' (Rowney 2017).

The reviews also comment on the formal choices of the series. Many identify the structure of the narrative and its similarity to the book and its movement 'through muted, unsettling chapters' (Ross 2017), and describe *the use of flashbacks* and the function they have in the development of the story:

Even the flashbacks, so rarely totally successful, work here. Because they are back to pre-Gilead (possibly round about now?), it feels like a brief respite, being allowed up for air for a minute, before pushed back down again with a boot on your head. And they act like warnings—to Offred, maybe to us too—against normalisation. It wasn't always like this, it's not ordinary now: don't let it become ordinary. (Wollaston 2017)

For this reviewer, the flashbacks disrupt the spatiotemporal contextualisation of the rest of the story in the here and now of Gilead. Interestingly, this reviewer uses the label 'push' for the felt experience of returning to Gilead, which is a term borrowed from computer science and used by researchers to describe the readerly experience of a deictic shift, the conceptual movement *into* a text or story (Galbraith 1995). Following this theory, encountering June/Offred's voiceovers creates another 'push' into the narrative, and a closer and more immersive alignment with her perspective. This viewing experience is further conceptualised as abrupt and seemingly violent, however; initiated by a 'boot on your head'. Other reviewers comment on the structural role of flashbacks in filling in the backstory (Stacey 2017), similarly setting up that contrast between then and now through the 'glimpses of Offred's old life' (Stacey 2017), which betray 'signs of things breaking down' (McKay 2018).

Finally, the reviewers indirectly acknowledge *divisions* or *depth of character* within the story, either in terms of the handmaids' roles, or in terms of the actors assuming the character roles. Critics comment on the divided roles of women in Gilead, noting how 'the patriarchy's great triumph is to persuade *the women* to police *themselves*' (Billen 2017, emphasis added). In Billen's conceptualisation, the women have divided roles: they are those who both carry out the policing, and those who are being policed, cast as both grammatical subject and (self-reflexively) as grammatical object. They further discuss Moss's performance of June/Offred, and the division invited by acting this role, with Moss as both literal and grammatical performer: Moss 'always lets us see the subversion behind Offred's placidity' (Billen 2017). McKay (2018) also particularly commends 'the performance of Moss, who inhabits the brutalised fury of Offred with frightening intensity', framing June/Offred's emotions as a container to be occupied (Sect 7.7.2).

7.3   Point of View Presentation: Novel to Screen

Stylistic studies of film and TV have traditionally placed emphasis on the analysis of dialogue from a pragmatics perspective (e.g., Bousfield 2007; Sorlin 2016; Statham 2015) and on the adaptation of book to screen (e.g., Forceville 2002), whereas film studies approaches traditionally explore visual cues alone. Recent accounts, however, have argued that a combined analysis of verbal and visual codes in film and other visual narratives would benefit from further exploration, especially given that language analysis has not historically been a priority in film studies (McIntyre 2008; Piazza 2010; Piazza et al. 2011). McIntyre's (2008) study of Ian McKellen's performance in *Richard III,* for example, identified that traditional film studies approaches overlook the use of dialogue and the interaction between language and non-language choices, and tend to fall at either end of the scale in terms of level of detail, exploring either macro-level issues of a film or a micro-analysis of specific frames. To provide an analysis that includes all these considerations, McIntyre applies ideas from deixis, discourse structure and pragmatics alongside a breakdown of the visual elements of McKellen's soliloquy scene. Through this account, McIntyre argues, firstly, that it is both 'possible and profitable to incorporate the analysis of production and performance with a more traditional, text-based stylistic analysis of drama', and secondly that such analysis produces a more holistic, stylistically nuanced discussion; for '[o]nly by doing this are we able to accurately describe overlapping elements of production and identify in detail specific stylistic effects' (2008, 326).

It could be argued that the more prominent stylistic effects in *The Handmaid's Tale* series relate to viewers' understanding of June/Offred's character, specifically, as the teller of the tale. However, though June/Offred narrates part of her story, film studies theorists also acknowledge the presence of a 'filmic narrator' (cf. Bordwell 1997) in telecinematic narratives. To refer to this role, Jahn (2003) uses the term 'filmic composition device' (hereafter FCD) instead, as this label indicates that 'the cinematic narrator is not a homogenous, monolithic agent with a humanlike voice' but rather can be seen as 'a separate agent or group of agents' (Ghaffary & Nojoumian 2013, 270) who put together what is seen on screen. In other words, there is not one single filmic narrator but a collective FCD, assembled by choices from several people, including the camera operator, the producer, the director and so on.

The FCD is strongly characterised in *The Handmaid's Tale* series, and viewers acknowledge the production choices as being particularly distinctive or stylised (see Yuan, 2017 for an account of some of the more striking style choices with accompanying commentary from director Reed Morano). The reviews surveyed in Sect 7.2 similarly comment on these choices, identifying the romanticised and Baroque style of the series, which 'looks beautiful—as classy as a Vermeer painting' (Billen 2017); and which 'looks extraordinary—stylised, choreographed almost, menacing' (Wollaston 2017). Such distinctive *mise-en-scène* style choices in the series relate to the use of colour, lighting, costume (Bordwell and Thompson, 2001) and the sustained use of symmetrical composition. In the series, lighting is manipulated in the Gilead and pre-Gilead narrative strands, for example, where Gilead scenes are filtered through a sepia tone and pre-Gilead is brighter and has a colder, bluer tone. Such a contrast suggests that these different states are filtered through contrastingly more realist as compared to more romanticised lenses by the FCD. Similarly, colours are manipulated in other *mise-en-scène* choices such as costume. The different social roles of the characters are represented through different uniforms, mostly set through primary colours, with the deep red of the Handmaids' clothes often foregrounded in otherwise colourless scenes. These general choices regarding lighting, arrangement and tone mean that that 'voice' of the FCD is distinct and 'striking' (Yuan 2017), and arguably never fully backgrounded.

There are many intersections between film theory and theories of narrative which make the examination of telecinematic choices through a stylistic approach a logical and synergistic endeavour. Indeed, Alber (2017, 280) touches on this in his account of perspective and consciousness representation, arguing that 'the overlaps between novelistic and cinematic strategies of consciousness representation are interesting and striking', but that 'they have hitherto been overlooked'. As a specific example, Alber suggests that interior monologues in film work analogously to those examples in prose, but while he categorises interior monologue as those examples in film which contain 'longer passages of uninterrupted direct thought', these are 'usually without any narratorial mediation' (2017, 280). If we allow that the narrator is formed by the FCD, then its marked presence throughout the series can be seen to, if not necessarily mediate, then certainly foreground, collaborate with and at times counter, the verbal content of June/Offred's voiceover. These ideas will be expanded on in further detail in the analysis.

7.4   Split Selves

The 'divided self' metaphor was first explored by Lakoff (1993, 1996) in his accounts of 'the divided person', in which a person's experience is described as fragmented by the component parts of Cartesian dualism, the rational-emotional divide. In such metaphors, a person is divided by their more rational 'subject' and their emotional or bodily 'self', apparent in phrases such as *I am not myself today* or *I made myself go for a run*. While both Lakoff and Demjen (2011) explore the concept of the split self in terms of explicitly metaphorical instances of language, Emmott (2002, 154) uses the term 'split selves' 'very broadly to include all cases of a character or real-life individual being divided and/or duplicated in any way in a narrative'. In her account, Emmott explores the duplication of both characters and real-life individuals, examining examples from both fiction and non-fiction medical life stories. These examples comprise individuals who 'perceived themselves to be "split" [...] because of a transitory sense of experiential discontinuity or because of a traumatic life change' (Emmott 2002, 170).

This idea is relevant for *The Handmaid's Tale*, in which audiences encounter multiple iterations of June/Offred's character. Gottlieb (2001, 103), for example, identifies the protagonist's division within the novel, which she narrates through 'a series of juxtapositions between her deprived, degraded self in Gilead and her former emancipated self'. She is similarly duplicated from the outset of the TV series. Audiences learn in episode 1, for example, that her name is June but also Offred, identifying her pre-Gilead names as well as conferring her status as belonging to the Commander Fred in Gilead. Of course, more superordinately, she is also the 'Handmaid' whose tale we are listening to. She is further duplicated through flashbacks in other episodes. In episode 4, for instance, she is shown in her former life with her husband Luke and daughter Hannah when they visit a fair, while also revealed to be in her bedroom in Gilead as she mentally recounts the memory. In these contexts, the division of selves is signposted through visual splicing as well as through verbal choices (for example, a shift in tense in the voiceover narration when returning to Gilead).

Emmott suggests that split self presentation might be 'inherent in the narrative form, since first-person narratives generally invoke a current self reporting on a past self' (2002, 153–154). Arguably, the inclusion of interior monologues in film, and the reflection of the current self on their previous experience, similarly always encodes a type of split self presentation. Interior monologues are used 'to convey a character's thoughts, feelings or motivations at the auditory level' (Alber 2017, 277). In the voiceovers in the series, the narrating June/Offred we hear (June/Offred1) at the auditory level is contrasted with the silent June/Offred we see (June/Offred2); and at times further compared with the 'enactor' (Emmott, 1992) of herself we might see in a flashback (June/Offred3). In such cases the representation of June/Offred occurs across modes and the voiceover is spatiotemporally displaced from the current visual narrative, which in turn also serves to foreground the FCD. Viewers may become aware of the artifice of the construction as the narrative is not a natural one, but rather one which has been edited or reframed by the FCD.

Mediation and the retelling of narratives are a central theme in *The Handmaid's Tale* novel. Like other Atwood narratives, the narrative has a reveal at the end of the story (Harrison and Nuttall 2019) which reframes the content of the rest of the tale: an epilogue describes a future conference, set in 2195, at which academics are discussing Gilead, long after its dissolution. It is revealed that June/Offred's story presented in the first 300 pages of the book were a transcription of a series of cassettes recording her account. This framing is referenced in the adaptation's first series, but not overtly. After the opening sequence of episode 1, which recounts June/Offred being captured and her daughter, Hannah, being taken away, there is a quiet (compared to the noisy chase scene which precedes it) but audible 'click' of an audio cassette recorder, just before June/Offred begins her first interior monologue voiceover. Consequently, it can be argued that a preoccupation with *The Handmaid's Tale* narrative, across both the novel and the series adaptation, concerns the owner-ship, or mediation, of voice, and the removal of (narrator) agency.[1] This theme is also identified in the title itself: the story is a 'tale', which is a label that 'removes it at least slightly from the realm of mundane works and days', while the term 'story', conversely, 'might well be a true story about what we usually agree to call "real life"'(Atwood 2014, 309). Audiences are therefore primed for a narrative removed from 'real life', even though the themes and content are highly familiar.

7.5   Methodology: Voiceovers

The data for the analysis in the following sections consist of the transcrip-tion of the voiceovers in the ten episodes of *The Handmaid's Tale*, series 1. In *The Handmaid's Tale* series, the number of voiceovers ranged from 1 to 14 per episode, with a mean of 5 per episode across the series. In the analysis that follows, each voiceover is referenced according to the episode and where it appears in the chronology of voiceovers for that episode (e.g., 10.4). Following Piazza (2010), for some parts of the analysis, key sections of the data (verbal text) are represented in tables alongside the corresponding production choices (visual text and notable paralinguistic choices). The anal-ysis will not consider the non-speech sound stream which makes up the third channel of communication in film and TV (Toolan 2014, 462) as this is beyond the scope of this chapter, though the diegetic and non-diegetic sound and music choices are also noteworthy.

The first episode comprises the highest number of voiceovers (14), which are mainly used for narrative exposition ('The knock is prescribed 'cause tonight this room is her domain. It's a little thing, but in this house, little things mean everything', 1. 11), or to voice June/Offred's response to the conversation that is not diegetically vocalised ('I kind of want to tell her that I sincerely believe that Ofglen is a pious little shit with a broomstick up her ass', 1.3). The function of the voiceovers changes across the series, however, and they become a means of suggesting June/Offred's rhetorical dialogue ('Am I not the first he's invited to this room? What happened? Did she say the wrong thing?', 4.8), or of signposting the introduction of a flashback ('She comes to me so clearly in the bath', 1.10). This happens most frequently in

---

[1] Such signposts suggest that this reframing will be acknowledged in the series as it continues. It remains to be seen how the epilogue will be addressed at the end of the TV adaptation, which, at the time of writing, is reported to be the forthcoming sixth series (2024).

episode 4, 'Nolite te bastardes carborundorum'.[2] In this episode, June/Offred has been banished to her room and has not been allowed to leave the house for some time due to a fall-out with Serena. June/Offred becomes frustrated and depressed, calling up memories as a means of coping with her present reality. In contrast, particular episodes have significantly fewer voiceovers, and this occurs when the episode departs from June/Offred's focalisation: episodes 6 ('A Woman's Place') and 7 ('The Other Side'), for example, are centred on Serena and Luke's backstories, respectively, and feature only one voiceover from June/Offred in each episode.

The next two sections of analysis build on these initial observations to explore the verbal and visual style choices that accompany the occurrences of the voiceovers, and to examine, firstly, how they function in the series; and secondly how they impact on the representation of split selves.

7.6   Offred Onstage

One of the most distinctive visual techniques used in *The Handmaid's Tale*, which frequently accompanies the use of June/Offred's voiceover (June/Offred1), is the prevalence of symmetrical composition shots to represent June/Offred2, the 'self' shown on screen. These are cinematic shots with near-perfect symmetry, popular with director Stanley Kubrick (Kolker 2015), and which work by drawing viewer's attention to a specific focal point at the centre of the scene. Such staging is seen to create a sense of uneasiness or dread because viewers can be positioned to wait for the focal point to be revealed, and because the uncanniness of the composition can indicate a sense of entrapment (Pezzotta 2013, 80). In *The Handmaid's Tale*, this composition can be frequently observed with June/Offred's figure or face forming the focal (or 'vanishing') point of the scene (Fig. 7.1). Although not typical in the scenes that accompany voiceovers, doors or windows also frequently form the centre point of a scene, which helps sustain the themes of imprisonment and surveillance that run throughout the series.

The Handmaid's Tale's use of symmetrical composition, however, differs from traditional applications of this composition as the depth of perception is often much shallower and subjects are not always placed far away from the camera at the vanishing point. Shallow focus is 'an approach in which several planes of focus are incorporated within a single image' (Mamer 2008, 19). When this occurs in conjunction with voiceovers, viewers are positioned

---

[2] Don't let the bastards grind you down.

Fig. 7.1 Symmetrical composition from episode 4, 'Nolite te bastardes carborundorum' (MGM & Hulu 2017)

close to a particular character (or object) in the scene, who is represented in detail and clarity, and other elements of the scene are backgrounded through schematisation or visual 'modalisation' (Kress and van Leeuwen 1996). This configuration can be seen in the shot reproduced in Fig. 7.2.

During voiceovers and in other scenes throughout the series, June/Offred's face is shown very clearly, very close to the camera. These close-up shots allow the audience greater emotional connection to a character but also increase the sense of claustrophobia generated by such an arrangement, and the close alignment with a character perspective (both literally and figuratively) can

Fig. 7.2   Shallow-focus shot from episode 1, 'Offred' (MGM & Hulu 2017)

become, at times, uncomfortable. It is this discomfort that means that the conjunction of a voiceover with a close-up of character face is typically associated with horror (Alber [2017, 277], for example, describes how the use of this technique in Hitchcock's *Psycho* is somewhat 'disconcerting'). Furthermore, such a close focus on the character's face narrows the visual field and therefore restricts the visual information offered to viewers. In turn, this physical constraint mirrors the metaphorical implications of June/Offred's limited perspective in Gilead.

Film theory states that when a character's gaze is off to the side, viewers are primed for a point of view shot (Branigan 1984). Also known as a subjective shot, this occurs where 'the camera assumes the position of the subject to show us what the subject sees' (Branigan 1984, 103). In these kinds of sequences in *The Handmaid's Tale*, viewers anticipate that the next scene will reveal the object of the character's attention. Instead, what happens here is that, rather than follow the line of June/Offred's gaze, the camera remains on her face for extended sequences. This heightens the intimacy felt between viewer and character and arguably further contributes to the feeling of claustrophobia generated by the series.

Both shallow-focus and symmetrical composition techniques can be observed in the shots that accompany the first voiceover of the first series (Table 7.1):

Table 7.1 Verbal and visual text of voiceover 1.1

Verbal text	Visual text
	(Symmetrical composition) June/Offred in bedroom sitting on windowsill, silhouetted against gauzy curtains. The colours are muted and details of the scene are unclear
A chair, a table, a lamp. There's a window with white curtains, and the glass is shatterproof. But it isn't running away they're afraid of. A Handmaid wouldn't get far. It's those other escapes	(Profile shot) June/Offred sits on a window seat in her bedroom. Details of the scene are slowly revealed or clarified
The ones you can open in yourself given a cutting edge. Or a twisted sheet and a chandelier. I try not to think about those escapes. It's harder on ceremony days, but thinking can hurt your chances. My name is Offred. I had another name, but it's forbidden now. So many things are forbidden now	(Profile shot) Zooms in so that June/Offred's face appears larger on the screen

June/Offred1's narration mirrors the opening sentences of the novel, which show a sequential ordering of items being listed in an atemporal ('A chair, a table, a lamp') and then present-tense narrative ('There's a window with white curtains'). Nuttall's (2014) analysis of this scene in the prose narrative identifies how this sequence of attentional frames can create a 'collage' or 'puzzle' effect (98), thereby challenging readers' conceptualisation of the fictional world. In the visual text of this voiceover, viewers' conceptualisation of the scene is challenged through the fact that the silhouette cast by June/Offred and the hazy light and contrasting darkness in the rest of the shot renders details initially difficult to discern. The sequential introduction of objects in the room is brought out visually, however, as the scene progresses—though these details relate to Offred/June (the colour of the dress, her facial expression), rather than those objects in the room she is describing. This creates a zooming-in effect where the camera moves closer and closer to June/Offred's perspective as the voiceover progresses, but without clarifying what she describes. Though she is the focaliser of the scene, she increasingly becomes the centre of attention. In other words, audiences contemplate her visually, while her voiceover dwells on items in her physical surroundings that are occluded from the audience's view.

These techniques both isolate June/Offred's position in space and create separation between her and her physical environment. This division occurs in the verbal text where June/Offred can be seen to separate herself mentally from her new situation. She distances herself from the rest of the hand-maids (she states, for example, that 'A handmaid wouldn't get far' rather than directly associating herself with that group), as well as the means of escape available to those in this group, as evidenced through the use of distal deixis ('it's *those other* escapes'), and even despite the fact this is a preoccupation of her thoughts ('*I try not to think* of those escapes'). The otherness of her new identity is also explicitly mentioned when she references that she had 'another name'. Given that the nominal profiles in the start of the voiceover relate to objects in a domestic setting ('A chair, a table, a lamp'), the reference to 'opening an escape' could initially be interpreted literally; viewers might think of opening a door to escape. However, the addition of 'in yourself' indicates the physical act June/Offred is describing, referencing the body as a kind of container in which pathways can be opened. The episode finishes with June/Offred stating 'My name is June', though audiences may be aware that the episode is entitled 'Offred'. Consequently, even at the macro-level of the episode, June/Offred's division of self is acknowledged.

At other points in the series, the visual text and the choices of the FCD work in concert with the verbal text. In voiceover 2.2 (outlined in Table 7.2) in the second episode, 'Birth Day', for example, June/Offred's verbal text similarly acknowledges a division and separation between herself ('us') and the rulers of Gilead ('them'), and she questions whether to categorise herself among the latter group ('There is an 'us'?). The verbal text moves from being epistemically modalised ('it seems imagined, like secrets in the fifth grade'; 'It doesn't seem as if it should be the true shape of the world) to more categorical assertions: 'Now, darkness and secrets are everywhere'. Unlike the visual choices in voiceover 1.1, however, there is some support from the FCD as to the content of the verbal text: namely, the bars of the gate she is standing next to are visible as she is talking about this societal division:

The rest of the verbal text mimics a political template. June/Offred provides exposition of the current situation and a comparison with the past by mentioning 'Now' in three successive declarative sentences, and by acknowledging the new Heads of State ('the Guardians of the Faithful') and the new capital ('Anchorage'). Despite these rhetorical choices which are hallmarks of spoken political discourse, as Fienberg (2017) observes in her review, Offred can reveal her thoughts 'via voiceover only'. This lack of freedom is foregrounded by the FCD on the visual level. One of the only discernible parts of the background are the bars of the gate, for example, and the camera follows her physical movement in front of, to behind, the bars of the gate. The FCD

Table 7.2 Verbal and visual text of voiceover 2.2

Verbal text	Visual text
There is an 'us'? It seems imagined, like secrets in the fifth grade. People with mysterious histories and dark linkages	*(Close-up)* June/Offred's face is shown to the right of the scene, wearing the white handmaid 'wings' The background is blurry but the thick, dark bars of the iron gate she is standing in front of are visible
It doesn't seem as if it should be the true shape of the world. That's a hangover from an extinct reality	*(Close-up; symmetrical composition)* Zooms in to June/Offred's face
Now, the Guardians of the Faithful and American soldiers still fight with tanks in the remains of Chicago. Now, Anchorage is the capital of what's left of the United States, and the flag that flies over that city has only two stars	*(Long shot; symmetrical composition)* June/Offred stands in front of gates Returns to centred focus shot on her face while she looks up Camera zooms out so that bars of gate can be seen again June/Offred closes gate
Now, darkness and secrets are everywhere. Now, there has to be an 'us'. Because, now, there is a 'them'	*(Close-up; symmetrical composition)* June/Offred's face is shown behind the bars of the gate

becomes collaborative at this point, unifying the voice of June/Offred1 with the visual presentation of June/Offred2.

Observing June/Offred visually while she contemplates other matters verbally creates a clash between the familiar and the impersonal, which is a phenomenon also brought about through the choice of shallow-focus shots alongside voiceover narration. Kozloff argues that voiceovers are a humanising device (1988, 128; Piazza 2010, 178). At the same time, however, shallow-focus cinematography is associated with unreality, since its use 'can create a purposefully less realistic image—one that manipulates viewer attention and suggests different planes of action both literally and figuratively' (Mamer 2008, 19). Consequently, the interplay between image and text in the scenes where a voiceover is accompanied by a shallow-focus shot of June/Offred's face creates an unsettling imbalance between artifice and reality. The voiceover humanises her, but the choices of the FCD detaches the audience from her character. Such a tug-of-war between the metaphorical and the humanised again exemplifies the division of the self represented here: June/Offred is both humanised to viewers, but also objectified within her current surroundings. The FCD shows her as an isolated character who narrates what is on her mind but does not visually reveal what she is thinking about. Though there are moments of collaboration where symbolic references are made in the visual text (as in the latter example of the bars of the gate), the objects of her contemplation are not revealed in detail to viewers.

This first section of analysis has demonstrated how the verbal and visual texts work together to represent June/Offred as someone divided and introspective; exploring the representation of how she channels her thoughts and agency inwards rather than outwards. Additionally, June/Offred is represented as a character whom audiences are invited to contemplate as the object of attention, even while she dwells on other topics. The next sections explore how June/Offred is further divided through audience address and recurrent metaphor choices.

7.7 Further Divided Selves

7.7.1 Addressing *you*

Given that the handmaid's 'tale' in the book is a recording of June/Offred's story, viewers may be expecting an intended recipient for her narrative to be revealed. However, June/Offred's isolation is further emphasised through the absence of a clear addressee, who remains ambiguous at both the verbal and the visual level. Across the series, June/Offred's gaze is rarely directed to the audience explicitly. This is unlike, for example, the character Francis Underwood in the *House of Cards* series who directly engages the viewer with second-person address and whose monologue is delivered on the same diegetic plane as the scene (Sorlin 2016). Despite June/Offred's central positioning and the direct close-ups of her face, her gaze during voiceovers is often just off-centre, looking at an unknown point out of sight (Fig. 7.2) and not directly at the audience.

Similarly, the verbal text also represents an ambiguous addressee, in that the you-referent changes across the series. At times, the address can be regarded as simply 'generalized' (Herman 1994), with June/Offred commenting on facts which are relevant universally in the world ('You can wet the rim of a glass and run your finger around the rim and it will make a sound', 4.6), or in Gilead, specifically ('The chances for a healthy birth are one in five, if you can get pregnant at all', 2.4). This type of 'generalized' you-address can also be seen in voiceover 1.1, mentioned in the previous section, where June/Offred mentions 'you', 'yourself' and 'your chances', although given the content of the verbal text here this could also be considered a form of telecinematic 'self-referential' address (Gibbons and Whiteley 2019) in which June/Offred relays potential options to herself via interior monologue. This dialogue between selves can also be seen at other points in the series where June/Offred more performatively assumes the role of different enactors. At the end of the third episode, for example, in reference to not being pregnant despite the hopes of the household, she admonishes herself with 'No ice cream for you this month, young lady' (3.4). At other points, June/Offred enacts other characters in the series. At the end of voiceover 1.13, for instance, she says (echoing Moira's words from an earlier flashback), 'Keep your fucking shit together'.

Occasionally, however, the 'you' has a clear referent within the series that is not June/Offred. In her only voiceover in episode 7 ('I love you so much. Save Hannah', 7.1) unusually she is absent from the visual text, which shows Luke reading the letter while June/Offred1's voice narrates. Similarly, June/Offred addresses the previous Offred through a voiceover in episode 4, in response to reading a hidden scratched message in a cupboard in her room: 'You had to be brave to do this. So, whatever it means, thank you' (4.1). These are examples of 'fictionalised horizontal address' (Herman 1994) which reference a character on the same diegetic plane of the story (rather than being, for example, a direct plea to the real-world audience). Occasionally, this horizontal address functions outside of the confines of the voiceover through either spoken discourse (on the same diegetic plane as the narrative) or through written text representation. This can be observed in episode 8, where, in response to a gift from Serena of a jewellery box with a dancing ballerina in the lid, June/Offred states via voiceover 'I will not be that girl in the box' (8.4), and then writes 'you are not alone' on the wall in the cupboard. A combination of both horizontal address and self-reflexive address can also be observed, as in the moment where she addresses Moira, but then switches in the final two directives: 'Moira, you wouldn't stand for this shit. You wouldn't let them keep you in this room for two weeks. You'd find a way out. You'd escape. Get up. Get your crazy ass up' (4.7).

However categorised, the you-references invite viewers to consider the addressee of June/Offred's tale, and therefore further evokes the transcription template revealed in the novel's epilogue. The performative aspect of the voiceover and the you-address are reminders that this is a tale about her life, which might be oriented towards a particular person or audience. Additionally, the number of characters directly addressed (Moira, Luke, past/future Offred) functions as signposts of June/Offred's multiple social roles: wife, mother, friend, Handmaid. At the same time, the use of self-referential address is a clear indication of her split selves. She has no one to talk to within the confines of Gilead, and therefore can ultimately only narrate thoughts to herself.

7.7.2   (Container) Metaphors

This final section of analysis explores how June/Offred's presentation of self is further split through the metaphors in the series. Building on the earlier work on self and container metaphors by Lakoff (1996), Emmott (2002) considers manifestations of how container metaphors are used in fiction and non-fiction narrative representations of the self. Looking at *The Diving Bell and the Butterfly* (Bauby 1998), for example, she examines how a building metaphor is reframed through different target domains: it is used as the source domain for comparisons with the body, ill-health, misery and the hospital/home, at different parts of the narrative (Emmott 2002, 165). Metaphor choices can provide information about the psyche of a central character, but more generally can also reflect central motifs across a film or book (Forceville 2002), or narrative universals of types of genres. Through analysis of Philip Roth's *Nemesis* and Ridley Scott's *Alien*, Senkbeil (2017), for example, explores how particular image schemas, such as infection, can form conceptual models inherent in the horror genre.

Key metaphors in *The Handmaid's Tale* relate to body parts and their metonymic relationships to the wider world. An 'Eye', for example, is the term for someone who spies for the Gilead authorities ('Maybe he watches me. Maybe he's an Eye', 1.4), and eyes are foregrounded in the visual text frequently (as in the final scene described in the visual text in Table 7.3). Similarly, hands are also referenced across both visual and verbal text. Of course, they form part of the term 'handmaid' itself, and the various refrains spoken to each other in greeting also echo both choices ('By his hand'; 'Under his eye'). While '[i]n Gilead, hands and feet are pronounced non-essential tools' (Staels 2008, 458), the concept of hands as representing agency is nevertheless acknowledged and is so poignantly in the line from the final voiceover of the series: 'I have given myself over into the hands of strangers' (10.5). These metaphors draw on culturally entrenched ideas of both agency and surveillance, and the isolation of body parts is also emblematic of the wider objectification of handmaids in Gilead. Such 'chains' of repetition (Forceville 2002) consequently support the de-humanisation of June/Offred, which is further acknowledged in comparisons she makes between herself and animals ('Washed and brushed like a prize pig', 1.10; 'We're two-legged wombs', 2.3) or inanimate entities ('This is what I feel like, this sound of glass. I feel like the word "shatter"', 4.6) and via explicit 'othering' through negation ('I don't want to be a doll, hung up on the wall', 3.3; 'I will not be that girl in the box', 8.4).

The most prominent metaphors though, like in Emmott's (2002) analysis, relate to a superordinate CONTAINER source domain. Table 7.3 outlines several different manifestations of this metaphor appearing in the verbal text and the visual text (and sometimes both) of voiceover 4.1. This voiceover continues after June/Offred experiences a flashback to a time pre-Gilead where she was with Luke and Hannah at a fair. The present tense 'I can't do this' marks a shift from the previous part of the voiceover, which is narrated in the past tense, and therefore shows a spatiotemporal lag. June/Offred is aware that she should not dwell on memories for the sake of her mental health (as signposted in the verbal text) and is reluctant to return to the present (as indicated by the delay in the visual text). Here, the discordance between the verbal and the visual texts suggests this reluctance, but also her disorientation in this episode. Despite her self-instruction, she is, in part, becoming 'lost in her memories' (see Giovanelli and Harrison 2024, 12–16, for a discussion of how the CONTAINER schema is frequently used to talk about emotional states).

The first METAPHOR observed here is A MEMORY IS A CONTAINER, which is evoked through both June/Offred's mention of memories as something you can 'fall in too far', and then later as something you can become 'lost' in. Charteris-Black (2006, 576) argues that '[t]he existence of a clearly

Table 7.3 Excerpt from voiceover 4.1

Verbal text	Visual text
I can't do this	*(Close-up)*
	June holds Hannah's hand and smiles
If I let myself fall in too far, I won't ever get out	*(Symmetrical composition)*
	June/Offred sits with her back to the shuttered window
There are things in this room to discover	June/Offred looks around room
	Shot focuses on the closed door behind her
I am like an explorer, a traveller to undiscovered countries	She shakily gets to her feet and moves to the door
That's better than a lunatic, lost in her memories	*(Close-up)*
	Bare feet walk across floor
	June/Offred moves into cupboard and switches on light
Words. It's Latin, I think. Someone wrote it. In here, where no one would ever see it	*(Close-up)*
	Hands trace the writing on the wall
Was it Offred? The one who was here before? It's a message, for me	Offred/June lies on the floor, looks at the letters and smiles
You had to be brave to do this. So, whatever it means, thank you	Flashback to looking through hole in bathroom toilet wall at Moira in the next cubicle. Close-up of eye looking through the wall
	Shot returns to cupboard; finishes with a symmetrical composition of June/Offred lying on her back, looking up at ceiling

defined container also implies a conscious controlling entity that fills or empties the container'. Like with some of the examples of self-referential you-address mentioned in the previous section, in this latter example June/Offred establishes herself in two roles: as the conscious controlling entity who populates the memory, and also holds control of her own movement within the container ('If I let myself fall in too far, I won't ever get out'). The reference to not being able to 'ever get out' further frames the idea of being contained as a negative experience; it becomes a country in which she can become 'lost', and therefore forms an additional kind of imprisonment. This idea is further evoked at the end of episode 4 where June/Offred references the woman who previously undertook the role of handmaid in Serena and Fred's household: 'There was an Offred before me. She helped me find my way out. She's dead. She's alive. She is me' (4.9). Within this description, June/Offred designates the agency to the previous Offred as helping her 'find [her] way out'.

Conversely, the latter sentences acknowledge a conflation of their roles: 'She is me' is an acknowledgement of their shared experiences in Gilead.

June/Offred further 'elaborates' (Lakoff and Turner 1989) of this first CONTAINER metaphor in her description of THE ROOM IS A COUNTRY. In this manifestation, there is a switch from her mental state to her phys-ical reality. She draws on different source domains, moving from describing her memories to describing her surroundings. She narrates how 'There are things in this room to discover', and casts herself as being 'like an explorer, a traveler to undiscovered countries'. This metaphor works by shrinking June/Offred's worlds. It adjusts the scope of her current situation of imprisonment by expanding the confinement of her room and the house to the scale of 'undiscovered countries', and conferring the specific role(s) of 'an explorer, a traveler' on herself. There is also a lack of specificity with the description; she talks about how there are 'things [...] to discover', but though the 'things' is schematic, the cupboard door is shown clearly in the visual text. The verbal text belies the fact that she knows all parts of the room very well, and enables her to maintain the performance of herself as an explorer rather than a prisoner in her physical environment.

Container metaphors can be seen elsewhere in the series, and the more superordinate metaphor THE SELF IS A CONTAINER is evoked, specifically. When June/Offred portrays Moira, for example, she describes how the self can be a container that provides protection: 'They didn't get everything. There was something inside her. That they couldn't take away. She looked invincible' (5.7). Equally, the idea that invasion into this container is a type of assault is suggested in June/Offred's reference to an Atwood poem: 'You fit into me like a hook into an eye. A fish hook. An open eye' (5.1). In a world that has stripped women of the physical right to own their bodies, the variations of container metaphors manifested in the series, and the idea that the mental sense of self is something that can be autonomously separated and contained, seem particularly apposite.

7.8   'If this is a story I'm telling, I must be telling it to someone'

The analysis in this chapter has combined concepts from film studies with ideas from cognitive stylistics to explore how the visual and verbal choices in this first series work to show the split presentation of June/Offred's char-acter. Building on the work of previous studies (McIntyre 2008; Piazza 2010), this combined approach has further demonstrated how ideas from these two disciplines can be synthesised to produce a holistic, multimodal analysis that captures the experience and interpretive effects elicited by telecinematic narratives. June/Offred is not represented as one character, but as many; and is represented through a division of mind and body, through her various social roles, and via the various enactors of her character through time. As the final part of the analysis observed, her divisions of self can be further explored through the metaphors she draws on to describe her feelings and mental states. While Emmott argues that instances of splitting are a phenomenon that 'arises[s] naturally from the nature of the human self and from the form of narrative' (2002, 161), in *The Handmaid's Tale*, this division seems to be a central concern of the storytelling.

The analysis has also argued that the performance of interior monologue through voiceover narration in TV and film always encodes a kind of split self representation. In such narration, the monologue is grounded in a speaking self who is spatiotemporally removed from the self shown on the screen. In *The Handmaid's Tale*, the world viewers see on the screen is experienced with a sense of immediacy (through the physically close camerawork, for example), but while voiceover narration is meant to be a humanising device (Kozloff 1988), it also creates a sense of artificiality as audiences are also aware that the verbal stream is grounded in a different time and place than the visual text. In this first series adaptation, this has the effect of distancing June/Offred from her own tale, making it seem as though she is a witness to events, rather than as someone experiencing them first-hand. This effect supports the witness literature categorisation of the novel (Atwood 2018), and contributes to discussions of reliability of accounts similarly raised in *Alias Grace*. The stylised choices of visual production (such as the *mise-en-scène* and the use of symmetrical composition shots) further mean that the FCD's role is never fully backgrounded, and this lingering presence creates an overarching theme of surveillance or narrative filtering. In other words, and as in the book, in Gilead your account is always one which is mediated; one which is never entirely your own.

References

Alber, Jan. 2017. The representation of character interiority in film: Cinematic versions of psychonarration, free indirect discourse and direct thought. In *Emerging vectors of narratology*, ed. Per Krogh Hansen, John Pier, Philippe Roussin and Wolf Schmid, 265–283. Berlin: De Gruyter.

Atwood, Margaret. 1985. *The handmaid's tale*. London: Jonathan Cape.

Atwood, Margaret. 2004. *The handmaid's tale* and *Oryx and Crake* 'in context'. *PMLA* 119 (3) *Special issue: science fiction and literary studies: the next millennium*, 513–517.

Atwood, Margaret. 2014. Acknowledgements. In *Stone Mattress: Nine wicked tales*, 309–311. London: Virago, Bloomsbury.

Atwood, Margaret. 2017. Margaret Atwood: *The handmaid's tale* sales boosted by fear of trump. https://www.theguardian.com/books/2017/feb/11/margaretatwoodhandmaids-tale-sales-trump. Accessed 17 July 2018.

Atwood, Margaret. 2018. Margaret Atwood teaches creative writing. Masterclass online.

Bauby, Jean-Dominique. 1998. *The diving-bell and the butterfly* (trans. Legatt, Jeremy from the French). London: First Estate. (Original work published 1997).

Billen, Andrew. 2017. *The handmaid's tale* review: Behind closed doors. https://www.thetimes.co.uk/article/tv-review-the-handmaids-tale-jane-austen-behind-closed-doors-nrgv2xg9h. Accessed 22 June 2022.

Bordwell, David. 1997. *Narration in the fiction film*. London: Routledge.

Bordwell, David, and Kristin Thompson. 2001. *Film art: An introduction*, 6th ed. New York: McGraw-Hill.

Bousfield, Derek. 2007. 'Never a truer word said in jest': A pragmastylistic analysis of impoliteness as banter in *Henry IV, Part I*. In *Contemporary stylistics*, ed. Marina Lambrou and Peter Stockwell, 195–208. London: Continuum.

Branigan, Edward. 1984. *Point of view in the cinema: A theory of narration and subjectivity in classical film*. Berlin, New York and Amsterdam: Mouton.

Chan, Emily and Rory Tingle. 2017. 'I keep forgetting to breathe!' Horrifying first episode of *The handmaid's tale* shocks viewers as dystopian drama finally airs in UK. https://www.dailymail.co.uk/tvshowbiz/article-4550904/The-Handmaid-s-Tale-shocks-viewers-UK.html. Accessed 22 June 2022.

Chandler, Abby. 2017. Stop saying that *The handmaid's tale* couldn't happen here—it's frighteningly realistic. https://metro.co.uk/2017/06/25/stop-saying-that-the-handmaids-tale-couldnt-happen-here-its-frighteningly-realistic-6730549/. Accessed 22 June 2022.

Charteris-Black, Jonathan. 2006. Britain as a container: Immigration metaphors in the 2005 election campaign. *Discourse & Society* 17 (5): 563–581.

Croft, William, and Alan D. Cruse. 2004. *Cognitive linguistics*. Cambridge: Cambridge University Press.

Debnath, Neela. 2017. *The handmaid's tale* review: What are the real-life influences and parallels of the TV show? https://www.express.co.uk/showbiz/tv-radio/821142/The-Handmaids-Tale-Trump-Margaret-Atwood-abortion-feminism-ISIS. Accessed 22 June 2022.

Demjen, Zsofia. 2011. Motion and conflicted self metaphors in Sylvia Plath's 'Smith Journal.' *Metaphor and the Social World* 1 (1): 7–25.

Emmott, Catherine. 1992. Splitting the referent: An introduction to narrative enactors. In *Advances in systemic linguistics: Recent theory and practice*, ed. Martin Davies and Louise Ravelli, 221–228. London: Pinter.

Emmott, Catherine. 2002. 'Split-selves' in fiction and in medical 'life-stories': Cognitive linguistic theory and narrative practice. In *Cognitive stylistics: Language and cognition in text analysis*, ed. Elena Semino and Jonathan Culpeper, 153–182. Amsterdam: John Benjamins.

Fienberg, Daniel. 2017. *The handmaid's tale*: Review. *The Hollywood Reporter*. https://www.hollywoodreporter.com/review/handmaids-tale-review-991871. Accessed 17 July 2018.

Forceville, Charles. 2002. The conspiracy in *The comfort of strangers*: Narration in the novel and film. *Language and Literature* 11 (2): 119–135.

Galbraith, Mary. 1995. Deictic shift theory and the poetics of involvement in narrative. In: *Deixis in narrative: A cognitive science perspective*, ed. Judith, F. Duchan, Gail A. Bruder and Lynne E. Hewitt, 19–60. Hillsdale, New Jersey: Lawrence Erlbaum.

Ghaffary, Mohammad, and Amir Ali Nojoumian. 2013. A poetics of free indirect discourse in narrative film. *Rupkatha Journal on Interdisciplinary Studies in Humanities* 5 (2): 269–281.

Gibbons, Alison, and Sara Whiteley. 2019. Do worlds have (fourth) walls? Text world theory, telecinematic stylistics and Fleabag. *Language and Literature* 30 (2): 105–126.

Giovanelli, Marcello and Chloe Harrison. 2024. *Cognitive Grammar in stylistics: A practical guide*, second edition. London: Bloomsbury.

Gottlieb, Erika. 2001. *Dystopian fiction East and West: Universe of terror and trial*. McGill-Queens University Press.

Grace, Sherrill. 1994. Gender as genre: Atwood's autobiographical 'I'. In *Margaret Atwood: writing and subjectivity*, ed. Colin Nicholson, 189–203. The Macmillan Press Ltd.: London.

Harrison, Chloe, and Louise Nuttall. 2019. Cognitive grammar and reconstrual: Re-experiencing Margaret Atwood's 'The Freeze-Dried Groom.' In *Experiencing fictional worlds*, ed. Benedict Neurohr and Lizzie Stewart-Shaw, 135–156. Amsterdam: John Benjamins.

Herman, David. 1994. Textual 'you' and double deixis in Edna O'Brien's 'A pagan place.' *Style* 28 (3): 378–410.

Hinds, Julie. 2017. Hulu's *The handmaid's tale* raises the bar for TV dramas. https://eu.freep.com/story/entertainment/movies/julie-hinds/2017/04/22/handmaids-tale-margaret-atwood-hulu/100714222. Accessed 10 July 2018.

Kolker, Robert P. 2015. *Film, form and culture*, 4th ed. Routledge: London.

Kozloff, Sarah. 1988. *Invisible storytellers*. Berkeley, CA: University of California Press.

Kress, Gunther, and Theo van Leeuwen. 1996. *Reading images: The grammar of visual design*. London: Routledge.

Jahn, Manfred. 2003. *A guide to narratological film analysis*. Available at: http://www.uni-koeln.de/~ame02/pppf.htm. Accessed 28 July 2018.

Lakoff, George. 1993. The contemporary theory of metaphor. In *Metaphor and thought*, 2nd ed., ed. Andrew Ortony, 202–251. Cambridge: Cambridge University Press.

Lakoff, George. 1996. Sorry, I'm not myself today: The metaphor system for conceptualizing the self. In *Spaces, worlds and grammars*, ed. Gilles Fauconnier and Eve Sweetser, 91–123. Chicago: University of Chicago Press.

Lakoff, George, and Mark Turner. 1989. *More than cool reason: A field guide to poetic metaphor*. Chicago: University of Chicago Press.

Mamer, Bruce. 2008. *Film production technique: creating the accomplished image*. California: Wadsworth Publishing.

McIntyre, Dan. 2008. Integrating multimodal analysis and the stylistics of drama: A multimodal perspective on Ian McKellen's *Richard III*. *Language and Literature* 17 (4): 309–334.

McKay, Alistair. 2018. *The handmaid's tale* review: just when you thought things couldn't get any darker, along comes a bleaker twist. https://www.standard.co.uk/culture/tvfilm/the-handmaid-s-tale-just-when-you-thought-things-couldn-t-get-any-darker-along-comes-a-bleaker-twist-a3843061.html. Accessed 22 June 2022.

MGM & Hulu. 2017. *The handmaid's tale* (TV series, series 1). Santa Monica, CA: Hulu.

Nuttall, Louise. 2014. Constructing a text world for *The handmaid's tale*. In *Cognitive grammar in literature*, ed. Chloe Harrison, Louise Nuttall, Peter Stockwell, and Wenjuan Yuan, 83–99. Amsterdam: John Benjamins.

Pezzotta, Elisa. 2013. *Stanley Kubrick: Adapting the sublime*. Jackson, MS: University Press of Mississippi.

Piazza, Roberta. 2010. Voice-over and self-narrative in film: A multimodal analysis of Antonioni's *When love fails*. *Language and Literature* 19 (2): 173–195.

Piazza, Roberta, Monika Bednarek, and Fabio Rossi. 2011. *Telecinematic discourse: Approaches to the language of films and television series*. Amsterdam: Benjamins.

Rees, Jasper. 2017. *The handmaid's tale* review: Night, episode 10, review. https://www.telegraph.co.uk/tv/2017/07/31/haidmaids-tale-night-episode-10-review-winters-tale-potent/. Accessed 22 June 2022.

Ross, India. 2017. *The handmaid's tale* review: A chilling new adaptation. https://www.ft.com/content/1d2e8528-26ac-11e7-a34a-538b4cb30025. Accessed 23 June 2022.

Rowney, Jo-Anne. 2017. Best TV shows of 2017 ranked: From *The handmaid's tale* to *Doctor Foster* and *Bojack horseman*. https://www.mirror.co.uk/tv/tv-news/best-tv-shows-2017-ranked-11768661. Accessed 22 June 2022.

Senkbeil, Karsten. 2017. Image schemas across modes and across cultures: Communicating horror in Philip Roth's *Nemesis* and Ridley Scott's *Alien*. *Language and Literature* 26 (4): 323–339.

Sorlin, Sandrine. 2016. *Language and manipulation in House of cards*. London: Palgrave Macmillan.

Staels, Hilde. 2008. Margaret Atwood's *The handmaid's tale*: Resistance through narrating. *English Studies* 76 (5): 455–467.

Stacey, Pat. 2017. *The handmaid's tale* review: 'It succeeds spectacularly on every level'. https://www.independent.ie/entertainment/television/tv-reviews/the-handmaids-tale-review-it-succeeds-spectacularly-on-every-level-35765634.html. Accessed 22 June 2022.

Statham, Simon. 2015. 'A guy in my position is a government target...you got to be extra, extra careful': Participation and strategies in crime talk in *The Sopranos*. *Language and Literature* 24 (4): 322–337.

Toolan, Michael. 2014. Stylistics and film. In *The Routledge handbook of stylistics*, ed. Michael Burke, 455–470. London: Routledge.

Wollaston, Sam. 2017. *The handmaid's tale* review: The best thing you'll watch all year. https://www.theguardian.com/tv-and-radio/2017/may/29/handmaids-tale-review-best-thing-youll-watch-all-year. Accessed 22 June 2022.

Yuan, Jada. 2017. How Reed Morano created the Emmy-winning look for *The Handmaid's Tale*. https://www.vulture.com/2017/09/the-handmaids-tale-how-reed-morano-created-its-look.html. Accessed 17 July 2018.

8

Future Readers

8.1 Introspection and Pre-closure in 'My Evil Mother'

At the time of writing, Atwood's most recent prose publication is the elegiac short story collection, *Old Babes in the Wood* (2023). Much like *Stone Mattress*, the collection features older characters as protagonists. The stories chart the shared life and marriage of Nell and Tig, and follows Nell in her life after Tig passes away. Short stories of other characters, framed through other genres and set in other times, intersperse the story of Nell and Tig, and make up the second, middle section of the collection. Notably, this middle section references the COVID-19 pandemic in its post-apocalyptic tales of 'Impatient Griselda', in which an alien tries to comfort a group of quarantined humans by telling them a story, and 'Freeforall', which was originally written prior to *The Handmaid's Tale* and addresses similar themes of reproduction challenges, brought on by widespread disease. Similarly, the stories in this section are more experimental in form. 'The Dead Interview', for example, is represented as a transcript of an imagined interview that takes place between Atwood and George Orwell, while 'Metempsychosis' presents a retelling of Kafka's *The Metamorphosis*, re-imagined through the perspective of a snail who turns into a human and struggles to adjust to life working from home during the lockdown. This collection of stories is both prescient and timely, though reflective in more personal ways. This was Atwood's first short story collection to be published after the death of her husband, Graeme Gibson, in 2019, and the reflections on shared lives and domestic routines, and on losing

C. Harrison, *The Language of Margaret Atwood*, Palgrave Studies in Language, Literature and Style, https://doi.org/10.1007/978-3-031-67640-6_8

loved ones, are framed in a way that captures both personal, and within the wider context of the pandemic, shared and more universal experiences.

Chapter 1 outlined how reader response research can support textual analyses that are both contextualised and naturalised, and the analyses across this book have drawn on different reader datasets to situate the discussion of stylistic choices alongside real reading experiences of Atwood's prose fiction writing. Up until this point, these datasets have been drawn from other readers' views on the texts. In this final chapter, I draw on my own responses, and so offer a set of views that are grounded in introspection. As Stockwell (2021) argues, introspection is inherently part of all empirical approaches to literary reading, working as a primary point for any analysis but also offering a valuable means of literary linguistic exploration. Here, I consider emotional effects that are not simply generated through analytical methods, though I do draw on these to account for the reflections that arose during my own introspective reading (Stockwell 2021, 175).

The fourth short story that opens the middle section of *Old Babes in the Wood* is 'My Evil Mother'. This story features a mother-daughter relationship through time, as narrated through the perspective of the unnamed daughter. She discusses growing up with her mother, a single parent, and describes her mother's eccentric and apparently witchy ways. Her mother instructs her to burn her hair to ward away evil, her cooking is described in terms of potion-making ('She kept a supply of such jars in the refrigerator. The goop in them was of different colours, and they were none of my business', Atwood 2023, 53), and her outfits are seen as a form of '[p]rotective colouration' (52) against detection within their respectable, suburban neighbourhood. As a young child, her mother tells her that her absent father is, in fact, their garden gnome; as a teenager, her mother urges her to break up with her boyfriend, Brian, after an allegedly portentous reading of his Tarot cards. As time passes and they both grow older, the narrator has a family of her own, while her mother's health deteriorates. Appearing towards the end of the story, Extract 8.1 outlines a final conversation between them at the hospital.

Extract 8.1

Her decline was now rapid. Shortly after this, she broke her hip – falling out of the air onto a chimney, she whispered to me – and had to be taken to the hospital. I tried to consult with her about her future: after they fixed the hip she'd go to a rehab place, then to a nice assisted-living facility…

"None of that will be needed," she said. "I won't leave the hospital in this body. It's all been arranged."

The arrangements included congestive heart failure. Final scene: I'm at her hospital bedside, holding her fragile, thick-veined hand. How had she become so little? She was hardly there at all, though her mind still burned like a blue flame.

"Tell me you were making it up," I said. Now that I was asking directly and not in anger – a thing I'd never exactly done before – surely she would admit it.

"Made what up, my treasure?"

"The hair burning. The pointing. All of it. It was like my father being a garden gnome, wasn't it? Just fairy tales?"

She sighed. "You were such a sensitive child. So easily wounded. So I told you those things. I didn't want you to feel defenceless in the face of life. Life can be harsh. I wanted you to feel protected, and to know there was a greater power watching over you. That the Universe was taking a personal interest."

I kissed her forehead, a skull with a thin covering of skin. The protector was her, the greater power was her, the Universe that took an interest was her as well; always her. "I love you," I said.

"I know, my treasure. And did you feel protected?"

"Yes," I said. "I did." This was somewhat true. "It was very sweet of you to invent all that for me."

She looked at me sideways out of her green eyes. "Invent?" she said. (Atwood 2023, 75–76)

For me, 'My Evil Mother' is an emotional short story. Like the other stories in *Old Babes in the Wood*, it reflects on the human condition, which here becomes a commentary on the changing dynamics between children and their parents. In particular, the story considers those revelatory moments where we question our elementary perceptions of a loved one's enduring strength and permanence within our lives, as we grow older ourselves.

In stylistics research, emotional responses to, and empathetic alignment with, texts are said to be context-dependent, arising from complex interplays between both textual and reader factors. As Fernandez-Quintanilla (2020, 125) argues, narrative empathy is

A character-oriented (emotional) response and perspective taking. The reader forms a mental representation of the character's situation and mental state(s) while maintaining a self-other distinction. In this way, readers re-enact, simulate, or imaginatively experience in a first-person way what they perceive is the character's mental state and mental activity.

Extract 8.1 invites perspective taking of the narrator through various means. Firstly, it comprises stylistic features consistent with the profile of high emotional involvement passages (Toolan 2013, 2016; see also Chapter 4), which illustrate the character's mental state and situation. The emotional weight of the scene at the hospital bedside is additionally exacerbated through its framing as a 'pre-closure moment' (Lohafer 2003; Toolan 2016) in the story. Following the work of Lohafer (2003), Toolan (2016) argues that readers expect 'imminent closure' when they read short fiction and respond to a series of 'pre-closure moments' in the text, to monitor moments where the narrative might, conceivably, end. The completion of the story is a key part of the experience of reading short fiction, as compared to reading longer fiction, and is something with which readers of short stories are more preoccupied. This is primarily due to the structural limits inherent within the brevity of the form: as readers, we are aware that, even if more open-ended, the story needs to reach a resolution, of a kind, more swiftly. Extract 8.1 presents a moment of pre-closure in various ways. It recounts a final conversation between the narrator and her mother at her death bed, and thus signals closure as a 'natural termination' (Gerlach 1985) of the story. It also signals a potential point of closure in the 'manifestation of a moral' (Gerlach 1985); it is the point in the story where the narrator finally confronts her mother about her past 'evil', witchy behaviour in order to elicit a confession.

As with other Atwood texts (see Chapter 5), the narrator here reflexively acknowledges the performative nature of her tale. She describes this conversation as forming part of the last part of a play, with stage directions outlining the visual details: 'Final scene: I'm at her hospital bedside, holding her fragile, thick-veined hand'. Consistent with dramatic performance, too, is the emphasis on direct speech from the two characters throughout this final exchange. Though still focalised through the narrator's first-person perspective, this discourse presentation frames the conversation in a more unmediated way, so that the utterances are displayed as more autonomous contributions (Stockwell 2021), increasing character vividness and authenticity (Toolan 2001, 130). This focus on externalised speech means that those instances where the narrator's internal reflections are outlined are automatically emphasised. Crucially, the continued lack of focalisation of the mother's perspective also means that the mystery of her mother's supernatural status is maintained until the end ('"Invent?" she said').

Returning to this extract again, it is my impression that other style choices within the scene further contribute to its emotional impact. The daughter hypothetically and hopefully projects a planned path for her mother's rehabilitation ('she'd go to a rehab place, then to a nice assisted-living facility'). As the extract continues, however, the decline of her mother's health is presented sequentially, in a compressed timeframe and within 'rapid' terms.

The second incident of her 'decline' occurred '[s]hortly after this', and then, the 'Final scene' swiftly follows. Consistent with their roles earlier in the story, the mother attributes her broken hip to a supernatural accident involving 'falling out of the air onto a chimney', and outlines her own plans for departure in enigmatic terms ("I won't leave the hospital in this body. It's all been arranged"). Despite the mother's more fantastical rendering of events, the prosaic reality of her situation is emphasised through the daughter's comparative use of medical language, in her descriptions of various locations for recovery ('hospital', 'rehab place', 'assisted-living facility'), and in the highly specified, and starkly realist, diagnosis of 'congestive heart failure'. The daughter's focus on more concrete realities is also apparent in her descriptions of her mother's physical frailty, where she is construed as quiet ('she whispered'), as 'fragile', and as diminished in size ('How had she become so little?'). While the daughter continues to frame her language in more literal terms, the metaphorical description of her mother's mind that 'still burned like a blue flame' is notably deviant. This foregrounding of a *heat/dimension word* (Toolan 2016) draws attention to her mother's relative mental strength in contrast to her physical health in these closing moments.

As with other high emotional involvement passages, there is *structural and lexical repetition* (Toolan 2016) at the significant point of revelation. The mother justifies her past actions by explaining that she wanted her daughter to feel that 'there was a greater power watching' and that 'the Universe was taking a personal interest'; a closing rationale for her previous eccentric, 'evil' behaviour. The daughter's response at this moment of confirmation is to echo the same lexical phrases used by her mother, repeated via a series of clauses: 'The protector was her, the greater power was her, the Universe that took an interest was her as well; always her'. These relational identifying structures place her mother as the central 'value' in the clause, with the preceding tokens, the comparators, successively increasing in scale, scope and magnitude: she was, in fact, 'the protector', 'the greater power', 'the Universe'. The repetition and comparative constructions serve to emphasise the narrator's progressive realisation, and direct acknowledgement, of her mother as her prevailing safeguard against 'harsh' realities.

Finally, there is an emphasis on *absolute/ultimate words* (Toolan 2016) that emphasise this point of resolution. This is the '*Final* scene', her mother confirms with high certainty that '*None* of that will be needed', the daughter asks questions that she had '*never* exactly done before', and, at the end, admits that the 'greater power' in her life was '*always* her' (emphasis added). This *absolute/ultimate* phrasing continues in the first sentences of the part of the story that immediately follows this extract, where the daughter introduces what is, in fact, the closing scene: 'And so I come to the end. But it's not the end, since ends are arbitrary. I'll close with one more scene' (75–76). As with her introduction to the 'Final scene' in Extract 8.1, the narrator again acknowledges the performance of the story and the formal, dramatic 'close' of just 'one more scene'. The story finishes with a conversation between the narrator and her own daughter, where the narrator unexpectedly finds herself taking on the role of her 'evil mother'. This ending forms a concluding reflection on the 'manifestation of a moral' (Gerlach 1985) that guides the story, which, here, can be interpreted as a commentary on the inevitability of the roles we take up throughout our lives. That familial relationships are cyclical and enduring, and that, ultimately, 'ends are arbitrary'.

8.2   The Style of Margaret Atwood's Contemporary Prose Fiction

This book has explored the complex interactions between authors and readers in Atwood's critical reflections on writing, and in her prose fiction writing. Atwood's continued contemplation of her readers is also apparent in her planned projects. Her involvement in the *Future Library Project* (Paterson 2014), for example, suggests an optimistic forecasting of her future readership. She is the first author to contribute to the Future Library, a 100-piece anthology which will commission a work from an author every year until 2114. More recently, Atwood's (2024) edited collection *Fourteen Days: An Unauthorized Gathering*, in which a group of contemporary writers contributes anonymous, 'unauthorised' stories, continues to reflect on current realities; in this case, the COVID-19 pandemic. This collection will continue to create ongoing DETECTIVE roles for readers, who will be invited to become forensic linguists who accredit, and 'authorise', each contribution.

A similar preoccupation with future readership can be seen in other comments, and in Atwood's continued reconstrual of established reading and writing metaphors. The following critical reflection, for example, draws on a description of the TEXT as a PIECE OF MUSIC:

> A book may outlive its author, and it moves too, and it too can be said to change—but not in the manner of the telling. It changes in the manner of the reading. As many commentators have remarked, works of literature are recreated by each generation of readers, who make them new by finding fresh meanings in them. The printed text of a book is thus like a musical score, which is not itself music, but becomes music when played by musicians, or 'interpreted' by them, as we say. The act of reading a text is like playing music

and listening to it at the same time, and the reader becomes his own interpreter. (Atwood 2015, 44)

To frame the closing comments through the language of this final metaphor, this book set out to explore the language and style choices of Atwood's contemporary prose fiction writing, 'the manner of the telling', as positioned alongside the reported experiences, the 'act' or the 'manner of reading', of real readers' responses to her texts. The book opened with an overview of the metaphors used by Atwood to frame her processes of writing, and the analyses have considered how, as well as combining to create central motifs in her work, these underpinning metaphors become part of the experiential processes of reading and interpretation, and of the dynamic and collaborative contexts of Atwood's storytelling. The cognitive stylistic approach to the language of Atwood's contemporary prose fiction has enabled an exploration of those ongoing interactions between the score of the text and the 'fresh meanings' readers continue to recreate, and to detect, in literary interpretation.

References

Atwood, Margaret. 2015. *On writers and writing*, first edition 2002. London: Virago.

Atwood, Margaret. 2023. My evil mother. In *Old babes in the wood*, 52–77. London: Chatto & Windus.

Atwood, Margaret, ed. 2024. *Fourteen days: An unauthorized gathering*. London: Penguin.

Fernandez-Quintanilla, Carolina. 2020. Textual and reader factors in narrative empathy: An empirical reader response study using focus groups. *Language and Literature* 29 (2): 124–146.

Gerlach, John. 1985. *Toward the end: Closure and structure in the American short story*. Tuscaloosa: University of Alabama Press.

Lohafer, Susan. 2003. *Reading for storyness: Preclosure theory, empirical poetics, and culture in the short story*. John Hopkins University Press.

Paterson, Katie. 2014. *The future library project*. https://www.futurelibrary.no/. Accessed 13 June 2023.

Stockwell, Peter. 2021. In defence of introspection. In *Style and reader response: Minds, media, methods*, ed. Alice Bell, Sam Browse, Alison Gibbons, and Dave Peplow, 165–178. Amsterdam: John Benjamins.

Toolan, Michael. 2001. *Narrative: A critical linguistic introduction*. London: Routledge.

Toolan, Michael. 2013. Is style in short fiction different from style in long fiction? *Style in Fiction Today* 4: 95–105.

Toolan, Michael. 2016. *Making sense of narrative text: Situation, repetition, and picturing in the reading of short stories*. New York: Routledge.

Appendix

Chapter 3, *Alias Grace* extracts

Extract 3.5

[1] Out of the gravel there are peonies growing. They come up through the loose grey pebbles, their buds testing the air like snails' eyes, then swelling and opening, huge dark-red flowers all shining and glossy like satin. Then they burst and fall to the ground.

[2] In the one instant before they come apart they are like the peonies in the front garden at Mr. Kinnear's, that first day, only those were white. Nancy was cutting them. She wore a pale dress with pink rosebuds and a triple-flounced skirt, and a straw bonnet that hid her face. She carried a flat basket, to put the flowers in; she bent from the hips like a lady, holding her waist straight. When she heard us and turned to look, she put her hand up to her throat as if startled.

[3] I tuck my head down while I walk, keeping step with the rest, eyes lowered, silently two by two around the yard, inside the square made by the high stone walls. My hands are clasped in front of me; they're chapped, the knuckles reddened. I can't remember a time when they were not like that. The toes of my shoes go in and out under the hem of my skirt, blue and white, blue and white, crunching on the pathway. These shoes fit me better than any I've ever had before.

[4] I watch the peonies out of the corners of my eyes. I know they shouldn't be here: it's April, and peonies don't bloom in April. There are three more now, right in front of me, growing out of the path itself. Furtively I reach out my hand to touch one. It has a dry feel, and I realize it's made of cloth.

[5] Then up ahead I see Nancy, on her knees, with her hair fallen over and the blood running down into her eyes. Around her neck is a white cotton kerchief printed with blue flowers, love-in-a-mist, it's mine. She's lifting up her face, she's holding out her hands to me for mercy; in her ears are the little gold earrings I used to envy, but I no longer begrudge them, Nancy can keep them, because this time it will all be different, this time I will run to help, I will lift her up and wipe away the blood with my skirt, I will tear a bandage from my petticoat and none of it will have happened. Mr. Kinnear will come home in the afternoon, he will ride up the driveway and McDermott will take the horse, and Mr. Kinnear will go into the parlour and I will make him some coffee, and Nancy will take it in to him on a tray the way she likes to do, and he will good coffee; and at night the fireflies will come out in the orchard, and there will be music, by lamplight. Jamie Walsh. The boy with the flute.

[6] I am almost up to Nancy, to where she's kneeling. But I do not break my step, I do not run. I keep on walking two by two; and then Nancy smiles, only the mouth, her eyes are hidden by the blood and the hair, and then she scatters into patches of colour, a drift of red cloth petals across the stones.

[7] I put my hands over my eyes because it's dark suddenly, and a man is standing there with a candle, blocking the stairs that go up; and the cellar walls are all around me, and I know I will never get out.

[8] This is what I told Dr. Jordan, when we came to that part of the story.

(Atwood 2017, 5–6).

Extract 3.6

[1.1] "In this new dream, I dreamt I was walking in a place I had never been before, with high walls all around made of stone, grey and bleak as the stones of the village where I was born, back across on the other side of the ocean. [1.2] On the ground there were loose grey pebbles, and out of the gravel there were peonies growing. They came up with just the buds on them, small and hard like unripe apples, and then they opened, and there were huge dark-red flowers with glossy petals, like satin; and then they burst in the wind and fell to the ground.

[2] "Except for being red, they were like the peonies in the front garden on the first day I came to Mr. Kinnear's, when Nancy was cutting the last of them; and I saw her in the dream, just as she was then, in her pale dress with the pink rosebuds and the triple flounced skirt, and her straw bonnet that hid her face. She was carrying a flat basket, to put the flowers in; and then she turned and put her hand up to her throat as if startled.

[3.1] "Then I was back in the stone yard, walking, with the toes of my shoes going in and out under the hem of my skirt, which was blue and white stripes. I knew I'd never had a skirt like that before, and at the sight of it I felt a great heaviness and desolation. [3.2] But the peonies were still coming up from the stones; and I knew they shouldn't be there. I reached out my hand to touch one and it had a dry feel, and I knew it was made of cloth.

[4.1] "Then up ahead I saw Nancy, on her knees, with her hair fallen over and the blood running down into her eyes. Around her neck was a white cotton kerchief printed with blue flowers, love-in-a-mist, and it was mine. She was holding out her hands to me for mercy; in her ears were the little gold earrings I used to envy. I wanted to run to her and help her, but I could not; and my feet kept walking at the same steady pace, as though they were not my own feet at all. [4.2] When I was almost up to Nancy, to where she was kneeling, she smiled. Only the mouth, her eyes hidden by the blood and hair, and then she came apart into patches of colour, she scattered, a drift of red and white cloth petals across the stones.

[5] "Then it was dark suddenly, and a man was standing there with a candle, blocking the stairs that went up, and the cellar walls were all around me, and I knew I would never get out."

[6] "You dreamt this before the event?" says Simon. He is writing feverishly.

"Yes Sir", says Grace. "And many times since."

[…]

"They said they were not dreams at all, Sir. They said I was awake. But I do not wish to say any more about it."

(Atwood 2017, 313–314)

Index

GPSR Compliance

The European Union's (EU) General Product Safety Regulation (GPSR) is a set of rules that requires consumer products to be safe and our obligations to ensure this.

If you have any concerns about our products, you can contact us on ProductSafety@springernature.com

In case Publisher is established outside the EU, the EU authorized representative is:

Springer Nature Customer Service Center GmbH
Europaplatz 3
69115 Heidelberg, Germany

The manufacturer's authorised representative in the EU is Springer
Nature Customer Service Centre GmbH, Europaplatz 3, 69115 Heidelberg,
Germany. If you have any concerns regarding our products, please
contact ProductSafety@springernature.com

Printed and bound by CPI Group (UK) Ltd, Croydon, CR0 4YY

29/04/2026

02099450-0017